THE SPECIALS

BY

A A PRIDEAUX

A CIP catalogue record for this title is

Available from the British Library.

ISBN 978-0-9930676-2-4

www.paganuspublishing.co.uk

First Published in 2014

Paganus Publishing

Ruthin

Wales

Paganus Publishing

Cover Designed by

Richard Fulke Paganus Prideaux © 2014

DEDICATION

To those I have known who would have been happy
to see me fail.

Fuck you, I didn't…

An old man is found dead in his home and DCI Revie and DS Jackson face the task of discovering who murdered him. At first, it appears that there is no reason the quiet widower should have been killed. But the investigation soon reveals that the gentle old man had been a long term and particularly deviant paedophile. As the story unfolds throughout the year and the body count rises, the police discover more people who have been living an apparently normal life while successfully hiding their past. The lives of all the people involved can never be the same again. The Specials reaches its dramatic conclusion in Snowdonia.

A classic whodunit

CONTENTS

CAST LIST

The Trewen family

• Edward Trewen married Janie and they had two daughters named Edith and Ellie.

The Prentice family

• William Prentice married Kathleen and they had a son named Michael.

• Michael Prentice married Edith Trewen and had five children.

• Eleanor the eldest daughter, married and divorced William and they had a son named Tom.

• Elizabeth the next daughter, married George and they had a son named Robert

• Andrew the only son, married Patsy and they had Mikey and Vikki.

• Emma the third daughter married Daniel and they had no children.

• Ellen, the fourth daughter, married Christopher and they had no children.

The Yates family

- Thomas Yates married Ellie Trewen and they had two sons
- Richard, the eldest son married Laura Kennedy and they had no children.
- Anthony, the second son married Tina Quigley and they had no children.

The Farrington family

- Ken Farrington married Kath and they had two children.
- David, the eldest son married and divorced.
- Debbie, the daughter is married.

The Neighbours

- Sylvia Lamb
- Alice Lamb
- Janet Banks
- Mrs Banks
- Judith Buckley

The Extras

- Natasha is the yard manager for Eleanor Prentice.
- Rachel is her stable girl.
- Billy is her stable boy.
- Pat is a neighbour.
- Shirley Rockford is a girl.
- Alan Hoguard is a boy.
- Sister Philippa is a nun.
- Sister Mary is a nun.

The Police

- DCI John Revie
- DS Dan Jackson
- DC Carol Eve
- DC Tony Pearl
- DC Plummer
- DC Griffiths
- DC Andrew Alexander (AA)
- DC John Petrie
- PC James
- SC Josie Swann
- Dr Jordan
- Mrs G is one of the forensics team.

CHAPTER ONE

Eleanor walked across the yard of her home. Today was going to be another glorious January day. Although she had lived here for three years, she still loved seeing the sea directly from the windows of her house and listening to the seagulls.

This morning she was a little later than usual starting work in her stables. The two girls and one boy in her employ had already begun feeding, mucking out and grooming. It was highly unlikely that they would make any comments on her lateness, but they might comment on her pale face and shaking hands.

The brick built stables on her left and facing the sea, housed her special horses. These four she had brought with her from her last house and they were always going to be her pets. But the mare, on which she was learning advanced dressage, was rapidly coming up behind them in the ratings. They all whinnied at her in anticipation of breakfast. Eleanor called gently to then as she walked to the feed room.

This room, large and built of stone, was several degrees colder than outside. Eleanor shivered and stopped by the bins to rub her arms.

"You ok, boss?" asked Natasha.

"I'm fine thanks, Tasha. Just felt cold as I came in here. Hope I'm not coming down with something before this weekend."

"Naaa. You're never ill. Must have been someone walking over your grave, that's all. Hey, are you really ok? You look very white."

"You know, I do feel as though someone walked over my grave. Perhaps we are being haunted. The old owner coming to see what we are doing here."

"If he's old enough, he should approve of the jousting set up."

"Yea. I'll be glad when that's finished. Then all those builders can go."

"I know someone who will be sorry when they do."

"Is Rachel still hanging around the hot builder?"

"Oh yes. She says this time she's in love!"

They both laughed and Natasha went back to the main stable block.

Eleanor filled up the feed buckets and put them in the wheel barrow, ready to take to the stables.

As she trundled it out of the door and into the bright early sunshine, she heard the radio blaring away inside the arena.

Billy was starting his schooling early today.

The news announcer on the radio was repeating the story which had given her such a shock while she drank her coffee in the kitchen.

The body of a 78-year-old man was discovered at his house in Applewyke near Leeds this morning. Thomas

Yates was found dead in a downstairs room by members of his family who had called to see him.

A widower and father of two, Mr Yates had worked for most of his life in Leeds. His family said that he had lived on his own since the death of his wife three years ago.

Police have asked for anyone with information to contact the police on the following numbers. They are treating his death as suspicious and are launching a murder enquiry.

When she heard the news, Eleanor immediately checked her phone to see what further information she could find out. It was definitely the man she thought it had been and he had been shot, but nothing was taken from the house. It seems his wife had been killed in an accident a few years ago, a domestic accident. Eleanor wasn't that bothered about her death.

She wondered if the police had any idea who had killed the bastard.

"Hello my babies, I'm sorry Mummy is so late this morning, did you think I wouldn't turn up? When do I ever not turn up? Mummy loves you all too much." The silly talk went on in this vein until the jobs were done and the clean babies had eaten breakfast and were happily munching on haylage.

Eleanor's phone was ringing in her pocket.

"Hi, Elizabeth!" she said.

"Have you heard the news?" was the quick question from her sister.

"Yes, I have. What do you think has happened?"

"Somebody killed him finally. Was it you?"

Eleanor laughed, "Like I've got time to drive all the way over there and shoot him."

"Is that what it was? A shooting?"

"According to the internet. It says that someone killed him in the front room. That room." Eleanor said with emphasis.

"Christ."

"I know. I wonder what happened?"

"Do you think they will come and question us?" asked Elizabeth.

"Shit. I hope not. Why would they question us? We don't know anything."

"Because they are bound to question anyone who knew him. That's what they do in all the stuff on TV."

"I suppose. Do you think we should tell them everything?"

"I don't know. If we tell them the truth, it will put us in the frame."

"In the frame? Have you been watching EastEnders again?"

They both laughed and the immediate tension was eased.

"Perhaps we should ask the others, because if one talks, we shall all have to." Eleanor said.

"Yes I know, but not all of them will want to talk. Then the police might want to know why we haven't said anything before."

"There wasn't any need to really. Life's been tricky enough to date."

17

"Well it's alright for you." Elizabeth couldn't help herself saying. She had yet to get over her sister's apparent good luck.

"Not always Elizabeth. I wanted more, expected more and got more. That's how life works." A familiar niggle was beginning in her stomach, because Elizabeth would always go down this road and it really wasn't fair. Life had thrown many obstacles her way and she had always managed to overcome them, with little or no help from her family and supposed friends. But now was not the time to mention that fact.

Another row would start.

"You certainly got plenty, Eleanor! Anyway, what are we going to do about this murder?"

"I don't know. I think we should ring the others and see what they think and then keep our eyes on the news. They might have already caught the killer and then we don't need to bother them at all."

"Shall I ring Emma?"

"Well I'm not going to. I'll end up accusing her of doing it. But I don't think she's got the nerve."

"And you can ring the Ellen?" Elizabeth was going to ignore the last remark, because she might accidentally let slip the fact that she had been talking to Emma again. Eleanor wouldn't be pleased about that. There had been a frosty atmosphere between those two since an argument about their father and money.

"I can't really tell Ellen this by email and I don't actually know her phone number."

"No, I don't either, but do it as soon as. Then ring me later. What time do you think you will be done?"

"Depends when I start, Elizabeth. I've got loads of things to do already today. We've got the show on Saturday."

"Oh yes. I forgot about that."

"Are you coming?" Eleanor already knew the answer to that question.

"Probably not, Eleanor. I've been meaning to tell you. I'm not feeling that well this week. I have a bit of a problem with my back." There was always something the matter with Elizabeth.

"Ok. Right, I'd better get on."

Eleanor ended the call and returned the phone to her pocket. She stared across the yard to the sea. This morning it was calm and the orange rays of the early sun shimmered across the ripples. The seagulls seemed to be making an inordinate amount of noise and Eleanor realised that someone must be ploughing nearby. She knew the birds like to follow the tractor. That's how Daphne du Maurier got the idea for her book, 'The Birds'. She saw birds following a tractor at Menabilly in their hundreds and imagined what would happen if they were attacking rather than scavenging.

That memory somehow seemed appropriate today.

Eleanor began grooming Esme, the beautiful grey mare she had bought a few months ago. Currently this mare knew more than Eleanor did. That was fine, Eleanor loved learning.

By the time she was walking Esme around the arena, the news was back on.

Police are repeating their request for information with regard to the body found at an address in Leeds. Apparently, the remains had lain undiscovered for several days. The police are treating the death as suspicious and the area will remain sealed off until the pathologist and forensic scientists complete their examinations.

"You were born in Leeds weren't you, Eleanor?"

"I certainly was Billy."

"Did you know who he was?"

"Who, who was?"

"The dead bloke they just found?"

"Don't think so, but I've not really been paying attention to the news this morning."

CHAPTER TWO

"You go down to your Uncle Thomas, Eleanor. He's waiting to see you."

Eleanor shifted from foot to foot, head down, trying to avoid the words coming from the mouths of her mother and auntie.

Eleanor did not want to go down and see her uncle.

"Go on Eleanor, your mother needs a break from you sometimes. She works very hard and all you do is demand attention."

Auntie Ellie, the odious woman after whom Eleanor had been named, pushed her niece out of the kitchen door and shut it behind her.

Eleanor was now standing on the driveway, stiff and tense with a weight so heavy on her shoulders that even her mother could not have coped with it.

Eleanor was three years old with a younger sister and brother and another sibling to arrive in a few weeks. Eleanor had experienced so little time in the spotlight with her family, that she felt special in no way whatsoever.

The kitchen door opened and Auntie Ellie came out and stood behind Eleanor. She smacked her hard on the bottom and said, "Get yourself down to your uncle right now or I'll hit you again."

Eleanor turned her face away and walked out of the open gateway and down the road. It was ironic that as her children got older, Edith Prentice would tell her children not to take risks, when their childhood had been one risk after another.

It didn't take long to arrive at the cottage which was home to the Yates family. Eleanor stood anxiously at the gate and looked at the shabby house. She was scared of the broken glass in the pale blue front door. She was scared of the scrap metal and rubbish lining the driveway and the terrifying sight of Uncle Thomas standing at the front window, beckoning her in with his long finger.

Eleanor knew that the best way to get through the next hour would be to get on with it. She moved her body down the pathway on stiff, wooden legs. The leaden legs took her to the foot of the steps which led to the kitchen door. This was the way she must enter. 'Up the wooden hill to Bedfordshire' came to her mind and seemed to help. Grandma would say that at bedtime. Kind Grandma.

The tatty back door pushed open easily and the smell hit her. It was a mixture of damp and cigarettes and hot lard. As she stepped inside the kitchen, her legs almost gave way. They had been tense for longer than most could bear. And now those little legs protested and began to wobble.

"Little Ellie! Come in here, I've got something to show you!"

Eleanor stood completely still, unable to move. Her eyes darted around the kitchen, noting the wet socks hanging from the grill on the gas cooker. Next to the cooker stood a filthy bin piled high with rubbish. Behind it were greasy skid marks where crap had been thrown against the wall in the vain hope that it would land in the bin. Much of it had missed and landed on the floor. The dishes were piled high in the sink and dirty plates and stinking food covered the counter tops. Eleanor knew from past experience that there *would be shavings from her uncle's razor on the edge of the sink.*

"Ellie! Come in here! Are you on your own?"

Eleanor blinked and a wave of terror overtook her and swept her forward. She shuffled stiffly out of the kitchen, through the dining room and gently pushed open the door to the living room.

Eleanor was three. But she remembered everything about these visits. Contact like this with her uncle, had been happening almost since she was born.

These mixed emotions of terror, anticipation and dread.

The smell of sweat, cigarette smoke and piss.

The massive wall of heat.

The lack of oxygen.

"Good little Ellie. In you come and shut the door behind you."

Eleanor stayed where she was, trembling on the stained carpet where her shoes stuck.

Thomas was sitting on the floor next to the gas fire and the television was on loud. As usual. The curtains now closed, let in only a small amount of light. The windows were closed too and it was almost impossible to breathe.

He was dressed in white, very tight jeans, a pale blue shirt and pointed leather shoes. His dark curly hair fell down to his shoulders and his fringe skimmed the top of his large glasses.

He patted the carpet next to him and said, "Come and sit down. We can have a special little cuddle."

Eleanor stayed where she was.

He got up from his sitting position and moved quickly on his hands and knees to where she stood. He sniffed her crotch like a dog. Grabbing hold of her hand, he pulled her over to the rug in front of the fire. The gas fire was on full blast and sent out plenty of heat. Eleanor stood stock still and stared at the television, her mind quietly shutting down. There was no point in fighting, it never made a difference. It was easier to shut down and accept her fate.

His hands were under her dress and at the top of her thighs, his fingers fiddling about. He lifted her skirt and looked at her knickers, which he was beginning to take down. He put his face between her legs and sniffed and licked.

"Oh, you wear such pretty knickers, little Ellie. Did you choose these especially for me? You always like to please me, don't you? Your very favourite uncle, Thomas."

He pushed her down to the floor and took off her knickers. He pulled his trousers down to his knees revealing some sort of hairy man with a long nose. Lifting up her dress with one hand and pulling her legs apart with the other, he positioned his body on top of his little niece. Eleanor felt his weight upon her and the pushing pain between her legs. She felt the stinging and the soreness. Eleanor was always sore between her legs and her mother told her to put cream on her 'nappy rash' when she complained.

She looked at the guitar leaning against the wall and thought of the times her uncle played 'Just like Eddie' and 'Peggy Sue.'

She hated him so much, but he was family and Mum said they must like him.

As the jumping about began, Eleanor retreated to her default position in the top corner of the room. She watched the whole event take place until he finally got up and lit another cigarette.

Up there it was safe from the pain and the heat and the squashing. She could see lights and sparkles and it smelled so nice and then...

A hearty slap to her face always brought her back to the room, lying on the floor staring up at the two faces of her uncle. And the funny smell that she hated, which somehow signalled the end of the experience.

Eleanor felt very tired and suddenly ashamed, as she felt the wet around her bottom. Had she weed herself again?

"Come on up you get, lazy bones. Stop lying around and let's go and get something to eat. What would you like?"

He was grinning and rubbing his hands together.

Eleanor pulled herself up slowly, wiped her dress down and followed him out of the room. She was very glad to be leaving the heat and stuffiness, but suddenly shivered as the cold atmosphere of the kitchen hit her.

Thomas lifted her up and plopped her on the kitchen side amongst the crumbs and stickiness. The cold marble on her bare bottom made her jump back up.

"Something the matter, Ellie? Do you want me to check?"

Eleanor was yet to utter a word since being told by her auntie that, "Uncle Thomas is waiting for you."

No one ever seemed to notice.

Eleanor shook her head violently and accepted the offered furry piece of cake.

The kitchen door suddenly banged open and both of them jumped as Auntie Ellie stormed in, shouting.

"Why the hell are the curtains closed in the front room?"

"Because the sun was shining on the television." Thomas answered mechanically.

Ellie rushed into the living room. There followed a scream and she came back into the kitchen holding her niece's knickers in her hand. She waved them in the air as she shouted,

"Why were these on the floor in there?"

Her husband shrugged his shoulders and ate his cake.

"Well miss. You must know why these are on the floor in my house?"

She pushed her face into her niece's face.

Eleanor considered crying but decided against it. Auntie Ellie always shouted at her and all young Eleanor could think was that she smelled and had hairy armpits. Dad laughed about that at home.

Home.

Eleanor wanted to go home.

"Well?"

Eleanor shifted and said quietly. "Uncle Thomas took them off."

The older woman stood up and looked at her husband who shrugged his shoulders again as if bewildered.

"You little liar. Why would he take them off?"

"He always takes them off when I come here. He likes to play wrestling on me."

26

Auntie Ellie, without warning, hit her as hard as she could across the face. With her other hand she pulled her niece by the hair and dropped her on to the floor.

"Get your stinking arse off my kitchen counter and put these filthy stinking knickers back on."

Uncle Thomas said, "She was saying she wanted a wee and I said, go up to the toilet and then I came in here to get something to eat. She must have weed on the carpet."

"Is that what you did, you filthy child?"

Eleanor said nothing. It was pointless saying anything. Ever. No one listened.

"I'll go and clean up," said Thomas and left the kitchen. He looked back at his niece and put his finger to his lips. He moved his finger across his throat.

Young Eleanor repeated, "He always takes my knickers off and I don't like playing with him."

She was rewarded with another hard slap. Auntie Ellie took hold of her niece's arm and swung her around the kitchen as she hit her. She had a rage upon her which need taking out on this lying little girl. She threw her against the pantry door, but still the little girl did not cry.

"Say you're sorry."

"I'm sorry."

"If you say anything about this to anyone. I will kill your brother and sister. I promise." Auntie Ellie opened the back door and threw Eleanor down the steps.

Eleanor fell on the concrete, cutting her knees.

She looked out over the valley, to the hills and the cottages and the trees.

27

She didn't cry.

The little girl got up, brushed herself down and ran back up the lane to home.

As she pushed open the back door, she saw her pregnant mother holding Andrew. Elizabeth was crawling around on the floor, sucking a rusk.

"Mum, Auntie Ellie just hit me," Eleanor told her.

"Well I expect you asked for it. You are filthy!"

"I didn't ask for it Mum. Uncle Thomas..."

"Get out of my sight, Eleanor. I have enough to do, without your whingeing and whining. Go and see what your father is doing."

Eleanor felt tears near to the front of her eyes.

Her bottom was stinging.

She saw her Dad sitting in front of the television, drinking a cup of tea. Eleanor walked towards him. She loved her Daddy. He was always kind to her.

"Oh come here my favourite little girl. Come and sit down next to me." He patted the carpet next to him. Dad was sitting in front of the gas fire which was on full blast.

The room was hot and stuffy.

"What's the matter, Eleanor? You've not been naughty, have you? Come here and let me cuddle you."

No, Eleanor didn't want any cuddles or anyone touching her.

"No."

She ran past her Dad and out of the room to the bottom of the stairs.

"Eleanor! Come back here!"

Little three-year-old Eleanor ran into her bedroom and fell on the bed.

She was hot and fevery, but she wasn't going to cry.

CHAPTER THREE

"What do you think of the murder?"

It had taken only one ring of the telephone before Emma answered.

"I think it's great news. I'm glad the old bastard is dead. Is it definitely murder? There must be loads of people who wanted to kill him. I wanted to kill him." Emma spoke rapidly.

"I didn't want to kill him." answered Eleanor.

"Why not? I thought you hated him?"

"I did at one time but to be honest I've not thought about him for years."

"Oh, I thought you had."

"No. Why would you think that I had?"

"Because you are always looking for trouble!"

Eleanor bit her lip to stop herself replying. Why did the family always act as if she was looking for trouble, when she never was? It was her they looked to when any family trouble needed sorting.

"Well, I don't care whether he's dead or not. What Elizabeth and I are bothered about, is the police contacting us."

"Do you think that they will want to see us? What can we tell them?"

"I'm just thinking that they will want to speak to us because we are his family."

"God, I hope not."

"They might not though. I mean they will want to speak to the people who knew him in Leeds, won't they?" said Eleanor.

"What about his sons?"

"They might be dead or abroad."

"It said on the news that Auntie Ellie is dead too."

"I heard that. From an accident or something?"

"I wonder what kind of an accident? I don't expect she drove or anything."

"Perhaps someone ran over her."

"They would need a tank."

They laughed and the previous argument was temporarily forgotten.

"She used to say a minute in the mouth, a month on the hips." Eleanor recalled.

"When did she say that?"

"Oh, one of those times we had to stay there and she was on a diet."

"She used to eat fish and chips on her diets."

"And dye her hair red."

"And she had hairy armpits."

"Yuck."

"So shall we just say nothing and see if the police get in touch with us?" asked Emma.

"Yes, because they asked for people with any information and we haven't got any information, have we?"

"No."

"Will you Skype Ellen?"

"Don't need to, they will be here tomorrow."

"Oh!" Eleanor was surprised because Ellen and Christopher weren't supposed to arrive from their home in America until next week.

"They decided to come here earlier. I can't remember exactly why."

"Right, we'll have a word with them. See what Daniel and Christopher think we ought to do."

Eleanor was the only sister without a husband, having already had two and divorced both.

"I will. I'll ring you tomorrow when the others are here."

"Great. Speak to you then."

Eleanor turned off the phone and put it against her mouth. She tapped gently in a subconscious attempt to keep her mouth shut. It would not do for any of this to come out.

The sisters used to have talks about whether to tell the police, but then decided that it would cause too much trouble for their parents. After all, the police would ask them what they knew and why they hadn't done anything about it at the time.

They decided that they would tell, as soon as their parents died.

But Andrew died first and so they told their parents. That caused a lot of trouble, but then Mum went too. Even though it might have been a good time to tell the police at that point, they decided against it.

Telling hadn't done any good at the time and chances were that it wouldn't do any good now. There would be interviews and one person's word against another and court cases.

Her mobile rang and Eleanor almost dropped it.

"Hello," she said.

"Mum. I've just heard the news. Is that your uncle who's been killed?"

"Yes, it is. Wonder what happened? Have you heard any more than has been on the news?"

"No, I saw it on Sky. I wondered why it was on there? Maybe there's something more weird than usual. They don't report all murders on there, do they?"

"I hadn't thought about it before. I've spoken to Elizabeth and Emma and they are going to talk to the others. Did you know that Ellen and Christopher are here earlier than they said?"

"No, why would I? What does everyone say?" asked Tom.

"That we should keep quiet. When are you home?"

"I'll be back tonight. Everything else ok?"

"Yea fine. Looking forward to seeing you later."

Eleanor pressed the red button and stared out of the kitchen window. She watched jet skis zipping across the water. The sun, almost at its highest position in a brilliant blue sky, put her in mind of holiday time.

She walked outside and down the path which led to the beach. This place was her field of dreams and had been paid for in full. She would never share it with a husband or a partner. Twice those selfish bastards had halved her hard work and she wasn't ever going to let it happen again. She and Tom ran several businesses, including a large property portfolio.

Plas Cerrig was an ancient stone hall, with over 200 acres of land running along the coastline. The horses and wealth she had pictured in great detail during those lean years after the second divorce were now hers.

Eleanor would allow nothing to ruin her life.

Nothing.

She walked onto the beach and looking at the brave, New Year holidaymakers, she suddenly felt incongruous in her jeans and riding boots. Some people looked at her, but most paid little attention. Eleanor would have had her dog with her usually, but today was a funny day. She walked down to the water alone.

"I love it here," she said to herself.

"Eleanor! Coooeee!!"

She turned around and saw Natasha waving at her from the gate. She waved back and walked towards the house.

#

Tom put his phone back in his pocket.

"What's going on with your Mum?" asked John. The two of them were running a course together. Eighty members of a well-known company on a team bonding exercise. Tom didn't usually attend these, but there was no one else available who could supervise today. They had 10 instructors to oversee.

Tom had heard the news and was surprised when he recognised the name. Tom had been brought up on statements such as, "Uncle Thomas is a pervy bastard" and "Auntie Ellie is a bitch." It was no surprise that he had spent no time at all with that branch of the family.

He asked once why he had been named Thomas if she hated her uncle so much.

"Because I wasn't technically alive when William named you. I wanted to call you Andrew, but by the time I came around from the anaesthetic, you were called Thomas. It seemed bad luck to change it."

His mother later said it was a cosmic joke that they had the same names as her hated uncle and aunt.

"Seems her uncle has been murdered."

"Cool."

"I know," answered Tom.

CHAPTER FOUR

Richard Yates had tried twice during the past week to raise his father on the telephone. But he hadn't tried any more than that, because he didn't really care whether his father answered or not.

The lifelong hate Richard felt for his father had doubled after death of his mother, as now he was no longer able to hate her.

But he still drove the ten miles from his home to discover why the old sod was not answering. The old man wouldn't always hear it ringing and when either of his sons turned up to find out how he was, he declared himself fine and dandy and said, "fuck off, I don't need your help."

Richard waited until the weekend, because there wasn't much point leaving work early and ruining a day having an argument with his father. He could always do that with his wife. His father was worse though, far worse.

Arriving at the family home, Richard sat in the car and leaned back in the seat. He closed his eyes. Whatever his father's problem, it could wait five minutes.

He began to remember....

"Mum, Mum!"

Richard ran down the drive towards the back door.

He ignored the rubbish on either side of the concrete drive, because he was used to it. The house had been built along with seven others in the corner of a stone walled field. Their house was at the end of the row and so most of the stone from the walls had been dumped in their garden. The stone was beautiful and useful and free.

But the Yates family had done nothing with it. Unless the addition of broken prams, bikes and parts of old cars were to be taken into account. The barbed wire which had replaced the stone was now rusting and broken and gave little protection from the horses which were kept in the field until they went to...

Richard never had discovered where. He knew that they sometimes escaped on to the lane and some men came and got them back in. Richard felt sorry for the horses, but he felt even sorrier for himself.

"Mum!"

Richard ran up the steps and into the kitchen.

"Mum!"

His Mum wasn't there.

Richard remembered that she would be doing a shift at the fish and chip shop down the road. She liked working there, or in the pub. And that meant that they would be getting fish and chips for tea!

He threw his school bag against the hall door and went over to the pantry. He wanted a drink and he knew that there would be Corona pop in there somewhere. He needed a glass.

Richard dragged a stool over to the sink and climbed up. The sink was full of pots and pans and hair from his Dad's razor. The latter always made him shudder. Why did he have to do that? None of his friend's houses looked like this house. And none of them stunk or were covered in rubbish and dust and fluff like his house was.

He turned round and looked at the kitchen with its bin and filth. When Richard got older he would recognise this feeling as the black curtain of doom coming down upon him. He would need to clean the house up a bit before his new friend came round.

Shirley had started their school three weeks ago and Richard was amazed how friendly they had become and how much they had in common. He liked Shirley so much, that when she said to him today, "Can I come round after school and we can do this project together?" He was ecstatic.

At 12 years old they were partnered in English to come up with ideas for an end of term play. The teacher had randomly chosen Shirley to partner Richard!! This was proof that wishes can come true if you believe in them hard enough.

But, he hadn't really thought the end result through properly, when he answered joyously, "Yes!"

Now, he was at home, Shirley would be arriving in less than half an hour and the house was a fucking tip. Richard jumped off the stool and went over to the bin and began jamming the extra waste through the already overfull flip top. There wasn't enough room for the stuff round the side of it and so Richard pulled the bin forward and tried to push the extra round the back.

It looked marginally better. Then he grabbed the dishcloth and began wiping the lid in an effort to remove sauce and tea leaves and whatever else was there.

He pulled some knickers from above the grill and threw them into the pantry. He jumped back onto the stool and ineffectively held the dirty pots under the cold tap. He filled one cup with water and tried to rinse away the beard trimmings. He looked at the kitchen curtains, the hem of one stuck in a bowl of dripping.

Could he possibly find an excuse to keep Shirley outside and give her some tea there?

That would be difficult.

He went into the sitting room. The room was filthy. Smoky and greasy and…. There was no way he could have Shirley in here and keep her friendship. His eyes shot up to the window and he saw his new friend walking through the gateway. He would have to stop her coming in.

Richard ran back through the kitchen and out of the door, just managing to reach Shirley before she started to walk up the steps.

"Hello Richard. Is it still alright for me to come in?"

"Well no, not really. I'm sorry. Can we do this another time?"

Shirley's face dropped.

"Yes, if you say so. What's happened?" Shirley's lovely eyes looked into Richard's.

"It's my Dad, he's ill you see and it might be catching so I don't want you to catch anything. Can we go for a walk to the park and talk about the project?"

"If you like." She looked disappointed.

Richard pulled the back door shut and gently ushered Shirley towards the gate.

The 77-bus pulled up at the stop outside and his father jumped off.

"What you up to, Richard?" he asked.

"We are just going for a walk."

"And who is this lovely little lady?" He leant over and touched the girl on her shoulder. His hand traced its way down the front of her neck, hoveringly for a little time above her breasts and then he pulled it away. Shirley recoiled and looked at him in disgust.

"A friend."

"And are you going to introduce your friend to your Daddy?"

"Shirley, this is my Dad."

"You are looking very well, Mr Yates. Richard tells me that you've been ill?" Was it Richard's imagination or was Shirley speaking in a posher voice?

"Not so you would notice, Shirley. You are looking very well, very pretty."

"Thank you, Mr Yates. I must be off. I have a lot to do tonight. We can sort out the project at break tomorrow, Richard."

She walked swiftly away, only looking back once in order to glare at Richard.

Since that project finished, the two had never really spoken. Shirley thought he was rude and not interested. Richard just didn't want to go through the embarrassment of inviting anyone home ever again.

Not into this pig hole that his parents called home

Richard opened his eyes and shivered. He got out of his car and began walking towards the back door. The drive way had been cleaned up by the family years before, following several letters from the council and complaints from the neighbours. After that, his mother turned her amazing hoarding skills into excessive cleaning and constant changing of the décor.

The house was 'immaculate within' as estate agents say. His mother became obsessive in her own hygiene, sometimes putting bleach in her bath and on at least one occasion, plucking every hair from her body with tweezers.

He pushed against the back door, but it wouldn't budge.

"Must be locked." Richard said. He walked around to the front door, which was almost never used by anyone. Richard couldn't remember why.

He tried the handle, but that just rattled when he twisted it. He moved the handle up and down hopefully, but to no avail.

Richard banged hard on the door and shouted, "Dad! Dad!"

Nothing.

He stepped back and looked up to the bedroom window, noting that the curtains were open. He looked at the downstairs window and those curtains were slightly open. Richard had a weird feeling overcome him and a long-forgotten sensation of tense, slow moving legs.

Something was going to happen.

He looked in through the window and saw his father lying on the floor in the middle of the room. There was a dark stain surrounding his body. The television was on and

Richard could see the changing screen flash against his father's oversized glasses.

Richard staggered back onto the lawn and half fell on to it. He felt sick and dizzy and thought he was going to faint.

His Dad looked dead. Was he dead? Could he be dead?

He was definitely silent. He imagined cold, dead, black eyes behind those glasses. The eyes that had forced Richard to...

Richard couldn't remember what the eyes made him do, just that he didn't like to do it.

Whatever it was.

Richard wretched and wiped his mouth.

"Hi, Richard. Are you alright? Dodgy pint last night?"

It was David Farrington. Their family had moved in within a few days of the Yates and the Prentices. Their parents had all bought their houses when they were built in 1967. All the kids were born there and they grew up together and went to the same schools. David had come back to live here after his divorce. The house had been left to him by his parents and he had been renting it out until he moved back in.

"No such luck mate. Look through that window."

David looked in through the glass and said, "Christ. Is he dead?"

"I think so."

"We'd better get ourselves in there." David made his way to the front of the house.

"I can't get in. Both doors are locked."

"That's weird. He never usually locks the doors, does he?"

"No. We'll have to break in. Have you got a crowbar or something?"

"Yea. There's one in the garage. I'll go and get it." David scampered off and Richard straightened himself up. He was still feeling dizzy and sick, but more able to deal with what was happening.

Within a few minutes the two men had broken open the back door and were in the house. Richard knew as soon as he saw his father lying on the floor that he was dead. There was blood everywhere.

There was a splattered ring of blood on the wall. Thomas was face down on the carpet surrounded by dried blood. He faced the television and there was blood all over his hair and hands.

Richard didn't bother to touch his father, especially when he noticed the dried foam and blood around his mouth.

"There's no point in mouth to mouth is there?" Richard asked tentatively.

David looked at the body. He wondered vaguely why he was humming 'Stayin Alive'.

Thomas's face was sticky and bluish.

"Naaa. I think he's dead, mate. Better call the police."

"Ok. Right. Erm. My phone's in the car."

David pulled his own phone from his pocket and handed it to Richard.

"You ring them please. I feel sick."

"Ok." David bashed in the number and gave the details to the operator.

43

"She said we shouldn't touch anything," he informed Richard after he had finished.

"I know. What the hell do you think has happened?"

"Your Dad's been shot."

"First prize for stating the bleeding obvious. Who's shot him? Did you hear anything?"

"No, I didn't actually, but it looks as though he's been shot with a small gun. You would think I would have heard that. Perhaps I was out, or asleep."

"A shot would've woken you up. The police will be asking when you were out, so they can narrow it down."

"Better think up a good alibi then."

"The room's a mess," said Richard as he looked around properly. Some of the furniture and ornaments and pictures were broken, or on the floor.

"He's not been doing too much about it since your mother died though, has he? I know Anthony has been round a few times and he didn't think that he was coping very well. Apparently, he's been having nightmares and wouldn't go upstairs to sleep."

"Yea, he's been telling us about nightmares. But, he also said that people have been breaking into his house at night and taunting him and I know that isn't true."

"He's probably going it a bit senile."

"Well he's stopped now," answered Richard.

"Yea. Sorry. Shall we have a look round upstairs? I mean once the police get here, you won't be able to take anything out and maybe there's some valuable stuff you want to get?"

Richard looked at his friend, initially thinking what a tosser he was. Then he thought that it was probably a good idea. There might be something he wanted.

They made their way through the door to the hall and ran upstairs. Richard remembered when the hall was filled with rubbish and the toilet smelled of piss.

Upstairs, everything seemed to be normal.

David went into the main bedroom and Richard went into the room he used to share with his brother Anthony. It still had the beds they slept in and bizarrely they were still made up. Richard realised that since his mother's death, he had never come upstairs when he visited. He looked at the pictures on the wall, Farrah and the tennis girl. On the chest of drawers, he noticed a Swiss army knife which his Uncle Michael had given him and he put it into his pocket.

"Mate! Come in here!"

Richard went quickly to his parents' bedroom and saw David at the dressing table.

"Do you want to take any of the jewellery away? And there's some money in the drawers. Do you want that?"

Richard looked at David and just said, "No David, I don't. Put it back."

They stared at each other.

The sound of sirens in the road broke the spell and they ran downstairs and back into the front room. By the time the first policeman arrived in the house, the two men were breathing heavily and looking sweaty with guilt.

CHAPTER FIVE

"There's something happening over the road." said Sylvia.

Her sister Alice manoeuvred her way across the furniture crowded room and looked out of the window. The sight of police cars and an ambulance caused her to feel an excitement in her lady bottom which she hadn't felt for many years.

The spinster sisters were in their late seventies and had spent their entire lives at the house. The large property had been built by their father just before the war. The sisters had continued living there after the death of their parents, having been unable to find husbands.

"I wonder what's happened?"

"The car's in the drive. Richard's car I mean. It hasn't been parked there for weeks." said Sylvia.

"I saw it there the other day."

"Did you? When? He doesn't come as often since his mother died, mind you he didn't come much before she died."

"It might have been Thursday or Friday. I can't remember. Maybe not Thursday, because we were in the garden most of the time. Was it Wednesday?" mused Alice.

"Oh look, there's another police car! I think they've blocked the road."

Could it get any more exciting?

The ladies organised themselves by dragging a small table to the window and moving two dining chairs alongside it.

They now had an excellent view and the heavy lace curtains meant that no one could see the sisters looking out.

"Fetch some tea and biscuits, while I get the book out." said Sylvia, her face shining with anticipation and happiness.

Alice scuttled off as Sylvia took the great brown leather book from the dresser.

Everything that happened within their experience had been noted down in this tome. They had started the book when they were children, but nothing much occurred until the houses were built over the road. Then, the years of comings and goings had filled the book and their lives, in the absence of family.

The sisters were soon merrily drinking tea and eating biscuits. The best china was in use and the cloth embroidered by their Gran, on top of the tray.

Today was going to be a brilliant day!

"I can see Richard there."

"Where is he?" Alice leant nearer the curtain.

"Over there in the Farringtons' drive. They must have gone round the back."

"We almost missed that."

"Yes. But it's written down now." Sylvia tapped the page with her fountain pen.

"That's good. Just think how much money we could make if it was published!" Alice exclaimed.

"No one would be interested in our little jottings. We will destroy it when we die, dear."

"No, we won't. We will give it to the vicar. He will know what to do. There's some interesting stuff in here."

Sylvia flicked through the journal. Hundreds of pages, filled with sixty years of notes.

"There's a lot in here about the Yates, but that's because we see them the most," said Sylvia, "and about everyone in that row of houses. I bet we could tell their life stories to anyone who asked."

"Like a newspaperman, you mean?"

"A newspaperman? Why would a newspaperman be interested in what's in here?"

"If something very exciting has happened over there," she said pointing at the house opposite,

"The papers might be interested."

"Maybe."

"They may pay us!" Alice said excitedly.

"This book is private and I don't think that we should let anyone see it. We have never told anyone about it and we should keep it that way." Sylvia looked sternly at her younger sister.

"No, we've never told anyone have we?" Alice was less sure, as over the years she may have hinted to a few people that the book existed. It didn't do any harm to keep notes about the comings and goings of the town and if a few people want to give her some cash for the privilege of looking, then where was the harm in that?

"A photographer has gone in now and they are putting up a tent outside."

"And a policeman is looking towards our house. Do you think he can see us behind these curtains?"

"No one else ever seems to." Sylvia commented.

The policeman wrote in his little book and turned his attention back to his colleagues. The road had been taped off.

"Go and fetch some more biscuits and tea Alice, we have run out already."

Alice trotted off and Sylvia kept her vigil. She wrote down a few more notes and thought about the extra money she had made by making suitable comments to neighbours about the things she knew. There was always a need for extra money to pay the bills, but she needn't trouble Alice with the problem. Besides, she enjoyed the power her knowledge gave her over the sanctimonious neighbours they had. By the time Alice arrived back with another pot and a plate of sandwiches, a body was being wheeled out of the house on a stretcher. The women imagined it to be a body, although it was covered by a large black bag.

"Do you think that's him in there?" asked Sylvia.

"Creepy Yates? Probably. We haven't seen him for a few days, have we? Not peeping through the curtains at us."

"No. Thank the Lord. Do you know that he's been peeping at us most days since they moved in there in…" Sylvia started to go back through the book. There was an index where she could check the year and find it by page.

"1967! They moved in a few months after her sister and her husband did. Time does go so quickly."

"Yes, it does. Do you remember when the little children used to go into his house and come out so different?"

"I don't want to talk about that, Alice. There are some things we shouldn't interfere with."

The sisters remained quiet for a time, drinking their tea and remembering. Sometimes Alice didn't think that they needed to write down everything that happened, because she felt as though it was in her head anyway. And some of the things they knew, really, nobody should know.

The body had been taken away now and they watched Richard as he stood by the gate, looking dazed.

"I thought he'd given up smoking! Doesn't he know it's bad for him?"

"Go and tell him then!" said Alice.

"That would go down well I should imagine."

They continued watching as Richard stubbed out his cigarette on the driveway and went to his car. He opened the door and reached into it, bringing out his phone.

"He's going to make a phone call. I bet he's going to call the rest of the family."

But Richard didn't have the chance. A policeman came over to him and held out a hand. Richard looked confused and then angry. He put the phone into the plastic bag which the policeman held out.

"They are putting him in the back of a police car now. I wonder if they are arresting him?"

Sylvia picked up the binoculars from the table and held them to her eyes.

"I can't see any handcuffs, so perhaps not," she noted.

"Do they still use handcuffs? Don't they laser people these days?"

"Don't be ridiculous Alice. Of course, they still use handcuffs. And its Taser not laser. I think, anyway."

More cars arrived and the police car containing Richard was driven away. David Farrington was put into another police car and driven away in the opposite direction. It passed Anthony Yates, who was trying to get under the tape but being held back by a policewoman. He waved his arms about and she called another officer over, who appeared to be trying to calm him down.

"He's crying," said Alice.

"Do you remember when he came over to play all those years ago? He fell in a puddle and got covered in mud and we had to carry him home."

"I held him out in front of me, all dripping and dirty," recalled Alice

"And his mother smacked him and shouted at him for getting dirty."

"Instead of saying sorry for allowing her two-year-old to toddle across a road and she didn't notice until he was brought home."

"Poor little Anthony. They never loved him, did they?" Sylvia said sadly.

"They never loved anyone but themselves," agreed Alice.

"I wonder what's happened over there. It can't be a normal death because there wouldn't be that many police around would there?"

"We know what happened, don't we?" said Alice. She took the tray back into the kitchen and left Sylvia writing and being nosy.

51

Sylvia thought about that last remark, because on reflection there had been some out of the ordinary events this past week. It was impossible not to know people after constant observation of their lives. The women probably knew their neighbours better than they knew themselves.

Sylvia thought that she ought to go back over the past weeks jottings, because then perhaps she could clarify in her head what she thought was wrong.

She stopped thinking, as there appeared to be further developments.

"Alice! Quickly! There are some television people coming!"

Alice came back into the room as quickly as her arthritic hips would allow and sat down on her chair.

"I've put the pie and potatoes in the oven to heat up for lunch. It should be ready in about an hour."

"Oh goody. I'm hungry with all this excitement."

"Is that the one from the news?"

"Where?"

"Over there by the tape. It is, it's that Kate." Alice watched the news every day.

"Oh yes. She's talking to Anthony."

"He would be better off talking to a journalist and getting a payment for his story. The television won't pay them," said Alice

"How do you know that?"

"Midsomer or EastEnders or Katie Price. I can't remember which one."

Watching a lot of television was educational, never mind what some people said.

"Anthony is talking to her, though. He's putting his arm round his wife and that reporter has a microphone in his face."

"It's funny how he's got his arm round her now and he's been chatting up that Janet Banks from opposite." Sylvia said,

"He's always been sweet on Janet, ever since they were children. He was always trying to persuade her to like him."

Sylvia had a soft spot for Anthony and his brother. When the boys were young her heart had ached to take care of them. Their parents had been lackadaisical and sometimes so cruel.

Alice reminisced, "Do you remember when Anthony was small? He must have been less than a year old."

"And he did all that screaming, for two days and nights. She just ignored him."

"It was only when her mother called round and made her take him to the doctors."

"Janie was a good woman and so was her husband. I miss them," said Sylvia. She had particularly liked Edward and had once mistaken his neighbourly kindness for something more. But it had all ended peacefully and no prisoners were taken.

"What was it that it turned out to be? Something twisted in his gut and he had to have an operation. The poor little mite must have been in such terrible pain."

"I know. That Ellie Yates was an unfeeling bitch. It's ironic she ended her life like she did." Sylvia said.

"She deserved it. God moves in mysterious ways."

"His wonders to perform," added Sylvia.

"What does that actually mean?"

"No idea. We'd better make sure we watch the local news, because all this drama will be on it."

"Oooooh!" squealed Alice, "It's a Sky News van!"

"That got here quickly. They must have had one in Leeds on another job."

"It will be on live now. Put Sky News on!"

Sylvia reached for the remote and pressed 501. A politician was being interviewed, but the banner across the bottom said....

A pensioner has been found shot dead at his home in Leeds.

"There's bound to be an interview on soon. I wonder if they will show our house?" asked Sylvia beaming.

"Depends which way the camera is facing. But from the look of it they are going to be aiming the camera the other way. They will want to get the murder house in shot."

They watched the reporter from Sky talking to the camera on the television and in the street at the same time.

The women were ecstatic.

"That's Jeremy Thompson, isn't it? He did that murder with the two little girls, didn't he?" asked Alice.

"I don't think he did the actual murder! Shall we go out into the garden and see if we can talk to him? I bet that he would love to talk to us, being neighbours and witnesses and everything."

54

"How are we witnesses? We don't need to be saying anything that will draw attention to us or get us into trouble."

"He's coming up the driveway!"

"Jeremy Thompson is coming here!" Alice brought her hands to her mouth.

There was a knock on the door and the women looked at each other.

"Shall we answer the door?" asked Sylvia

"Yes, but put the book away first. We can't have them filming that."

CHAPTER SIX

Eleanor finished riding and decided that now would be a good time to catch her father and give him the news.

Michael lived in a cottage on land owned by Eleanor a little further up the coast. It took less than five minutes to walk there, so she took the dogs and set out.

Michael had known Thomas since he had become engaged to his sister in law Ellie. He never liked Thomas and often commented on his pasty white face and blood red lips.

It had been many years before he had any idea of the trouble Thomas had caused his children, because they had sworn not to tell him. He had been horribly upset when he found out and had wanted revenge in some form.

But still the family had agreed to keep quiet.

Eleanor pushed open the gate to the cottage and shouted to her father. As it turned out, he wasn't inside, but down on the beach fiddling about with his boat.

Michael had always loved boats and since he moved here, at the invite and insistence of his daughter, had enjoyed himself immensely. A youthful 72, he had blossomed since the loss of his wife, several years earlier.

Michael waved at Eleanor and soon they were sitting on the decking looking at the sea.

"Wow. So, he's been shot then. What a way to go."

"Yes. I won't be going to the funeral though."

"I shouldn't think that any of you will be going?" Michael looked directly at his daughter and she felt almost hypnotised by him.

"No, we won't Dad."

"I still think you should have let me do something."

"No point Dad. You would just have got in trouble."

"After Andrew, when your mother and I worked it out, we didn't want to say much to you because you all seem to be getting on with your lives so well."

"We all remembered though Dad."

"I suppose we felt guilty too," whispered Michael.

There was an unusual silence between them. Eleanor never wanted this conversation with her Dad, because there was the danger that they would touch the knotty subject of guilt and blame. In the early years, Eleanor rebelled against the parents who had let this happen to her, with drink and drugs. But they never talked about it, because no one did back then. They probably don't these days either. As she got older and had a child of her own, she realised that to be a guiltless parent was impossible.

Michael stared out to sea and Eleanor said, "Dad, I've got to nip home because someone is bringing a couple of horses soon. Come with me and we can chat." She was desperate not to upset their relationship.

"Darling, you go back. I've got some jobs to finish on the boat and I will come over after that."

Eleanor kissed him and said, "Are you sure?"

"Of course." He kissed his daughter and watched her walk back along the coast path.

He had been suspicious of Thomas by the time Eleanor was 11 and from then on kept her away from him. But calling the police? That would have caused more trouble, with court appearances and interviews and notoriety. No, far better to move on with life and ignore it.

He leant back in the chair and dozed.

There was that lady again.

She was standing on the pavement across the road and smiling at him in that lovely way. She was the only person who had ever smiled at him. The sad thing was, Michael did not consider it unusual to reach ten years old without ever having been smiled at.

Dressed in blue and white, the tall and beautiful lady seemed to follow his life and he had no idea who she was.

He told his mother about her once and she screamed at him and sent him to the nuns at his school and told him to repeat his story.

When he did, Sister Philippa dragged him by the arm and took him into her office.

"Stand there, boy" she shouted at him.

Michael stood defiantly by the desk and braced himself for the punishment he knew was coming. Sister Philippa took down the cane from the top of the cupboard and said,

"You are going straight to hell, Michael Prentice. It does not matter what you do for the rest of your life, you are going to hell for blaspheming against the Holy Virgin Mary."

This was confusing as Michael had no idea to what she was referring. But he was used to beatings, both his father and mother giving him regular punishment. Father used his belt and mother used whatever was handy. He rarely knew why he was being beaten and accepted it as part of his life. He had been told he was going to hell many times and took that fact for granted. Perhaps hell was not such a bad place, because judging by the people who told him they were going to heaven, he would prefer hell.

This beating lasted longer than usual and only stopped when Sister Mary came into the office and took the cane from her fellow nun.

"Get out, Michael and go home. I shall expect to see you in class tomorrow morning."

Returning home, Michael considered his life and thought that it would not be so bad if it ended early. He knew he had a twin sister who had died at birth and was told by his mother that she wished that she had lived and Michael died. Michael wished he could join his sister. He kicked a wall miserably.

Turning the corner into Grange Street he felt the familiar sinking feeling he always did. No 27, where he lived, looked cruel and cold. Other children were running about the road, playing football as they did most nights.

There were net curtains at all of the windows and he knew that his mother would be watching him through them, so there was no point in dawdling.

"Coming to play, Mike?" asked one of the boys.

"No, I can't," he answered. The truth was that the other children thought that Michael was a bit stuck up, which was ironic as they knew full well that his father was drunk more often than sober. William Prentice would stagger his

way down the street with his legs plaiting, singing and sometimes being sick or peeing in the gutter.

Michael went in through the front door. The house was tiny, so the room he entered was the one where his mother and father were both standing, waiting for him to come home.

"What did the Sisters say?" asked his mother.

"That I was going to hell."

"So you are, you little heathen. Your mother told me what you said. I told you not to lie like that."

"I don't lie," answered his son.

William reached to his trousers and began undoing his belt. Michael felt giddy and sick again.

"But they already beat me Dad," he said.

"Take off your jumper." Michael did as he was told and his parents did not flinch when they saw the blood that was seeping through his shirt.

"Good," said William.

William grabbed his son by the arm and raised his belt as far as his own arm would reach and brought it down with a whack on Michael's buttocks. He did this ten times until he felt weak. Michael did not scream, just stood passively with a red face and silent tears streaming down his cheeks.

"Get to bed, you little shit," William said and sat down by the fire demanding his wife fetch him another drink.

Michael went upstairs and took off his clothes. His shirt and underwear had already stuck to the blood on his back. He wiped himself as well as he could and left his bloodied clothes on the floor. Climbing into bed, Michael felt as he had done virtually every night of his life.

He wished he was dead.

The guilt issue started not long after this episode. Going to church with his mother one Sunday they stopped to talk to a neighbour and Michael took an offered sweet.

"Don't eat anything before Mass, boy. You know the penalty," his mother told him.

But he was hungry and ate the sweet on the way to church.

When he sat down and listened to the priest droning on and on about punishment, he began to feel guilty and evil and scared. So began an issue with food which would haunt Michael for the rest of his life.

Then there was Christmas. Michael knew that there would be no Christmas presents this year, because there never were. He came downstairs and ate the barely warm porridge his mother placed in front of him.

He knew his friends would be enjoying themselves with their families and there would be noise and colour. He had to sit and read the Bible.

After a lunch of badly cooked pie and mash he started to go upstairs, when his father called to him.

"Have you seen your present then?"

"No, what present?" Michael tried hard to keep the excitement from his voice.

"Out the back. It's a bike."

Michael rushed through the back door and saw a bike leaning against the wall. How could he have not noticed it before? It could only have been put there after he had gone to bed. It was not a new bike, but seemed alright nonetheless. He examined it thoroughly and liked what he saw.

Remembering his manners, Michael ran back into the house.

"Thank you, Dad, it's great," he beamed.

"Here is the book for you. All you have to do is keep up the payments and the bike is yours!"

"I don't know what you mean, Dad." said Michael.

William began to get cross.

"The book, stupid, the book!"

Kathleen joined in. "That means you will have to earn the money to pay for the bike and have it knocked off the bill at the shop."

"But I don't have any money Dad," said Michael.

"You little bastard," answered his father. He took hold of his sons arm and hit him time and time again.

Michael was sent upstairs.

He began to cry only when he was alone in the room. Christmas was rubbish that was for sure.

He looked out of the window covered which was covered in frost on the inside of the panes. He rubbed the ice until it melted and looked out at the fields beyond. It had been snowing and Michael watched a shepherd feeding his flock. His eyes wandered to the field next to that which had horses in it that looked sad and cold.

There she stood again.

The beautiful lady, dressed in blue and white and smiling at him.

This time she waved too and Michael could not stop himself waving back. She put her finger to her lips and Michael understood immediately. This was to be their secret. He blew her a kiss and slowly she faded away.

When Michael was allowed downstairs the next day, there was no bike and no book.

It was never mentioned again.

Michael had seen the lady a lot these past few days and had been slightly unnerved by her presence. It was not surprising that he hadn't noticed the abuse of his children with an upbringing like that. Surely, he wasn't to be punished for it?

He wandered back to his boat on the beach and fiddled about with it for the rest of the afternoon. Michael wanted to work out the story he would tell the police if they asked what they had all been doing for the past week.

He had a horrible feeling that things were going to get worse before they got better.

CHAPTER SEVEN

When Elizabeth put the phone down after speaking to Eleanor, she felt cross.

Just when her life had begun to finally settle down after 40 years of dramas, Uncle Thomas had gone and got himself killed and that was bound to create trouble. It had certainly brought up bad memories for her.

Their loving uncle had systematically worked his way through his nieces until they became older and wilier. Each girl would hide, run away and find an excuse, until the next in line would be encouraged to visit. She suspected that Thomas preferred a younger child, because he stopped paying attention to any of them as they reached around 11 years old. He must have gone elsewhere when they all reached their teens, but none of them cared where.

The bizarre fact was that each child kept their terrible story to themselves, neither telling an adult, nor each other. It was not until the children grew up that they finally compared stories. Except Eleanor, who triumphantly told them all that she must have avoided the abuse, until a near mental breakdown when she was 40 and the subsequent therapy, uncovered her secret tale.

How could their parents not have known? They weren't stupid people or uncaring?

"What the fuck..." Elizabeth said out loud.

"What's up Mum?" Robert was home from university and unperturbed by his Mum's utterances. He was used to them.

"My uncle has been murdered."

"Was that the bloke they've been on about on the television? The one who's been shot?"

"Yes."

"Wow. Are you ok?"

"I'm fine. Put the telly on and we'll see what they are saying about it now."

The reporter was part way through a story.

Police are asking for anyone with information to come forward. But so far this morning there has been a lot of activity at the address. Some family members have arrived. Neighbours say that they had not seen Mr Yates for several days, but did not suspect that anything was wrong as he kept himself to himself. It would appear that one of his sons found the body when he came to pay a visit.

Little information is available at this time, but we understand that he had been shot in the living room at his home, probably several days ago. This is a quiet street where nothing usually happens and so there is a sense of disbelief amongst the neighbourhood.

The reporter went on in a similar vein for a minute, showing shots of the Yates house and surrounding area. Elizabeth recognised the house and the street. She felt sick and sat down until the feeling passed. Memories of her childhood swam over her and she felt as though she were drowning.

"Hello Lizzie! I'm glad you came to visit me. Are you on your own?"

"Yes," was all the young girl could manage to say. She had been sent down to stay with her uncle while her mother and aunt went shopping in Leeds. Sometimes she managed to wangle one of her siblings coming too and so long as they stayed together, she would be safe.

Today her siblings were all playing football in the field at the back of the houses. Thomas's two sons were playing too.

The scene was set. Elizabeth had no chance.

Uncle Thomas had become slicker and quicker as he perfected his art over the years.

"Up we go!" he said brightly. "We haven't got much time to play, so let's get on with it. Do you want to wee first?"

"No." answered Elizabeth. She didn't want to go into the toilet where the seat and the floor were covered in wee and the place stunk.

She preceded him up the stairs, hearing his breath and feeling his hand on her back. Elizabeth was already mesmerised by the process.

Thomas pushed her into his bedroom and told her to lie down on the bed. She obeyed as usual and he walked over to the window. He looked up and down the street and then dragged the curtains shut. The noise affected her ever after. That sound of metal curtain fastenings moving along metal tracks. It set her teeth on edge and her mind on scramble.

When he turned back to face her, all Elizabeth could see was a black shadow man against the thin blue curtains. She *could no longer make out the big glasses and the tight trousers, but she could smell. He smelt, the room smelt, the bed smelt and she felt sick. The atmosphere in the room was chewy and airless and filled with anticipation.*

Elizabeth knew what was coming.

He moved over to the bed and the talking stopped. It always did when he was getting near to the main event. He undid his belt and unzipped his jeans and moved onto the bed. He put his hand on her face and opened her mouth and then climbed on top of her.

Elizabeth was unable to breathe and began to choke and splutter, but that didn't stop him. She tried to struggle and scratch him, but that just spurred him on and he used his weight to prevent her wriggling. His thigh on her chest meant she could no longer heave her lungs to take in air through her nose now that her mouth was full.

Suddenly, he finished and Elizabeth found herself looking down at her immobile frame on the bed. Her uncle was slapping her face and shaking her hard. "For fucks sake, wake up, you stupid child!"

He shook and shook and Elizabeth thought that she would stay exactly where she was and watch him suffer.

She could hear her mother downstairs talking to Aunt Ellie. As soon as she thought, 'Mummy,' she was back in her body receiving another slap.

"Thank God for that. Now go to the bathroom and wash your face and go downstairs. Say anything about this and I will tell your father what you have done. He will be ashamed of you."

Elizabeth did not want to experience her father's shame and scuttled out of the bedroom into the bathroom. After trying to wipe the stickiness from her hair, over and over and over and over again, a knot of fear in her middle, she went down the stairs.

"Where's Uncle Thomas?" asked an angry looking aunt.

"Uuuupstairs," she stammered.

"And have you been with him?"

"No, he's in bed." Elizabeth ran to her mother and held tightly onto her legs.

#

"I'm sure she thought he was having affairs with his nieces, you know."

"Who?" asked Robert.

"Auntie Ellie. I mean, she must have known what was going on, but she was always cross with us, as though we had been leading him on. Horrible, horrible people."

"Yea, well he's dead now. Someone must have finally got their revenge."

"Yes."

Elizabeth would have to think about this, because she knew several people, mostly family, who could now be under suspicion of his murder. She was one of the main ones.

"Do you want some coffee, Mum?"

"Lovely darling. Yes please."

He handed her a cup and said,

"I'm going out now to meet Andy in town. Then I'm back to Leeds. Are you going to be alright?" Robert was always worried about his mother. They had been through a lot together. He wanted to protect her against any trouble. When he was a boy he was incapable of helping, but now a man, he could if necessary. He trained and fought and trained again and was now a fit and lean fighter.

"Of course I am, you go off and enjoy yourself."

Robert left and Elizabeth cleared the kitchen.

She heard a deafening knock on the front door and went to answer it. The knock sounded as though the police were trying to break in. As she moved her hand towards the doorknob, the hammering started again. But she couldn't see anyone through the glass.

"Hello?" she said. "Who's there?"

No one answered and so Elizabeth decided not to open the door.

"Probably Jehovah's…." she said to herself.

The noise stopped, so she nipped up to the loo. Halfway through the deed, she heard George playing the guitar in the sitting room. He only knew the 'Smoke on the Water' riff and he was playing it over and over. Then she realised that George was not at home.

Elizabeth stopped pissing and listened, all her nerves on edge. The riff played again. Elizabeth got up and went to the top of the stairs. From there she could see the front door, which was thankfully still closed.

The guitar continued to play.

It took all of her courage to start walking downstairs while that guitar was playing. But Elizabeth was much harder than she looked. She crept quietly downstairs. Peeping round the sitting room door, she saw the guitar leaning against the wall on its stand, exactly where George had left it. The music had stopped and everything was as it should be.

She remembered that Uncle Thomas played the guitar. "Oh shit," she said.

CHAPTER EIGHT

Anthony Yates arrived at his father's house, or rather arrived next to the tape which blocked off the road in front of the house.

Richard had rung him from David's phone soon after he called the police.

"He's dead Anthony. Someone shot him."

"Fuck, Richard. Who would have done that?"

"I don't know, Anthony."

"Has anything been stolen?"

"I don't think so, but it's hard to tell if anything has been moved or whether it's just a tip."

"I'll come round now. Where is he? In the house, I mean."

"In the front room."

"In front of the fire?"

"Yes."

"I might have guessed. I'm on my way mate."

But by the time he arrived, he couldn't get further than the tape and Richard and David appeared to have been arrested.

Their father had been a rubbish father and a horrible man, but Richard would never have been involved in his death. He must tell the police that, straight away.

"That's my father's house, I want to go in!"

The demands were in vain, because the policewoman would not let him go beyond the tape. She informed him that the house was now a crime scene and no one could enter aside from police. His angry insistence was getting him nowhere and only a sharp warning from a sergeant about his potential arrest ensured that he backed off.

Anthony nervously smoothed the hair on the back of his head, unsure what to do next. His eyes flicked round as he tried to take in his surroundings. He saw the police moving inside and outside of the crime scene. He saw the police cars and vans. The cars belonging to forensic people and administration people, parked further and further up the road. The vehicles blocked the driveways of the residents without care or consideration. There were newspaper people and television people in their vans with metal things sticking out of the top.

Anthony thought he recognised the woman reporter who was talking to a camera and there was a man doing the same to another camera whom he was sure was on Sky News, but he couldn't think of his name. He spoke briefly to one after a microphone was pushed into his face, but couldn't remember what he said.

He looked at the house opposite his father's and saw the net curtains moving. He guessed that the two elderly women would be watching carefully. Anthony's wife Tina told him that she was going to work and he could ring her there if he needed her. She said she didn't have time to hang around here all day.

He watched her go with little emotion.

"Anthony, come with me." He swung round and saw Janet. She took his arm and led him back to her own place, two doors up from his father's.

"Thanks. They won't let me past and they've taken Richard and David. But I don't know why."

"I don't know why either, but it's probably because they were there when the police arrived. Come on in and sit down. I'll make some coffee, or do you want tea?"

"Whisky, but it's probably not a good idea yet. Make me coffee, please." Anthony put his head in his hands on the table.

Janet busied herself with the coffee, not wanting Anthony to think any more about whisky.

"Here you are, Anthony. Do you want anything to eat?"

"God no, Janet! My father has just been killed and you are trying to get me to eat! Leave me the fuck alone!"

"Alright," said Janet and backed off immediately. The two of them were very familiar around each other and knew what the other was thinking. This fact was becoming increasingly obvious to Anthony's wife, Tina. Janet wasn't worried about Tina.

"Do you know what's happened to my Dad?" he asked her.

"I don't, no. I mean I know he's dead and someone shot him, but I don't know what actually happened. Do you?"

"No, of course I don't." He picked up a spoon and stirred sugar into his coffee. "But he probably asked for it."

Janet looked at him," Anthony?"

"Yes?" he said, knowing what was coming next.

"Has it got anything to do with your mother's death?" She looked frightened.

"Maybe, but I don't think so."

He got up and stood at the door drinking his coffee. From there he could see the road to his right and also straight across the shared driveway into the Farrington's side door. This was open and he could see into the kitchen. If David had gone off with the police, then there shouldn't be anyone in the house. Anthony started to walk across the driveway, to close the door. He was met by another policeman.

"Can I help you, sir?" he asked.

"I was going to shut David's door. He's not here at the moment."

"And who are you, sir?"

"I'm Anthony Yates. I am the son of your murder victim and I want to go into the house."

"I see, well I'm afraid you won't be allowed to go in just yet. We shall need to speak with you."

"Where have you taken my brother?"

"I believe he has been taken to Leeds in order to help us. I expect they will want to speak to you too, sir. Perhaps you can give me your details?"

This Anthony did and gave the policeman his card.

"I shall be here for a little while if you need me," he said, pointing his finger at Janet's house, "and then you will get me at home."

"Thank you, sir."

Anthony went back into the house.

"What did he want?" asked Janet, looking nervous.

"My details," he answered shortly.

Anthony sat down again. In truth, he wasn't registering what was going on today. He knew his father was dead, but he wasn't actually feeling it. He had felt the same when his mother died. But he was pissed that day.

Ellie Yates had been fiddling with the washing machine, which apparently shorted while she was poking the electric cable with a knife. She died almost immediately and was found by her husband when he got home from some meeting or other in town.

Anthony was dropped off at the gate behind the ambulance and ran up the side steps and into the kitchen. His mother lay on the floor with two paramedics working on her. She had something in her mouth and a machine attachment on her chest. She was a funny colour and Anthony noticed a weird smell. The washing machine was out of its designated hole and had a scorch mark up the side of it.

"How is she?" he asked the men.

"We are doing what we can," said one without stopping what he was doing.

Anthony went into the front room to see where his Dad was. He found him smoking and staring at the television, which was turned off.

"What happened?" asked Anthony.

"She's electrocuted herself," he answered while thumbing in the direction of the kitchen. "I came back and found her on the floor with a knife in her hand. The knife was all scorched and the plug and the washing machine all burnt. Stupid cow was always prodding about when she didn't think it was working properly."

"Well, why didn't you get it fixed for her?"

"Kitchens are women's places, not men's. It's not for me to sort out. It's her own fault." He took another pull on his cigarette.

"Don't you care Dad?"

"Not much," he answered.

The room was neat and tidy, save for the full ashtray and dirty plates on the table next to his father's chair.

"How did Mum manage to electrocute herself today though?"

"She was doing her usual of nagging me all morning. Telling me I'm dirty and should change my clothes and tidy up and stop shaving in the kitchen and it all got a bit violent." Thomas stubbed his cigarette out firmly in the ashtray.

"So I threw a knife at her and she threw it back and I gave her a clout and she gave me one back."

"Dad! Why were you doing that?"

"Because she's a nosy, noisy cow. Then next door's dog came into the kitchen and as you well know, dogs are vermin. I said, if you want it to be so clean in here why are you letting in vermin? She didn't have an answer for that and so I went out. Then, when I came back in she was on the floor all smoky and singed."

"Then what did you do?"

"I called 999 and waited until they got here. Oh and phoned you."

"Did you try and help her?"

"God. No! Not with all that sick and stuff coming from her mouth. I could have caught something nasty."

Anthony looked at his father in disgust and went back into the kitchen.

The paramedics were putting his mother onto a stretcher and getting ready to take her away. They were not surprised at the lack of emotion shown by her family members, having seen a lot worse on their shifts.

"Is she dead?" Anthony asked.

"We are taking her to the hospital in Leeds. Perhaps you can make your way there."

"Can't I come in the ambulance?" Anthony asked. Then he thought how inconvenient it would be to be left in Leeds without his car.

"I'll follow you."

Anthony decided he would take his mother's car. He considered briefly whether to shout his father and take him to the hospital, but thought better of it. Instead, he rang Richard and told him to meet him at the hospital.

By the time he arrived, parked the car and walked to A & E, there was no sign of his mother or the paramedics who had brought her. An enquiry at the desk led him to the relative's room, where he was told to wait until someone came to see him.

There were four other people in there, split into two groups and apparently very upset. Anthony looked away from them, embarrassed. God forbid that they ask him what his reason to be here was. Luckily, he didn't have to wait long before Richard arrived.

There was no man-hugging or hand shaking, just a nod and a half smile as they sat next to each other.

After half an hour, the other two groups had been collected by staff wearing their sympathetic faces and taken out of the room.

"So it's us next," said Richard.

"Hope so, I hate this waiting. I mean it's one thing sticking us away from everyone else, but no one tells you anything, do they? I bet if we went out and asked, they would just say, I'll send someone along." Anthony was getting irritated.

Eventually, a doctor arrived and he said, "I'm very sorry to tell you that your mother has passed away."

Both men had risen from their chairs when the doctor asked them their names but now sat down abruptly. It doesn't matter what you feel about your mother, it still a very shocking moment when you hear that she has died.

"Can we see her?" asked Anthony.

"If you would like to come with me, you can see her."

Richard and Anthony followed him down the corridors, right, left, and then straight on for a very long time. They passed people they would never see again and everyone kept to their tracks.

These people don't know that my mother is dead, Richard thought.

They travelled along another corridor to where a man stood next to a door, his head bowed. Richard felt a shiver down his spine and almost grabbed hold of Anthony's hand, because it reminded him of the Edgar Allen Poe films

78

his father used to force them to watch late on a Saturday night.

The nurse turned, beckoned them into the room and opened another door. With horror, they saw their mother lying on her back on some sort of slab. There was a contraption in her mouth and a smell of vomit in the room.

"She can't be comfortable," said Richard as he leant over to touch her. "God, she's still warm!"

"She hasn't been dead that long, she's bound to be warm."

"It feels like she's still here, Anthony. I don't mean in her body, I mean standing here with us."

"She's not happy, is she?"

#

The coroner ruled accidental death by electrocution and allowed the funeral to take place. Anthony found it difficult to accept the way his father acted. So upset in front of authorities and neighbours and then laughing and carefree when at home.

Anthony had become more convinced that his father's version of events that day was a lie, but couldn't get to the bottom of it. He confided in Janet and she was sympathetic, but said that he must stop dwelling on it and get on with his life.

Instead, he increased his drinking. He had always drunk plenty of alcohol, but after his mother's death, it became less of a leisure activity and more of a career.

"I'm going," Anthony said suddenly to Janet and got up, knocking the chair over. Janet ran across and picked up the chair.

"Do you want me to drive you, Anthony?"

"No, I should get back to my family and let them know what's going on."

He went without acknowledging her, leaving her with tears in her eyes.

Janet, used to side swipes such as 'my family' let him go without saying a word. She knew he would be back. She folded the tea towel neatly and put it on the radiator. She cleared the kitchen and pushed the chairs back under the table.

"Well you got what was coming to you, didn't you? You pervy, child molesting bastard." Janet said to no one in particular.

CHAPTER NINE

Police are still no nearer to solving the mysterious killing of a Leeds man last Saturday. Mr Yates was shot dead in the living room of his home and appears to have lain undiscovered for several days. What police have described as a cold and callous murder, has upset the local community who now feel unsafe in their homes.

The appeal for information has been renewed, although police say they are currently following several leads. Two local men, who were helping police with their enquiries, have now been released.

Anyone with any information can contact Crimestoppers or their local police.

Sylvia turned the radio off.

"I had a call from the police this morning Alice and they are going to come and interview us this afternoon."

"Oh, how wonderful! We must tidy up and then make biscuits. Policemen love biscuits."

"Do they? How do you know that?"

"Miss Marple, or something."

On this useful piece of information, the old women prepared themselves and the room.

They had updated the book during the week, but now made sure it was secure in its place on the library shelves. They tucked it inside the dust jacket of a book about old womens' medical problems which they were pretty sure would not be opened by anyone. They were not as stupid as they liked to pretend.

Once the scene was set and the police settled on the sofa, the questioning began.

"Have you found out who did the murder yet?" asked Alice.

"Not yet, madam," answered Detective Chief Inspector Revie.

"Do you have any clues though?" enquired Sylvia.

"We have some leads we are following," said Detective Sergeant Jackson.

"Do tell. We have a few ideas of our own if you are interested in those." Alice informed him.

"Well if you could just answer some questions, we would very much appreciate it Miss Lamb," said the sergeant in a voice he saved for flattering elderly ladies, even though it hardly ever worked.

"Oh, we would love to answer some questions, we like questions because we have all the answers," said Sylvia importantly.

"I'm sure you do, Miss Lamb," answered the sergeant

"Call me Syl, all my friends do."

"No, they do not. Who calls you Syl? " asked Alice.

"Well that man who used to come to the Mecca called me Syl and he promised to take me to London."

"He called you Dill and London wasn't where he wanted to take you," Alice sniggered and smoothed her skirt.

"Ladies please! We would like to know if you saw anything out of the ordinary during the past week."

"You mean to do with Creepy Yates?"

The policeman looked at each other. The original house to house enquiries had given them very few leads, but these follow up personal interviews were giving them much more useful information.

They were beginning to form the opinion that rather than no one having a motive to kill the man, many people had.

"Tell us what you know, please," asked Chief Inspector Revie.

"Depends what you want to know?" Alice didn't want to make it easy for the men, in case they left too quickly.

"Did you see anyone out of the ordinary? Has anyone called at the house opposite, or your house who you weren't expecting?"

"No, I can't say that there has been anyone out of the ordinary. I think that we know most of the people who come here and I haven't seen anyone strange over the road," said Sylvia.

"Not that we watch his house all the time," Alice tapped her sisters knee, to make sure they were making the right impression.

"No, goodness me, no. We don't watch all the time. We have a great deal to do and many friends who call." Sylvia smiled.

"Were you friends with Mr Yates?"

Now it was the women's turn to look at each other and they answered in unison, "No."

"Had you had an argument with him?" asked the sergeant.

"No, not an argument. We hardly ever spoke to him, or them."

"Them?"

"Him and his wife," said Alice.

"Yes, she had an accident a few years back, didn't she?" Revie asked.

"Yes, an accident. That's what they called it, but she had been doing the same thing for years without managing to kill herself." Alice folded her arms.

"We aren't saying that it might not have been an accident," Sylvia reassured.

"No, I'm sure. If we could get back to this incident, it will help us greatly."

"We did see Richard arrive that Saturday morning and he waited in his car for a bit, then he went in."

"Then David went round from next door. They stayed in the house for a while and went upstairs and seemed to check around there and then the police and ambulance arrived." Alice listed the events.

"You've let them go now, I hope?" asked Sylvia, "It's absolutely ridiculous imagining that they would have been up to anything like that! They were more likely to do something bad when they were much younger, but not now."

"Bit naughty when they were younger?" asked the sergeant, although his enquiries had discovered only fighting after football matches and David being cautioned for careless driving a few years ago.

"Not so much naughty as getting into trouble with their parents. Ellie and Thomas decided that very little constituted trouble and they punished their children a lot." Alice said.

"Hard on their kids, were they?"

"They didn't consider themselves to be hard, sergeant. They thought they were being fair."

"But they were just cruel," said Sylvia, "Do you know that they would lock the boys in that little cupboard thing next to the outside steps? The one with the door facing the driveway? It was supposed to be for coal and lawnmowers, but they put the boys in there if they were getting in the way."

"Oh dear," answered Revie.

"But I suppose it's better than the things he used to do to the little girls who used to visit, or be made to visit. It was disgraceful, but no one seemed to stop it."

"They seemed to encourage it," added Alice.

"Who did?"

"Ellie's sister. I don't know what she actually knew, but they had to go down there regular as clockwork and they didn't seem happy about it."

"When did all this take place? Was it recently?" asked Revie.

"No. More like the late 60s, but I could check for you if you like." Alice was rewarded with a kick, which the police did not appear to notice.

"How will you do that?"

"She can't check anything, Chief Inspector, her memory isn't that good!" Sylvia tittered away at her own statement.

"So, do any other members of the Yates family live near here?" asked DS Jackson.

"Not for a long while, sergeant. Not for years. I gather some of them have done quite well for themselves. Well so Ellie Yates said to Mrs Banks and she told the doctor's wife."

"And she told us!" finished Alice.

"One of the girls is that famous writer."

"Do you have any of their addresses or telephone numbers?" Sergeant Jackson prepared to add to his notes.

"No idea," said Sylvia.

The sergeant asked, "Which famous writer?"

"The one who wrote that book that's been on at the pictures. About murders and stuff."

"With that woman who has been on Hercules Poirot and I think it was set in Leeds. Eleanor something." Sylvia was unconsciously demonstrating how writing things down in her book as they happened, was better than relying on her own intermittent memory.

"Do you mean Eleanor Prentice?" asked the sergeant amazed.

"That's her!" said Alice, sitting back further in her chair and clapping her hands.

"Eleanor Prentice used to live here with all her family?" the Chief Inspector asked. This was no place to admit it, but he was a fan of her books and had seen the film in question three times. He liked the way the police had been represented and felt empathy with one of the characters.

"Years ago," began Alice." Ellie Yates's sister and her family lived up the road with all her children and the kids suffered certain assaults at the hands of Thomas Yates until they moved away."

"We don't actually know if they were assaulted, we can just assume it because of the things we saw."

"Well yes and all the other children we saw going in and out of the house over the years."

"Has this been reported to the police? Or investigated by them?" asked Jackson, conscious that none of this information had shown up on their records.

"I doubt it very much. Things like that weren't reported back then and it's private really, isn't it?" said Sylvia.

"And I'm sure that the families would not like any of this to come out and get in the newspapers. I should imagine that they would do or pay almost anything to ensure that didn't happen." added Alice.

"Do you have any actual evidence of these offences?" asked Revie

"You mean like times and dates and what people said at the time and afterwards? All written down and in the order the things happened?" asked Sylvia.

"I don't know of anyone who has that sort of information," Alice said firmly.

"Do you have any of their addresses, or know of someone who has them?" asked the sergeant, trying to hide his irritation. He didn't like old women.

"Normally you would expect cousins to have each other's information, but in this case, I don't think so."

"And you don't have any more information that might help us?" asked the Chief Inspector.

"No, but, we could write down everything that happens over there from now on and let you know?" asked Sylvia.

"I don't think that level of detail will be necessary, but if you hear or see anything which you think may be of importance, please let us know."

Chief Inspector Revie got up from his chair and went towards the book shelves.

"You have quite a collection here," he said and began to run his fingers along the titles.

"Quite a few first editions too," said Sylvia. "But perhaps you would like some more tea?"

"No thank you, ladies. We must be going now."

There was more fussing and chirruping while the policemen took their leave. The ladies watched them from the window as they walked back to their car which was parked on the Yates's drive.

"You nearly told them about the book," said Sylvia.

"There's a part of me that thinks they should know about it."

"They aren't very good policemen if they need our little scribblings to help them find a murderer." Sylvia didn't want the police to find out that some of the information had already been used and paid for.

Sylvia went to the dresser, because she had more to write in her book.

\#

"Those old birds know more than they are letting on," said Revie.

"You think so sir? I think they are just dotty and want some attention from us. Bit of excitement in their dull old lives. My Gran's like that," answered Jackson.

Revie grinned at his young sidekick. "You'd be making a big mistake if you think that older people are daft. Those women have spent most of their lives watching what goes on, up and down this road. I bet they know something about what went on, whether they are aware of it or not."

"They are just obsessed with people on the telly!"

"With detectives on the telly. That's different."

"Do you want to interview them again?"

"Yes, but not yet. I want to see other people first, particularly this missing family of his. I want you to find out where they are all living."

"They could be anywhere."

"They probably are, but I'm sure that you will be able to find them and then maybe we can get some more information. Because there's not a lot of direction at the moment." `

"I wouldn't mind interviewing that writer." Jackson said, half to himself.

"I will be doing that interview myself. Chief Inspector's perk."

They arrived at the car.

"I think we'll have another look inside the house, just in case we've missed something."

"Ok sir, do you have the key?"

"Yes, I do," he said and took a plastic bag from his pocket.

He handed it to his sergeant and motioned him to open the back door. Revie looked round in order to take in the surroundings. Standing in the driveway, he faced the house. To the left he could see the other half of the semi where the Farringtons lived. Further left, he could see the similar line of semis, all built at the same time. To the right and at the back of the property was a sweeping estate, finished sometime in 2005 on what used to be a field with horses, the Chief Inspector remembered. Behind him on the other side of the road were more houses, built at various times with cul-de-sacs and semis and the old stone house where the doctor used to live. Dr Brown, he thought he was called. Next to the doctor's, lived the Lambs.

Many of these householders would have a good view of the Yates' house and the Yates' life. Revie was surprised that he had no more information coming to him. He was aware that people were busy and used to going about their own lives, but really, something must have been seen.

He was shouted by his sergeant and they made their way into the murder house.

In the kitchen they noticed the smell of death which still pervaded the air. The body had been removed several days ago, but as it had lain undiscovered for a few days and begun to decompose, that smell would probably never go.

"God, it still smells in here," said Jackson.

"They say that when there has been a murder, the atmosphere in a house keeps the memory of it and that's why people don't like living in a murder house," commented the Chief Inspector.

"Probably as much to do with the rotten smell. I heard that even when the obvious smell leaves, there's still an underlying smell that the brain recognises, even though you don't actually smell it as death," answered Jackson, the more scientific one.

"A very good point. But it smells now. I wish I still smoked, because I could light one and only smell that."

They made their way into the front room, which looked similar to their last visit, except for the fact that there was no body on the floor.

The smell was bad in here.

Chief Inspector Revie looked at the blood stains on the carpet and on the wall above the gas fire.

"Whoever did it, had to be right in the room with their back to the opposite wall. They would have been in front of the sofa." He mused. "Have they decided whether the shot was fired by someone sitting down or standing up?"

"Standing up I think. Or a very tall person sitting down. The shot seems to be in a straight line, rather than angled."

"So the murderer was let in and allowed to get into that position first. There is no sign that the old man tried to run away."

"No and he dropped down dead. No wiggling about."

"He must have known his killer."

"Perhaps that's why the neighbours didn't see anything out of the ordinary. They saw someone they knew coming to the house and thought nothing of it," offered Jackson.

"That's a good point. Let's go upstairs."

They went through the hall door and walked to the bottom of the stairs.

"And the front door was locked?"

"And the back door and the only keys were hanging up on that key rack thingy in the kitchen," answered Jackson.

"Except for the keys his family had."

"And next doors apparently. But they've known each other for 40 odd years."

Upstairs it was a tip. In the bedroom, nothing seemed to be out of place. Revie moved things around on an ornate shelf unit on the dividing wall.

"Sir, I don't know if this is something or not."

"Go on."

"Everywhere is covered in dust, layers of it, but up here on top of the wardrobe, parts of it are clean, like someone's been here."

"Did forensics check it out?"

"I expect so, I'll ask."

Jackson rummaged around on top of the wardrobe, saying, "old suitcases, sandals and some old snaps or something. Everything is quite old."

"Pass me those photographs down, Jackson."

This was soon done and Revie looked through them quickly.

"All these children don't look very happy about being photographed, do they?"

Jackson took them back and agreed. "The kids are naked in all of them. Oh my God. Look what they are doing. That's fucking disgusting."

"Yes, it is. Bag them all up and see if you can find anymore. Perhaps we can identify some of them, even though they will be grown up now."

He walked over to the window and saw one of the Lamb sisters standing in her bedroom window with what appeared to be binoculars. When she saw him, she swiftly closed the curtains.

"Yes, I think I need to speak to those old ladies again. But not now, no time."

CHAPTER TEN

Because Eleanor Prentice always ignored calls that came to her mobile and were marked 'Unknown', it was two days before she finally spoke to Chief Inspector Revie.

When he finished explaining who he was and why he was telephoning, Eleanor asked, "Are you related to Don?"

"No," he answered, "I wish I was. He was the greatest manager of all time."

"Yes, he was. I used to have a rabbit named Revie. He was a white rabbit," she replied. "You want to come all the way over here to speak to me. That's quite a trek for a policeman from Yorkshire. Can't I talk to a local man?"

"I would rather you talked to me first," he said, "We can get straight to the point."

"We shall look forward to seeing you. If you get lost on the way, please call and we will try and get you here safely. You do speak Welsh?"

"No. I expect there will be one or two people who speak English there?"

"Everyone can speak English. I'm just not sure that everyone will!"

She put down the phone on this witty remark and immediately stopped smiling. This was not going to be much fun. Eleanor didn't want to be reminded of her past. The past had been dealt with and placed in an appropriate part of her mind.

She dialled her father's phone.

"Hi Dad. I've just had some Chief Inspector on from Yorkshire and he wants to interview us. He says he's going to interview all of us eventually, about Uncle Thomas."

"When is he coming?"

"Tomorrow about 11, he says. Are you going to come over here? Or do you want him to come to you?"

"I'm coming to you. I'll get there early. Shall I go to Pwllheli first and get some lunch stuff?"

"Yea, that will be good. I'm going to ring Elizabeth and see if she wants to come here too. Then we can all get our stories in at once."

"Is he going to see Emma and Ellen?"

"I expect so, but I don't know when. Are you coming over here after, Dad? I want to show you a new horse I fetched the other day."

"Yes. I'll see you later."

She clicked 'End 'and rang Elizabeth.

"Hello Eleanor."

"A Chief Inspector is coming here in the morning."

"Is he really?

"Yes. He's going to see Dad too. And he says he's going to interview everyone, so I don't know if you want to come here and get it over with."

"I don't know if I can get over to you tomorrow."

"You could if you wanted. Don't you want to get it done?"

"Of course! But I don't think I can come tomorrow. It's too difficult."

"Ok. I just thought it would help."

"Not really. I have lots to do. Perhaps after he's seen you two, he won't want to be bothered with me." Elizabeth said hopefully.

"He said that you were his number 1 suspect."

"He didn't, did he?"

"No. I'll telephone after he's been, shall I?"

"Yes please."

Eleanor put down the phone without entering into any further conversation. She had too much to do. Her version of a lot to do and Elizabeth's were two totally different versions.

Eleanor made a cup of coffee and walked out of the kitchen and onto the terrace. She sat on one of the benches and stared out to sea.

This was her way of meditation and often the ideas which had made her millions came this way. Meditation was also handy if she needed to escape. This was the method she had used throughout her childhood and her marriages.

"They should be here soon!" said mother, as the children looked out of the window. The Prentice family had moved from Applewyke a few years previous and reduced the contact with the Yates family to high days and holidays. Thomas Yates upped his game and enjoyed finding opportunities to be alone with his nieces without any other adult suspecting.

"What day are they going home?" asked Ellen.

"Goodness me! They haven't even arrived yet and you are trying to get them home!"

The children said no more as it would be pointless to explain why they hated their relatives. They didn't really understand it themselves and had settled on trying inventive escape plans when the visits were upon them.

By the time the visitors had poured out of the car and suitcases taken up and tea laid out, an hour had passed.

Thomas lit a cigarette and announced, "After that long drive, I could do with a leg stretch. Any of you kids want to come for a walk with me up Rowe Lane?"

There was a scuffling of feet and several children managed to get out of the kitchen before their mother said, "Go on Eleanor, you go for a walk. You can show him that pony that's at the top of the lane."

"You wouldn't even be able to walk if it weren't for me and auntie. We taught you to walk, didn't we?" He looked across at his wife for support.

"Yes, we did! You took your first steps with us! While your Mum was working!" agreed Auntie Eleanor. The perfect auntie.

"Come on little Ellie. Off we go."

"Don't forget the camera Tomkins," his wife reminded him, "you can take a picture of her horse."

Eleanor Prentice, now in a hypnotic trance of bewilderment, followed her uncle out of the house and down the driveway. It only took another minute or two to reach the lane.

Rowe Lane was little more than a narrow track, suitable for pedestrians or a confident horse rider. The hedges fell to the centre of the track and formed a dark canopy over their

97

heads. Below grew numerous plants, creating a fairy grotto where little animals and birds played.

At the far end of the lane was the horse which Eleanor would often go and visit on her own. She didn't like sharing the experience with anyone, least of all this man.

"How far up are we going Eleanor? It seems like a long way to me."

"Nearly there," she answered quietly. She was feeling less and less comfortable the further they went.

"Let's stop here for a rest, I'm worn out! Does anyone else come here at all?"

"No," she said and quickly realised her mistake.

"Well I think it's time you gave your old uncle a cuddle, don't you?" He moved towards her and grabbed her arms. "You wouldn't believe how much I miss seeing my little nieces now you've moved. The other girls on the road aren't a patch on you!" he said cheerily.

But the entire time he talked, he expertly forced her down into a kneeling position by pressing hard on her shoulders and putting his leg behind her knees.

"What are you doing?" she asked.

"Cuddling", he answered. And he held her down with his left hand and undid his trousers with his right. He forced his damp penis into her mouth and as he moved back and forth, he sang, "With my little stick of Blackpool rock..."

Eleanor finished retching into the hedgerow and Thomas lit yet another cigarette.

"If you're not feeling well, perhaps we should go back," he said.

He told the family that Eleanor had suddenly got sick and seemed pale and faint, so he brought her home. Her mother told her off for eating too many of the sweets that her Gran had sent and said what a shame it was that she should spoil Uncle Thomas's walk.

Eleanor managed to keep well away from them during the rest of the visit and vowed never to let it happen again.

She was 13.

But another event occurred that Christmas when they were sent to stay with their auntie and uncle for a couple of days. Eleanor never connected the two events until therapy, a lot of expensive therapy, made it clear.

Eleanor had gone to the toilet and held her breath for as long as she could because of the smell in there, when she noticed something on her knickers.

Blood.

She had no idea why this should be and shoved toilet roll inside her knickers, thinking that perhaps she had cut herself. Sometimes she did get sore down there. After checking again an hour later, she noticed with horror that there was even more blood and she almost fainted.

She would have to tell her auntie because she may be dying.

"You've started your periods!!" Auntie Ellie announced with excitement.

What the hell did that mean?

It was explained to her that she must wear this pad thing and as her auntie put it, 'no longer play with the boys.' There was much merriment at this last statement, but

Eleanor couldn't see how playing football had caused this trouble.

"Every month? For the rest of my life?" There had been surprisingly little sex education at her girls' school.

Eleanor noticed her uncle standing behind her auntie, grinning like a Cheshire cat. Then he walked into the front room and never touched Eleanor again. She buried these linked memory events away and was left with a fear of her periods and childbirth for the rest of her life.

And she hated wearing knickers.

Excellent case study, Mr Psychologist.

Eleanor opened her eyes, called her dogs and walked over to the stable yard. Eleanor always felt safe with animals.

\#

When the Detective Chief Inspector sat down with a cup in one hand and a chocolate digestive in the other, he was smiling. The journey hadn't taken as long as he had been led to believe and he and Jackson were both quite fresh.

The house and yard were far grander than they expected and 'so clean and tidy!' said Jackson.

They were led through the entrance hall to a central hall, with a sweeping oak staircase and from there into a room which overlooked the sea.

Eleanor said, "You could have come by the back door and through the kitchen, but this way is so much more impressive, don't you think?"

They both agreed and changed focus from the lovely hostess to the lovely view. Which was better?

"Now then Chief Inspector, do ask your questions."

He finished his biscuit and put his cup down on a coaster.

"You will be stopping for lunch, I hope?" asked Michael.

"Well, we were going to stop off in town and eat. Is there a town?"

"Of course, but please stay here. Although we won't be having anything exciting."

The DCI had worried that lunch might be like the telly food rich people seemed fond of and was glad when the meal would be ordinary. He didn't have much experience of rich people, or he would have known that they don't do anything fancy, unless forced by occasion.

"I would like to know whether you have seen your uncle recently, Miss Prentice."

"No, I haven't. I would think that it must be nearly 25 years since I have seen any of them. I'm sure it was at my brother's wedding and I was pregnant. The families have not got on for a long time."

"Why is that?" he asked.

"A lot happened and our family moved on and theirs' did not," said Michael.

"We move in totally different circles," added Eleanor.

"Did they come to your mother's funeral?" asked Jackson.

"Funeral?" asked Michael. "My wife isn't dead, she's just missing."

"Oh, I'm so sorry sir. We were told that she died years ago."

"By whom?"

"Errr…." Jackson was flicking uncomfortably through his notes.

"Where is she now, Mr Prentice?" asked the DCI, endeavouring to deflect attention from his sergeant.

"We don't know. That's the problem. She took my brother's death very badly and sort of deteriorated mentally. Then one day she went for a drive and we haven't seen her since," said Eleanor.

"How long ago was that?" asked Revie

"About three years. The police were informed and after making some enquiries, decided that there was nothing further they could do," she answered.

"What did she take with her?"

"I'm afraid she cleared out our bank accounts of £250,000 and took the Range Rover and her dog. The Range Rover turned up a year later, but there has been no sign of the money, my wife or the dog since."

"And you are still missing the dog?" muttered Jackson.

"I beg your pardon?" exclaimed Eleanor.

Jackson obviously thought that he had thought that last remark and not said it out loud, and looked abashed.

Revie continued, "Do you have any information about your uncle's death?"

"No, I do not. Otherwise I would have contacted you. But it sounds as though he had a most suitable end, rather like his wife. I cannot pretend that I am sorry he is dead, but I have no idea who did it." Eleanor looked coolly at the policeman.

"Do you have any idea?" asked Michael.

"Not at the moment sir, we are still making enquiries. Perhaps you can both tell us where you were from the Thursday to Saturday when the body was found?"

"Here. Both of us were either at this house or my Dad's or town or riding out. We certainly didn't go very far afield."

"Can someone vouch for you?"

"Dad and I can vouch for each other; we spend a lot of time together. Thomas was killed in Leeds and it's a three-and-a-half-hour drive to his place with the wind behind you. Someone would have noticed one of us was missing."

"Because," added Michael. "That would be, there and back, seven hours. Plus murder stops, plus pee stops. So, about ten hours?"

"Yes, thank you sir."

"Do you recognise any of these children?" Jackson handed over the bag of photos, each picture in its own sleeve, so they could view without touching. They had chosen the least disturbing to show.

"I must warn you that the pictures are not very nice," said the Chief Inspector.

Eleanor began to look through the pictures and then handed them to her father.

"Where did you find these?" she asked as she looked.

"We found them on top...." started Jackson.

"Let's just say we found them," interjected Revie.

When they finished looking, Eleanor took the pile back from her father.

"I never knew he took photographs," she said, "Fucking, disgusting pig of a man. I hope he's burning in hell while pieces of his flesh are being carved slowly off. Fucking hell."

"Are you alright love?" Michael came and put his arm round his daughter.

"Of course I am. We have some evidence at last. Now we can do something."

"The others might not agree."

"They might not but fuck, I've been the black sheep before. I can manage it again. Plus, I'm rich, so it's ok now."

"Do you know who these children are?" asked Revie.

"Yes, that's me and so is that and that's Janet Banks and that's Richard and that's Anthony. There's Judith Buckley and…" Eleanor continued until she had identified most of them, including her brother and sisters.

"I don't know who the others are, but that will give you something to do Inspector." She put the pictures down on the table and walked over to the window. Michael followed her and put his arm round her.

"I'm so sorry," he said.

Eleanor spun round and said, "It's not your fault, Dad! Don't ever think that. We've been through it and the only ones to blame are the Yates and they are dead. This way there won't have to be a court case or anything. But I'm going to have to tell the others about the pictures. They haven't gone on the internet, have they?"

"I don't think so, Miss Prentice, but we have someone checking into it. I don't think it will affect your career," added Revie

"Oh, I'm not bothered about that. If anything, people will buy more of my books if they find out and I can rescue more horses."

"I'm glad you are taking it so well. You are a strong woman." said Revie

"Well you don't get to be this strong without having plenty of adventures along the way to strengthen your resilience muscle," she said.

Jackson, having no idea what she was talking about, answered, "I see."

"Unless there is anything more you wish to ask us, perhaps we can get a sandwich?" asked Michael.

"Just the statements," said Jackson.

Statements were written and signed and afterwards they ate in the kitchen. The Chief Inspector smiled a lot at Miss Prentice, Jackson noticed.

But she didn't seem to notice, merely looked thoughtful.

When they took their leave, Revie said, "Thank you for your help and your statements, I shall contact you again if I need any more information."

"And will you be bothering my other children?" asked Michael.

"I will have to speak to them I'm afraid and have them confirm their identities in the pictures."

"They may not take it as well as me," said Eleanor.

"I'm sorry this happened to any of you," Revie said, caught off guard, because she had smiled at him.

"Well I expect I shall get another book out of it," she said.

They waved them off and went back into the kitchen.

"They will look into Mum's disappearance now Dad."

"Yes, they will," he answered, "Perhaps they'll get my money back. I expect the dog's dead."

Eleanor hugged him.

"Don't worry Dad, I'll make sure the family are alright. Let's have a walk on the beach. Dogs!!!"

CHAPTER ELEVEN

When they showed the photos to Janet Banks, she sat down smartly before her legs gave way. Chief Inspector Revie showed her only the pictures as yet unidentified, or of her.

"There are a lot more, but we have already identified those," he said.

"Where did you get them?" she asked. "Did you find them at the Yates house?"

"Yes, we did. Were you aware that they existed?"

"No, God. I had no idea. Do these have to come out? I don't want people seeing them! Oh God!"

She began to shake and Sergeant Jackson said, "Would you like a drink or something? Are you alright?"

"She will be fine in a minute. It's the shock. Make her a cup of tea, with lots of sugar. Make us all some tea while you're there," instructed Revie.

Janet began to settle as she drank and so did the men. They hadn't enjoyed her discomfort.

"It started when I was quite small. I would go and play with the boys and he always seemed to engineer that we were alone together. He was a creepy old man, always touching."

She continued, "It's funny because I've always thought of him as an old man. When I was little, he seemed so old when he did things, but I don't suppose he could have been

107

much above 20 or 21. I never knew about the photos though."

"Do you recognise the children on the other photos? We have already identified some."

Janet took her time and answered in the negative.

"I don't know if it's better that they find out they were filmed or not," she murmured.

"Have you had much to do with him as you got older?"

"Not really. I left for university and then got married and lived near York for years and rarely came home. Then I got divorced and my Dad died, so I came home a year ago."

"Did you see Mr Yates much then? It's been said that you are quite friendly with Anthony Yates."

"Oh, you've been told that have you? We've been friends since we were children and we are friends now."

"I've heard you are more than friends."

"What does that actually mean? We are friends and help each other out. Anthony is married and I'm not, so anything more than friends would be inappropriate."

She put down her cup.

"I didn't mean to offend you, but I need to know what you were doing from Thursday through to Saturday last week."

"I was here, or at work in Leeds. Just normal things. But I didn't see anything out of the ordinary as I told your officer when he came before. You want to ask the Lamb sisters. They are always nosing at everyone. They seem to know everything."

"And your mother, can we speak to her?"

"You can if you want, but it won't do you any good. She's not quite with it anymore."

She got up and beckoned them to follow her upstairs. She put her finger to her lips.

"Please don't say anything, you will scare her. She doesn't understand our world anymore."

Janet opened a bedroom door and the men peered in. The bed appeared to contain an old woman who was now fast asleep, or unconscious. There was an oxygen cylinder and mask to one side of the bed. Covering the dresser and chest of drawers were medical items, Tena lady pads and other nursing paraphernalia.

"Does she still recognise you?" asked Revie.

"Rarely," she answered curtly.

"That's very sad."

"It's bloody hard work, I know that."

They went back downstairs.

Revie gave Janet his card and said, "Please ring this number as soon as you can and arrange to call in and do a statement for us."

"I will," she answered.

"Thank you, Miss Banks. I will let you know how we get on."

"Don't hurry in catching his murderer. They deserve to get away with it."

With that she closed the door.

The two policemen got back in their car, so they could drive further up Waterloo Lane and see Judith Buckley.

They were met at the door by an average looking woman holding a small dog, which she deposited on a cushion in front of the fire.

Her reaction to the photographs was similar to Janet's. Utter shock, followed by the confession about visits to his house as a girl.

"I was great friends with Eleanor Prentice at one time. She's quite famous now you know," she said, pointing to one little girl.

"We do know. Can you identify any of the other children?"

She flicked through the pictures and shook her head.

"I'm sorry, no."

The Chief Inspector noticed that so far, none of the victims had made any effort to conceal their own identity and without thinking, made that point to Judith.

"I should imagine that we want the truth to come out. Back in the 60's, a child didn't have a voice and as they grew up, talking about it was pointless. When you are the person affected, you don't want to talk about it because it's stopped now. If that makes sense."

She handed back the photos.

"It does make sense," he answered.

"Who are the others involved? I would expect his sons, probably the Prentices, maybe Janet Banks? They are the ones who come to mind straight away."

"Will you make a statement?"

"I will. You know my mother thought she was protecting me when I was a girl? She thought that we were a cut above the others in the road. But of course, we weren't.

My father had the barbers at the top of this road, next to the bank on the corner."

"I remember that place!" said Revie suddenly. "My Dad went there and he used to take me for a horrible short back and sides. Oh, I'm sorry."

"Don't worry, I don't think he was an artist by any means, he could use razors and clippers and that was it. My Mum didn't really refer to his business much, but we did have quite a bit of money. I think he used to take bets too."

"Yes, I heard that."

Jackson looked at his boss, surprised again by some of the things he was saying. Revie knew more than he gave him credit for.

"Anyway, I had better dresses and a swing and pocket money. I got the dolls and the ribbons. But I still got Thomas Yates."

"And your parents?"

"Mum died when I was ten and Dad sent me to her parents who were old, but sweet and I got married and lived in Scotland. Then Dad died and I inherited, so I could get divorced and come back here."

"Seems quite a few of you women don't like marriage," said Jackson.

"Ex victims don't like being controlled. We probably choose a controlling husband because that's what we are used to and then we still don't like it. Then we either stay single or find a nicer husband. I'm a counsellor," she added.

"Are you happy now?" Jackson asked suddenly.

She looked at him as though she had just seen him, "I would say that you are a controlling man sergeant. Be careful that your wife doesn't get fed up of you."

He blushed.

Revie raised his eyebrows, but was careful not to grin. How could she know that his sergeant was going through some marital difficulties at the moment?

"Please come down to the station and make a statement, will you? If you ring this number beforehand, we shall make sure that everything is arranged so you don't have to wait too long," said the Chief Inspector.

He handed her his card, which she took before showing him the door.

As they walked down the path, she said. "Petticoats."

"Pardon?"

"I had lots of petticoats. That made me different from all the other little girls. That bastard said he liked the petticoats and he was glad I wore them for him. I haven't worn them since then."

She smiled and closed the door.

"They all seem a bit screwed up," said Jackson.

"I'm not so sure about that," Revie answered, "I think they are just different. No, not different. Special."

They climbed in the car and drove back to Leeds.

#

David Farrington was leaning against the back of his van, smoking.

He had watched the police arrive at the Banks and then drive off up the road. He had only had a cursory nod from the sergeant, but he hadn't nodded back. David felt that his treatment at the police station had been more like a suspect than the discoverer of the body. He wasn't going to forget that.

The sun beat down on the concrete driveway and he could hear birds singing. He put out his cigarette and walked over the low wall which separated his front garden from the Yates.

On a whim, he looked in through the front window. Inside, it looked cold and spooky and he could still make out the bloodstains on the carpet.

His mind travelled back to his childhood, when he and his sister Debbie lived here with his parents and grandparents. At the Yates were the two boys and Thomas and Ellie. Often his mother and Ellie Yates would go out together, but the men never did. Men didn't seem to get on with Thomas Yates. He remembered how the women would knock against the wall in the living room when a song they liked came on Top of the Pops. He remembered how the children rarely went to each other's doors to ask about coming out to play. A knock on the front window and a shout sufficed.

Yea, a lot of it was fun back then. There would be football with the Prentices and the Yates and Judith and sometimes Laura and Janet. Who else? Alan Hoguard wasn't it? He and his sister would come over from the estate.

Cupping his eyes against the window, he could almost see and hear how it used to be and he felt tears in his eyes. He even missed the tough times. Now, nearly everyone was either dead or moved and it was so sad.

113

What's the point in living your fucking life and getting all these memories together, good and bad? Because you just die at some undetermined point and who cares? Who fucking cares?

He stood back from the window and knew he was in a bad temper. His ex-wives always complained about his bad tempers.

Well. Fuck them too!

He walked back to his van and closed the door. He had to price up a job in a minute and he needed the work. He needed the money.

Turning round he could see one of the Lamb sisters watching him from her bedroom window.

"You nosy cows," he said. "Always fucking looking at everyone's business."

As he got into the driver's seat, he said, "They must have seen something. They see everything. I wonder if they've said anything to the police? No, they can't have."

With this thought, he reversed out of the driveway without looking and sped off up the street.

Sylvia Lamb smiled and moved away from her window.

CHAPTER TWELVE

Police are renewing their appeal for help in solving the murder of Thomas Yates. If anyone has any information, however insignificant, please contact the police.

A press conference is scheduled for this afternoon and although investigating officers will be attending, it is not yet clear whether members of his family are.

"I doubt they can get anyone to say anything good about him," said Michael, as he stood in the yard watching Eleanor tack up one of the horses.

They were listening to the radio when another Yates news item came on.

"They aren't having much luck finding out who killed him are they?" said Eleanor.

"I hope they don't find out." He patted the horse. "It will probably be better for everyone if they don't."

"How do you mean?"

"Because I expect the person who did it had a good reason and if the police find out, they will be punished again. I think that if I knew anything about the murderer, I would keep quiet."

"Yes, I would too. But perhaps they won't find out. It would be handy to know what the police do know."

"You could get that inspector bloke to tell you. He seemed quite smitten."

"Well I'm afraid I'm not going to act like a simpering idiot for anyone. Except you ponies," she said, changing her voice to a lighter note and rubbing her horse's mane.

"Ha-ha. Right I'll watch you for a bit and then I'm off to sea for the rest of the day."

"Anyone going with you?"

"Perhaps I will have a little friend with me. It's the last chance I will have to see Flora, once everyone arrives here for the show."

"I'm looking forward to that. The visit, I mean. I know you will be upset about Flora. Tash! I'm going in the school now; do you mind waiting?" Eleanor knew that she would mind, but she couldn't really say anything to the boss.

"Oh, ok. I'll go in the outside school then." Tash answered.

"Thanks. I'll be about an hour I should think."

Eleanor and Michael went in, chattering all the while.

"I wonder when the funeral will be?" Eleanor asked.

"Christ, you're not thinking of going, are you?"

"No, I'm not Dad. I just wondered, that was all."

"I might be interested in making sure he is dead and buried or burned or whatever. But I couldn't sit through the hypocritical church service about how lovely he was and how he will be missed. He's lived there for over forty years, so I expect there will be quite a few people at his funeral. Although, I expect most of the older ones will be dead or in homes."

"Thanks for that!" joked Michael.

"You know what I mean! You are the lively exception to the rule!"

But Eleanor was wrong.

The body was released to the care of his relatives. That meant that Richard and Anthony Yates were in charge of their father and they didn't care much about his funeral arrangements. They knew that he should be buried with their mother. But as their parents hadn't got on that well in life, they weren't sure that they would want to be together for eternity.

"I don't think it actually means that they have to spend forever and ever amen together. It's just cheaper and what people expect," said Richard reasonably.

"True. Tell the funeral directors to sort it out then. What about the do afterwards?" asked Anthony.

"I'm not sure who will be coming. Everyone will have read about it and I know the police are going to come, but I've only got Laura coming. I'm not sure the neighbours want to, they don't want to take time off work and stuff."

"Has anyone from the road said that they are coming?"

"No. Everyone seems to be busy. I don't think we should bother organising catering, because it will be embarrassing," confided Richard. It seemed that Thomas's passing wouldn't be marked with much ceremony.

But then he had been a shit.

"What about the Prentice lot? Do they even know?" Anthony had fond memories of his cousins, even though there had been no contact in well over twenty years.

117

"I wouldn't even know how to get in touch with them. Eleanor is famous, so she wouldn't bother coming. They probably only know he's dead if they've seen the news."

"They are bound to have seen the news. But they haven't contacted us, so we should probably leave it," reasoned Anthony. "Though, it would have been nice to have a catch up."

Two days later, a hearse containing the coffin pulled up outside the Yates house. The funeral director had rung Richard the night before and asked where they should come and Richard couldn't think for a minute. He said the house, because he assumed that was the usual thing to do. Then he realised that the front room hadn't been cleaned properly. So he told the Chief Inspector, who had asked to be informed about the funeral date and time and he told Richard that the police didn't want anyone in the house just yet, because it was still a crime scene.

So, on the morning of the funeral they all stood on the driveway. Richard and his wife Laura, Anthony and Tina, David Farrington, who had been told by Richard that he had better come, and the Lamb sisters, who wanted to follow the story through.

This was the only response to the notice in the paper. The notice also asked for donations to the NSPCC, rather than flowers. They ended up with neither.

The men solemnly got out of the hearse and opened the back door. They took the three wreaths presented to them and placed them on the coffin. They could not have been more dignified had there been a huge crowd waiting.

"Perhaps a chara' has turned up at Greenwood crem." said Sylvia Lamb, with no hint of irony.

The guests all managed to squeeze into the black family car and they set off.

"Well this is exciting!" said Sylvia, "I wasn't sure what to wear, so I put on this old lace thing."

"Actually, it's very beautiful," said Laura Yates, "Its proper lace, isn't it? Not manmade?"

"No, its proper Nottingham lace. It must be about fifty years old, I should think. It used to be ivory, but now it's gone coffee coloured. With this black shawl, I thought it would do. It's hand made by a designer, you know."

"It looks absolutely fabulous," said Laura, who was by now coveting the outfit. The dress was quite obviously antique, but in such good condition. Must be worth a fortune, and Laura was thinking that perhaps she could fit into it.

Alice was dressed in a beautiful black satin coat and a skirt of purple which was revealed beneath when she moved her legs. Laura thought that these two old dears must be quite well off. She wondered vaguely who were their heirs.

Suddenly embarrassed at her musings, she stopped looking at the ladies and shifted her gaze to David and realised with shame that he had been watching her. He looked as though he knew what she had been thinking and she blushed. He smiled at her and winked.

"You both look lovely, ladies," he said, "It's a good job you came to bolster the numbers up a bit."

"Don't be rude," said Richard, so David stopped.

The ladies grinned. They seemed to be enjoying themselves.

Everyone remained silent until they reached the cemetery.

119

"There's that inspector and his sergeant. I wonder why they are here?" asked Anthony.

"They will be looking to see if the murderer is attending. Apparently, the murderer often comes to the funeral." Sylvia informed them.

"Well they are going to stand out here, aren't they?" said David. Then added, "sorry, that just came out."

Laura giggled and Richard glared at her.

Next to the police were two men who looked like a reporter and his camera man. There were some more reporters sitting on the church wall. None of them had much to do.

The funeral attendees followed the coffin into the church and everyone sat at the front. Richard noticed some people he didn't recognise. There was an old couple sitting near the back and another quick glance revealed that the only other person present was the vicar.

The vicar blithered on for ten minutes about Thomas Yates's life. He had gleaned the information from a short conversation over the telephone with Richard and containing really only the important times and dates in his life and his tragic death.

They were soon out and noticed that the next funeral was ready to come in. A hearse, followed by a family car was sitting waiting for their turn.

They all trooped out after the coffin and waited around the graveside while some more words were said. The old couple were nowhere to be seen. The police stayed away from the group, but watched in silence from another gravestone.

Anthony Yates said to the group as they walked away, "We haven't arranged a do as such, but if you would like to go back to The Globe, we can have some food and a drink back there."

There was a general assent to this and they headed back to the family car. The newsmen had gone, but the police were still there.

"We are going back to The Globe, if you want to come," said Richard.

"No thanks sir, we have to get back to the station." Revie smiled as he watched them all climb back into the car.

"Not much of a turnout," said Jackson.

"No. Interesting that. There are usually quite a lot who come to the funeral of a murdered man. His neighbours are either shy, or really don't like him."

"Who was the old couple?"

"That, I don't know. They seemed quite old and were all bent and quiet, then as soon as the funeral service was over, they scarpered."

"I noticed that, but I didn't see where they went. I'll get the CCTV, shall I?" asked Jackson.

"That would be a good idea," said Revie. "See to it then, lad."

He watched the family car drive off and thought that this was a very peculiar case.

He looked at the people coming to visit graves, or just have a walk around. Greenwood was a particularly beautiful place. Old and full of Victorian stones and memorials, surrounded by yew trees and with the grass planted with bulbs and flowers.

He saw a middle-aged lady carrying a bunch of flowers and an old man with a small dog on a lead. Then he realised that the next funeral was already on its way out of the church.

Like a conveyor belt of death.

CHAPTER THIRTEEN

It seems so sad in this day and age, that an old man can be murdered and left undiscovered for several days. And to make it worse, there were less than ten people at his funeral. This picture was taken just after the funeral service and shows how few people seemed to actually care. Where were his friends and neighbours? He went to school, raised a family and retired from a job he worked at for 30 years and only 9 people came to see him off.

The police have not arrested anyone in connection with the murder of Thomas Yates. The two men taken into custody following the discovery of his body have now been released. The news conference and routine police enquiries have resulted in several leads which are being followed up. The police are asking for anyone with any information to contact them.

This item, on a commercial news station, began a discussion amongst several guests about the sad plight of the elderly in our modern world.

Emma said, "Do you mind if I switch this off Eleanor? It's doing my head in, all this bollocks about the poor old man."

"No, turn it off. We can start on the table for lunch. Shall we have it out on the terrace?"

"Oh yes. We can't waste this lovely weather."

The family were visiting.

The family consisted of three sisters and their husbands and several nephews and nieces, including the children of her dead brother. It was an annual event and lasted for at least a week. It coincided with the local Winter Agricultural and Horse show which had been held on the land for years before Eleanor owned it.

Everyone joined in and everyone loved it. The show lasted for the weekend and there was a fete and a fair and a barbeque and a dance. The horse show brought people from miles around.

Such fun!

Today was Thursday, almost two weeks since the murder and the day after the funeral. The show committee and staff at Eleanor's yard were getting the field ready. This year it was dry and that helped considerably. The horses would be competing in the indoor and outdoor arenas.

Eleanor and her family were helping and everyone seemed to be enjoying themselves. So far, they hadn't thought about nor discussed the murder.

Lunch took place around the large table, eating and drinking and laughing. The weather was glorious and thankfully appeared set fair for the next couple of weeks or so. No snow, frost or heavy rain forecast.

"I love coming here, Eleanor. Love it," said Emma.

"I know you do. So, why don't you move over here? I've asked you often enough," asked Eleanor.

Daniel glanced at Emma and Eleanor saw him give her a, 'don't you dare say you are moving here' command. Eleanor loved them both and wouldn't dream of pushing the subject, so long as they knew the offer was always open.

The table was a happy table. Everyone was using the time to catch up and become the people they were when the kids were young. They had all changed so much since those days.

Eleanor had her work published and became rich. The husbands had done well in their careers and the sisters moved away, one right across the world. Their brother died in an accident and they lost their mother, literally. Dad came to live near Eleanor, so everyone knew he was safe. Their children grew up and became nice young people who loved being near their family.

There was such a lot of noise that sometimes people on the beach looked up to see what was happening. The staff kept away during the mealtimes, not by instruction, but because they knew this family time was important. There were nightly barbeques however, where they came and drank and partied with the family.

Suddenly Michael banged the table with his spoon and said, "Everyone, I think we ought to have a talk about this murder and what it might mean."

The table became silent and they all looked at him.

"Just make sure that side gate is shut and then we will know if anyone comes," said Tom.

"What does it matter?" asked Mikey.

"Some things need to stay within the family," replied Tom.

The side door was checked and a quieter mood settled around the table. The younger ones sat in excited anticipation of what may be revealed.

"The police have already interviewed most of us who used to know Uncle Thomas, so you kids should be safe. None of you youngsters met him, did you?" asked Michael.

"They haven't interviewed us," said Christopher. "We just got a phone call saying that we would be contacted shortly. But they had better do it soon if they want to catch us before we go back to America."

"When they came to see me, they just asked about where we were when they thought he was killed and if we had heard anything from him or the others recently," said Elizabeth.

"That's pretty well what they asked us, isn't it Dad?"

"Yes, but they didn't really tell us much, did they?"

"You mean about what they know?" asked Emma, "They might not do that, because they will get into trouble."

"They asked about Mum," said Eleanor.

"What did you say?" asked Christopher.

"They thought she was dead," began Michael. "They seemed surprised that she was only missing."

"Surely they've got records of it?" said Ellen.

"Must have, but those two didn't know," answered Eleanor.

"What happened to Gran?" asked Vikki. She had been very young when Gran went missing and most of the kids hadn't thought much about it. It was never talked about in front of them.

"She just left one day, taking her dog and a car," said Eleanor.

"And a lot of money," added Michael.

"But, why did she go?" asked Vikki.

"I would like to know that too. No one ever tells us," said Mikey.

The adults looked uncomfortable and waited for someone else to talk. Really it was up to Michael to tell, wasn't it? They all still felt as though these children shouldn't know, even though they were aged between 15 and 22.

Michael started, "Gran became very insular and focussed when Andrew died," he smiled at Vikki and Mikey, Andrew's children. "She couldn't accept that his death had been an accident and became convinced that he had been murdered."

"Wow! I didn't realise that! I thought she just ran off with someone," Mikey looked genuinely shocked. "Mind you, she was a bit old to do that."

"She couldn't get it out of her mind, but there wasn't any proof that he was murdered," said Eleanor.

"And it's upsetting for people to hear about it," added Ellen.

"But tell us how Dad died, I really need to know!" demanded Vikki.

The sisters looked at each other.

Elizabeth spoke up.

"He got up one night and went downstairs because he thought he heard something outside. He went out and slipped on the ice and banged the back of his head on the stone step when he fell."

127

"I knew that already, so why did Gran think it was murder?" asked Mikey.

"She said that he had been getting some funny phone calls or something and she thinks that he was hit on the head by someone and then fell."

"But that's not what the police said, is it?" said Christopher.

"No. There wasn't any evidence that anyone hit him on the head. Apparently, all the evidence pointed to just a fall. A horrible accident that couldn't be helped," added Daniel.

"But did anyone else think it was murder? Any of you lot?" asked Mikey.

They looked shifty and embarrassed.

"I thought it was a bit weird that he could just fall down like that," said Eleanor. "He was so fit."

"He slipped," said Elizabeth. "Anyone can do that."

"I once slipped on the ice in a hospital car park," said Ellen, "I fell straight onto my head, without hitting my bum on the way down and I had a massive swollen egg at the back. It started to bleed and I had to go back into A and E and I only went to visit someone!"

"But you didn't die, did you?" said Eleanor.

"No," she answered. "I didn't die."

"Well there you are, it's not as easy to die as people sometimes make out."

"Do you really think it was murder, Eleanor?" asked Vikki.

"Oh, I don't know that it was murder, it just seemed odd, and that was all. But Mum was sure that someone killed him and kept pestering the police and asking us to look into it."

"We did check his phone and his friends and your Mum, but no one thought that anything funny had happened," said Christopher, "if there had been anything wrong, we would have got to the bottom of it."

"But your Gran couldn't be convinced and she just got more and more anxious about it as time went on," said Michael.

"She got crosser with all of us, because we wouldn't see it as murder," said Eleanor.

"Oh, how sad if she thought that and nobody supported her," said Vikki quietly.

"It wasn't quite like that," said Michael. "Your Gran got a bit odd before she disappeared."

"In what way?" asked Mikey.

"She thought someone was following her and trying to stop her uncovering the murder. Then one day I came home and she wasn't there. She took money, the dog and the car as I said. But she left her clothes and books and glasses and everything else. We never heard from her or saw her again," Michael said sadly.

"Change of subject required, I think!" said Christopher brightly.

"Can't be done," said Michael. "We have to anticipate what the police might do."

"Why?" asked Robert.

The sun shone down on the party, which was now a much more subdued affair. No one from the beach looked up at the party anymore.

The side gate rattled and Tash shouted, "Eleanor, are you coming over soon?"

"Bit of family business Tash. Do you mind? I will be over later!"

"No probs," she answered and there was the sound of her retreating footsteps on the gravel. Eleanor realised that she hadn't heard the footsteps arrive.

"Better crack on with this," said Daniel, "Get it over with."

"Tea or coffee anyone?" asked Emma, ever concerned for others.

Orders taken, she and Ellen sorted out drinks. It took a further ten minutes before everyone was sitting down again.

"Do you think she went off with someone?" asked Vikki.

"I don't think so Vikki, she wasn't like that. Not like that at all," said Michael.

"Sorry, Grandad."

"It's alright lovely."

"How long after Dad died did she vanish?" asked Mikey.

"Two months, that's all," said Elizabeth.

"The thing was that just after Andrew died, your Gran finally found out all about Thomas Yates and everything that he had done to our children when they were little."

"What sort of things?" said Vikki.

"He sexually abused each and every one of them."

"Oh my God!" said Mikey, "I wasn't expecting that. How horrible, what a bastard! No wonder none of you care that he's dead."

"Mum told me a bit ago," said Tom.

"I knew too," said Robert.

"Well we didn't know. Did he touch my Dad as well?" asked Mikey.

"Probably," said Tom.

"I'd kill him if he wasn't dead," said Vikki and Eleanor put an arm around her and squeezed.

"Anyway, once she heard that, on top of Andrew dying, she blamed herself for not looking after her children. She said that she had been a poor substitute for a mother and started to get depressed. I told her that I was as much to blame as her, but she wouldn't have it and everything went downhill from there," said Michael.

"Do you think she went off to kill herself?" asked Robert.

"Then why did she take so much money?" asked Ellen.

"No idea," answered Michael.

"So, if I've got this right," said Mikey, a young man so sharp he might cut himself, "My Dad dies in suspicious circumstances three years ago and then my Gran disappears two months later with a load of money. Then two years after that her sister dies in a suspicious accident and two weeks ago the abuser is murdered. Basically, nothing to see here!"

CHAPTER FOURTEEN

"You've heard about his wife then?" asked Eleanor. "We only knew about it when they said on the news that she was dead. Was it a car accident or something?"

"No," said Mikey. "She got electrocuted!"

"Did she? Electrocuted by what?" asked Ellen.

"By the washing machine. Did you really not know? None of you? It didn't take me long to find out." Mikey was genuinely surprised.

"We haven't had anything to do with them for years and stopped thinking about them. I doubt they know anything about us either," said Emma.

"But they definitely count it as an accident, don't they?" asked Christopher, "There was never any doubt?"

"Why do you ask that?" said Michael, turning to his son in law.

"Well, Mikey is right. It is a bit odd, all these things that have happened. I was starting to wonder if there was a common denominator."

"Like what?" asked Elizabeth, alarmed that Christopher of all would see that there may be a problem. Christopher was always so, well, unemotional.

"Perhaps we should ask the police for more details," said Michael.

"They are not likely to give us any. We would be better off trying to find out by ourselves," said Eleanor.

"But to what end?" asked Elizabeth.

"We have lost Andrew and Mum, so if there is something connecting the deaths, we ought to know. I don't care about the others, but I care about our family," said Ellen.

"What could possibly connect them? There had been no contact between any of them for years before Andrew died," said Eleanor.

"True. But Mikey is right. It's all a bit odd." Mikey hadn't expected his Grandad to back him up.

"Tell us again about what you thought when Mum vanished. I mean really thought," Emma had asked the question of her father and everyone was interested.

"I can't remember what I thought exactly, because now it feels like years ago."

"Dad, it was years ago!" Eleanor wanted to lighten the mood because she didn't like to see her father upset. He was a fit man, but no longer a young man. They all liked to use a black humour to cheer people up and often that could be misunderstood.

"Just tell us what happened Dad," said Emma.

"After we heard that Andrew had died, neither of us could believe it was true. None of us could believe it, could we?" He looked round his family for support and they all nodded their heads in agreement.

"Your mother kept saying that he was murdered and wouldn't accept any other version. When we asked why she thought that, she just said that she knew it because Andrew had been getting phone calls telling him that he was being watched and that he should keep his mouth shut."

"Who had been ringing him?" asked Mikey.

"Keep his mouth shut about what?" asked Tom.

"I have no idea. I asked her over and over again and she said that Andrew had told her one day when he was upset. But he hadn't told anyone else about it and she wasn't very clear because she was so emotional."

"We did look at everything that happened very carefully and the police were convinced that it was just an accident," said Elizabeth.

"I agree that it was odd, but odd things happen all the time," said Eleanor.

"Then your Mum started saying that someone was bugging the house and she could hear voices all the time."

"I didn't know that!" said Daniel.

"Because everyone started talking about what happened with Uncle Thomas when we were kids, she got worse and worse. She said that we were all being watched and it was up to her to find out who was doing it. Then I'm afraid she went to the police several times and by the time she had written a statement telling them about microphones in the house and an unknown person murdering her son who was intent on murdering everyone else. Well, they thought she was a bit bonkers to say the least. We all managed to talk her out of causing any more upset and she sort of just shut up."

"Did you all know that this was going on? Because it doesn't look like we did," said Vikki.

"Don't get sulky," said Eleanor. "We weren't that keen on everyone knowing what Mum was like. To be honest, Dad has only given the edited highlights. The full story is way more stressful and it was starting to cause trouble in our own lives and careers and we all wanted it to stop."

"Causing trouble in your career, don't you mean Eleanor? Wouldn't have helped your book sales to have a barmy Mum?"

"Elizabeth, don't be a bitch. Having a barmy Mum would have helped. Look how the publicity played out in my favour! Anyway, none of that is what we are talking about, because if we go down that road, I think that you will find I did the most for her."

Michael intervened. "Your Mum got quieter as time went on and we couldn't get her to talk about Andrew or anything. One day I got back home after I'd been sailing for a couple of days and she wasn't there. I thought she had gone in the car with her dog. After an hour or two, I rang round and we gradually began to realise that she hadn't been seen for a while. She didn't have a mobile, so we couldn't ring her. I started to think that she might be home after dark and when I hadn't heard anything, I called the police."

"It was a scary time for us," said Elizabeth.

"When they got me to check to see if she had used her cards, I discovered that she had taken a huge chunk of our savings the day before she went missing, so that meant that she had planned it."

"When did they find the car?" asked Mikey.

"It wasn't found for a few months, but apparently she had been driving it around up until then, because they saw her on CCTV and she got done for speeding and parking in various places. In Yorkshire and in Blackpool for example."

"How do they know she was driving it? The car, I mean?" asked Vikki, who couldn't decide if she was becoming more confused or less.

"She's on some of the film. But once the car was found, there has never been any trace of a sighting of her," said Michael.

"Do you think that she's dead?" asked Tom.

"I suppose she must be. There is no way that she would have kept away from us if she were still alive."

"But, you said she had started to go bonkers. Maybe she just lost her bearings a bit and now she doesn't know who she is."

"Could be, Tom, could be. I don't know whether I feel she is dead or not."

"I don't know if she's dead either, and you would think her children would know instinctively, but we don't," said Ellen.

"I don't think you can know, if someone is bonkers when they die," Mikey laughed. He was known as Bart, because of his bouncing and provocative comments.

"Thanks for that," said Grandad.

"I'm wondering whether we really ought to find out some more about how Aunt Ellie and Uncle Thomas died. Just in case it's connected in some way," said Christopher.

"We can give that job to you," said Michael.

"We will be going home soon, so we can't really."

"Christopher, you can do it. Living abroad gives you plenty of excuses not to help with family stuff and so this is a great opportunity for you both to do some catching up," said Eleanor.

"We will do our best," said Ellen. She was feeling much cooler towards Eleanor than she had a minute ago, but decided to say nothing. Eleanor could be very harsh when crossed.

She also knew full well that neither she nor Christopher would be doing any research. They had their own lives to live.

"We had better get some jobs done," said Tom, rising from his seat.

"And some thinking done," said Michael, rising from his.

The party split up and Eleanor and her sisters cleared the table and went into the kitchen to wash up and sort the place out, ready for the party later.

"That was a mean thing to say, Eleanor," said Ellen as they carried dishes to the washer.

"I didn't mean it to come out like it did, Ellen. All this talk about Mum and Andrew has got me a bit uptight, I think," she answered.

"Ok," murmured Ellen, although she was still upset.

"Do you think Mum is dead?"

"She must be Eleanor. We would have heard something," answered Emma.

"What if she has lost her mind? She might be in a home somewhere," said Elizabeth.

"I don't think you can put someone in a home without having their history," reasoned Elizabeth.

"I wonder what she did with all the money? That was mean of her taking it, because if it hadn't been for you, Dad could have lost the house," said Emma.

137

"She can't have been thinking straight to do that, can she?"

"No, but it's hard to see when Mum was ever actually thinking straight," said Elizabeth.

"Let's not say anything negative, because we'll bring it back on ourselves," said Eleanor.

"Ok," the sisters almost said it in unison, being used to Eleanor's pearls of wisdom regarding 'vibes'.

"And what about Andrew? Murder or accident?" asked Elizabeth.

"Up until just recently, I haven't thought about it much since it all happened," said Ellen. "I suppose I haven't wanted to. We needed to get on with our own lives."

"But what do you think now?"

"I really don't know, it could have been either way," she admitted.

"I'm going to ask his wife about it again." Emma said.

"Don't. That will start all that trouble up again." It had been a horrible time after Andrew died, because his wife had tried to stop the children seeing his family and there had been even more trouble over money. But Mikey and Vikki had their own ideas and spent time with their Prentice relations and stayed away from their mother. It had been a tense time and nobody wanted all that again.

"Perhaps someone should mention it to the police," said Eleanor

"Which police?" asked Elizabeth.

"The ones investigating the murder. It might all be connected somehow," answered Eleanor.

"What if it turns out that Mum killed your Aunt Ellie and Uncle Thomas?" said Tom, who had come into the kitchen and been listening to the conversation.

He was rewarded with open mouthed stares from his Mother and Aunties.

CHAPTER FIFTEEN

Patsy Prentice looked from behind the blinds of her front room window, nervously awaiting the arrival of the police at her house.

She couldn't work out why police investigating a murder in Yorkshire, wanted to talk to her about the death of her husband three years ago.

But whatever the reason, she was worried.

Patsy had cleaned and ironed and straightened everything in the house after she got the call yesterday.

"Good morning, Mrs Prentice, would it be convenient for me and my sergeant to have a few words with you tomorrow at about 11?"

"Yes, yes, of course," she answered, surprised at how she scared she felt.

She had even considered carefully what she should wear, not wanting to give the impression of being a merry widow.

Or a guilt-ridden victim of life.

The car arrived and two men got out. Soon Patsy had them sitting in the lounge with a tray of tea and cake and biscuits on a plate.

"Do you live alone?" asked Chief Inspector Revie, noting the drab, pale interior of the house.

She looked around and thought how disappointing it all seemed, "I do live alone now, yes."

Revie took another drink from his china teacup and asked," your children have moved away?"

Pat lit a cigarette without offering the packet. "My children left me a while ago Chief Inspector. Though I doubt that is why you are here."

"No, no it's not," he answered. "We wanted to ask you about the death of your husband."

"What about his death?" She was unable to keep the fear from her face and the policemen noticed it.

"We would like you to go over exactly what happened the night he died," said Jackson.

"Why do you want to go over all that again? It's finished with as far as I'm concerned." Patsy sounded almost peevish.

"Please humour us, Mrs Prentice. Just tell us what you can remember."

"Andrew came home from work as usual and had his tea and a few drinks and we watched telly. There wasn't much on, so I went to bed and Andrew stayed down to watch the football. He came to bed about midnight I think, I was half asleep so only noticed him getting into bed."

"Then he got up again?" asked Jackson

"Not straight away. We must have been asleep for an hour or so and there was this noise downstairs."

"In the house?"

"I'm not sure; it could have been outside or inside."

"What kind of noise was it?" asked Revie.

"Well, it's hard to describe really. A sort of howling noise."

"Like a dog?"

"No, not a dog. More like a wolf or a ..."

"Or a what?"

"Like a werewolf or a vampire. The kind you see in films."

This time the policemen could not hide their feelings from their facial expressions. They were trying not to look amused.

"I'm not mental you know!"

"No, Mrs Prentice, it's just that you didn't mention anything about this at the time. I think you said..." Revie skimmed through his notes, "You said it was a banging noise, followed by shuffling."

"Yes," she admitted and took another drag on her cigarette. "But you would have thought me nuts. I'm sure I was already under suspicion about his death and I didn't fancy saying I heard a werewolf. But I did hear it and Andrew did too. That's why he went downstairs that night," she sniffed.

"Because he heard a werewolf?" asked Jackson.

"You think I'm joking sergeant, but I'm not. I know that Andrew thought that the noise was somehow otherworldly."

"So that night wasn't the first time you had heard the noise?" Revie was interested in this line of enquiry.

"No. We had heard it more and more regularly in the weeks before he died. We couldn't tell anyone about what the noise sounded like exactly."

"No. I can see why you would want to keep that to yourselves. So, what happened when you heard the noise that night?"

"Andrew said that he had had enough and was going to sort it out once and for all. I told him to be careful and he said he would. He took the baseball bat from under the bed. He had only started bringing that to bed when the noises began. He put his jeans on and a sweatshirt. I got up too and put on my dressing gown. When he went downstairs, I looked out of the bedroom window."

"Did you see anything outside?" Jackson tried to get the image of a play out of his head, because he had no idea what was coming.

"I saw a shadow of a man or something by the eucalyptus tree. It was quite easy to notice that, because of the snow and ice. The street lights meant that it seemed quite light in the front. I sort of loud whispered to Andrew that I thought someone was on the lawn and he must have gone outside then, so really his death was my fault."

"What happened next?" asked Revie, anxious for Patsy to move on with her story. She talked so slowly and in such a depressed way.

"I was looking out of the window and I heard Andrew shout, so I ran downstairs and there was Andrew lying on his back just outside the door with his head on the stone step. He was bleeding and his eyes were just staring up at the sky. It was so unreal, with the snow starting to come down and the blood on the step and his eyes not blinking."

She seemed to go into a trance at the memory.

"Did you see anyone about, Mrs Prentice?"

"No, I didn't see anyone. I knelt down and tried to shake him and then tried to stop the bleeding and I think then I was just screaming. The neighbour came round and he called the police and an ambulance. Everyone sort of did things for me and took me in the house and then someone was telling me that Andrew had to go to hospital. A policeman drove me there and then after we had waited at the hospital a while, they told me that my husband was dead. My life ended there."

Patsy Prentice was crying and the men felt awkward.

"You don't appear to have told the police this version at the time," repeated Revie.

"I didn't because of the reasons I said before. But I did say that there were noises outside which there were and that Andrew went out to check on it and I found him like I did. The only thing I didn't mention was that the noise sounded like a ghost. It's up to you to do what you want with that information. When Andrew died, he was the only dead one. But since then his mother has gone missing and now I read about his aunt and uncle. I know Andrew hated them, not his mother, but the others. Anyway, a lot has happened since he died and perhaps if he had been the last one to die, I might have mentioned werewolves, but as it was, I didn't."

"I can perhaps understand your logic in that. What involvement did you have in the disappearance of Andrew's mother?"

"She used to be ok, but soon after the funeral she came round or called me and asked me about his death and said that he was getting phone calls. I didn't know about any phone calls and I didn't tell her about the noises because I thought she was going a bit senile or something with the shock of Andrew's death. It was obvious she was grieving, but she seemed so..." she searched for the right word, "intense."

"Do you have any idea where she could have gone when she went missing?"

"I expect she jumped into the sea or something. She came here the day she left home, although I didn't know that she had left at the time. She was wild eyed and upset and said she was going to get to the bottom of Andrew's death once and for all. She was sure her husband knew what had happened to Andrew, but I don't think he did because he would have said. She said that she knew who had been calling Andrew before his death and to leave it to her. I offered her a bed, but she told me that she was going to go home now and speak to Michael. But apparently she didn't."

"Do you have any idea where she could have gone?" asked Revie

"No, not really. No, I don't. I was asked that time and time again, but I don't know. And now they don't speak to me, haven't for years, because they aren't sure that his death was an accident."

"Have they said that to you?"

"No, but I know what they are thinking. They ended up getting my children to leave me and Eleanor helped them with her money and they didn't want to know me. I wasn't good enough." Patsy was starting to sound quite bitter.

"You don't see your children either?"

"No, they won't have anything to do with me. Would you two like something a little stronger than tea?"

145

"It's a bit too soon after breakfast for me, I'm afraid," answered Revie.

"Well I'm going to have some," she said and shakily poured out a large whisky. The men were beginning to see why she no longer had a relationship with her family. After drinking the glass contents quickly, she poured out another, larger than the last.

"Has life been difficult since your husband's death? He left you alright for money?"

"Oh yes, he left money and I got this house, but I have never had any peace. Not one day's peace."

"What do you mean?" asked Revie.

"The noises outside never stopped," she answered.

"You mean they are going on now?"

"Yes sergeant, the noises are still going on. They go on night after night and sometimes I get phone calls from I don't know who and its driving me nuts."

"What? So it hasn't stopped since Andrew's death?"

"Since before his death. I haven't seen anyone, but I've heard."

"What does the person say on the phone?"

"Just mutters. They never leave a number and I still haven't told the police until you just now. Mainly because I'm afraid I will end up the same as the others."

DCI Revie looked at his notes and asked. "Two questions, Mrs Prentice. Do you think your husband's death was an accident and do you think that your mother in law is still alive?"

146

"I don't know and no."

As they walked back down the path, Jackson said, "I think she's hiding something sir."

"I agree, but I'm not sure what it is that she does know. I think it might be an idea for someone to keep an eye on the place for a day or two. See if these noises are real or if she's just a pisshead. Also, have a word with the local police and see if they can tell you anything."

CHAPTER SIXTEEN

We have some breaking news.

Police in Yorkshire have said that a body has been discovered in Applewyke and they are treating the death as suspicious.

The body of an elderly woman who lived with her sister was found by a neighbour earlier this morning. Her sister has been badly injured and is currently having emergency treatment in hospital. Police have not said whether or not these injuries are life-threatening.

It appears that this incident has taken place exactly opposite the house where the murder of Thomas Yates took place six months ago.

We can go to our reporter who has just arrived at the location. What do have for us Bill?

'From what we can gather, the neighbours had become worried when they had seen neither of the Misses Lamb this morning and went to the house. They were not answering their phone or the door and so they broke in. After discovering one sister dead and the other severely injured, the police were called. The curtains were closed, we have been told and the assumption is that the attack happened during the night as both ladies were dressed in their nightclothes. They had been seen earlier in the evening by friends and appeared to be in their usual good spirits.

It can't go unnoticed that the sisters lived opposite Thomas Yates, who was murdered a few months ago and were friends with him. They were two of the few people who attended his funeral.

We currently don't know what form the attack took and the police are keeping an open mind as to any motives. I am sure they will want to have words with the surviving sister as soon as doctors allow.

The area has been sealed off for the second time this year and the local residents we have spoken to are worried that there may be a serial killer on the loose.'

When Eleanor finished schooling all the horses she needed to that morning, she noticed that she had been called by Elizabeth three times, her son twice and Emma once.

Something was definitely afoot.

Without bothering to check her voicemail, she rang Tom immediately.

"Heard the news, Mum?"

"No, I haven't, what's happened?"

"More murders, well one at least and an attempted one."

"Who? Who has been murdered now?"

"Some old woman who lived opposite your Uncle Thomas and her sister. One is dead and the other has been injured."

"That must be the Lamb sisters," Eleanor said quietly.

"Did you know them?"

"Not very well. I mean I can remember them living there when I was young. They used to complain that Thomas stared at them from his bedroom window. But, from what I can remember they used to stare at people a lot too. So they have been attacked? Do they know who has done it?"

"They are talking about a serial killer. I bet the police are going to have to investigate everything properly now."

"Yes. It's all a bit grim," answered Eleanor, "It seems to be getting out of hand, don't you think?"

"You sure it wasn't your Mum?"

"I'm sure it wasn't my Mum. Not unless she's done some sort of SAS training since she disappeared. And she's a bit old."

But the truth was that Eleanor was wondering if this could be attributed to her Mum. Could it?

"Well, perhaps she has. But now, even the press might start asking us all questions if they link any of the stuff in Leeds to our family. It could be quite interesting. Maybe I will get a TV career out of it."

"I thought you wanted to be an explorer?"

"I do, but if the BBC want to pay me to explore, even better!"

"Let's cross one bridge at a time, Tom. We had all better think up our alibis at this rate. What time are you back?"

"Probably not until tomorrow night, now. I'm staying at Matts and then I'm going up Tryfan. I'll ring you."

"Take care and I will see you tomorrow."

"Ok, Mum. Bye."

As soon as he was off the phone, she rang Elizabeth.

"What the fuck is happening now, Elizabeth?"

"I know! Have you only just heard?"

"Everyone rang while I was riding and I've just spoken to Tom. It's a bit mad, isn't it? Do you remember the women?"

"Only vaguely, then mostly from what Mum and Dad said. But, nothing very exciting."

"Me too, but who do you think has killed them?"

"Only one of them is dead so far. Tom says Mum did it!"

"Very likely. But apart from her, it makes you wonder if they saw something to do with Thomas's murder, doesn't it?"

"I know, I thought that."

Eleanor and Elizabeth weren't the only people wondering that. The police were too.

As soon as he got the news, Chief Inspector Revie shouted for Sergeant Jackson and they went to the scene of the crime at Stone House, Waterloo Lane, Applewyke.

There was a natural sense of déjà vu for the men when they pulled up alongside the tape separating the crime scene from the rest of the road. The same satellite trucks and reporters and probably the same voyeurs appeared along the road.

"I wonder if he's watching us," said Jackson.

"It wouldn't surprise me. Have a good look around to see if you recognise anyone. Before that make sure that everyone who is standing around is being photographed. We can't afford to miss anything." Revie instructed. "There was to be no joking or messing around now. The old man

151

opposite might have been a nasty old git, but these ladies were harmless."

The sitting room, where he had been drinking tea with the ladies back in January, was now filled with forensic scientists and police. Drawers had been turned out and chairs and tables knocked over. There were papers and books everywhere. This scene was repeated all over the house with even the kitchen cupboards relieved of their contents.

They were directed upstairs to the bedrooms, where Miss Lamb's body remained. There was blood over her and on the bedding. Blood spattered the headboard, the walls and the carpet.

Her face was unrecognisable.

"Do we know which sister she is?" he asked Dr. Jordan.

"Sylvia Lamb. Alice Lamb is at the hospital and we've identified her from her driving licence."

"Is she in any condition to speak to us?"

"Apparently not yet and I'm not sure she ever will be able to. She's in a bad way."

"What do you think has happened?" asked Revie.

"I can't give you exact times. But I do know that the house has been ransacked. Sylvia Lamb was shot with a handgun while she was sitting up in bed and Alice Lamb was shot on the stairs and probably had her arm in front of her face."

"That's horrible," said Revie.

"Yes, it is," agreed Dr Jordan. "You need to catch this person, John."

"I intend to."

Sergeant Jackson joined him in the bedroom and they both looked at the gory scene.

"She didn't deserve to die like that. Poor thing," Jackson said.

"No, she bloody well didn't!" he answered. "Did you see anyone outside who attracted your interest?"

"A few people I didn't recognise, but I saw Richard Yates standing in the window of his Dad's house, David Farrington in the window of his house and Anthony Yates standing next to Janet Banks in the window of hers."

Revie raised his eyebrows and said, "That's odd!"

"I know. They looked like the people who had been hypnotised in that film. Except I think it was only the women."

"The Stepford Wives?"

"I think so."

"We will talk to them all again. In the meantime, have a good look around here. If it turns out that it was the same gun that killed her, then we have the same person that killed Yates. Sylvia was killed for a reason. Either that, or they are all connected in some way that the murderer feels as though he has to eliminate them..."

"Or the women knew something about the Yates murder and he had to silence them," said Jackson.

Revie walked out of the bedroom and looked over the banisters.

"What's different about this murder to the one over the road?"

"There's a survivor? Do you mean that?"

"No, I mean this time he was looking for something. We don't know if he was going to kill the women anyway, or just try and steal from them."

"The other house was a tip."

"His sons said that it was always a tip though. This house was very neat and tidy when we were here. They haven't turned it into this in a few weeks."

"They could have done, if they had lost something and were looking for it," added Jackson.

"And the murder was separate to that?"

"Well yes, I suppose that's what I mean. It's possible, isn't it?"

"It's highly possible, sergeant. I'm impressed! Perhaps you stand a chance with promotion after all."

If Sergeant Jackson had a tail, he would have wagged it.

"In the meantime though, see if you can find out if anything obvious is missing."

Revie went back into the bedroom and looked at the bloodied body of the lady who had been so hospitable to them a few months prior. This room had been turned upside down like the others, but her surprisingly large screen television was hanging safely on the wall and her mobile phone sitting neatly on the dressing table next to her handbag. So, if it was a robbery it wasn't a normal one. He walked over to the dressing table and opened a jewellery box. A dancing ballerina shot up as he opened the lid and a tune began playing. He opened the little drawer underneath and saw that it was empty. So was the drawer under that one. Sylvia Lamb had been wearing jewellery when he last saw her. Revie looked around the table and opened some more drawers. There was plenty of stuff for hair and face and nails, but no jewels.

"Are there any rings or necklaces on the body?" he asked Jordan.

"No, there aren't any that I can see."

"There aren't any here either. I will look in the other rooms." As he turned to leave he noticed the curtain billowing into the room, although the window appeared to be closed. He thought he felt someone brushing past him and he suddenly had an idea to check the wardrobe. On doing that, he saw that there were several empty coat hangers. These weren't pushed to one side waiting to be filled, but spaced in the position of having recently held an outfit.

Revie went into the room belonging to Alice and saw that was in a similar state of untidiness. A cursory glance around the room gave him the same impression as next door.

Jackson returned to his side and said to his boss, "You are looking very thoughtful. Come up with an idea, have you?"

"I'm beginning to wonder whether this murderer is a woman," he said.

"Why is that?"

"Because I think clothes and jewellery have been stolen from the ladies' rooms."

He made his way downstairs.

"But how would a woman carry a gun, shoot two people and then calmly pack up clothes and jewellery and carry that and a gun outside without anyone seeing?"

"She could if there were two of them. Two women, or a man and a woman."

"Or the women had a clear out for the jumble, before they were murdered."

"Has there been a jumble sale?" asked Revie.

"Dunno sir. Do you want me to ask?"

"No, I don't."

The men arrived in the hallway after carefully circumnavigating the blood and the men attending to the forensics there.

"I've been thinking that it was a woman doing the stealing because of the clothes and jewels, but down here there has been a systematic search. The TV and electrical stuff are still here and untouched, so it's not that. But all the drawers and cupboards have been turned out. I wonder what they had, that was so important?"

He cast his mind back to their interview and suddenly remembered how Sylvia Lamb's eyes flashed when he had commented on her interesting library.

"Bring down those books, one by one," he instructed. "Carefully mind and have a look inside every one of them.

CHAPTER SEVENTEEN

Richard Yates was staring in disbelief at the scene playing out on the other side of the road.

He got the news from some local kids, whose mother had tried to raise the sisters that morning. She was supposed to meet them to discuss a local project and had then fetched another neighbour to help her get in. They took the spare key from the greenhouse and unlocked the kitchen door.

The bleeding body of Alice Lamb was enough to make them scream and call for the police. According to the boys, they didn't bother to try and help Alice, choosing instead to run outside and telephone.

Richard heard some updates on the news and here he stood, watching the story unfold from his window. He knew that David was watching from next door, but as the two men were no longer friends, he had no intention of calling him to compare notes.

It turned out that David had been having an affair with Laura. They both denied that it had been going on for very long, but Richard wasn't convinced. Laura hadn't been paying much attention to him for a long time. The eventual admissions of an affair with his best friend, made utter sense.

Richard had set off for work one morning as usual. He sat in a traffic jam, drumming his fingers on the steering wheel and dreading the presentation he was to give this afternoon to some Head Office people.

"Fuck, fuck, fuck," he said and slammed his hand against the wheel, accidentally sounding the horn and causing several drivers to look at him. The man driving the car in front leaned out of his window and shouted, "It's not my fucking fault mate!"

"Sorry! I've just remembered I've forgotten something," Richard shouted back.

The man raised his hand in acknowledgement and brought his head back in the window.

As soon as the traffic started moving again, Richard left at the slip road and made his way back home. He thought of telephoning Laura to ask her to look for the folder, but he couldn't quite remember whether or not his limited porn collection was in the same drawer and he didn't want her to see that.

He parked the car on the road outside. He was unable to get on the drive as it was blocked by David Farrington's van. Had he come to start on the new kitchen today? No, that was next week.

Richard didn't go through the front door, choosing instead to go in through the kitchen door. Laura and David should be there, but they weren't.

He picked up the post from the hall floor. It was then that he heard noises coming from upstairs which made him stop, half stooped, hand outstretched.

He could hear his wife making sounds he had not heard come from her since the early days of their marriage. Richard went out of the kitchen, into the hall and began walking up the stairs. He held onto the banister for support, as his legs were trying to buckle underneath him.

There was a faint reminder of childhood as he crossed the landing, but he ignored it, because now he could hear his long-time friend shouting Laura's name.

Richard pushed open the bedroom door and saw the two of them on the bed.

"You couldn't even shut the fucking curtains," was all he could think of saying. "Now all the neighbours will know."

Laura screamed, "Richard please! I can explain!" giving the well-worn answer to being caught red handed.

"Rich, mate. Please, let's talk. Put that down!"

Richard looked at his hand as David pointed and realised that he was carrying a knife. He must have picked it up in the kitchen. He raised it to shoulder height and said, "Well my faithful friend and loving wife. How long has this been going on?"

"We just had a moment that was all. It hasn't happened before. This is the first time, Richard. Oh God, please don't do anything," begged Laura.

"I want to do something to you both. I want to stab you and let you slowly bleed to death while I watch. I want you both to die a horrible death, but chances are that I will get caught and I don't want to go to jail."

Laura was sobbing and David stared at him, not in fear, but with hatred.

"What I do expect is that you leave my house today, Laura. When I get home you will have gone. If you choose to try and get any money out of me, I mean any money Laura, you will live to regret it."

"You can stay with me, Laura. Don't worry, my solicitor will sort it out for you," said David.

159

"And I will let everyone know what I know about you, David. I doubt your business will survive that."

Richard brandished the knife at the pair again and walked out of the door, saying as he went, "By the time I'm home tonight, Laura!"

As he drove away, Laura got dressed shakily.

Oh my God, David. I don't want a divorce, I want to keep my life."

"You can't be very happy with it Laura, or you wouldn't have just let me fuck you," he sneered.

Laura stopped her dressing and looked at David. For a moment, she thought that she could see danger in his eyes. Or was it evil?

David laughed and pulled her to his chest. As he kissed her, Laura forgot herself.

"Come on, let's get some clothes and stuff together and take them back to my house."

"I'm not so sure I want to give up on my marriage just like that, David."

"Yes you do, Laura. I have plans and have been getting some money together. I'm going to move to France, do you want to come to France with me?"

"Yes, I want to come to France with you, David."

Laura kissed him and she remembered how much David had inherited and if he sold the house he lived in now, well that would be a tidy sum. Perhaps it wouldn't be such a bad idea to jump ship.

She packed some clothes and told him which other things to put in boxes.

"Good job I brought the van, isn't it? Though we might need to do more than one trip. Are you taking the big screen telly?"

Yes, I'm taking my big screen telly and we can come again at the weekend. There's not much of this shit I want anyway. Especially when I know that you are going to buy me all new stuff!"

"We are going to be rich, Laura Yates, soon to be Laura Farrington!"

"Are you asking me to marry you?"

"I certainly will as soon as your divorce comes through and you get your half of the money. Because added to mine, we should be able to get a pretty decent place in France."

"Oh. Right. It's just come as a bit of a shock that's all. I wasn't expecting another marriage when I got up this morning."

"Let's see how everything pans out, love. Don't forget your bank cards because we should probably clear any accounts before he gets to them."

And after Laura had got herself a solicitor, Richard found himself ordered to leave his home and move into his father's place. There was apparently no money left in any of the accounts for him to use and he was being forced to pay all household bills until an agreement could be reached.

There had been no more conversations between the two friends since that day, two months ago, when he had caught them shagging.

#

Anthony wasn't so pleased about Richard taking over the old house, as he had plans to move in there himself.

Janet shouted to Anthony, "Coffee?"

"Yes please," he called back.

Anthony had been without a drink for three months. He had called his wife 'Janet', in a drunken stupor and had been thrown out of the house.

Janet welcomed him into her house with open arms and a glad heart. Janet Banks had wanted this for ever. Anthony Yates wasn't so sure and had been trying to find a way out of this mess. When the marital home and his Dad's house sold, he intended to go and live somewhere else.

In the meantime, needs must, and he was going to have to stay at Janet's, or else he would have to move in with his brother and he didn't fancy that.

"Anything else happening?" asked Janet as she came back into the room and joined him at the window.

"It looks like they are taking a body out of the house now,"

"Oh no. Who do you think it is?"

"I don't know which one is injured and which one is dead," said Anthony.

"Shall I go out and have a better look?"

"People might think you are being nosy, but who cares? Go and find out what you can."

Anthony was glad that he was on his own for a while. Janet had hardly left him alone since he moved in. He needed some breathing space.

Janet put down her coffee and went outside. Anthony picked up his phone.

"Richard, are you watching this?"

"I am. Oh, I see you've got Janet checking what's going on."

"It won't take long before she finds out something."

"No, she's good at that."

"How are you today? Heard any more from the solicitor?"

"No, but he seems to think we will get an agreement. Anthony, I've been thinking that when I get my money, I will buy this place. What do you think about that?"

"I think it's a good idea, if you think you can pull it off. When everything is settled I want to move right away."

"From Yorkshire?"

"Yes. Is that alright?"

"I can't say anything about it, Anthony. I will miss you though. Christ, it feels as though my whole life is falling apart."

"That's why I want to get away, Richard. Nothing is the same and I want out of it. I just want to collect as much as money together as possible and move on."

"I don't blame you. How's the non-drinking going?"

"Still no drinking and I feel better for it. I can think clearer now."

"Janet's on her way back in."

"I'll pop round later."

Anthony put the phone down.

"Sylvia is dead, Alice is at death's door and someone has ransacked the whole place." Janet informed him.

"Christ," answered Anthony.

"I saw David and Laura round there yesterday evening. You don't think they were anything to do with it, do you?" said Janet.

CHAPTER EIGHTEEN

David shouted upstairs, "Laura! Can you see anything?"

"I'm not shouting down to you. Richard will be listening through the wall. Come up here."

David did as he was told and joined Laura at the window. He put his arms around her and she cuddled up to him. They saw a body being put into the back of a big black van.

"That will be Sylvia," Laura said quietly.

"I wonder if Alice will make it?" asked David.

"It would be better if she didn't."

"It would."

David turned to the bed where the clothes and jewels which had formerly belonged to the Lamb sisters lay strewn about.

"Have you tried them on?" he asked.

"I've only held them against me. I'm going to get them dry cleaned before I wear them."

"We had better pack them up and move them while the police are around."

"They aren't likely to come up here, are they?"

"I don't know. But I expect they will be questioning everyone again."

"Not today though. We will be safe today," said Laura with confidence.

But for once, she was wrong.

They moved away from the window, stripped off their clothes and fell on the bed. The clothes were thrown unceremoniously onto the floor. If Richard didn't hear the noise Laura made, he must be going deaf. They both enjoyed the extra thrill of knowing he would have his ear pressed against the wall. Listening. But their fun also meant they missed seeing Chief Inspector Revie and Sergeant Jackson coming out of the Lamb house carrying a large book. This was handed to a uniformed officer who, after being given instruction took it away in his car.

They also missed the police looking across at the houses opposite and making their way to David Farrington's house. The policemen knocked loudly on the front door and after getting no response, went round to the back.

They indulged in another minute of knocking and were eventually rewarded for their efforts, when the door was opened by a dishevelled David.

"Hello officers. What can I do for you?" he asked, with what he imagined was a winning grin.

"You know there has been a serious incident across the road, Mr Farrington?"

"It's hard to miss. They are dead, aren't they?"

"Do you mind if we come in?" asked Jackson.

"Do you have a warrant?"

"Do we need one?"

"No. Sorry, I'm being a dick. Come in." He ushered the two men into the kitchen.

Sergeant Jackson immediately asked if he could use the bathroom. The hesitation from David was obvious, but he could hardly say no.

"Yes, if you must."

Jackson smiled and went upstairs. As he reached the landing, he saw Laura Yates standing there, in an almost see through housecoat.

"Hello," he said.

"Hello," she answered. "Are you that copper who arrested my husband and David?"

"I didn't arrest either of them. They were only helping us. Are you no longer with your husband?"

Jackson knew perfectly well what had happened, as the team had been keeping an eye on everyone connected with that murder.

"We have differences which may result in a divorce," she answered carefully.

"Irreconcilable?"

She laughed and Dan Jackson, the man, could see that this tousled haired woman could cause trouble. She was striking looking, if not classically beautiful, but sexy with a capital X.

He also noticed through the partly open bedroom door, the clothes strewn across the floor.

Laura followed his gaze, "A bit untidy I know. Richard didn't like it, but David doesn't mind."

"Perhaps you would like to come downstairs and answer a few questions for us?"

"I thought you wanted the loo."

"Changed my mind."

Laura moved behind him and followed him into the kitchen. Jackson could smell her.

"This is Laura Yates sir, I found her upstairs."

David folded his arms and said, "Laura is living with me until she sorts out her marital problems."

"You and Mr Yates have separated? That is sad. I hope you manage to sort it out." Revie gave her his best avuncular smile.

"Thank you," answered Laura and received a frown from David.

"So, as I was saying Mr Farrington, is there anything you can tell me about the incident over the road?"

"Like what? We didn't hear or see anything weird last night. But we had the curtains closed and the telly on, probably like most of the people in the street."

"You didn't hear any loud noises at all?" asked Jackson.

"Like a gun you mean?" asked Laura.

"No one has mentioned a gun," said Jackson.

"No. But my father in law was killed with a gun and no one heard that either," reasoned Laura.

"What were you watching?"

"Don't you police watch the telly? It was the opening ceremony last night. There was loads on," said David.

"Ah, the Olympics, I tried to get tickets, but failed sadly. So, there was music and fireworks?" commented Revie.

"And dancing. And loads of singers. Take That were on. I love Gary Barlow!" said Laura with her hands across her heart.

"I see," said Revie.

"You didn't see anything suspicious or different during the past few days you said? These three houses are the only ones with a direct view into the Lamb house. Everyone else's view is obscured by trees and walls," said Jackson.

"We can't help you I'm afraid. While we are on the subject, have you found out who killed Thomas? Do you think the same person did for them over the road?" asked David.

"Too early to tell," answered Revie.

"Look, can I use your bathroom please?"

"I thought you'd already been?" said David.

"Not yet," answered Jackson and he ran up the stairs before drawing any more attention to his toilet habits.

"Perhaps you two could just tell me exactly what you were doing all day yesterday and during the night. In detail, please." Revie took out a notebook and began to write.

Jackson opened and closed the bathroom door, but remained on the landing. After a cursory check over the banister he sneaked into the front bedroom. The covers on the bed were ruffled and the room untidy.

He picked up the clothes from the floor, one by one and thought how exquisite they were. They were well made and classic. Almost old fashioned.

No. They were vintage. The labels were vintage and designer. Jackson had been brought up by a fashion designer mother and had learnt a lot from her. It was an expertise he never bragged about and the information certainly had not been written on his police application forms.

He went over to the dresser and opened the top drawer. Inside were several pieces of good jewellery. Expensive, classy and nothing like he would expect the voluptuous Laura Yates to wear. He shut the drawer and walked to the bay window, so he could look at the Lamb house. He saw the CSI people and the police and the neighbours. Glancing to his left from the bay, he realised that he could see into the upstairs side bay of the Yates house. Standing there looking at the same scene was Richard Yates. Jackson noted that the top window was open as was the one next to him. There was barely a metre separating them.

"Christ, they must be able to hear everything in each other's bedroom," he muttered.

Richard turned to look at Jackson, but gave away no emotion on his face. Jackson looked to his right and could see the Banks house and the bedroom window where Anthony Yates looked back at him.

Sergeant Jackson felt unnerved and vulnerable for a moment until he regained his composure, shook himself and made his way to the bathroom. Creeping in, he flushed the loo and went quickly down the stairs.

"You were a long time, got a gippy tummy, have you?" asked David facetiously.

"I'm fine thanks," he answered.

Jackson scribbled on his notepad and handed it to Revie. After reading it, his superior asked, "Do you mind if we have a look round?"

Laura and David looked at each other and David answered, "Why would you want to do that?"

"Just for the sake of elimination sir, to help us out. We shall be asking everyone in the street."

"You need a warrant, don't you?" asked Laura.

"Not necessarily," answered Revie ambiguously,

"I would like to get a different aspect of the Lamb house. Your house is opposite and a detective likes to get an all-round view."

"Perhaps you could come back later Chief Inspector. I haven't tidied up yet and would be embarrassed if you saw any of my dirty underwear!"

Revie nodded his head and said he would be back in an hour after talking to Richard Yates.

The policemen left the house with David Farrington almost shutting the door on their backs.

"Sir?" said Jackson as they walked up the drive.

Revie held up his hand and pressed a few numbers on his phone. He made a request which had Jackson smiling when he heard it. He relaxed his shoulders.

They walked over to their car and opened the doors. But they didn't have time to sit down, because Revie received a phone call. After beckoning over three officers, they made their way back down the drive of the Farrington house.

Revie knocked on the door and David answered, "You said an hour, Chief Inspector."

"Plans change, I'm afraid sir. We would like to come in now, if that's alright with you. This time we have a warrant."

Five minutes later, Richard Yates watched the police take away his screaming wife and sullen next-door neighbour,

171

handcuffed and in separate police cars. Laura looked up at Richard and shouted something to him which he couldn't quite make out, but he doubted that it was friendly.

CHAPTER NINETEEN

After organising a search of the Farrington house, Chief Inspector Revie and Sergeant Jackson called round to see Richard Yates.

Richard had the front door open as soon as he saw them making their way down the drive.

"You've arrested my wife," he said.

"Let's just say that we need to ask them both a few questions," answered Revie as he made his way into the kitchen through the hallway.

"Have you managed to get everything cleared away here, Mr Yates?" said Revie, jerking his thumb in the direction of the front room.

"Mostly. I had to get cleaners in and take away the furniture and carpet. How come we have to pay for that?"

"Perhaps your insurers could help? I could give you the number of someone at the station that may be able to advise you."

"Don't bother. Do you want some coffee?"

"That would be very nice of you. It's been a busy morning so far." ·

"Can I use your bathroom?" asked Jackson. Now, the need was genuine.

"Help yourself," Richard answered.

This time there was no one on the landing and the bedroom doors were all wide open. A quick glance into the rooms showed nothing out of the ordinary. It was apparent that Richard Yates was using his parent's old room, the others held only storage boxes and old beds. The rooms had a stale smell which Jackson recalled from their original search after the murder. It was a smell of unwashed things, whereas the toilet smelled strongly of piss and the bathroom of damp.

He washed his hands and decided against drinking anything that had been made for him downstairs.

His boss and Richard were chatting away in the kitchen and as Revie looked at him when he came in, Jackson was able to shake his head very slightly to convey the message that there was nothing of interest upstairs.

"Mr Yates tells us that he saw his wife and David Farrington visit the Lambs late last night."

"About two in the morning," added Richard.

"You saw them at the house?" Jackson asked.

"I did," he confirmed.

"Did you see them go in?" asked Revie.

"I think they must have gone in round the back, because I didn't see the front door open."

"How come you were watching the house?" asked Jackson.

"I wasn't watching the house, I was watching them," Richard said simply.

"Just tell us what you saw and why you were watching at all," demanded Revie.

"Ok. Look, you know that my bitch of a wife is having it off with David Farrington? I don't know how long it's been going on, but I do know that it's going to cost me a lot of money. She didn't have anything when we got together. Now she's after everything. I can't go into my own house, because her solicitor has prevented me even though I'm paying for it. And she's after my share of this place."

"What has this to do with last night?" said Jackson.

"I'm afraid I keep an eye on them. I don't sleep much with the stress and the noise they make in the bedroom doesn't help." Richard looked angry.

He continued, "Sometimes I stand nearer the window than perhaps I should and I can hear everything they talk about and do in there. Laura has been going on and on about the valuable clothes that Sylvia Lamb has and telling David she wants them. She always goes on and on and on until you give in because it's easier to."

"So, you are saying that you heard them discuss taking the clothes?"

"I did and I will swear to it. I can't swear that David agreed to take them because I didn't hear him agree. But I saw him go with her and she wasn't dragging him along."

"You heard this on other nights?" asked Revie.

"Other than last night you mean? Yes, I did. Last night I heard her say it had to be tonight because everyone will be watching the telly all night and David said, tonight it is then. Then, I didn't hear anything for an hour because they left the bedroom, but I watched them go over the road and they were going there in a way that meant they didn't want to get seen."

"What did that look like?" asked Jackson, imagining them rolling across the road, army style.

"Just quickly, heads down and into the driveway."

"Were they carrying anything?"

"David was carrying a big, leather Gladstone bag. I bought it for Laura years ago. He had it over his shoulder and walked quickly. When they came out he was still carrying it on his shoulder but wasn't walking so quickly. Laura kept looking back at the house, and when they got under the street light, that one there, she looked scared. I saw her hold on to the post and David sort of prised her fingers off it."

"You didn't think of calling the police?" asked Revie.

"No, I didn't know anyone had been killed then. I thought that I would ask her about it this morning. But instead I'm telling you."

"Do you think that your wife is capable of causing harm to someone to get what she wants?" enquired Jackson.

"Not physically. Her harm is mainly emotional, like nagging. But she doesn't have a conscience and I could see her making him do it."

"You think that David is capable?"

"Oh yes, he's always been like that."

"Can he shoot?"

"Yes, but he doesn't own any guns, legally that is. But I'm sure he's got some from before the amnesties. His Dad used to have them, I know that."

Jackson scribbled away and then asked, "Did you see anyone else around that night?"

"No just the usual people getting on and off the bus and some people walking their dogs, one was Judith Buckley, I think."

"But no one going into or coming from the Lamb house?"

"Not that I saw, but I went to bed after Laura and David came home."

"Were they excited when they got back?"

"I only heard some muffled talking. They didn't seem excited or angry or anything unusual," he answered.

"Will you put that in a statement for us please sir?" said Revie, "If you would find time to go to the station today, I can arrange for someone to meet you."

"I will do," he answered, and began to show them out of the door. "Are you going to talk to my brother?"

"We will indeed, I think he is staying a couple of doors up the road?"

"He is. He's with Janet Banks for a while because his wife has decided that she wants a divorce too. It's not serious between them though. Not for Anthony anyway. I'll go to the station this afternoon," Richard shouted after them.

The police walked up the path out of the gate and back into next door's.

"How's it going?" asked Revie as he made his way through the kitchen.

"We are a bit thin on the ground, so won't be finished for a while yet," said Mrs G, their favourite CSI officer.

"Do you have anything for me to go on?" asked Revie.

"Sadly, all we have are the clothes and jewellery that I imagine came from the Lambs, but I can't guarantee that until we do some more tests."

"Any murder weapon?" asked Jackson.

"No guns found so far. But we shall know more when those two have been swabbed and tested. I would have thought though, that if either of them had killed her, there would be a lot of blood on their clothes. And as we haven't found any blood, then perhaps they changed and burned the stuff they wore."

"Thank you very much," said Chief Inspector Revie, "and I won't quote you until you have made everything official. Which should take ages?"

She patted the side of Revie's face in a friendly way, forcing Jackson to raise eyebrows at his boss.

Revie said, "Make sure someone checks that lamp post outside here. They both touched it last night."

"Anything for you!"

"Next door," said Revie to Jackson, who was grinning.

Chief Inspector Revie was blushing.

Next door at the Banks house, they were received with friendliness, cups of tea and chocolate biscuits.

"Couldn't just nip to the loo, could I?" asked Jackson.

Upstairs, as downstairs, was immaculately clean and tidy.

Almost obsessively so.

The main bedroom was definitely being shared by two people judged Jackson, by the clothes in there and the impression that both bedside tables were being used. He only peeped around the door of old Mrs Banks room, where he could see no change from their last visit. The other bedrooms were set up as a guest rooms and an office.

The bathroom and toilet smelled only of some sort of flowery perfume, which was quite a pleasant change from piss.

Jackson came into the kitchen and began drinking his tea.

Janet was in the middle of speaking to his boss, "So when I noticed them going over the road, I thought that they can't be up to any good at that time of night. I only noticed because I had nipped to the toilet and happened to look out of the window before I got into bed. Looking out of the window is a habit I think most of us have when we come into a room isn't it? I always do it anyway." She stopped to take a drink and Revie encouraged her with a nod.

"I saw David and Laura coming back down the Lamb's drive and David was carrying a big bag and Laura was sort of hurrying and she had her hand up to her mouth. Like she was laughing."

"What did you think they were doing there?"

"I don't know really. I can't think of a reason, but Laura has always been ready to cause trouble, so I suppose I thought that she might be playing a joke on the Lambs. But to be honest I didn't think any more about it until this morning."

"Did you see or hear anything else yesterday evening?"

"No, we were watching the telly."

"Thank you. Did you see or hear anything unusual, Mr Yates?"

"Absolutely nothing at all. I didn't even know about Laura and David going over there until about an hour ago."

"Have the Lamb ladies been frightened or worried lately?" asked Jackson.

179

"No. Just their normal selves. Gossiping with people and watching out of their windows and going up to the shops. Just normal, you know."

"Yes, I've only seen the same people calling on them that I usually do. But to be perfectly honest, Chief Inspector, I don't spend that much time looking over the road," interjected Janet.

Revie ignored the fact that her recent evidence seemed to prove the contrary and said, "You two have lived in and known this street and the ladies for a long time."

"All our lives. My brother and I were born here and my parents moved here after the Lamb family arrived, so I've always known them," said Anthony.

"Same here. My parents moved here almost the same week as the Yates. Everyone in this row of houses did, because they were all finished at about the same time. The same man built them all. The Lambs are very nice ladies, a bit nosy, but kind. They probably know everything about everybody in this street," added Janet.

"Probably about everyone in this town," said Anthony.

Janet took another biscuit and said, "I wonder if they saw who killed your Dad, Anthony?"

Anthony looked at her sharply and snapped, "You think that Laura and David killed my Dad and then went on to kill the Lambs?"

"Well no, I don't know. Sorry Anthony, I wasn't actually thinking that through. I just sort of said it. I'm not saying that they did it." She stopped abruptly, realising that she was making no sense.

"Shut up then Janet, if you don't understand what you are talking about."

She hung her head and Jackson felt sorry for her, she looked like a victim.

"Could you please arrange to come in and make a statement later today?"

"Yes of course, Chief Inspector. Is Richard going too, I see you have interviewed him?" asked Janet.

"He is."

"We'll ask him for a lift. No point us going to the same place separately," said Anthony, who appeared to have suddenly cheered himself up.

"We shall speak again, but do call me if you remember anything else," said Revie.

Outside he said, "Back to the station I think. I want to have a look at that book and a talk to that pair. And I expect you need the loo again."

"Ha-ha," Jackson said.

CHAPTER TWENTY

Later that afternoon the two men were back in their offices, reading the book they had found at the Lamb sister's house. Detective Chief Inspector Revie had refrained from doing a dance when the book was found. It would have put him in danger of losing dignity and standing in front of his subordinates.

They had carefully taken each book from its place on the shelf and Revie opened and shook them. Upon doing this to a book entitled 'Recognising Embarrassing Complaints of the Elderly Woman and how to deal with them', a leather-bound volume fell from the dustcover and he managed to catch it before it hit the floor. It was a large book and well-handled and when he opened it, he saw that the book was almost full of writings in the small neat hand of an older woman. The date on the first page was 27th September 1952.

Back at the office, Revie saw that the notes were made regularly, commenting on local events and giving the names of anyone who called at their house or who walked past its gates.

He turned the pages of the book to nearer the present day and saw that the jottings were in much greater detail and although written in some sort of shorthand or code, gave times and dates of recent events.

"It looks like it's mainly Sylvia who has written in the book," said Jackson. "But Alice has written in it sometimes."

"I know. As soon as she is well enough to speak to us, she will help us decipher some of this shorthand." He continued to look over the work.

Revie loved puzzles and he loved history and this book was the two combined.

"We ought to get someone to write it up properly," said Jackson.

"There is a danger that words will be missed and some of the sentences transposed incorrectly. I agree it should be done, but not yet a while."

He continued to read and write notes.

"Miss Lamb seems confused about the death of Thomas Yates, because she didn't see anything out of the ordinary when he was killed. Although she says she saw Richard Yates visit his father two days before the body was found," noted Revie.

"He told us that he hadn't seen his father for days before he discovered the body," added Jackson.

"I think that we will find a few things in this book, which will alter what we thought we were going to find out."

"Boss!" DC Griffiths said.

"What is it?" he answered, still reading.

"They've finished taking all the samples from your suspects and their solicitors are here."

"That was quick with the solicitors," commented Jackson, "especially for a Saturday."

"It'll be because there's potential for a serial killer here. They want the kudos." Revie closed the book and said, "I think we should interview them and find out what they did and what they saw. I will read through this later."

Revie returned the book to a plastic bag, put it into a briefcase and finally into his safe.

"This book could be dynamite," he said, "I don't want any harm to come to it."

They made their way to the interview rooms and Revie decided to speak to David Farrington first, deciding that Laura Yates was the stronger person.

David Farrington sat with his arms folded and a petulant look on his face. His solicitor looked stunned and Revie imagined that they had exchanged words before this interview.

Preliminaries over, Revie began his questioning.

"Perhaps you can let us know how you came to be in possession of the belongings of the Misses Lamb?"

The solicitor looked at his client who shrugged his shoulders and began.

"Look. We had nothing to do with the murders, but we did take the clothes and jewellery. I didn't want to, but Laura insisted. If you knew Laura, you would know that you don't resist Laura." He smiled as though they were all in this together.

It wasn't going down well.

"Were the ladies fine about you being in their house?"

David's face dropped, "Yes, but they were asleep. I know they were alright when we left." Revie flicked through the notes in front of him.

"Then, how do you account for their deaths occurring at the same time you were in the house? Are you sure they were alright when you left?"

David unfolded his arms and pushed his chair away slightly from the desk.

He looked uncomfortable.

"Bit tricky is it, not having Mrs Yates with you?" asked Jackson.

"What do you mean by that?"

"I imagine that she could come up with some answers for you. You probably can't think very clearly on your own. How long have you two been involved?"

"We are not really involved. Laura and I have known each other most of our lives. We all went to school together."

"All?"

"Me, Richard, Anthony, Janet, Judith, Laura, Tina and a few others."

"What about the Prentices?"

"The Prentices? What made you think of them?"

"They are relatives of the Yates, aren't they?"

"Well yes, I suppose so. But they left years ago. I mean back in the 80s and I can't remember any of them coming back here since."

"You never talked about them?"

"Might have done. But they went all posh, so I don't expect they would even bother with us now."

"Hmmmm," said Jackson.

185

"We haven't heard from them for years, like I just said."

"And you are still telling us that you and Mrs Yates aren't involved?"

"Not really involved, she's a bit homeless at the moment. Richard is divorcing her you know."

"Because of you, I gather. And she has stopped his access to the marital home, hasn't she? Mr Yates is not allowed there."

"That's because she's frightened of him."

"But she feels safe enough living next door to him, with you?" said Jackson incredulously.

"I'm there to protect her, aren't I?"

"I see. So perhaps now you would like to go back over what happened last night. From the time you went to the house, to when you got home."

"It was nowhere near the time of any murder," he started.

"Do you know the time of the murder?" asked Jackson.

"No, no I don't know. Look if I admit to what I know, what will happen to me, to us?"

"Depends what you actually did," said Revie, "Your solicitor will tell you that I can't make any promises."

"Can I have a word with Laura?"

"No, you can't, not yet."

"I'm not sure what to do now," said David.

"You are in a lot of trouble David. Think of yourself not her, because I'm sure she isn't thinking of you," said Jackson.

David leant back and closed his eyes for a minute.

"Laura is very insistent. I've told you that already, but honestly you have to be with her to know what she can force you to do. You can try and say no, but before you know where you are..."

"That's what happened last night, is it?"

"Sort of. By the time I was walking across the road with her, I was already pretty near pissed."

"Did you take a bag at all?" asked Jackson.

"I took a bag of Laura's. Some big leather thing."

"Did it have anything in it?" asked Revie.

"Like a gun you mean? No way, I told you I had nothing to do with that. I'm not a murderer." He folded his arms again.

"Just asking. Please carry on with your story," encouraged Revie.

"As I say, we went over to the house. We had arranged to pick up some stuff I'd bought from them. They said we should just come in. The front door was locked, but we didn't bother with it too much because the key to the conservatory is left under a statue there. It was a bit weird because the lights were on all over the house, but we just assumed that is what they normally did."

"You didn't notice if they kept their lights on at other times?"

"I don't think I ever paid that much attention."

"Did you see or hear anyone?" asked Jackson.

"No one, other than ourselves. I went in and collected the stuff from Alice Lamb. Laura particularly wanted a dress of Sylvia's. I don't know which one because I'm not interested

187

in clothes. I didn't mind being interested in jewellery because I can understand that being worth something. You know, like money."

"What about Sylvia Lamb. Where was she?"

"In bed asleep apparently. We were very quiet and didn't disturb her and she never came down."

"You didn't see her at all?" Jackson asked.

The police looked at each other.

"I let Laura put the clothes she wanted in the bag and I took jewellery from Alice." He stopped and grinned.

"How long were you there?" asked Revie

"I didn't fancy hanging around any longer than I had to and to be honest we wanted to get back home. Don't fuck about, get in and get out."

"So you are used to doing this then?" said Revie.

"What?"

"Going into people's house late and taking their stuff?"

David scowled, "I'm not a thief you know."

"Did you shoot either of them?"

"No. I fucking didn't!" David got up from his chair ready to face his accuser.

"Sit down, Mr Farrington," said Revie calmly. "I want to make sure I have all the facts."

"Well I don't like you accusing me of something I didn't do. We got out of there pretty quickly after we got the stuff we wanted."

"Why did you cause so much damage?"

David looked confused, "We didn't! I told you, we went, got the clothes and jewels we wanted and came home. Laura kept laughing and I told her to stop in case she upsets the old dears. I bet we were back at my house in less than half an hour. Probably less than that."

"What did you intend to do with the stuff you fetched?" asked Revie.

"Laura wanted them. Just to wear, I suppose. I haven't really thought about it. We could sell or wear the jewels, but now I expect we will have to give them back?"

The interview ended and they went straight to talk to Laura Yates.

"Do you think he's telling us the truth?"

"I don't know sir, I mean he acted as though they were still alive and uninjured while they were there and I'm not so sure that he's clever enough to make it up."

"But they were there around the time of the attack, so if they are telling the truth, the Lambs were injured just after they left."

"And if they didn't search through the house, then who did that?"

"Two separate incidents?"

"Let's see what Laura Yates has got to say."

CHAPTER TWENTY ONE

The demeanour of Laura Yates was totally different to David's.

The policemen listened to her version of the events of the previous evening. Reluctant at first, she soon began to talk. Especially when told that David was insisting the whole job had been her idea.

"Cheeky git, how dare he say that? He was the one who decided that we should go in. I was worried that we would frighten the Lambs, but he said they wanted us to come in the evening. Sylvia said that I could have the dress she wore at Thomas's funeral, I was going to pay her, but then she went all funny about it, said she wanted more money. So I went to get it that's all." She folded her arms.

"That doesn't make any sense at all. Why would they want you to go in the middle of the night and why would you take all the other stuff?" asked Jackson.

"Because the ladies are often up and about at that time. We talked about it and agreed a deal for the lot."

"You agreed to buy the stuff?" asked Revie, "You are telling us that this was a business deal and not a theft?"

"Of course, it wasn't a theft. Whatever made you think that?"

"We thought that it was a theft. David seems confused about the whole thing."

"Well, David is an idiot. Haven't you worked that out yet?"

The policeman refrained from glancing at each other.

"You actually spoke to the ladies while you were there?" asked Revie.

"Not both, just Alice. Sylvia wasn't well she said. In bed with a headache or a bad stomach, I can't remember what it was. But we discussed the stuff and agreed what I would pay her. She said that they didn't mind waiting for the money until after my house sale has gone through."

She stopped talking and bit her nails.

"Does this mean I'm supposed to give the stuff back? Or pay straight away? How's it going to work?"

DCI Revie said, "You are telling us that contrary to all the evidence, you and David Farrington only went over to the Lambs house to do a deal on some items and that you came home with those items after agreeing to pay them at a later date?"

"In a nutshell, yes."

"And that you did not see Sylvia Lamb, only Alice Lamb and as far as you are concerned, they were both in good health when you left?"

"I can guarantee that Alice was, but I don't know about Sylvia."

"How do you explain the attack on them?"

"I don't know anything about that. There was no dead body in the house when I went in and there was no body in there when I came out."

"What did you think when you saw the police this morning? When you heard about the attack and the injuries? Weren't you curious?" asked Jackson.

This question appeared to unnerve her, "Not really, a bit maybe. I didn't think about it much."

She hesitated and then said, "To be honest I thought that if the police came and found that stuff, they might not believe me when I said that we did a deal. It's got me arrested, hasn't it?"

"Because you have no proof that the items were bought and not stolen." asked Jackson.

She leant forward and was all smiles and big eyes. She seemed to squeeze her arms together and her breasts looked much bigger.

"Exactly, Detective Sergeant Jackson. I knew that you would understand! So, can I please leave this horrible place now? Please!"

Jackson looked at his boss who raised his eyebrows. Laura's solicitor touched her arm as if in restraint.

Jackson said, "Not for a bit yet, Mrs Yates."

The interview ended and the policemen went out into the corridor.

"She's got a nerve!" commented Jackson.

"She certainly has and it looks as though she will drop Farrington in it, if she thinks that she can get away with it."

"But they are totally avoiding the murder question," said Jackson.

"There's always the possibility that someone else came in afterwards and killed them," mused Revie.

"Taking advantage of seeing those two go in and out you mean?"

"Either of the Yates brothers had the opportunity to do that I suppose."

"If we work on that theory though, then anyone could have done it. It doesn't even have to be someone from the neighbourhood."

"Someone already intending to do damage and then having to wait for those two to get lost." Revie looked thoughtful. "Another intruder must have had a different motive, because they searched the rest of the house."

"We don't know if they found anything, because nothing else seems to be missing."

"Their housekeeper will turn up tomorrow, so we will get her to go through the house and see if she notices anything," decided Revie. "But I'm thinking that one or other of these crimes is to do with the murder of Thomas Yates."

"Do you think that we should have a cup of tea and have another look through that book?"

"Aaah. Getting a bit more interested in the book, are you?"

"I was always interested," said Jackson.

DC Griffiths walked towards them and said, "Can you ring Dr Jordan please, sir?"

"I will," he answered and did so immediately.

"Just an update which may help you, John," she said.

"Fire away."

"Both women were shot where they lay," she said.

"Not moved after that?"

"No, not possible. There is one set of bloody prints upstairs in the house. I need to check if they belong to your people."

"Can you tell who was shot first?"

"No. You need to pray that Alice Lamb makes it and you can get some better information from her. Bye." She finished the call.

Putting the phone back in his pocket he said, "Dr Jordan says that the women were shot where they were found."

"Yes, I see."

"Are we going back in there?"

"Not just yet. I think we should go back to plan A and have a look at the book."

Coffee drunk and biscuits eaten, Revie was dictating some entries in the journal for someone to write out.

"Last night, all she wrote in here was that they were looking forward to Mrs Brown calling in with a list of the helpers for some fete they were doing next week. She was coming this morning, so that makes sense. There's quite a bit about Richard Yates looking out of the bedroom window, just like his father. Also, about Anthony Yates looking out of his. They didn't seem to approve of all this marriage break up and blame Yates senior for the way they were brought up."

"So, there's nothing about meeting Laura Yates to do a deal?"

"Not that I've noticed yet, but the ladies write quite a lot. Oh, there's some woman who called on them yesterday afternoon to see if her dog had come into their garden because she had lost it. They thought they recognised her, but the lady said that she wasn't local and had only stopped the car to take the dog for a walk because it was desperate for a pee pee."

"Funny place to stop, there's not a lot of grass around here," noted Jackson.

"Hmmm."

"What about if we go through the book and check the dates of the murder," said Jackson.

"I'm going to do that next."

He flicked the pages back several months.

"It seems that they saw Thomas Yates looking through the downstairs window on Thursday afternoon and then the curtains were closed as usual and in the morning, they were open again. But it seems that they didn't see him at all and the curtains were never closed fully after Thursday night."

"They write in that much detail?"

"They don't always. They reminded themselves and rewrote it after they found out he was dead."

"And if they are writing what actually happens, that means he was probably killed on Thursday night."

"And the murderer opened the curtains to distract attention."

"They've got David Farrington coming home on Thursday night, staying in and going back to work on Friday morning."

"He's the one with all the opportunity," said Jackson.

"But what motive?" asked Revie.

"Money. Not that there seems to be much. Perhaps he thought that the Lambs saw him at the Yates that night? But they only wrote that he went to work and back."

"Besides, we've still got to get through this maze of their stories today. Let's go back to talk to them."

David Farrington looked surprised when asked if he wanted to change his story in light of what they had been told by Laura Yates.

But he recovered quickly and said, "She's told you that she did a deal with the Lambs, did she?"

"You tell us," answered Revie.

"I didn't know if was going to say that or not. That's why I told you the other story first. I told you that she's very persuasive and she said that if I didn't take the blame then she was going to say everything was my fault."

"When did she tell you that?"

"This morning, when we saw that there had been a murder."

"So why has she decided to tell us that story just now?" asked Jackson.

"I have no idea," he answered, "it's got me thinking about her motive. She's very tricky and even when you think a few steps ahead of her, she still seems to catch you out."

"We need to know about the blood on your shoes and whether you went anywhere else in the house," said Revie.

"I didn't look anywhere else and as for the murder, I have no idea. Perhaps the murderer was in the house, but we only saw Alice. Maybe she killed her sister before we got there. Did you find the invoice?"

"Invoice?"

"She gave us an invoice. Laura put it somewhere."

Ten minutes later, Laura was adamant that there was no invoice and the agreement had been verbal.

I told you that the Lambs were quite happy to do a deal on some of their old things. They were short of cash I believe."

"But they weren't getting the money from you for a while, were they?" asked Revie.

"I doubt it would take long for the house to sell and I was intending to get some cash out of Richard before then."

Jackson asked, "How much?"

"Pardon?" she said.

"How much did you agree to pay for the Lambs things?"

"Err. £300."

"That's cheap," Jackson answered.

"Might have been £500."

"Still seems cheap for all that jewellery."

"I don't think it's worth that much."

"Those clothes will be worth a bit too, they are vintage."

"You know about clothes then, do you?"

"A bit, my mother worked in fashion," said Jackson. Revie looked at him and gave a tiny smile.

"I know what I like and if you compare them to prices in High Street shops, it's a good price."

"Not if you compare them to the prices collectors are prepared to pay," reasoned Jackson. He wasn't going to let this drop.

"I don't know anything about that. Can I go now?"

"No, but you can go back to your cell while we check out some other stuff," said Revie, folding his notepad and getting up.

Laura Yates became agitated and asked, "How long are you going to hold me?"

"You can talk to your solicitor about that," he answered.

Revie and Jackson were soon back in their office, with Revie thumbing through the book and Jackson leaning against the window.

Jackson said, "There must be something we don't know."

No one answered.

Revie suddenly broke the silence and said, "Sylvia says that she saw Edith Prentice just before Thomas Yates was murdered."

"Who's she?" asked DC Eve.

"She's the sister of Ellie Yates and the mother of Eleanor Prentice and she's been missing for three years."

"Christ!"

"Sylvia also says that she saw her last week. Thursday night."

"How can she?" asked Jackson.

"Sylvia says that Edith was wandering about the place, visiting people. I think I'm going to have to go right through this journal. You go and see if any other neighbours have told the house to house lot anything and go and see Judith Buckley."

CHAPTER TWENTY TWO

Edith Prentice pootled about every morning, drinking a cup of tea and smoking a cigarette and then drinking another cup of tea, until she felt ready to go and have a shower and do her hair.

Edith had become obsessive over the years. It was as though she couldn't do the next job on the list until she had a cigarette and a drink first, tea during the day and whisky in the evening. Like the person who has to wash her hands over and over or go back to check the lights or the gas fire.

But she didn't consider it to be a problem. The fact that she would get up to go to the shops and then immediately think, "Oh I'll just have a quick ciggy," didn't register with her. She achieved virtually nothing constructive during the day, merely living in a constant cycle of smoking and drinking.

At the beginning of her married life, she had to find ways to feed the ever-growing family on a limited income and progressed to becoming a part of her husband's very successful company. The family moved several times until they owned a large property in Wales and a villa in Portugal. Money was easy and arrived frequently, but Edith felt more insecure the more secure she became.

It didn't make sense.

Three daughters married and remained happily so. Her eldest married and divorced, but seemed happy with that. Her beloved son married a woman who no one liked. It wasn't that she did anything nasty. It was just that she didn't fit in. Patsy couldn't understand the lively constant Prentice humour, the in jokes and the witty banter.

Patsy maintained a sullen silence in the beginning which progressed to a refusal to attend family events or being snippy and miserable when forced to. Andrew became more nervy and on edge, as he tried in vain to keep his wife happy. His family and friends had already started to ask why he remained in the marriage.

Andrew confessed to his mother shortly before he died that he wanted to leave his wife and come home to the family.

Edith joyfully said to him on the telephone, "Come home now son."

"I can't, not just yet, Mum. I need to get one or two things cleared up first."

"Like what?"

"Well, someone keeps phoning me and I'm not sure who it is."

"What do you mean phoning you? About what?"

"Saying that they have been following me and I should watch what I'm doing."

"I don't understand. Why don't you call the police?"

"Because I'm sure it's something to do with Patsy. She knows I want to leave her and she's frightened that she will end up without any money."

"Tell the scheming bitch that we will set our solicitors on her!"

Edith, furious that this dreadful woman should be orchestrating threats against her son said, "Has she got someone else, Andrew? Someone she's getting to frighten you?"

"I don't know Mum. I think she's been seeing someone, but I don't know who. Look, don't worry about me. I will be fine."

"I can't help worrying about you. I worry about you all. When are you coming home?"

"This weekend Mum. I'm going to tell her tonight. We'll sort it out from there."

"But, what about this person threatening you?"

"It'll be alright. I will probably come home at the weekend with all my stuff in a van and then let the solicitors sort it out."

"I'm not happy about all this, Andrew."

"The only thing that's going to happen, is me coming back home and then I can be free to start again. Love you Mum."

"Love you son. Ring me tomorrow."

"I will. I promise."

But although her phone rang in the early hours and the screen told her that it was Andrew, there was no one there when she picked up.

And at 3am came the news that Andrew had been killed in an accident. Edith didn't believe a word of it. She was convinced that his wife had something to do with his death, pointing out that as a result of this event, Patsy got the house, the money and the furniture. Everything Andrew had and nothing left to the children.

Edith waited in vain for the mysterious other man to turn up at Patsy's side. But that surprisingly, never happened. It was during the grief which followed, that Edith learnt about the sexual indiscretions of Thomas towards her children. She couldn't understand why she had been kept in the dark about it, not understanding their explanation of not wanting to upset her. Upset her! They should have gone to the police!

They said no one wanted to give evidence, because a child's word against an adult's wasn't worth a lot. And later, now they were adults, the police would want to know why they hadn't mentioned it before.

Edith couldn't reconcile all the information and the events of those days. She had felt as though her mind was dissolving.

She had been most surprised to find herself renting a cottage in the Yorkshire countryside with her little dog and suddenly there was no sign of her family.

Perhaps they were dead, she couldn't work it out.

Edith lit another cigarette after her shower and decided to sit outside in the little garden and look across the fields. It reminded her of when she was a young girl.

"You've won a scholarship!" was the excited cry of her mother when she read the letter.

It was closely followed by, "How are we going to afford all the stuff you need for this school?" Edith's mother had high ambitions and no spare money.

Her father looked up from his paper and said quietly and calmly, "We'll manage. I'm proud that a daughter of mine is going to Greenwood."

203

And Edith knew that it would be alright.

It was many years later when she discovered that her sister Ellie, was so incredibly jealous of her elder sister's success that she tried to scupper her progress at every turn.

Once her uniform and all necessary accessories were purchased, Edith began her first term in September 1946. But she had to walk to school and back every day in order to save money. She learned pretty early on, that mentioning her humble upbringing at school was not a good idea. It wasn't that the other girls or teachers looked down on her. No, it was because the school ethos was to focus on what you want to become. Although she was a bright girl, this had been the hardest lesson to learn. She was accepted unquestioningly by the staff and students at Greenwood, whereas the children in her street considered her 'stuck up.'

It didn't stop her worrying or trying to impress. There was one terrible day when she had finished a particularly complicated piece of homework and trudged through the snow to her school. Upon arriving at the gates, she realised that she had dropped it somewhere on the journey. She had the choice of turning back and trying to find it and arrive late. Or go to her class and give her excuses. She tried the latter and was allowed another chance.

She joined the choir, the drama society and scored high marks in all her exams. She sang on the radio and took a big part in the school's centenary celebrations. She reached her goal of becoming a prefect.

Her final day, when the girls signed each other's books and promised to keep in touch for ever, was the best and the saddest of her life to that point.

When the party finished and she left to walk home, ready to begin her nursing training, Edith Trewen never felt clever or important again. Her schooldays had been the best of her life. She made friends who swore lifelong allegiance, but as soon as they all went their separate ways, those golden bonds were broken for ever.

Edith was clever, well read and educated and no one asked her opinion on anything. She married soon after completing her training and within a few years, the mother of five watched her husband take the credit for virtually everything.

Edith hoped that Andrew would call in and see her this afternoon. Then she remembered that he couldn't, because he was dead and that bitch of an ex-wife was to blame for that.

Cow.

And all the things Thomas had done to her children. How could she not have noticed that? She was even trained in noticing and she hadn't noticed a thing. He had always been so understanding with her. Eleanor said she had told her auntie what her husband had done and she just hit her. Why didn't she say anything when she was a child? When it was happening? But Eleanor said that she had and wasn't believed. Edith couldn't really remember that.

In truth Edith couldn't remember much of what had happened since she got married. Always pregnant and working at the hospital, she could hardly keep her mind on what she needed to do, let alone notice when it was going wrong.

And what was wrong with trusting her sister and her husband to look after the children? They were family!

Perhaps she would go to town now and take the car. Edith suddenly remembered that she had left the car somewhere once and never found it again. She hoped that someone had found it and was looking after it.

"Betty!" she shouted to her dog, but no dog came. That was because Edith had left her dog somewhere. Hopefully someone was looking after Betty too.

Edith lit a cigarette and flicked the switch on the kettle. She would walk to town after a cup of tea. She could get a taxi back. That man from the taxi firm was always nice to her because she tipped him so well. Ken took her all over the place and she was glad to give him the money, because with his young family and the wife that refused to go out to work, he often struggled to pay his bills. He reminded her a bit of Andrew.

She went upstairs to her bedroom and pulled her suitcase from underneath the bed. Moving aside a picture of her family, three bottles of whisky and some crystal glasses, she pulled out a box and opened it.

Inside the box, were thousands of pounds in cash. Edith took out some notes and closed the lid. The box was not fitting neatly back into its place, so Edith had to move the gun and box of bullets out of the way. Then it fit neatly, so she patted it, locked the suitcase again and put it back under the bed.

Edith decided to have another cigarette and a cup of tea before she went out to the shops.

CHAPTER TWENTY THREE

Michael was in the kitchen with Eleanor as she talked on the telephone. She looked upset and confused in equal measure.

"What's the matter?" he asked, when she put the phone down.

"That was the DCI from Leeds. He just told me something weird."

"What do you mean?"

"He said that someone has seen Mum."

"Who has seen her? Where?" he asked.

"I'm not sure, he didn't say. But he's asked if we can go and speak to him at the police station."

"Here? Or there?"

"At his, in Leeds. I've said that we will."

"When do we have to go? Just us two?"

Michael was asking questions and barely listening to the answers, because he couldn't really get his head around what he was being told.

"Anyone can come I think, but all he wants to do is talk to us. I want to find out what's going on because from the little bit he told me, I'm not sure when someone has supposed to have seen her."

"It might be a mistake," Michael said, "I mean she would have been in touch with us, wouldn't she?"

"You would have thought so. I'm going to ring the other two now and see if anyone else wants to come. We'll go tomorrow and leave about 9. Is that alright for you?"

Eleanor had the phone in her hand and looked at her father, expecting a positive answer.

"Yes. I'll be ready for 9. How long are we staying there?"

"Late afternoon? I don't fancy stopping there too long, unless you do?" Eleanor hadn't thought of hanging about, but perhaps her father might want to visit old haunts.

"No, not particularly. I was just thinking that if they really have found your mother, we might want to stay."

Eleanor had not considered this possibility and didn't speak for a moment.

"Well, I suppose we could take an overnight bag, just in case and I'll make sure the animals are looked after. But we could bring her straight here, or perhaps she may want to stay there?" she said.

\#

It was only Eleanor and her father who set off to Leeds the next morning.

"We should miss the traffic," Michael said.

"That's what I thought," said Eleanor. "Dad, do you think it's likely that Mum might still be alive?"

"That's hard to say. The way things have been going lately, anything's possible."

They talked about the changing scenery and said how lucky they were to live in Wales. Eleanor's favourite dog sat on her knee, happy to be travelling with her Mum.

Michael leant back in the passenger seat, enjoying being driven for once. He had been the driver all of the time throughout his married life, Edith refusing to take a test. She drove, but refused to take a test.

Silly moo, he thought. But he had missed her these past few years.

After a pit stop at the services, they drove east on the A55 and talked about the times they used to drive down to Cornwall for their holidays. They were such happy days. Except when Mum would smoke constantly on the journey, causing the children and the dog in the back to be sick. They loved this time together and they talked about Andrew and Mum as the conversation veered between nostalgia and sadness.

They drove into Leeds, which was busy as usual. The vehicle they were in suddenly seemed too large for the bus lanes and traffic lights.

"I can see why people in cities buy small cars," Eleanor muttered.

They finally found somewhere to park and Eleanor put her dog in her bag and slung it over her shoulder.

They were ready.

"So, all you have to go on, is what Sylvia Lamb wrote in her journal? Isn't she a bit daft?" asked Eleanor.

"She's dead, Miss Prentice, and I wouldn't say that she was daft. I spoke to her only weeks before her death and she was perfectly sane then," answered Chief Inspector Revie.

"I'm sorry, I shouldn't have said that. I'm not really sure why you wanted us to come here," said Eleanor.

"When I first checked Miss Lamb's journal, I noticed a couple of mentions of Mrs Prentice. Miss Lamb thought she had seen her walk past the house opposite. She knew her from the time your family lived here, I believe."

"Yes, Edith lived at the other end of town as a girl. When we married, we moved a few doors up from the Yates. We only stayed a few years though, because we had ambitions and plans and not many people in that village did," said Michael.

"I'm glad you did Dad. I wouldn't have wanted to grow up there," said Eleanor with feeling.

"But I've had time to read through more of the book since then and she mentions that your mother first came back several years ago. That time she drove here in a Range Rover."

"Are you sure that she didn't get that information from the papers?" asked Eleanor.

"She could have done, but to be honest, all she was doing was writing it in her journal and not calling the police. Maybe she didn't know that Mrs Prentice was missing, she certainly didn't write about that. Miss Lamb is just recording the fact that she saw her and adding that she hadn't seen her for years," said Revie.

"How many times does she mention her?" asked Michael.

"I've checked the dates that your wife went missing and she seems to turn up here the day afterwards, park in the lane next to the Lamb's house and go across the road to the Yates house."

"Mum actually went to see him?" asked Eleanor.

"That seems probable, as she was seen going in and coming out again. And she has been seen at different times since then. She was seen the night of Thomas Yates murder. The last time recorded was the day before Miss Lamb died."

"We have to find her!" said Michael.

"What we intend to do Mr Prentice, is put out an appeal in the local media and see if we come up with anything," said Jackson.

"We still have some posters we had printed when she first went missing. Would you like those?" asked Eleanor.

"Thank you," said Revie. "And with your permission we intend to send details out to the media today."

"That means the public will assume that Mum has something to do with all these deaths!"

"We shall make no mention of that. It's just as likely that they think she may be in danger," said Revie.

"Is she in danger?" asked Michael.

"We have no reason to believe so," said Jackson.

"No, it sounds like you have more evidence that Mum has been involved in the deaths," said Eleanor. "Does it say if she was anywhere about when my aunt died?"

"That death is on record as being an accident," said Revie.

"I would have thought that you will be investigating all deaths now. The Yates, the Lambs, and my brother."

"Miss Alice Lamb is not dead," said Jackson.

"No, but she's not likely to make it, is she?"

"She's certainly unwell," added Revie.

211

"Has she said anything yet?" asked Michael.

"I don't think so. Nothing worth commenting on," answered Revie.

"Does the journal mention any other member of our family?" asked Eleanor.

"Not that I've discovered as yet, Miss Prentice. Not in recent years. But the journal goes back over 50 years, so I imagine that there will be something about your family in it."

Michael dropped his glasses and phone.

"Oh, it hasn't broken has it sir?" asked Jackson. "I dropped my phone not long after I got it and the screen smashed. I had to pay £150 to get it fixed!"

"No, its fine," said Michael putting everything back in his pocket.

Eleanor deflected them from her father's discomfort.

"Those people you arrested? Are you going to charge them?"

"They were only helping with enquiries and have been released," said Revie, displaying none of the frustration he felt over having been forced by a superior to do that.

"You are quite happy with us putting out an appeal on the TV and the radio?" asked Revie.

"I suppose so. Are you ok with that Dad?"

"I suppose so."

As the two left the station Eleanor asked, "Do you want to go into Leeds for lunch, Dad?"

"I think lunch in a nice restaurant and then a drive into Applewyke to have a look round," he answered.

"That's a good idea," said Eleanor. "Go to the scene of the crime."

"That's it," he answered.

As they walked towards the city centre, Eleanor asked, "Do you think that Mum's got anything to do with these deaths?"

"Not a chance. Can you see her shooting anyone? I mean really?"

"No, I suppose not," she answered.

CHAPTER TWENTY FOUR

If driving into Leeds felt nostalgic, then driving along Town Street in Applewyke was positively exciting.

"Wow, the old Rugby Club!"

"And that's where we used to catch the bus to Blackpool with Gran when we were kids," said Eleanor.

"They ruined it when they knocked down all those old stone shops and buildings," said Michael.

"And then put up all this concrete crap to replace it. Look at that! It's horrible!"

"You used to be able to see fields and animals and now all you can see are buildings."

"I try and avoid telling people where I was born," said Eleanor. "It's not that I'm ashamed of being born where I was, it's just that this place looks nothing like the place I was born in."

"I know what you mean. Turn right at the traffic lights. The bank is still on the corner!" he noted with satisfaction. "I might still have an account there."

"Do you want to call in and check?" asked Eleanor as she turned into the street where she was born. The street was a mile long and their old house was approximately half way down it.

"No, I don't! Do you remember the barbers that Norman Buckley ran, opposite it?"

"Vaguely, yes. He used to frighten us. He used to peep out of the window from behind the pole when we walked to

214

the infants, then he would give money to Judith when she went in. God, the pole is still there."

"Don't think it's a barbers though," said Michael.

"No. It looks like an insurance office or something."

"That's where the Buckleys lived," Eleanor said pointing to the left. "I wonder if that woman is Mrs Buckley?"

"It's more likely to be Judith Buckley."

"Oh yes. When I go back to a place I know, I always expect everyone to be the age they were when I left."

"That's because it makes you feel younger."

"I am younger. Surgery!" she said patting her smooth face.

They both laughed.

Eleanor began to slow up as they neared their old house.

"Dad, it's so little!"

"It is," replied Michael, "You wonder how we all fit in it. The garden is so tiny too."

"We were smaller then Dad and we did move."

"Yes, we did. Shall we walk the next bit? Park here?"

"Alright. If you think so, I'll park here."

They climbed out of the car and Eleanor slung her bag over her shoulder. They walked past three houses and then Eleanor said, "That's the Banks house."

"Doesn't look like anyone's in."

"No, but there's someone at the Farrington's. I wonder if it's David? Thomas and Ellie's house looks empty too. The DCI said that Richard was living there now. Perhaps he's at work."

"It looks a bit tidier than when we last saw it. But I don't like it now that all those houses have been built in the fields. There are hardly any green areas left in the town."

They turned around, in order to look at the Lamb house.

"I forgot that their house was quite a bit bigger than everyone else's," said Eleanor.

"That's because it was built much earlier and would have looked out onto fields and the hills and now it's squashed in by all the other houses."

They talked in a similar vein for a few minutes until they were disturbed by a shout.

"Hey! Hey!"

They turned round in response.

A man standing in the driveway of the Farrington house was shouting them.

"I think it's Ken Farrington!" said Michael.

"You are making my mistake Dad. That must be David."

"Hey!" he repeated, "Eleanor Prentice?"

"Err yes," she answered.

"I thought it was. I'm David, David Farrington. You remember me, don't you?"

"Of course," Eleanor said and wondered why she felt on red alert, "You remember my Dad?"

"Hello, Mr Prentice," he said holding out his hand to shake. "I sort of remember you. You were always at work, weren't you?"

"Yes, I was. How are your parents, David?"

"Dead, I'm afraid, Mr Prentice. They died a while ago."

"I'm sorry to hear that. Do you live here now? Are you married?" Michael wondered why he felt the need to ask so many questions and could only assume that he was embarrassed and wanted to get out of the way.

"I'm divorced and I live here on my own. Except, I've got Laura Yates living with me on and off at the moment. She's getting a divorce from your cousin."

"Oh, I see," said Eleanor. "I'm afraid we haven't been in touch for many years, so I don't know who is married to whom."

"Well, we all know about you. What's written in the papers and stuff and on the internet. You aren't married, are you? But you are very rich, we all know that." He grinned at her.

"I got lucky with my work," she answered.

"Would you like to come in for some coffee or something? We could chat about old times."

"No, thank you," answered Eleanor, "We have a long drive ahead of us."

"Oh," David sounded disappointed, "I could fill you in on what's been happening around here lately. You've got to be interested in that."

They decided that they were and agreed to have a quick drink with him before they set off home.

The television was on when they walked into the kitchen.

Police are asking people to look out for Edith Prentice, a 77-year-old woman who may be living somewhere in the Leeds area. This picture was taken almost four years ago and she may have changed her appearance since then.

217

Police are stressing that Mrs Prentice is not wanted for any crime, nor is a danger to the public. She has been missing for a number of years and her family are anxious for her safety.

Please call any of the following numbers if you think you can assist the police in their enquiries.

"Wow, is that your mother?" asked David. "How long has she been missing, Eleanor?"

Both Michael and Eleanor felt uncomfortable with a question which they felt invaded their personal space.

"A little while," Eleanor replied tentatively, "Why? Have you seen her?"

"No, no I haven't. I wouldn't recognise her anyway. That photo actually looks like her Mum."

"Of course, you knew my grandparents, didn't you?"

"I did. It was sad when they died. The town missed their friendly faces," said David.

"We all did, but it was a long time ago now. Everyone dies eventually," said Michael.

"They do. Tea or coffee? Sugar, no sugar?"

"Coffee, no sugar," said Michael.

"Twice please!" said Eleanor.

David left the room and Eleanor said to her father,

"People will assume that Mum has done something wrong."

"I don't know that they will, she looks too feeble," answered Michael.

"But you and I both know that she's not."

218

"She wasn't the last time we saw her anyway," commented Michael.

Eleanor walked to the window, looked out of the bay and remembered the times as a child she had played here. They had been quite a gang, close knit and loyal. She hadn't thought about that until just now.

Looking left she could see into the Yates house and had a shocking experience of déjà vu.

There was Uncle Thomas staring through the side window and beckoning to her. It felt as though that long bony finger could almost reach her. She gave a scream and both her Dad and David ran to her side.

"It's Uncle Thomas," she said pointing to the window.

David looked where she pointed and said, "No. It's not. That's Richard. You remember Richard, don't you?"

Eleanor was still shaking and trying to stifle sobs. Her dog, still in her bag began to yap in sympathy.

So, she was still affected after all these years. Thousands of pounds of therapy and he still got to her. Bastard. She was so glad he was dead.

She went to her father and he hugged her tightly.

David stood by the window waving to his neighbour. "I'll get your coffees," he said.

"You know what," said Michael, "I think we'll just go. It's been a long day."

"Yes, I want to leave now," said Eleanor.

David put his hand on her shoulder and she shrugged it off unconsciously. David grinned and waved them goodbye, but oddly shouted after them, "I've never forgotten how special you are, Eleanor! Don't be a stranger!"

As they walked back to the pavement, Richard Yates was waiting by his gate.

"I'm sorry Eleanor. I didn't mean to frighten you. Would you like to come in?"

Michael was about to answer when Eleanor interrupted him, saying, "Yes, we will come in, but only for a minute."

"Are you sure?" asked Michael.

"Yes, ghosts need putting to rest," she answered.

"You mean my Dad, don't you?" asked Richard.

Eleanor smiled at her cousin. They were the closest in age of all the family and had spent a lot of time together as children. They kept up some letter writing during adolescence, but that soon stopped. Mainly on Eleanor's part she seemed to remember, because she thought that Richard had always particularly liked her.

CHAPTER TWENTY FIVE

The house smelled exactly the same as Eleanor remembered, although the kitchen appeared to be only a few years old.

"Do you remember visiting us, Uncle Michael?"

"Crikey, I haven't been called Uncle Michael for about a million years!" he said, startled at the thought. These two Yates men were his only nephews and he hadn't seen them since, he couldn't remember when.

"I forgot, but don't you have brothers and sisters?"

"I had a sister, but she died when we were small I'm afraid. You and Anthony are my only nephews."

"I have always wondered why we lost touch. What happened? No Christmas or birthdays or weddings or anything. I missed everyone, because we used to have such fun, didn't we?" said Richard.

"For some of the time, but not all of it Richard. That wasn't your fault though," said Eleanor.

"No," he answered.

"What about Anthony, how's he?" asked Michael.

"He's fine. He's getting divorced too and he's living at Janet Banks house for the time being."

"Oh! Is he with her now?"

"No Eleanor, not really. It's just a place to stay until he gets his house sold. After that he tells me that's he's going to move away. I hope he doesn't," he finished sadly.

"Oh, dear! You've got your problems too I hear," Michael jerked his thumb in the direction of next door.

"My dearest Laura you mean? Yes, she's decided to throw in her lot with David. I wish she had married him in the first place, it would've turned out a lot cheaper for me."

"Are you going to stay at this house, Richard? I thought that you would have wanted to leave it?"

"I thought about it, but now I've lived here a while again I sort of feel like I'm home, even though everyone's gone."

"I'm sorry that you've had to put up with all these horrible deaths. The papers said that you found your father's body?"

"I did Uncle Michael, in the front room."

"Please, just call me Michael!"

"Ok. I will. Now come into the front room and I'll show you where he was killed. I'm sure you want to know."

He walked through the doors and Michael and Eleanor followed him. Very few people can resist the urge to visit a murder scene. The television and three-piece suite were in the same position that they remembered from years before, although of course these items were far newer. The carpet looked and smelled brand new.

"I had to change the carpet and redecorate in here. Do you know I had to pay for it?"

"Did you?" answered Eleanor. "I would have thought that someone else would pay. I don't know, maybe the insurance?"

"He wasn't insured, but at least it looks alright now. That's what got me to thinking I would buy out Anthony, because

222

when I started decorating and buying new things, I thought that I could finally make the place acceptable."

"Yes, I can understand that," acknowledged Michael.

"When I'm here, I think about Grandma and Grandad and all your family and mine having Christmas together. Even though there were some tricky times, we did have fun, didn't we?" He looked at his relatives and Michael was reminded of the little boy he once was.

Michael patted his nephew on the shoulder and felt almost tearful.

"We did, Richard, we did."

"Dad was shot against this wall," he said pointing to the shared wall with the Farrington house. "In front of the fireplace."

"Do they know who might have done it?" asked Michael.

"They have no idea, but I imagine that there are a lot of people with a motive," he said.

"I imagine there are," agreed Eleanor.

"My brother and I have motives and a few others. Did either of you kill him?" he asked unexpectedly.

"No," they answered in unison.

"You know. If you had, I wouldn't tell?"

Eleanor thought that she believed he wouldn't.

"What actually happened, Richard?" asked Michael.

"I arrived on the Saturday morning. I hadn't been able to get hold of him for a day or two on the phone and couldn't get in. The doors were locked which was weird, but when we finally got in, we found him shot on the floor there."

"Hadn't you seen him for a while before you found him?"

"To be honest, Uncle Michael," he nodded an apology. "I called in on him on Thursday and ended up having a row with him as per bloody usual. But I didn't tell the police because they might think I had something to do with his death. But I didn't!"

Michael suddenly recalled how Richard would come to him and ask what he should do about friends and school and the little problems he had as a boy. He came to Michael where he should have gone to his father. Michael felt guilty for not having been a better uncle through the years.

"I don't imagine that you did Richard," he comforted him.

"He was alright when I left him on that Thursday night. I wanted him to tell me what really happened to Mum, but he said that it was nothing to do with him. Then it just got worse and worse and we ended up arguing badly and I left."

"He wasn't expecting anyone else to come?"

"I don't think so. He was saying that Anthony was a better son than me and he was going to ring him and change his will and all that bollocks."

"Do you think he would have done?" asked Eleanor.

"Probably, he was enough of a twat," said Richard.

"So it was just a coincidence that you were here that night. Or perhaps someone was already here and waiting for you to leave."

"I don't know, Michael. I've thought about it loads since and I'm always looking out of the window thinking about it."

"What happened to your mother?" asked Eleanor.

Richard's mouth moved in a circle.

"I just know that she was on her own and the washing machine wasn't working properly. She tried to fix it with a screwdriver and poked it in the wrong place and got electrocuted. I know she wasn't much of a mother to us, but she didn't deserve to die that way."

"No, she didn't," said Michael. "I first met her when I was courting Edith, she was a lovely young lady, about 17 I think. She had a bit of a crush on me apparently."

"She always talked fondly of you," said Richard, "I don't think she cared at all about my Dad though. But then, he cared enough for himself."

"It's horrible losing family, isn't it?" said Eleanor.

"We heard that Andrew died around the same time as Mum, didn't he? He had an accident too," said Richard.

"Yes, he apparently slipped on the back steps one night when he thought he heard a burglar outside. He banged the back of his head and died almost straight away," said Michael.

"Horrible."

"It was," agreed Eleanor.

"Funny all these accidents and deaths in our family over the years, isn't it? With Grandma and Grandad dying in that car accident all those years ago and Mum and Dad dying in mad ways. Then, Andrew dying and your Mother going missing and the women over the road too."

"When you put it like that, it does sound a bit mad," agreed Eleanor.

225

"You could put it in a book," pointed out Richard.

"I think I'm going to," said Eleanor.

"I saw the appeal a bit ago on the television. Who has seen her?"

"I don't know," answered Michael.

Eleanor's mobile rang and she spent several seconds trying to find it underneath her dog in the bag.

She listened, saying only a few words and finishing with, "Oh my God, we will be there as soon as we can."

"Trouble?" asked Michael.

"They've found Mum." she answered.

CHAPTER TWENTY SIX

Within ten minutes of the appeal going out on the local media, the station telephone started ringing.

The details were brought to DS Jackson and he skilfully began to classify them. There were the usual enquiries about missing persons, potentially identifying Mrs Prentice as their relation and people saying they had seen her on a ferry, on the telly and all over the United Kingdom.

But there were also several calls identifying the same woman living in a village on the Yorkshire border. Her name was Sally Lally.

"That's five different people who have given me her name and address," Jackson told Revie, "And here's her telephone number. Shall we call round or ring?"

"Ring as we drive there," he answered and got up from his desk. "You drive."

The address would take 40 minutes to reach normally, but following a traffic car with blues and twos going should take them less than 30.

Revie dialled the number and let it ring.

"There's no answer," he said.

"Is there an answerphone?" asked Jackson.

"Yes, the network one, I'll try again and leave a message."

This he did, but they arrived at the village before any answer came.

"They ought to turn the lights off, it might frighten her," said Revie.

As if they heard him, the lights and sirens became still and they cruised to the front of the cottage.

In the front garden was an elderly looking lady tending the borders. At the first approach of the cars, she looked up from her work, trowel in hand and smiled. As the officers left their car she walked towards the gate.

"Hello! Has my father sent you?"

"No, he hasn't. Can you tell me your name please?"

"Can I speak to my father? He's the Chief Constable you know, your boss!"

Revie made his way to her and said, "shall we go inside? Easier to talk there I think?"

His jovial, friendly manner encouraged her to acquiesce and taking the trowel from her hand, he carefully led her back into the neat cottage. Jackson followed, after directing the uniformed officers to look around the outside of the property. By now villagers had made their way towards the cottage as news spread.

Edith received her guests, showing no surprise that they were police.

She put on the kettle and brought out mugs, then asked, "tea or coffee?"

"Nothing for me, thank you," said Revie. "Perhaps we can ask you a few questions?"

"Of course you can!" she answered and sat down opposite him.

"Now, could you tell me your name please?"

"Yes, I can!"

"Then what is it?" he asked, after waiting for ten seconds for the smiling lady to answer him.

"Well it's..."

She stopped, unsure how to answer. She leant forward conspiratorially and said, "I'm not sure that I should give you my proper name. Its classified you know." She sat back in her chair, smiled and nodded.

"I understand that, but all the same I would very much appreciate you letting me know. It will help my enquiries a great deal."

"The name I've been using is Sally Lally, but it's not my real name. I had a school friend called that and I'm afraid I borrowed her name."

"And what is your real name?"

"You must guess!" she answered cheerfully.

"My first guess," Revie said, "Is Edith Prentice."

"That's a very good guess, but I can't confirm whether or not it's correct. I'm working under cover and until I finish the job I've been set, I cannot use my real name."

"What is your job?"

"I have to investigate something which happened a long time ago and it's not yet done. I might not have even started it," she added as she leaned forward again.

Jackson opened his eyes wide at his boss and shrugged his shoulders.

"Perhaps you would allow us to look around the cottage?" asked Revie.

"I will do better than that," she answered. "I will take you round myself."

She got up and beckoned them to follow her. Deciding that this would be the best way to discover what was going on, they obeyed.

They found the cottage to be neat and tidy. It was comfortably furnished with the usual ornaments and pictures about the place. When the tour finished upstairs, Revie noticed that there was nothing in the home which constituted a family life. No photographs and only one set of everything. It seemed no one stayed over either.

"Do you have family Miss Lally? Do they visit?"

She looked perplexed when he asked this question and answered, "I can tell you nothing of my family and you must mind your own business." She drew herself up as tall as she could.

They were now in her spotlessly clean and tidy bedroom. There was no evidence of family or pets. It was not a home.

Perhaps she wasn't Edith Prentice?

"I know something you may be interested in," she said suddenly.

"Oh, what's that?" answered Revie.

She knelt down and moved her arms around underneath the bed.

"Shall I help you?" asked Jackson and as she moved aside he brought out a large suitcase.

"Is there a key?" he asked her.

"No, all you need to do is open it."

When Jackson saw what the suitcase contained, he gasped.

"It comes in handy does that," she said, pointing to the cash.

"What about the whisky?" asked Revie jovially.

"I love whisky. Shall we have one now constable?"

"Oh, I think we had better wait until I'm off duty," he answered.

"There's something else in here," said Jackson and brought out a diary. He handed it to the Chief Inspector. There were notes on different pages, detailing birthdays and anniversaries. Revie recognised names from the Prentice family. There was also a copy of Andrew's funeral brochure and this seemed to seal the deal.

"Anything else, sergeant?"

"Not that I can see sir," he answered.

"Mrs Prentice, I would very much appreciate you coming to the police station with us. There are some more questions I would like to put to you. Would you mind doing that?

"Not at all," she replied. "Will I be going in the police car?"

"No, that won't be necessary. You can travel in our car with us," said Revie kindly.

"Oh. I was rather hoping for a trip with the blue lights flashing." She tapped him on the arm. "I'll get my coat and bag if I may."

"Of course."

"Will someone feed the dog for me please?"

"Dog?" asked Jackson.

"Yes dog, constable. Oh! Silly me, I forgot. I left her somewhere..."

"Where did you leave her?" asked Jackson immediately, an animal lover.

"Somewhere, it was years ago. The park or the vets or somewhere. I can't be expected to remember everything you know."

She remained cheerful and chatty as they went down the drive. She waved to some neighbours, who waved back.

"You alright, Sally? Need anything?" asked one of the women.

"No thanks. I will be back later today."

Revie had a word with one of the uniforms and he pulled a face, but stayed where he was.

"I've asked him to stay here until we finish a search," he said to Jackson.

"Do you suspect her of something?" asked Jackson.

"I don't know," he answered. "But just to be safe, I think we should check it out."

He made a phone call before climbing into the car, where Mrs Prentice sat happily.

"Sorted," he said to Jackson.

"What about the family? Are you going to tell them?"

"I will ring when we get to the station. I'm not sure if they've set off for home yet."

"They said that they were going for a little drive around first, so we might catch them," answered Revie.

"That meeting is going to be very weird," he replied.

"It is. Are you alright there in the back, Mrs Prentice?"

"Yes I am. I like being chauffeured about. Thank you, Constable."

CHAPTER TWENTY SEVEN

When Eleanor and Michael arrived back at the police station, it was late afternoon. They had made phone calls home, arranging for the animals and houses to be sorted out. They didn't expect to be back until late, or possibly tomorrow. Eleanor also started the family phone tree by speaking to Elizabeth and promising to call back later when they knew more. She text her son, who was currently working abroad.

They had an initial meeting with DCI Revie where they were warned that Edith seemed to be a little eccentric. They took deep breaths and walked into the room where Edith sat.

They saw a white haired, elderly lady sipping tea and sitting on a comfortable sofa. She was dressed smartly and wore sensible flat shoes, entirely unlike any she would have worn when they saw her last. She looked at least 20 years older.

"Mum?"

"Edith?"

Edith turned to look at her husband and daughter and smiled.

"Hello!" she answered brightly. It was obvious that she didn't recognise either of them.

"Mum? Don't you know who we are? It's me, Eleanor," her voice trembled and she sat down next to her.

"Eleanor. Of course I do dear. You used to work at the library, didn't you?"

"No Mum, I'm your daughter."

"So nice. But I'm afraid I don't have a daughter. I don't have any children at all. I think they are dead." She carried on drinking tea.

"Edith, do you recognise me love? I'm your husband."

Edith looked at her husband of almost fifty years, gave him another of her happy, beaming smiles and said, "No dear. I'm not married, but if I were. I wouldn't mind it being to a handsome chap like you!"

The conversation continued in a similar vein for a few minutes until they were joined by DCI Revie and a professional looking lady.

"This is Dr. Alison Cross and she would like to have a few words with Mrs Prentice, would either of you like to stay?"

"I'll stay with her," insisted Michael and Eleanor got up to leave the room.

"Do you think she's gone senile or something, Chief Inspector?" she asked when they were in the corridor.

"The doctor will make some sort of initial assessment, but she seems to have been managing alright at the cottage she was renting."

"Did you find anything there which gave you an idea of why she left us?"

"There doesn't seem to be anything that we've found as yet. I do know that she's been renting the cottage since she left home."

"So much for all that initial publicity then," Eleanor said with irony.

235

"Would you like to wait in another room for a while?" asked Revie.

"No, I think I would like to go for a walk," she said. "I've got some phone calls to make."

The doctor told Michael that Edith was suffering mentally, but without further tests could not say whether or not it was to be a permanent condition. Michael wanted to take her home, but Edith could not be persuaded, believing that she was not part of the Prentice family.

The doctor also said that Mrs Prentice was not doing harm to herself or anyone else and for the time being should just be monitored.

"I was hoping that if she came back with us, then she would start to get her memory back when she saw the family again," he said to Eleanor.

"But none of us live in the same places that she knew, so I don't think that will work," she replied.

"Let's take her back to her cottage and spend the night there and see if we can make her see sense," he said.

"I thought that you had got used to life without her Dad. I didn't realise that you missed her so much."

"Well, I have missed her, probably more than I knew. It's not nice getting older and people that you knew aren't here anymore. They've died or moved away and then there are hardly any people left who know about the old days. I want her home where she should be."

"Ok Dad. Let's see if we can persuade her." She rubbed his shoulders.

DS Jackson had checked out the cottage while everyone was at the station, but came up with nothing. As a result, the police were happy to allow them to return there for the night.

Edith was excited to be getting a lift to the cottage with her new-found friends.

"It's very nice of you both to take me home. My usual taxi driver will be jealous if he finds out that I'm having lifts from other people. He likes to take me everywhere I go!"

"Really, Mum? Does he live near you, or is he from town?"

"I've got his number next to my phone somewhere at home. You keep calling me Mum! Your own Mum will be upset if she hears you doing that!"

"Do you mind if we stop at your place tonight? It will help us a lot. We don't want to drive all the way back to our houses and hotels are so expensive here," asked Michael.

"No, of course not, it will be lovely to have company. I'm looking forward to having a dog in the house again too. I don't know what happened to my dog though."

They were pleasantly surprised when they arrived at the cottage and found it so clean.

"Where shall I put my things?" asked Eleanor. "I don't mind sleeping on the sofa. In fact, it will make it more like a sleepover."

Eleanor was finding it surprisingly exciting to be with her mother after all these years.

"Wherever you like, dear. I've got a suitcase here somewhere too. I keep my things in there, in case I have to nip off on another mission."

"Mission? What sort of mission?" asked Eleanor.

Edith tapped the side of her nose, "Can't say. All I can tell you is that Andrew will be glad when it's all been completed."

They stopped what they were doing and looked at her, "Andrew! You remember Andrew, do you?" asked Michael.

"Well of course I do. He's my son!" As she said this, she sharply drew in her breath and put her hand on her mouth. "Oh, I'm sorry, I shouldn't have said that. I will be getting into trouble now and I want to keep everyone safe."

"In trouble with who Mum?"

"I can't say anymore because we won't be able to keep safe. So, no more."

She walked away from them and started to hum. They recognised this habit of Edith's, used primarily when facing a tricky situation. They decided to carry on as normal so they could quietly get to the bottom of this problem.

"You sleep in the spare room Eleanor and I will sleep here," said Michael.

"Dad. Let's sleep on opposite sofas. I would feel more comfortable then."

"If you prefer. Now, what about fish and chips or a Chinese?"

"Fish and chips for me please!" said Edith.

"And me!" agreed Eleanor.

"Looks like I'm on driving duty then," he said. "It's like the old days!"

"We always thought Yorkshire fish and chips were the best, didn't we?" said Edith.

"Yes, we did Mum."

Eleanor walked out to the car with her Dad. "I think we should try and persuade her to come home. She is starting to open up a bit, isn't she?"

"She is. But you know what? I think that someone has been talking to her, telling her crap about keeping secrets. I'm going to speak to the Chief Inspector about it."

"Leave it until tomorrow Dad. We might find out more tonight."

When Michael had gone, Eleanor approached her mother again.

"Mum, why do you feel you need to keep your family safe?"

"It's complicated, Eleanor. If I don't follow the rules, then we could all be in trouble," She pulled Eleanor over to her and whispered, "Walls have ears and we have to be careful what we say."

"Is someone threatening you Mum? We can tell the police and they will help you. Tell me who it is and I will help you too."

"You have always been helpful, haven't you? And clever too. I haven't forgotten that you have done very well for yourself. But don't forget that it was me that taught you how to write in the first place." Edith stroked Eleanor's hair and they were suddenly transported back forty years.

"Mum, please come back with us. Whatever the problems are and whatever you are worried about, we can sort it for you. We live right next to the sea. You love the sea, don't you? You can walk from either of our houses and be on the beach without even crossing a road."

Eleanor saw tears in her mother's eyes, "I miss Andrew so much and I want him back with us. Someone made him go away and I have to make them pay."

"Perhaps Mum. But in the meantime, come home."

"We will see." And she got up from the chair and walked into the kitchen. Michael arrived back at the same time and the house was filled with food smells and voices and it all felt lovely.

"It's pouring down out there!" he exclaimed, "But there wasn't much of a queue in the chip shop."

He wiped his feet on the mat.

Edith took the bags from him and said, "That will be because of the price of it. Fish and chips used to be cheap, but not now."

"And you don't get half as much. Fish used to be loads bigger!"

"Here's the salt and vinegar," said Edith. "Bread and butter?"

"Please," answered Michael.

Eleanor noticed that her Mum was paying a great deal of attention to her dog.

"Are you going to come back with us, Edith? We can sort out all the lease stuff and move your belongings."

Edith put her fork down on the plate and said, "this is my home and I don't think that I can give it up just like that."

"No, no, I understand Edith. I don't want to push you. It's just that I want you to be safe. I've missed you." He patted her hand and she held his. He noticed that she still wore her wedding and engagement rings.

"No one wants you to give up your home, perhaps when you come to the seaside, you might end up preferring that," said Eleanor.

"I'm worried about all my arrangements here if I go. My landlord and my taxi driver and shopkeepers. Such a lot of people and things to worry about."

"We can sort all those things out for you Mum. We can take all your documents and ring people when we get home. Or you can just come for a holiday and we can come back and sort stuff here."

"A holiday, I would like a holiday very much. I haven't had a holiday for years."

Eleanor left her Mum and Dad chatting away, and took her dog outside for walk in the garden. She telephoned home, her son and then her sister Elizabeth.

"We are trying to persuade her to come back, to me or Dad."

"So, does she know what trouble she has caused?"

"No, I don't think so, she's sort of a bit senile. Not totally like Great Grandma was, but she knows us sometimes and then not others. She's taking care of herself, you know feeding and washing and managing the house, but doesn't seem to have any concept of who or what she is."

"Has she said why she did it?"

"No, because she doesn't think that she has done anything at all. It's as though she's living each moment brand new. Though we've noticed that now she's spent some time with us, she's recognising us a bit more."

"That's good. If you persuade her to come to you, then we'll come up and see her too."

"One thing, she's kept all her cash in her suitcase under the bed. She spent a lot though, paying rent and things. Compared to what she took, there doesn't seem to be much left. We don't know where the dog went, which is a shame."

"Yes, it is. She was a lovely dog."

"We are hoping she will come for a holiday at least, and then hopefully we can persuade her to see a doctor."

"Because if she was just happy being apart from the family, that's one thing. But if she is having some mental issues, it's our responsibility to look after her, isn't it?"

"Yes. I suppose. Look I'll text you in the morning and let you know what's been decided."

Back in the kitchen, she found her Dad sitting alone.

"She said she was tired and went to bed," he said. "But she still says that she's coming with us tomorrow."

"Does she know us really?"

"I think she's suffering from some sort of delusion and we need to get her to a psychotherapist or someone."

"Do you think that someone has been threatening her? I sort of can't get it out of my head."

"I'm not sure. It could be her delusions or real or a bit of both."

"If someone is threatening her, who could that be?"

"No idea. I hope it's not anything to do with these murders though."

"You know I had forgotten about all that with the excitement of finding Mum. I don't expect my mind can deal with it."

"I know what you mean."

"I wonder whether it would be wrong to search the house while she's gone to bed?"

Michael considered very briefly before agreeing. They started downstairs, trying to cause as little noise as possible.

"This feels wrong," said Eleanor

"But it's necessary isn't it, to help her?"

They searched the whole place, except for Edith's bedroom and found nothing out of the ordinary. All her bills were paid with cash and the receipts were kept in leather boxes. Her landlord called for the rent every month but there was no name or address for him, only a phone number.

They put the boxes together in the corner of the hallway, ready to load in the morning.

"I'll have a quick look round her room, when she's in the bathroom tomorrow," said Eleanor.

"Sleep now, love. Too much for one day."

CHAPTER TWENTY EIGHT

"They've taken her back to Wales with them this morning," said Revie as he put the phone down.

"Mrs Prentice? Is that OK? I would have thought that she is still a suspect," said Jackson.

"She is, she is. But that doctor said that she might be suffering some sort of mental anguish as she put it and so we will have to tread carefully with her. We will keep her in mind, but eliminate everyone else first."

"Who are our actual suspects now then?" asked Jackson as he sat down opposite the boss.

"Until we have an explanation about Edith Prentice's whereabouts these past few years, she has to be up there. She knows all the victims and if what we have heard about old man Yates behaviour is right, then she also has a motive."

"But she's nuts."

"She's acting nuts, but we don't know if she actually is. Richard and Anthony Yates also have motives. Their parents weren't up too much and those two inherit the house now they are dead."

"Are we assuming that Ellie Yates was murdered now?"

"Not necessarily, but it is a possibility. Have we heard any more about the condition of Alice Lamb?"

"Yesterday, the hospital said that she was critical, but stable. We aren't allowed to talk to her though. They said they will let us know as soon as."

"I'm pretty sure that the Lambs were attacked, because of what they knew or saw," said Revie.

"What about that cock and bull story of the sales deal with them?"

"I want those two to feel comfortable for a little while, let them feel safe while we keep an eye on them."

"And the Prentice clan?" Jackson continued reading from his long list of possible suspects.

"Not sure. There's no evidence, but they all have a motive."

"Do you think that the brother's death was an accident?"

"Again, don't know. Get the details of his death and we can go through them and the details of any investigation into Edith Prentice going missing."

"Ok. Now what about Miss Banks and the other woman, Miss Buckley. They both hated Thomas Yates."

"And a few others probably. I don't know if I prefer no suspects and lots of evidence or loads of suspects and not much actual evidence," mused Revie.

"You always tell me that there is something somewhere in the evidence we already have. That it will become obvious in hindsight, so check and check again."

Revie looked at him over the top of his reading glasses, "You remembered that?"

"Yes, of course. I remember most of the rubbish you tell me."

Revie grinned. "I also think that we need something else to happen. So, we can move on a bit. I don't mean I want a murder, but something."

"I would think that with the amount of stuff that has been going on, there's bound to be another event."

"Mmmm."

"Right, I'll allocate some of these jobs amongst the team."

Jackson left the room and Revie tapped the table with his pen. He must be missing something and he would guarantee that if he didn't have the missing piece of the puzzle amongst this evidence, someone was bound to.

DC Eve brought in a folder.

"It's the report from CSI about the Lamb case sir."

"Thank you," he answered without looking up.

"Sir?" she said.

"Yes Carol, what do you want?"

"I was wondering if you would let me go round the Lamb house please."

Revie leant back and asked, "Why should I let you do that?"

"Because I'm finding this case really interesting and complicated."

"I agree. Do you think that you can help solve it?"

"I'm doing all the usual research, but I'm thinking that if it's so complicated, then the answer should be quite simple," she said.

"Right."

"I expect you think that I'm jumping the gun, but I have a feeling for this one sir and I thought that I should like to go to the house." She stood in front of him, arms behind her back.

Revie wondered for a moment whether DC Carol Eve was particularly ambitious. He knew she was clever and methodical and that she had never asked to do anything like this before.

"Take someone with you," he said. "Don't go alone and don't get behind with your other work."

"I won't sir," she said and skipped out of his office. He looked after her and smiled.

He opened the file and began reading. After a while, he shouted "Jackson!" and was rewarded by his arrival a few seconds later. He kept on reading the file and so did not notice the scowl on his sergeant's face.

"I've been through this file," he said and pushed it across the desk. "The gun that shot these ladies was definitely the same one that killed Yates. They think that Miss Alice was shot first on the stairs and then Miss Sylvia shot next. There wasn't much time between the two shots. It seems a silencer was used."

"So Alice disturbed them and Sylvia could have sat up and shouted and they went straight in and shot her."

"Or she didn't hear anything and someone just came in and shot her. But, whatever way it was horrible thing to do," said Revie in an unusual show of emotion.

"Anything on the road or the lamp post? Or at the Farrington house?"

"No blood or gun, just the clothes and jewellery. Their story could be right, but I don't believe them."

"I agree. I saw Eve and Pearl go off to the Lamb house just now, what are they up to?"

247

"They want to have a look round. Eve thinks that she might come up with some ideas. She's a bright spark."

"She might be a bit too sparky for her own good. She's the sort to get herself into trouble," said Jackson.

"Do you think? I'm hoping fresh eyes might give us a clue."

The two sets of fresh eyes were pulling up outside the Lamb house in the pouring rain.

"I want to solve this one myself," said DC Carol Eve.

"How you going to manage that?" asked DC Tony Pearl.

"Find a clue that no one else has found, that's how," she answered.

"Think it will help your promotion?"

"It will."

They stood on the drive and Eve took the house keys from the bag. She held the arm of her colleague to prevent him striding off.

"We have to imagine that we are murderers," she said.

"If it's a burglary that's gone wrong we would have a different attitude to a murderer."

"Yes, but the gun is the same one that killed him across the road," she said and pointed to the Yates house. She started when she noticed that someone was watching her from the window there and brought her hand back down to her side.

"Who's that?" asked Pearl.

"Don't know, probably the son."

Bringing her mind back to the task in hand, she walked slowly down the drive.

"We would creep in and try not to be seen, but I'm not going to do that. We will just go round to the kitchen door and go in there." She looked right and left as she did so, endeavouring to take in the entire scene.

"Forensics has already been here," said Tony Pearl, who was not as thorough nor as ambitious as Carol.

"I know, but we aren't looking for those sorts of clues."

They went into the kitchen.

"Apparently there were no splatters of blood on the clothes of Laura Yates or David Farrington and none in their house."

"How do you know that?"

"I read the file before I took it in to the boss."

"Clever."

"Now down here there has been a proper search, but so far nothing has been found to be missing. The Lambs had a lady cleaner and she went through the place. She confirms that the only things gone were the things found at the Farrington house."

"Everywhere is so neat, isn't it?" noted Pearl. "I mean, I know there has been all this disturbance, but underneath, it's so tidy and in order."

"Hmmm. The house feels wrong because it's untidy. I imagine that everything would always be just so. I see that their normal everyday crockery is up market and sort of old fashioned."

"It's horrible what they did to those old ladies. I'd like to nail them for it."

"We can't approach this as though we think those two did it. We must keep an open mind," said Eve.

"Yea. They did keep everyone's secrets in that journal of theirs. Perhaps they used to blackmail people with it."

"True, it's just that you wonder if it's connected to the murder over the road. If they've been blackmailing someone over that, you think that they must have been blackmailing all the time. And no one's killed them until just now," said Eve.

"I like this blackmailing idea. I'm going to bring that up."

DC Eve scowled at him. It was a bloody good idea and she wanted it to have been hers.

"Let's get on with it," she snapped.

She didn't see her colleague pulling faces behind her back, but guessed that he probably was.

"So, we are searching in this room and suddenly notice Alice Lamb on the stairs," she continued.

"We wouldn't notice her from here," reasoned Pearl.

"Alright, maybe she calls out, or maybe we have gone into the hall and see her then."

"And after killing Alice, they had to go and shoot her sister."

"So, they must know the layout. They knew Sylvia would be in bed and couldn't allow her time to raise the alarm," said Eve.

"How do we know that she didn't shout out?"

"Because she only sat up in bed, as if suddenly disturbed. She hadn't tried to get out of bed or move the covers or anything. They went into the room and shot her straight away." Eve's thoughts were flowing and she didn't want them interrupted.

"That means getting past the bleeding sister on the stairs and that would cover the murderer in blood."

Eve stopped. That was another good point. "And the report said that there were no bloody footprints, except caused by the first copper."

"So they must have gone up and down another way," said Pearl in a matter of fact tone.

"Yes." she agreed. "Let's find it."

"Could they climb up the outside of these banisters? Then hurl themselves onto the landing?"

"Not unless they were Chinese acrobats. Plus, there wasn't any mention of smears on the blood on the wooden banisters."

"Right. You read this report thoroughly, didn't you? How long did you have it before you gave it to the boss?"

"An hour."

"Fuck! You'd better not let him find that out."

"I don't intend to and if he does find out, then I know you told him."

Pearl didn't seem worried by this threat. Instead, he led the way through the ground floor to look for an alternative route upstairs.

"There are only these windows which lead to the outside," said Pearl as he turned the catch and opened them.

"This'll do!" he announced while pointing upwards.

"A fire escape!" Eve said. "Let's go up and try it!"

She wanted to be the first upstairs to look and not allow Pearl to score another point from her.

The door at the top of the iron spiral staircase led them to the end of the landing. Before entering it, she looked around to see who could see them and who they could see. The answer appeared to be no one.

They walked along the landing to Sylvia's room and had a look in.

"Sylvia Lamb was shot here, so open the door and bang, bang."

"I thought it was just one bang?"

"Report says two bangs," she informed him. "One smack in the middle of the chest, then she started to fall back and the next one skidded along her chest and hit her under the chin and came out the top of her head."

She walked to the bed and pointed to the headboard. "There's the hole where the bullet ended up"

"Whoever did it was a bloody good shot," commented Pearl.

"I know. Not really the act of someone in a panic who wasn't used to shooting."

"Any footprints up here?"

"Not footprints as such. Just smears of blood that goes from here to the other end of the landing." She followed the marks which brought her to a pine dresser with a marble top.

"That's just like the one in the kitchen," she commented. "It's lovely. Look, it doesn't have legs at the front. It's fixed to the wall."

The open drawers revealed only a large mat, which she assumed was for putting under a vase, a packet of wet wipes and some large carrier bags.

"Hmmm, always useful. Do you know I went to Wales last week and you have to pay for plastic bags? Even the ones you put fruit in." She shut the drawer on this piece of information.

"I'm nipping in here," said Pearl as he went into the bathroom.

She looked into the other rooms upstairs, but saw nothing interesting. When Pearl came out, they walked back to the inside staircase and descended.

"It's a big house, isn't it?" she said.

"I wouldn't mind it," he admitted.

Walking back through the kitchen, she pointed to the similar dresser, "see!"

"Yeah lovely. You sound like my girlfriend. She's always pointing out furniture and stuff. I'm not interested in that either."

"She must be so proud when she talks about you," said Eve, locking the door behind them.

The wind suddenly picked up and a carrier bag which had been tangled on a branch, untangled itself and hit him in the face. He pulled it off and handed it to Eve.

"Keep hold of this one," he said, "in case you go back to Wales!"

CHAPTER TWENTY NINE

"There are more coppers at the Lamb house," said David Farrington as he walked into the kitchen.

"What do they want now?" asked Laura, who was half-heartedly looking through cupboards wondering what she ought to make for tea.

"No idea. They were laughing and didn't even look at me as I drove in. Mind you, I did drive up the road to turn round when I saw them and then came back."

"Why? Do you think they've found anything out? The solicitor said that they can't prove we stole those clothes. And they can't tie us up with the murders, can they?"

"I don't think so. But you never know with the police."

"Perhaps we should give them reason to look in another direction," said Laura, jerking her head towards next door.

"Richard?"

"Why not? If he went down I would get the house, both maybe. He and Anthony always wanted the old man dead, they hated him."

"Everyone seems to have hated Thomas," said David quietly.

"Don't tell me you liked him? There was no one he left out when he was playing at kiddy fiddling was there? He got to a lot of people, one way or the other."

"I'd rather not talk about it."

"Richard always said that. I think if it had been talked about more..."

"We would all have been put in care or something and that wouldn't have helped anyone."

Laura went quiet, she hadn't wanted to talk about the past.

David said, "You know Laura, I miss talking to Richard and Anthony. It's a shame that we can't be friends anymore."

"Whatever," she answered.

"I forgot to tell you," he said suddenly. "Eleanor Prentice and her father came round yesterday."

Laura stood up from her crouching position and began looking in the freezer, "You mean my ex cousin in law or whatever she is? What did she want with you?"

"I don't think they were actually coming to see me. They had to go to the police in Leeds and came here for a drive afterwards. They went to visit Richard and then sped off."

"I saw on the news that they've found their mother after years of being missing," she said.

"Yes. The story is getting more and more complicated, isn't it?"

He made some coffee and sat at the kitchen table where he was joined by Laura.

"If it turned out that Richard killed his Dad, then he might have had a reason to go and kill the Lambs too," she said.

"What reason?"

"Maybe they saw something. I've heard that they get money from some people because they know their secrets. If we told the police that, they are bound to investigate.

Especially if they found out he wasn't at home the night Thomas was murdered."

"How do you know that?"

"Because I had arranged to meet you and told him that I would be out and then you let me down…"

"I was working late."

"So you said. But I went home early and Richard didn't come home until late and he'd been rowing with someone. I can always tell and I would guess it was with his father, because he always acted the same way when he had been rowing with him."

"Why didn't you say before?"

"At the time I didn't want to get involved with the police at all and then I forgot."

"You must tell the police now then, it may be important. It will get them off our backs."

"Do you think so? Perhaps I will then."

"Ring them now, before tea. I've got some phone calls to return."

"Not to that Eleanor? You always fancied her, didn't you? I bet she didn't look at you twice now she's all posh and rich."

"She was very pleasant to me, as was her father. No, I have to ring some customers back."

Next door Richard and Anthony Yates were talking in their kitchen.

"I saw more police over there today. I wonder if they are definitely connecting the Lambs with Dad?" asked Richard.

"I don't know, but I've heard that they are trying to find out who fixed the washing machine back when Mum died."

"Christ! I've no idea, have you? Was it next doors? It's unlikely though that Dad would spend money on it. If anyone killed her, I wouldn't bet that it wasn't Dad."

"Do you think he would really?" asked Anthony.

"When Alice Lamb comes round she will be able to clear up a lot," said Richard.

"It has to be Laura and David, doesn't it? The Lambs had something on them and they knew it. Perhaps they killed Dad. Laura expected more money from the inheritance and was going to keep up the pretence until you got a divorce. But you caught them out too early."

"Laura was home that night," said Richard.

"That means it was David and she encouraged him. What about that?"

"Anything's possible just lately. Nothing would surprise me. Oh and talking of surprises, Eleanor and her Dad came round yesterday afternoon."

"Cousin Eleanor? Were they looking for Auntie Edith round here? I saw it on the news."

"They found her the other side of Leeds last night. Didn't you hear?"

"Who? Auntie Edith?"

"Yes. I'd like to get to know the story behind all that," said Richard with feeling.

"I loved it when we all a proper family," said Anthony. "When we spent Christmases and holidays at their houses, it was such fun."

"That's because they always lived in posher houses than us, Horses and fields and loads of rooms," remembered Richard with an overwhelming nostalgia. Richard had aspired to be like his cousins and when he married the feisty Laura, his childhood friend, he had imagined that they would soon be living the high life. But it never came to pass and instead he lived the life of the ordinary man. That life now included the infidelity and divorce and subsequent splitting of assets.

"I haven't seen them for years and years. What did they look like? Uncle Michael was always really nice, I remember. He used to take us to football."

"Yea. He's still nice you know. Didn't seem that different, except older of course. Eleanor looked only a bit older, but sort of..." he struggled for the correct word to describe her, "styled."

"They didn't stay long though, which was a shame. Probably won't see them again," Richard added sadly.

"Oh well, we've got enough to keep us occupied."

"Have you heard anything about your divorce?"

"Only that apparently there's a buyer for the house, for God's sake. I don't know of anyone who has sold their place so quick, but it's not a very good price. If I want to move on, I should probably accept it."

"Have you told Janet?"

"No, I haven't. I don't want to live with her or be with her. I'm going to leave and I don't know how to tell her."

"Come and live here then, until you are sorted out. That way you are making a break with Janet before you go and start a new life."

Anthony looked at his brother and felt like crying, "Thanks Richard, I think I will."

"Look," started Richard. "Can I tell you something and you promise not to call the men in white coats?"

"Of course you can. What do you want to tell me?"

"Since I moved back here," he stopped and his colour rose. "I've been hearing things in the house."

"What sort of things?"

"Like growling or muttering. If it was a horror film, I would say it was a monster. You know, like the ones on Hammer horror, that kind."

"Shit! Where have you heard that?"

"Sometimes downstairs and sometimes outside. I swear it's been happening more often and to be honest, it scared me."

"What do you think it is?"

"I think it's Dad."

"What?"

"I just think it sounds like Dad, like when he used to be outside our bedroom door, you know?"

"I hope it's not his ghost! Perhaps I should move in earlier?" said Anthony.

"I wish you would. We should stick together with all this fucking shit going on. I've got a feeling that the police are going to try and involve us in more interviews and somehow it feels like it could get awkward," said Richard quietly.

"I was thinking that. Perhaps we should be clear with each other up front," said Anthony.

"What do you mean?"

"The night Dad was killed, I came round here because I was going to ask him about moving in for a while. But I couldn't get an answer, so I ended up going round to Janet's. I thought he was with someone because I could hear him shouting, but no one answered the door."

"That could have been me. I was rowing with him that night, but I haven't told the police. He was alive when I left and someone must have come in after me."

"Did you come in your car?"

"Yes, but no one has mentioned it yet."

"I'm mentioning it now. I was waiting for you to say something because your car was parked in the garage. I saw it."

"And you haven't told anyone?"

"No. I wanted you to tell me. If you were involved, then I'm not going to be the one who shopped you."

"Why not?"

"You're my brother and I hated the old shit as much as you. If you shot him, then he asked for it."

"I didn't shoot him Anthony, I promise I didn't. A few reasons, I'm a coward, I don't own a gun and I couldn't shoot one anyway."

"That's what I thought," said Anthony and smiled.

CHAPTER THIRTY

After a police appeal yesterday afternoon, the mother of the well-known author Eleanor Prentice was found safe and well. Edith Prentice, who had been missing for over three years, was living at a cottage near Leeds, seemingly unaware of the continuous attempts by her family to trace her.

Mrs Prentice went missing shortly after the death of her son, who had apparently died in an accident. Police are currently investigating the murder of her brother in law and murder and attempted murder of two ladies who lived in the village where she was born. Mrs Prentice was the sister of Ellie Yates, who died in another apparent accident shortly after Mrs Prentice went missing.

Police are not commenting on whether any of these incidents are related.

Eleanor Prentice and her family have been helping police with their enquiries. Miss Prentice has said that there will be statement released through her solicitors later today.

The television piece then showed an ugly scrum of reporters surrounding Eleanor's car as she left the gates to her home.

"You look really annoyed there," said her son as he watched the television with her.

"I was bloody well annoyed! Cheeky gits. That little piece there makes it sound as though we are mass murderers!"

"You should ring that inspector and get him to say something."

"What like? He's probably thinking that we are something to do with it all anyway."

"It says you are making a statement later."

"Well I'm not!"

"Perhaps you should," said Tom.

"You do it then, I can't be arsed."

"So mature, mother," he said, endeavouring to lighten the mood a little.

"Write one for me and send it to the media lot. They should stop bothering us then," she said.

"Will do."

Eleanor flicked the switch on the kettle as her mother wandered into the kitchen. Since they arrived home yesterday afternoon, Edith had settled in well. She loved her room with its en-suite and the wonderful view she had of the sea. There had been no question of her going to Michael's cottage, as she wanted to stay in this hotel. She invited her husband to stay there with her, but this offer he declined.

It was strange, because Edith was not stressed in any way about being taken from her cottage and seemed to take each moment as it arrived, with very little connection to past thoughts or actions.

"We need to get a doctor or psychiatrist to see her soon," Eleanor told Elizabeth on the phone.

"Will she go do you think?"

"If I make up some story about checking her wellbeing, I'm sure she will. I'm taking her privately, so she won't feel so weird. I'm thinking we ought to get some sort of idea, especially as the media are making comments."

"I noticed that. We are going to come up this weekend if that's ok with you?"

"Love you to come. Perhaps you will get some story from Mum, but somehow, I doubt it. I think she's got Alzheimer's."

"Brilliant. I'll see you the day after tomorrow. Oh, we'll be staying a few days."

"Stay as long as you want, you know that we love to see you. Emma and Daniel are arriving on the Monday when he can get time off and their place can be looked after."

"Lovely. Ring me if you need anything!"

The kettle boiled and Edith said, "Oooooh, lovely darling. Shall I make some tea?"

"Yes please Mum. Did you enjoy your shower?"

"I had a bath, not a shower. I used the bubble bath and all those smellies on the side."

"All the smellies?"

"Only a bit of each. The hotel makes enough money out of us I should think, so it's only fair to use some of the stuff. But I couldn't find out how I called the reception."

"There's no reception Mum. I own the place and you can use whatever you want and eat or drink whatever and whenever you want."

"Oh, that is kind of you. You've done very well for yourself, owning a hotel right by the sea."

"Yea Mum, I have." Eleanor decided not to pursue the conversation.

Tea made, they sat at the kitchen table drinking and dunking rich tea biscuits, just like back in the day.

"Don't forget to ring my taxi driver," said Edith.

"You mean the landlord Mum?"

"That's right dear, let him know where I am, he's bound to be worrying."

"Do you think you will want to go back there Mum? I was thinking that you could stay here now. You can live here from now on. Or you can live with Dad, but there is loads of room here and always something going on."

"I see that you have lots of people working here and all these horses and dogs. I used to have a dog you know."

"I do know, what happened to her?"

"I left her somewhere, but I can't remember where. In a taxi I think."

"Oh dear. You can have another dog and keep her here if you want Mum. You can keep her in your bedroom."

"Oh!" her eyes lit up and she clapped her hands like a little girl, "Would you let me get a dog? I wasn't allowed dogs at my cottage, the landlord said that Betty bit him, but she didn't. She just didn't like him, I think."

"Mum, of course you can!" Eleanor remembered being allowed a dog of her own when she was little and how her Mum helped her choose one and make the puppy's bed in the corner of her bedroom. She almost jerked her body forward as she endeavoured to prevent a cry of emotion come from her mouth. Yes, Edith had returned to being an

265

innocent young girl and the family would cherish her as such.

Eleanor wanted everyone to be safe.

Michael walked into the kitchen and put his hand on Eleanor's shoulder. Eleanor looked up the mobile number she had noted down at the cottage and rang it.

"Hello!" said the male voice when he answered.

"Oh hello. This is Eleanor Prentice. My mother is Edith Prentice, who rents a cottage in Yorkshire from you."

"Is she with you now?" he asked.

"Yes."

"Yes, she does rent from me. I saw on the news that she has gone to stay with you. It was a surprise to see my place on the telly. I hope no damage has been caused?"

"No, not at all, it is in an excellent condition. What I wanted to do was tell you that Mum will be staying with her family from now on and wishes to hand in her notice. How long is her notice?"

"Notice? She can't leave. Mrs Prentice has been an excellent tenant for years and I don't want her to go."

"Well that is nice to hear! But I'm afraid that she will be leaving the tenancy. In fact, she will not be returning to the cottage and we will arrange for her things to be collected. She is sitting with me now and has agreed that it will be best for everyone for her to stay here. There has been so much police and media interest that she will be better off with me."

"Oh, that's a shame. But the terms of the tenancy are three months' notice."

"Oh!" said Eleanor, ever the business woman. "I don't have a copy of the tenancy agreement, perhaps you could send me a copy and I will get my solicitor to look it over. I thought the normal term of cancellation was one month? I gather that Mum paid you in cash each month?"

Her suspicion that the landlord had not declared anything to the taxman may have been correct as he said, "ok, one month. If you leave the keys and cash at the cottage when you call, that will be fine."

"That is kind, perhaps you could leave an inventory too so that we don't take anything which isn't hers?"

"Yeah, I can do that."

"Perhaps you could also give me your name and address? I haven't been able to find it amongst Mum's stuff."

He hesitated and Eleanor added, "I would not like you to feel as though you will ever be out of pocket."

He said, "you can use the address of the cottage. I will always be able to pick up any mail or messages there."

"Have I ever met you?" asked Eleanor.

"I don't think so, Miss Prentice, I would remember if I had. The truth is I don't like my wife finding out about the rent and I would rather not involve my home address, if you don't mind."

"I see," said Eleanor, not really approving of his manner on the phone. She would be glad just to get her Mum out of this situation and move on to the next stage of her life.

"Ok. I will sort it for you and I expect that we will come sometime next week." She hoped that she could persuade a couple of her visitors to help her move the stuff on a day's turn around next week.

"I'm going for a walk now," interrupted Edith.

"Ok Mum, Take care."

Michael asked, "Where's your Mum going?"

"She's gone for a walk on the beach. Before you go after her, I want a word. This landlord, he's odd you know? I sort of feel like I know him, but probably don't."

"Ok. What did he say?"

"I told him that Mum would be leaving and agreed to pay him one month notice and that we will fetch all her stuff next week. But he wanted three months, cheeky git! Anyway, I don't think he's been paying tax, so when I mentioned my solicitor he agreed."

"Wow! But, I suppose he has been good to her until now, tax or no tax."

"I know, so I'm just going to get her stuff and go. The girls and their families are all coming during the next couple of days, so I thought we could take a couple of them to the cottage while the others stay with Mum here. What do you think?"

"I think you have done a lot. What does Mum think about giving up the cottage?"

"I haven't actually mentioned it to her. I thought it best just to sort it and if she asks, we could say that he has decided not to rent it out anymore. As it is, she seems to have got through an inordinate amount of money, unless she's left that somewhere too. Have I done wrong, Dad?"

"No love. I think it's best to keep her here where we can keep an eye on her. That way no harm can come to her, or anyone else. You've done right."

"And I thought that if I take her to a friendly psychiatrist, he will agree that the best place is here with her family."

Michael looked at his daughter with renewed respect.

She appeared to have covered everything.

She hoped she had.

CHAPTER THIRTY ONE

Detective Chief Inspector Revie put the phone down following a long phone call with his boss. He felt cross and underappreciated. He couldn't work any more hours than he already did and even when he went home he thought about the job he was working on. Over the years he had gained promotions and respect, but lost his wife and family like so many other senior officers. Now that fucking fast tracked twat was telling him he needed to work harder and solve the case soon, as though he didn't want to solve it.

"Jackson!" he shouted at the top of his voice.

When Jackson put his head round the door he said, "Is it really necessary to bellow at me like that?"

"No," Revie answered, "but I'm naggy after that call with my boss."

"Oh, I see. Giving you a hard time, is she?"

"Wants the case solved. Get everyone together and we'll have a meeting. Let's pool our information."

"Ok. Good idea boss."

An hour later, the team were collected and Revie stood in front of them.

"I want us to go through the main suspects and I want you lot to pitch in with any comments or ideas you may have. We want to get a wriggle on before he strikes again."

"Is he likely to?" asked DC Pearl.

"We aren't sure how many times he's struck already. Right, Thomas Yates, his eldest son Richard has to be right up there. Any observations?"

Jackson began, "He found the body, so DNA and the rest was on him. He inherits the house with his brother and doesn't appear to like his father. Since the murder he has split from his wife, who now lives next door with his ex-best friend who discovered the body with him. He has left the marital home and lives in his parent's house. Chances are that the affair was going on before the murder. Quite a few of the suspects in this case have known each other since childhood. Since the separation from his wife, he spends a lot of time looking out of the window, just like his father. He hates his ex-wife and his ex bezzy mate."

"Who told you that he is acting like his father now?" asked Revie.

"Someone did, Laura Yates I think." He started to flick through his notebook.

Revie continued, "So Laura Yates next. She is a fan of money and a dead father in law brings more money to her. She probably didn't expect Richard to find out about her affair as soon as he did and planned on getting a bigger share in a divorce settlement later."

"Probably rules her out of being in cahoots with her husband too. But she could have arranged the Lamb murder with David Farrington," commented DC Alexander.

"True," said Revie, "Now, do we have a motive for Farrington?"

"Unless it's one that we don't know about, it could be that he's in league with Laura Yates, banking on getting her divorce settlement," said Andrew Alexander.

271

"Thank you, AA. Anthony Yates has similar motives to his brother, including splitting up with his wife after the death. So that could bring Janet Banks into the frame. She lives next door to the Farringtons and has also known everyone since childhood."

"Plus, we know that Thomas Yates appears to have abused most of the young girls in his family, as well as lots of the neighbourhood children. That's a powerful motive, but you wonder why they would wait until this year before they killed him. That means there would have to be a trigger we don't know about yet," said Jackson.

"Does the book mention the names of all the girls who went into his house over the years?" asked DC Eve.

"Mostly the Prentice girls, Laura Kennedy as she was then, Judith Buckley, Janet Banks, Shirley Rockford. Then there was Tina Quigley, who married Anthony. After they all grew up or moved away, he must have gone elsewhere for his kicks, but as yet we don't know where."

"And then there are all these photographs that he had. There were pictures of all those girls and some we haven't identified," said Jackson.

"He's a disgusting pig! Who took the photographs?" said Eve.

"We assume he did. But don't let personal opinions get in the way of your detection abilities," instructed Revie.

"Ok boss, sorry," she said.

"We don't know whether he acted alone when he was abusing, although the earlier victims say that he did. We don't know if he was involved with anyone else later on. Certainly no one has come forward," Revie continued.

"What about Mrs Prentice? She's been missing all these years and we don't know why. She came to live not far away," said Jackson.

"And the Lambs recorded seeing her about over the years. Have we checked the dates of the sightings to any of the attacks?" asked Eve.

"One of the jobs on the to-do list. Would you like the job, Eve?"

"Yes, please Sir. I would love that job! Can I go through it all?"

"Write up whatever you want, so long as you do it quickly," said Jackson.

DC Eve beamed. This was what she wanted.

"Anyway, Mrs Prentice has gone back to live with her daughter, so we know where she is. I'm not entirely sure that she is operating in our universe, so let's hope we find out that someone else did it. Now let's talk about the Lambs, any news about Alice Lamb, AA?"

"When I rang this morning, they told me that she is still unconscious and we aren't allowed to see her. I'm not so sure we are ever going to get anything out of her before she pops it."

"Did they say she was going to die?" asked Jackson.

"No, it's just his female intuition," joked Pearl.

"Enough of that now. We know that Farrington and Yates were definitely in the house around the times the women were attacked, but have nothing to prove that they did the shootings. I'm not so sure that we can even get them on theft because they've turned up with an agreement to buy the clothes and jewels and pay later. They've offered to give the stuff back to the estate or pay. But we would know a damn sight more if Alice would talk to us. So, if they shot the ladies, did they do it for the jewels or because they knew about the journal?" said Revie.

"When Tony and I went in there, we couldn't really work out how it was done. We couldn't see any blood downstairs and after Alice had been shot and lay on the stairs there was no room to get past her without getting blood all over the place. Then we thought that there must be another way to get upstairs. We went up the only other way, which was by using the outdoor staircase and got onto the landing there. That must be the way the killer got up and downstairs, but it seems wrong somehow."

"What do you mean?" asked Jackson.

"I don't know what I mean. It's like the scene is wrong, like we are missing something really obvious," answered Eve.

"Well keep on top of that idea. There may be something in it," said Revie.

"Are we going to bring in the other deaths to the plot?" asked A A.

"Like Andrew Prentice and Ellie Yates?" said Pearl.

"I would say we have to put them into the mix," said Jackson.

"Agreed. Ellie Yates, you checked into the details of her death didn't you AA?"

"Yup. She was electrocuted by the washing machine while she was alone in the house and was discovered by her husband when he came home. Apparently, she had a habit of fiddling about with it if it wasn't working properly. It was decided that her death was accidental. I checked the notes and one of the investigators said that, electrocution is usually caused by the fact there is no earth on the machine. So, if she was touching the machine and something wet like the metal sink at the same time, that would do it. But when the machine was checked, the earth was definitely connected."

"Could someone have fixed it after she died? Is that possible?" asked Revie.

"Anything's possible, but at the time they ruled it out as unlikely and no one had a motive to kill her. But I did discover that almost 2000 people die in the UK every year from home accidents and many of those are by electric shocks," Andrew informed them.

"What, from washing machines?" asked Pearl with surprise.

"No, all sorts of appliances. There are a lot of kids and pets killed by getting trapped or being put in machines," he continued.

"No! Please don't say anymore," said Eve. "I can take anything about murders, but don't start talking about horrendous things happening to animals!"

"Ok then. I just thought it was interesting," he replied.

"I once went to a house where they had these dogs that just kept having puppies and when they thought there were too many puppies they took them and…" began DC John Petrie.

"I swear to God, if you say one more thing I will punch you," said Eve, fingers firmly in her ears.

"May I say that if the public could see how the murder investigation team operate, they would sleep very safely in their beds," said Revie solemnly.

There was a good deal of sniggering and not one look of shame amongst the team.

"We should put Ellie Yates death on the list as a potential link to these," said Jackson and began putting pen to the white board behind him.

"That means we should also put on the death of Andrew Prentice, that's an unusual death too," said Revie.

"I've checked on that," said Pearl. "The wife says he felt that there had been someone coming to the house at night and making noises. She said it sounded like a werewolf. Anyway, this one night he went out to check who was there and she heard a shout and when she got down he had slipped and fallen. It was a frozen night and he fell and hit the back of his head and died pretty well straight away."

"Wasn't his mother convinced that something funny was going on?" asked Eve.

"She wouldn't let it drop, because he had told her that he was being followed and was worried about it. It was looked into at the time, but to be honest it seems to me that the officers thought that she was just a daft woman in deep grief for her son."

"What about the werewolf comments? I mean, that's not usual, is it?" asked Eve.

"She didn't tell the investigating officers it was a werewolf at the time. She described the noise as that of cats or foxes or something. At the time they made absolutely no connection to any form of attack," said Pearl.

"To be fair though, it's only adding all these stories together that's making some sort of mystery. Those deaths may well still be accidents and we should only concentrate our minds on these recent murders," said Revie.

"But sir, if we add it up in the order we have decided, a suspicious death of Andrew Prentice, followed by his mother convinced that there was a problem with his death. She complains, is ignored and eventually goes missing along with several thousand pounds in cash. She has learnt after her son's death about the abuse her brother in law inflicted on her children. She moves to a cottage only a few miles away from Applewyke. Then her sister, who she also blames, dies in an accident only a few months later. A year later her brother in law is murdered, and then the Lambs get attacked and or killed. It's worth connecting, isn't it?" said DC Eve, with passion.

The room had listened to her intently and most nodded their heads in agreement.

"And I've been thinking that if we can check to see if there have been any other suspicious events occurring during the same time, either to the players in our story or written in the journal, then maybe we have something to go on," she continued.

"Do you think that Edith Prentice is the murderer?" asked Jackson.

"No, because she had no reason to kill her son, that was the trigger for her to leave. Someone else killed Andrew. Maybe Edith pursued the murderer and that has resulted in him being aggravated into committing more. Or she now has organised someone to pick them off one by one. The people she considers to be her son's abusers. She could be paying them?" suggested Petrie.

"How would she do that?" asked Revie.

"Well we know that she took several thousand pounds cash with her when she left and from we gather there are only a few thousand pounds left. Maybe she has been paying someone," said Eve.

"Good! Well done Eve!" said Revie.

DC Eve smiled broadly, while Petrie scowled. Hadn't he just said that?

"But even so, we must keep open minds. I'm leaning on the side of one of the sons. The main motive for murder is money and they inherit. Both sons are in need of money, and this is a good way to get it," said Revie.

"Are we looking at those two as our main suspects?" asked Jackson.

"Not main, but high up there," said Revie. "I think now we have a clearer idea of the story we need to unravel. You are checking the journal, Eve?"

"Yes sir," she answered.

"Pearl, I need you to look through records and list any deaths during say, the past five years of any members of the families of our players. That should include any childhood friends of the Yates. The rest of you follow up on the leads we already have. Let's ask for a miracle so that we can clear all this up quickly."

The meeting closed.

CHAPTER THIRTY TWO

We have a breaking news story. Richard Yates has been found dead at his home in Applewyke.

Richard Yates was the eldest son of Thomas Yates, who was murdered eight months ago. His killer is still at large. This family is closely related to the writer, Eleanor Prentice. Her mother was found shortly after an appeal by the police investigating the murders of Thomas Yates and his neighbour. There is no information as to how Richard Yates died, but neighbours say that he was seen alive last night. He was also seen out shopping earlier in the day.

Police are still waiting to interview Alice Lamb, the surviving sister of another murder in the same street. They hope she will be able to shed new light on the recent suspicious deaths.

The police are making no comments at this time and have told us that they will make a statement later today.

"Well that has confirmed our theory, hasn't it?" asked Jackson.

"What theory is that then?" said Revie.

"Richard Yates being suspect Number 1?"

"Because he's killed himself?"

"And left a suicide note by way of confession," reasoned Jackson.

The two men were racing to the same street they had visited way too many times in recent weeks.

Revie had taken a phone call from his boss asking what the hell he was actually doing with all the resources he had been given, at the same time Jackson was being informed over the phone that Richard Yates had been found hanged on the banisters at his home.

"Maybe this death will help us solve these crimes. We need a fucking break."

"I don't know sergeant. I have a horrible feeling that we have a long way to go yet."

The house was crawling with people when they arrived and they were led directly into the hallway through the front door.

"Get a tent up over the door," instructed Jackson, "and get those voyeurs out of the way!"

"The tent is on its way Sarge and we are putting up tape. We needed access for the ambulance until just now."

They saw the remains of Richard Yates hanging by a rope from the middle banister.

It was always the smell that got to Chief Inspector Revie with these types of death. Once the body drops, it loses control of its bowels and Richard had certainly done that. His body stretched down, face lolled to one side and blackening tongue endeavoured to escape from his mouth. This corpse bore very little resemblance to the man Revie had been talking to recently.

Revie also noted the tee shirt and jeans that Richard Yates wore. There were no shoes or socks on his feet.

"What a stupid thing for him to do," muttered Jackson. He had a cousin who had thrown herself in front of a train and ruined her parent's life.

"Who found him?" asked Revie.

"His brother Anthony. He's gone back up to next door but one. He's in a bit of state," said one of the uniforms.

"Anything out of the ordinary, constable?" asked Revie.

"Not as far as we can see, sir. It looks like he climbed up the stairs, put the rope round his neck and jumped over. But here's the note he left." Constable James handed the letter to DCI Revie.

"It's typed," he said in surprise.

"Yes sir," answered James.

Revie read the note.

I can't handle the guilt any longer. I have tried to live with it, but I can't.

I hated my father and the things he did to me and everyone else was disgusting. It's been hard enough dealing with all his favourites when I was a child, but lately it's been difficult. So he had to go. I've done everything for him for years and thought I was special, but it turns out I wasn't.

I enjoyed killing him and Mum, but when I realised that the Nosy Parker Lambs knew what I did, they had to go too. I hoped Alice would die, but she hasn't yet and that hasn't helped.

I have decided to kill myself. I still want my darling wife Laura to have my share of the estate and not give it all to Anthony. He will understand.

Sorry

Richard Yates

"Does that note make sense?" asked Jackson.

"No. It sounds wrong. It doesn't sound like he wrote it somehow," agreed Revie.

"It's from a computer, anyone could have done it," said Jackson.

"Let's go and see Anthony Yates. Let me know if they come up with anything new," said Revie as they made their way out of the door.

"I'm getting fed up of dead bodies," he said as they walked up the street.

A couple of journalists pushed microphones into their faces and he roughly pushed them aside.

As they walked towards the back door of the Banks house, it was opened immediately.

Janet Banks said, "Come in, we've been waiting for you."

Anthony Yates sat at the kitchen table, staring at an unopened bottle of whisky.

"He hasn't had a drink in months and if he starts again now, he will kill himself," said Janet.

Can we have a word please, Anthony?" asked Revie gently.

"What's the point?"

"We would like to know what happened this morning when you found your brother," said Jackson.

"I found my brother dangling from the banisters, so now I have no family left. I'm finished now officers, finished."

He unscrewed the bottle cap.

Revie took the bottle from his grip and moved it to the sink, "Don't start drinking again, Anthony, or you will be finished. You help us and we promise that we will find out who is doing this."

"Promise?" Anthony looked at them through red swollen eyes.

"I promise," said Revie. "Now Miss Banks, coffee all round please and perhaps some toast?"

Jackson and Revie led Anthony Yates into the front room and gently helped him to a sofa. Within a couple of minutes, they were being served by Janet, who then sat down.

"Perhaps you feel well enough to tell us exactly what happened."

Anthony sipped his coffee, "I went round to see him, that's all. I'm always going round to see him. We had some things to discuss. I went in round the back door and shouted Richard. He didn't answer, so I thought he must still be in bed. He hadn't been sleeping that well and sometimes he stayed in bed late."

"Don't either of you work these days?" asked Jackson.

"I got sacked months ago and Richard was on sick leave."

"What happened next?" asked Revie.

"I noticed a smell first and there was a different sort of silence, like I was being watched. I thought at first it was the ghost of my Dad, Richard said he thought Dad was haunting the house. Richard said he was frightened of the noises he used to hear."

The policeman looked at each other.

283

"Anyway, I pushed on the hall door and felt some weight against it and I couldn't get it open properly. So I went through the front room and got into the hall that way. That's when I saw my big brother hanging from the banisters with a rope around his neck. Why would he do that to me? Why would he? There are only us two left? Now I'm all alone," he sobbed.

Janet got up from her chair, took the mug from his hand and put her arms around him.

He shrugged her arms off and glared at her, "I don't love you, Janet, I was going to move out this weekend and move in with Richard. Then once my divorce comes through, I'm going to France. I'm not going to be with you Janet. Never!"

Janet stood back from him, but didn't alter her expression, "I know, Anthony, but I am still your friend and I want to help you through this. After that, you can live your own life. But, if I let you go on your own now, you will end up drinking again."

Anthony looked at his friend and frowned, he hadn't expected that reaction.

Revie and Jackson let the moment pass and when it had, Revie said, "Did you notice anything out of the ordinary?"

"No, I didn't."

"Where did you find the note?"

"Note? I didn't see a note!" he answered.

"Your brother left a note confessing to the killing of your father and Sylvia Lamb and the attempted murder of Alice Lamb."

Anthony was angry, "That's bollocks!" he said.

"You don't think he did it?" asked Jackson.

"Of course, he didn't! Richard couldn't hurt a fly! I don't believe he wrote any such thing!"

"We do have a note, I'm afraid."

"Let me see it. Let me see what it says."

Jackson handed him the note, now sealed inside a clear bag and after reading it quickly, he said, "That's printed on cream paper and I happen to know that the only paper Richard had was white, because I was using his computer yesterday afternoon."

"So, you think that someone else wrote this letter? Who would that be?" asked Revie.

"The person who murdered my brother! This supposed suicide note proves it was murder. Christ, Richard wouldn't kill anyone and he wouldn't kill himself. Now do something about it!"

CHAPTER THIRTY THREE

The next call was at David Farrington's house, where they found Laura Yates still in residence, but crying uncontrollably.

"I can't get her to stop," said David, "I didn't think she cared about him that much. At all, really." He stood, hands twitching and a face expressing confusion at her reaction.

"Do you think she will talk to us?" asked Revie.

"No, she won't talk to me, so I don't know how she can talk to you. She just cries. You will have to go and come back another day."

"Noooo! I want to talk! I want them to find out who killed Richard! Why kill Richard? He wasn't harming anyone. He was just a bit slow sometimes. He didn't deserve to die, David."

"I know Laura. But, he didn't have to die. He chose it himself, he chose to die!"

Laura turned on him, "Get out of my fucking sight and leave me with the police. Go on, fuck off right away."

"Perhaps if you stepped outside for a little while, Mr Farrington. But don't go too far away, we shall want to speak to you too," said Jackson.

"I think I should stay here, in case you need me," said David.

"I don't need you. I can manage on my own. Go away," she said, wiping her nose and regaining her composure.

This he did and the policemen sat down opposite her.

"How did you hear about Richard's death?" asked Revie.

"I heard Anthony shouting for help, screaming for help. We got up and went outside. Then we saw that Anthony was on the front lawn, sort of whimpering. David stayed with him and I went in and saw Richard," she began sobbing. "I saw Richard hanging and his tongue was out and he was dead. It was horrible."

"Did he mention killing himself?"

"No, he didn't and he wasn't the sort. We have had some issues and are separated, but he wouldn't have killed himself," she said.

"He left a note," said Revie.

"Did he?" she seemed surprised. "I couldn't find a note anywhere."

"You looked for a note?"

"Of course I did! He wouldn't do that and not let me know why. He still loved me you know and he wouldn't want me upset."

"But you didn't think he would kill himself, at all?"

"No. I said so."

"So why did you look for a note?" asked Jackson.

"Because I wanted to know why he did it!" she screamed.

"Why do you think he did it?" asked Revie.

"I don't know. What does the note say? Does he mention me?" she added almost hopefully.

"He says that he killed his father and Sylvia and that he attacked Alice," said Jackson.

Laura stopped her sobbing and stared at the men, "That's rubbish. He didn't kill them. I know he didn't kill them,"

"How do you know?"

"Because Chief inspector, he hasn't got it in him. Why would he? Find me a motive that will convince me!" she challenged them.

"We have none and we are keeping an open mind. There has been too much going on to make any snap assumptions. You must trust us, Mrs Yates."

She looked at him and her expression told them that she didn't trust them.

"Can I see the note please?" she asked.

Revie handed it over for her to read and she said, "That isn't the way Richard talked and I don't understand why he would write it on the computer and then print it off all nice and calm. No, it doesn't sound like Richard at all, in fact it sounds..."

She stopped.

"Yes?" encourage Revie.

"Nothing. I was just thinking that it sounded sort of childish, that was all."

"Did you hear anything unusual from next door, during the night?"

"No, but I was out until quite late and when I got back in, the street was in silence. I just went to bed."

"Thank you, Mrs Yates. We will want to talk to you again. Now, could you call in Mr Farrington, sergeant? We will talk to him in the other room."

"Don't worry about me Chief Inspector. I'm going up to the shower and then I'm going to my sister's house."

"I see. We would like her address please. Write it down there. Thank you."

Laura did as she was bid and went upstairs.

Her mind went back to the first time she met Richard back at school. She realised that her first impression of her dead husband had also been the smell. Back then it was the smell of the unwashed. Today, it had been that terrible death smell.

The Yates boys were known for living in a less then caring home and sometimes this had meant that they were bullied and harassed. But his cousins stopped the bullying, especially Eleanor who took him under her wing until their family moved away. Gradually, the bullying stopped and throughout the rest of their schooldays, their gang grew into Richard, Anthony, David, Judith, Janet, Tina and Laura. Sometimes, there were new faces that hung around the group and then they dropped away again.

Laura knew that David always wanted her and that Richard worshipped her. It felt good to be that attractive. She was never shy, like other girls of her age.

She knew she was sexy.

There was one new boy who had taken a shine to Laura and she returned the flirting. Both seventeen years old, they laughed and giggled together. When the group went to dances or the pub, those two would engineer to sit together.

But there was no real dating. Pete said he didn't want to upset the group. Laura hadn't understood what that meant, but accepted it.

One weekend they arranged to go to Blackpool. They were staying at the boarding house of an aunt of the Yates. While they were at the Pleasure Beach, Pete took the opportunity to persuade Laura to go for a walk on the sands with him.

"Come on. Let's get away from everyone Loll. I want to be on my own with you."

Laura, happy to be attended to in this way, grabbed the proffered hand and ran along with him. It was so romantic, with the stars and the moon and the laughter coming from the fairground rides. There followed much touching and kissing and finally she was persuaded on this night to follow him under the pier. Down there, with the tide out, it was cold and dank. They leaned against a metal pillar. Pete kissed her and began to squeeze her breasts hard.

"Stop that," she said.

"Why? Don't you like it?" he asked.

"No. I'm not like that!"

"Of course you are," he said and continued to push his body against hers with increased vigour. His fingers had found the zip on her shorts and he quickly had them pulled down over her thighs. He put his leg behind hers, knocking her off balance and she dropped heavily onto the sand.

Pete was on top of her like an animal and she said over and over, "Stop, please stop. I don't want you to."

"You are a prick teaser, Laura. You know you've wanted this since we met. Now lie back, shut the fuck up and take it!"

"Please! Stop!" she sobbed.

He didn't stop because she asked him to. He stopped because Richard Yates lifted him bodily from her. He then proceeded to hit Pete so hard, time and time again, that Laura had to grab his arm.

"You'll kill him Richard! Stop it, or you'll be in trouble. Let's go."

They went away from there, Richard holding her in his arms and saying, "I won't ever let anyone hurt you again Laura. I love you."

It was this memory that Laura could not get out of her mind and it made her cry and cry. Richard had always loved her, in spite of her faults and skirmishes elsewhere. She knew that if she had gone round to see him and begged for forgiveness, he would have taken her back. Perhaps that's why she had let David talk her into staying with him. She could be near Richard.

Oh God! He shouldn't be dead! Left with David Farrington, a man who constantly needed reassurance, she knew she would have to daily instruct him if they were to get anywhere in life.

She undressed ready for the shower, intending to pack her things and leave.

Downstairs, David Farrington was still highly agitated when he was summoned to speak.

"What has she been telling you? Don't trust what she says, she's a fucking liar."

291

"That seems a funny thing to say about your girlfriend," said Jackson.

"Sounds like she's not going to be my girlfriend for much longer, does it?"

Sitting down in his own front room with the two policemen did not help his mood and he said, "So what are you going to accuse me of now?"

"Not of anything, but we would like to know what you saw this morning. Did you go into the property?"

"Yes. When we heard Anthony, we went outside and he told us that Richard was dead. It didn't seem real when he told us. Laura went in first and then I followed. She sort of screamed and then kept going on about a note. She was touching Richard and telling him not to be dead. Gross. I told her to go outside and she did."

"Did you stay long after she left?" asked Revie.

"No, not long, just to get used to him being dead. Because like I said, it doesn't seem real somehow. That he's dead, I mean."

"I can understand that," said Revie.

"There's been so much death lately and it's all people I know, it is starting to make me wonder whether I'll be next. Because until you find out why he's doing it, well we are all in danger aren't we?"

"Did you notice anything out of the ordinary when you were there?"

"Like what?"

"Something that just seemed wrong."

"No I didn't, apart from my friend being dead. Although I don't suppose he was my friend at the end."

"He did leave a note. He confessed to the killings."

"Did he? That's a surprise. But then he did hate his father, so maybe he finally cracked," said David, leaning back in his chair and smiling. "So my friend Richard was the murderer, who would have thought it?"

CHAPTER THIRTY FOUR

"Who is actually coming this morning?" asked Eleanor as she poured tea into four cups on the draining board. She used the method taught to her by her father, that of pouring tea without lifting the pot and achieving the result much more quickly. The cups did need wiping before they could be put onto the table, so really it was questionable whether any time was saved at all.

"Me," said her son.

"Daniel and I," said Emma.

"We are going to stay here with Mum and Dad," said Elizabeth. "You don't mind, do you? I'd like to spend some time with Mum."

"Of course, I don't mind," said Eleanor. "I think it's a good idea. All this family contact is helping her, I'm sure."

"When I told her that we were going to sort her cottage out, she said that we should make sure we sorted out her debts. She seems to think she owes the local shop some money for deliveries, the window cleaner and the taxi driver."

"She's always on about the taxi driver," said Eleanor. "I didn't see a card for him at the house, but it may turn up today."

"There may be some more bills that have been posted. And then we can tell the landlord to forward any other bills," said Daniel.

"Is there going to be enough room in the Range Rover for her stuff?" asked Emma.

"Should be, we brought her cases back last time and apparently all the furniture belongs to the house. The landlord said he would leave an inventory. If there is anything large, we shall have to arrange for someone to tip it, but I think it's just a few boxes. We could split it up and put it in the recycling bins. There's bound to be enough of them."

"I'll go and get some boxes from the storeroom," said Tom.

After an uneventful journey, they arrived at the cottage at almost lunchtime and Daniel volunteered to fetch food from local shops.

The landlord had left an inventory on the kitchen table along with instructions to leave the rent in the envelope he had provided and put it in the empty ice cream carton in the freezer. Eleanor thought that she might use that idea in her next book which would be probably be based loosely on what was going on in her life at the moment.

She handed sheets to Tom and Emma and told them to get on with two rooms. She started in the sitting room, feeling that her brother in law would prefer to do the kitchen.

She took out a dustbin bag and began with the pile of newspapers and magazines. She threw them in willy-nilly, until one caught her attention. It was a story about Ellie Yates's death.

"Hey! Come here! Look what I've found!"

Tom and Emma quickly came downstairs and Daniel walked into the house with two carrier bags full of lunch.

"She knew about Eleanor's death," said Daniel.

"There are a few papers with the story in it. And a magazine with a story entitled, 'How I warned my aunt about the washing machine'," said Tom.

"What the hell?" said Emma and she took the magazine from her nephew.

"It's written by Judith Buckley. God, that's a blast from the past. Why has she said aunt?"

"Because she used to call her Auntie Ellie, didn't she? We had to call Judith's Mum, Auntie Kath, even though she wasn't our auntie." said Eleanor.

"Oh yes." Emma looked at the article. "Do you think we should tell the police about this?"

"Maybe," said Eleanor.

Tom looked through the rest of the papers and said, "There's stuff about Uncle Andrew's death too."

"She was obsessed with his death, perhaps she came back here after she went daft. And she started to collect any story that mentioned names she recognised," said Eleanor.

"That makes sense," said Daniel.

"There's another report here about Anthony Yates losing his licence from drink driving," said Tom.

"When was that?" asked Emma.

"September 2009, according to this. That's about the same time Ellie got electrocuted." noted Tom.

"I wonder if that's relevant?" asked Emma.

"Perhaps we should do a timetable?" suggested Daniel. "Of all these events and deaths, I mean."

"Shouldn't the police be doing that?" said Eleanor.

"I expect so," he answered.

"Daniel likes doing all the grizzlers and crozzles in the papers, so he should be able to work it out quicker," said Tom and they all agreed that this was true.

"Perhaps we should keep all the papers then, instead of throwing them away," he suggested. "Because it looks as though Edith had some reason to keep them."

The papers were removed from a plastic recycling bag, folded neatly by Daniel and transferred to one of the boxes.

"Lunch," said Tom, "I'm starving."

They took the food out to the garden table where the sun streamed down beautifully.

"It's a nice place, this," said Emma.

"Yea, peaceful," acknowledged Eleanor.

The peace however, was soon shattered by a loud, "Hellooo!!"

A face popped over the fence and the body it was joined to, appeared to belong to a middle-aged woman of jolly demeanour.

"Are you Edith's family?" she asked.

"Yes, we are," answered Tom.

"I'm Edith's neighbour, Pat. How is she? We were very surprised to hear that she had been missing for all that time."

"She's fine thank you. Did you have much to do with her while she lived here?"

"We spoke over the fence mostly and sometimes, if I saw her at the shops. We used to offer her a lift but she always had one sorted out. I saw the police here that night when they fetched her. It was very exciting and quite out of the ordinary! It was on telly too."

"Yes, there was quite a scene I gather," said Eleanor.

"One of her daughters is that famous writer. Is it you?"

"No," said Eleanor.

"Oh well. When will Edith be coming back here to live?"

"She won't be, we are clearing out her things now and then she will be living elsewhere."

"Well that is a shame. My husband and I will miss her. Give her my best, won't you? Tell her Pat said hello. I know that she could be forgetful sometimes, but then we all can, can't we? I know that I often forget where I... Oh, I've just remembered, I've got a box of her stuff in the house. It's not much, just papers I think. Shall I fetch them round for you?"

"That would be very kind," said Eleanor.

Pat came through the side gate into the back garden, before they had finished eating. She carried a red leather suitcase. It seemed heavy and Tom went forward to take it from her.

"Your Mum was always back and to, adding things to this case and taking them out. I was asking my husband just now how we came to look after it for her and he said, don't you remember? Edith thought that someone had been going through her things? And I said I can't remember that! I told you we all get forgetful!"

"Thank you very much Pat, would you like some tea?" said Emma.

"No thanks love, I have to get back to my husband, he's a bit of an invalid you see. It's nice to see the garden being used, to tell you the truth. We used to feel sorry for Edith with no visitors and her sitting here all alone. The only one who came was the landlord, I think."

"We didn't know where she was," said Daniel, "or we should have come to see her."

"I know that. But she bought this garden table and chairs not long after she arrived and she said it's for when visitors come round and of course they never did. I think that they are beautiful and hardly ever been used, it's such a shame."

"Would you like them?" asked Eleanor on impulse. The others nodded and agreed.

Pat looked a little tearful and said, "Thank you so much! Shall I fetch them today?"

"Of course, please do!"

"I remember when she fetched this here in her car. A big one like yours it was and we helped her take it out of the back. She was much fitter back then. It took some putting together, I can tell you!" She chuckled at the memory.

"You remember her car? Do you know what she did with it?" asked Tom.

"I think she said the landlord wouldn't let her keep it, or dogs. She had to get rid of the dog, too. We thought it was because she couldn't afford to keep them and so we didn't ask any more questions. Anyway, the landlord always took her around after that. She used to call him her taxi driver."

The family looked at each other and Daniel asked, "So the landlord is the same man who took Edith everywhere?"

"Most places, she rarely went out if she didn't get a lift and I didn't see her get another taxi."

"Do you know him?" asked Eleanor.

Pat looked puzzled, "I don't remember the name, but the cottage used to belong to his father before he died. Your mother was his first tenant in ages. I've seen him about, but not to speak to if you know what I mean. Look, I'll give you my phone number. Then if there is anything else I can help with, you can always get in touch with me."

"Thank you very much. Perhaps Tom and Daniel will bring the furniture round when we've finished here? Will that suit?"

So it was arranged. The remainder of the afternoon was taken up with finishing the house and putting Edith's few belongings into the back of the Range Rover.

"Weird isn't it, that she didn't have things around her from the family. At home she was always keeping stuff," said Emma.

"I know. But then, the whole thing is weird."

They counted out the money required by the landlord and placed it where he had instructed.

"Perhaps he's scared of burglars too," commented Eleanor.

They tried to open the leather case, but decided instead that they should take it home. If Edith had a key they could use that, otherwise they would force it open.

Then, closing all windows and doors, the keys were pushed back through the letterbox and they returned to the car.

"Who fancies a drive around the murder houses?" asked Eleanor

"So long as we don't stop anywhere," said Emma. "I don't fancy being murdered."

CHAPTER THIRTY FIVE

"Blimey! There are police all around the Yates house." said Eleanor. "What's gone on now?"

They pulled up a few yards from the police cars and media vehicles.

"Go and ask, Tom. I can't get out in case someone recognises me," said Eleanor.

This he did and soon came sauntering back up the street with shocking news.

"Your cousin Richard has hung himself," he informed his startled family.

"Why would he do that?" asked Emma.

"Lots of reasons, I expect," said her husband reasonably.

"Highest on the list appears to be the rumour that he's the murderer and he's killed himself because of the guilt," said Tom.

"I hope he is the murderer," said Emma.

"Why?" asked her husband.

"Because if he's not, then someone is still after members of our family and that's not good!"

Eleanor noticed DCI Revie leaving the Farrington house and walking to his car. She flashed the headlights at him and he turned in her direction.

"Hello, Miss Prentice, heard the news? Or were you here anyway?" He poked his head in through the window and acknowledged the occupants.

"No. Well, we came today to clear out Mum's cottage and pay her outstanding bills, like the rent and stuff."

"We forgot to pay the shop," said Emma from the back seat.

"Oh bugger," said Eleanor. "Now, we shall have to drive back."

"And you heard the news and drove over here?"

"No, as I said we were clearing everything away and then we thought that we would come here on the way home for a sort of a…"

"Nose," said Tom unabashed.

"I see," said the Chief Inspector.

"Is there somewhere we could talk?" asked Eleanor.

"We can go to the local station and have a word there. It's on Town Street," he said.

"Great, now we are going to be really late," said Emma.

"We might as well get it out of the way," Eleanor reasoned. "We'll only have to deal with it again."

Half an hour later, the four of them were sitting opposite DCI Revie and DS Jackson in a meeting room of some sort, with coffee and biscuits on the table between them.

"I've been looking forward to this," said Revie.

"Why did Richard kill himself?" asked Eleanor. "Do you know?"

"He left a note saying that he did the murders," he informed them.

"I said that was it," said Daniel.

303

"Do you think that's likely?" asked Tom.

"I don't know. We are keeping an open mind, as always. Now, you are telling me that it's just coincidence that you all travelled here today," he asked innocently. "Did you stay overnight?"

"No, we set off this morning and have to be home tonight," answered Eleanor.

"How is your mother coming along? Has she settled in now?" asked Jackson.

"She gets better each day. But a psychiatrist is seeing her regularly and we are hoping that she will get back to her old self," said Emma brightly.

"But, it's not very likely," added Daniel. "She's a bit far gone, although she's alright."

"I'm sorry to hear that. Did you find anything at the cottage to show why she went missing?"

"No, not really. Although we did find out that her landlord made her get rid of her car and her dog and he used to give her lifts everywhere. He was the taxi driver. And he's probably trying to fiddle the taxman because he's taken all the rent in cash," Eleanor told him.

"That's not unusual, except for the car bit. Did you meet the landlord when you were at the cottage?"

"No, he said he couldn't come. We left his cash and keys there."

"Nothing else interesting of your Mum's?" he asked.

"No, it's a bit sad. All we still know is that she went missing, got rid of the car and the dog and thousands of pounds of cash. That's about it. I wish we did know more," said Eleanor.

"How is the other lady that was shot?" asked Tom.

"Still critical I'm afraid, but alive," said Revie.

"I hope that she recovers. For her own sake and also for everyone else's," said Eleanor.

They got up, ready to leave. There appeared to be nothing more anyone wanted to say.

When the family stepped back into the evening sunshine for the walk to the car, they saw David Farrington coming towards them.

"What are you doing here?" he asked sharply.

"Probably none of your business, David. What do you know about my cousin's suicide?" Eleanor asked, rather more sharply than she had intended to.

"Nothing, you fucking, stuck up cow! Don't come here pretending you are friends with us all. None of us here have seen you for years and then you turn up causing all this trouble. You think you are so special don't you?" He stalked past them and Daniel put a restraining hand on Tom, who was going to punch him.

"What was all that about?" asked Emma.

"I have no idea!" answered Eleanor.

They watched David stagger off across the car park and into the shopping centre.

"Perhaps he's drunk," said Tom.

"Perhaps, he was Richard's friend. But then he had been sleeping with Richard's wife, so I'm not so sure they were that friendly," said Eleanor.

"What do you think of that suicide note? Saying he was the murderer?" asked Emma.

"He didn't look like a murderer when we saw him the other day, but to be perfectly honest I don't know what he was like. It's so many years since we've seen any of them. And I don't know what a murderer looks like anyway."

"Is that why we didn't bother telling the police about our thoughts on the newspapers and the articles?" asked Daniel.

"I don't know. There's isn't really anything to say is there? It's just a possible idea. We can tell them if it comes to anything, can't we?"

Tom was in the driving seat of the car and called the others in.

"Come on, I want to get home tonight," he said.

Everyone climbed in, Daniel in the passenger seat and the sisters in the back.

"Drive back down the murder street," instructed Emma, "We can go home that way."

As they did, Eleanor suddenly shouted. "Pull over here. There's Judith Buckley in her garden!"

"Do you think ours was the only family who moved away from this street?" asked Emma.

"Seems like it," agreed Eleanor. "Shall we go and speak to her? Pretend we've just seen her in the garden?"

"Well we have, haven't we?" said Daniel.

"We can't all go in," said Tom. "Daniel and I can wait here, while you go in."

Daniel smiled at his nephew and added, "and don't be long!"

Judith was very surprised and very pleased to see Emma and Eleanor and invited them in for a cup of tea.

"We can't stop long," said Emma, mindful of her instructions.

"I expect it's because of all these deaths that you are here, isn't it?"

"Yes and because of Mum," said Eleanor.

"I saw that on the news. Is she alright now? I used to see her about from time to time."

"Did you? Recently?" asked Eleanor.

"Yes, over the past couple of years I've seen her in the town. I thought it was her mother to be honest, but of course I knew that she was dead."

"Was this before or after Aunt Ellie died? I know that you had a lot to do with her, because we've seen that story in the magazine."

Judith put the kettle down and looked embarrassed. "I'm sorry about that, but they did pay me £250 and I needed it at the time."

"Was she always taking risks with the machine?" asked Emma.

"That's what I told the reporter, but I don't know whether she did or not. Ellie was always a mean cow and she didn't change much over the years. I saw her sometimes and once when I was there she told me that the washing machine was playing up and she was going to get someone in to fix it. But she can't have done, because she was dead a couple of days later."

"You know that Richard has killed himself today?" said Eleanor.

Eleanor didn't mention the note, as the police had asked them to keep it quiet.

"I know, I heard. That's really horrible."

"Do you think Richard was the type to kill himself? He never seemed like that before," said Eleanor.

"No I don't, but so much has gone on round here recently, that anything is possible."

They chatted for a few more minutes before Emma reminded Eleanor that they still had a long way to drive.

Eleanor wanted to have a look at the garden, because she remembered how they played there as children.

"I've still got a photograph somewhere of us and Anthony and Richard on the swings. We were so jealous of your swing!"

"Were you? I was jealous of the way your family were so close." Judith hesitated before she said, "I saw the photographs. I didn't know he took photographs, did you?"

The sisters looked at Judith and Emma said, "no, we didn't. I'm glad the rotten bastard is dead. If Richard killed him, I don't blame him, do you?"

"No, I don't. But I wished him dead myself many times, so maybe I did play a part in his death."

"That what you wish, you get you mean?" asked Eleanor.

"I wanted him to die sooner than he did though," answered Judith.

"I hope all the dying stops now. I have such depressing memories of this place and even now it feels like hell still. I don't want to stay here any longer than I have to, in case I get infected again," said Eleanor.

A dog yapped loudly somewhere.

"Oh," said Judith. "My dog wants his supper."

As they talked by the gate, David Farrington walked past them again. He glared at the group and said viciously, "Witches gathering? Always the same!" He stalked off.

"Laura is leaving him because she blames him for Richard's death," said Judith. "She called in here on the way to her sister's and it doesn't look like he's taken it very well."

"He always was a sulky, misery arse," said Eleanor.

"And a devious sod," agreed Emma. They watched him stagger down the street.

Judith hugged them both and said, "give my love to your Mum. She was always nice to me when I was a girl. I've never forgotten her kindness."

They promised and got into the car.

"How come she never mentioned that article to the police?" said Eleanor.

"Perhaps she's just an attention seeker and now she doesn't want to get blamed," suggested Emma.

CHAPTER THIRTY SIX

David Farrington stomped and staggered his way down the street.

"Fucking women, fucking witches," he muttered as he walked.

As he neared his home, he saw that the road was now open. But the door at the Yates house was sealed with tape, forbidding entry. A bored looking policeman stood on guard.

David shouted to him, "Oy mate! Are you there to protect the street or the house?"

The policeman merely nodded, half smiled and turned away.

"Fucking coppers," David muttered as he walked down his drive, hands in his pockets rummaging for the house keys.

He glanced to his left and saw Anthony staring at him from the downstairs bay window and he flicked the V's at him.

"Fucking twat!" he shouted.

He put the key in the lock of the back door and before he could turn it, he felt a heavy thud on the back of his head and he was on the tarmac.

Standing over him was Anthony Yates.

"Who's the fucking twat now? I know you had something to do with Richard's death, you cunt. I'm going to make you pay." he snarled.

David rubbed his head and attempted to sit up.

"No, I fucking didn't and now I'm going to call the police and have them arrest you for assault!"

"Do it. See if I care! It's only your word against mine and you are already under suspicion. Why did you do it, David?"

"I haven't done anything except shag his wife and trust me she was up for that. She said you Yates were a poor lot. You went out with her a few times, didn't you? She told me and said your father made a better job of it than you did. She must be the only woman in the world to have it off with a father and both his sons!"

Anthony dropped to his knees next to David and began punching him. David fought back and soon they were rolling along the drive, punching and shouting.

They stopped when the cold water hit them. Janet was hosing them down and shouting, "Stop it, just stop it. Why are you doing this? It's pointless!"

They jumped up and held out their hands to stop the flow of water.

"Ok. We'll stop!" said David and Janet turned off the tap.

"You pair of idiots! Anthony, get in the house and David, grow up! Aren't you in enough trouble already?"

The policeman, who had sauntered round the corner for a look, grinned and went back to his post.

Janet followed Anthony into the kitchen saying, "If you've woken mother and started her off again, there will be hell to pay."

She slammed the door behind them.

David pushed open his back door and went into the kitchen. Putting the keys on the side, he began to empty his pockets. His phone seemed okay and he put it on a towel just in case there was any water in it. He reached inside his other pocket and took out a second phone and placed it next to the first. Then he took out his cigarettes and lighter, but the cigarettes seemed to have fared worse and there would be no way he could light one.

"Fucking twat," he said.

He stood for a moment staring out of the window. The view had been nice when he was a kid. There used to be fields behind and there had been an uninterrupted view to the old baths on the hill. Now, he could only see a high wooden fence and the upstairs windows of the houses behind. There wasn't a field left in the town now.

"Fucking progress," he said out loud.

Realising that he was cold, David made his way upstairs. He undressed, leaving the wet clothes on the bathroom floor and had a long hot shower. He put on his dressing gown, the one that Laura had bought for him and went into the bedroom.

This room at the front of the house had belonged to his parents, while he and his sister had separate rooms at the back.

He stared out of the front window and thought about how much of his life had revolved around this street. All his friends lived near here. Being able to look outside and know pretty well what everyone was up to, was comforting. In Applewyke, most people kept the same routine, without knowing it. In fact, if anyone tried to change their routine, everyone noticed straight away.

But now, his parents were dead and his sister moved away, probably never to return. Opposite, the Lamb sisters who had noted every moment of his life, everyone's life, were dead. Alice would die, he was sure of it. He looked into the side bay window of the Yates. He could shout if he wanted to be heard. He and Richard had thrown things across to each other when they were children, until Richard was caught by his mother and beaten.

Once, they had all been playing round at David's when his parents were out. Anthony brought in cigarettes and they smoked them. When David's father came home, he asked if they had been smoking. Richard, used to thinking on the hoof, said, "No, Mr Farrington. There was a bonfire up the road and we've had the doors open, so I expect that's the smell."

But Mr Farrington hadn't believed them and David had put up with the humiliation of being beaten with a belt in front of his entire gang. They had stood in silence throughout the punishment and afterwards didn't mention it. It seemed better that way.

David felt that it was always him who was badly done to and not the others. That's why he was trying to make money from his other schemes and then he would leave this shithole once and for all.

Trouble was, he was still here, divorced and even Laura had left him, so he could probably say goodbye to her money. Now Richard was dead, there would be a packet to come to her.

He would use Plan B to call in money urgently. He really wanted to start a new life.

313

He remembered how Thomas Yates had looked back at him from the bay window and winked and smiled. Thomas had tried to teach him to play the guitar, but David hadn't been any good, so he gave up. Then he had transferred his interest to Andrew Prentice, teaching him to play. Those Prentices seemed to have everything their way. Now Laura was all upset that Richard was dead. David suspected that she had been thinking of going back to Richard anyway. Good job she hadn't had time to tell him before he hung himself.

"Fucking bastards, the lot of them," he said.

Why couldn't things stay the same? Their childhoods might have been shit, but at least it was their shit. Familiar shit. Everyone knew what was going to happen next, even if they didn't like it.

David wanted to take the control back in his life. He was going to get Laura back. That's what he was going to do. She had been pleased when she saw how he got that deal done with the Lambs. Laura was the same as him, whatever she said.

He must get hold of more money.

Next door, Anthony was in the shower. He had been furious about Janet soaking him as well as David. Couldn't she see that David asked for it? There was no doubt in his mind that he was going to leave Janet and move into his old house as soon as the police said it was alright.

He was pretty sure that now Richard was dead, the whole Yates estate came to him and none to Laura and also that Tina couldn't have any of it either. Served them right. Both women off with someone else, while he and Richard had been willing to compromise with them. Yes, he had been

314

seeing Janet, but anyone in their right mind could see that he wasn't serious about her!

 "Anthony! Do you want some tea?" shouted Janet from downstairs.

"Yes please!" he shouted back.

Janet must know that he didn't love her, but she kept on being nice to him. She reminded him of how a mother should act with her son. Perhaps that's why he stayed here, even though he didn't really want to.

Janet's mother couldn't possibly be long for this world. There were very few daughters who could bear to do for their mother what Janet did. She would probably die sooner if Janet stopped looking after her.

When the old cow died, Janet would inherit a lot of money he knew for a fact. Old Mr Banks had owned the ironmongers on Town Street and left an absolute packet when he died. That was reason enough to stay, to get his hands on that. But he wanted to go to France and Janet wouldn't want that would she? Janet had become so mumsy and dowdy since she became nursemaid. Not much to write home about, as the saying went.

He went downstairs and into the kitchen. Janet had placed a pot of steaming tea, two bacon sandwiches with the sauce bottle next to the plate and a home-made chocolate cake in the middle of the table.

She might be dowdy, but she knew what he liked.

"Look, I'm sorry about before, Anthony. But you know what David's like. If it wasn't for him, you would not have lost your licence. It was his fault you were driving on a wild goose chase. He didn't take any blame, did he? You've got a record and I don't want anything happening to you."

"I know you don't."

"It might affect you being able to go to France."

"You know I still want to go?"

"You've wanted to go as long as I've known you."

"Well, I apologise. Thanks for stopping me. I might have killed him today."

"He deserved it. He's always caused trouble so that he can get his own way. You know, Anthony, I wouldn't mind going to France with you."

"I thought you wanted to stay here?" He was very surprised to hear this news.

"Only until Mum goes and when she does, I'm going to live my life properly. I will have enough money to, more than enough. It's just Mum who's holding me back."

"And when she dies, you would sell up and move abroad?"

"To wherever you want, Anthony. Mum can't last much longer. The doctor said that she can't."

"No, she can't possibly last much longer," agreed Anthony.

"I was thinking of moving my stuff to Dad's house and getting it sorted out," he said.

"Were you Anthony? Well perhaps we ought to give it a proper cleaning and decorating now. Throw everything out and start again. Get rid of the ghosts. If you are going to live there, that's by far the best idea. If you are going to sell it, it needs doing too."

Janet wasn't going to give Anthony up that easily.

316

CHAPTER THIRTY SEVEN

Dr Jordan sat down opposite Chief Inspector Revie and waited until he had finished reading.

"So that was murder too," he said, closing the folder.

"The rope that hung him had previously been used to strangle him. It is highly likely that Richard Yates was dead before he was strung from the banister, but if he wasn't, he wouldn't have lasted long."

"Whichever way, its murder and not suicide."

"Yes, no question. I'm not going to record it as murder yet. But I'm pretty sure it was."

"And it means the note was bollocks too."

"Someone has gilded the lily, I would say. Maybe that's the mistake that will lead to his capture."

"What about the note, how's testing going with that?"

"Should know more tomorrow, there's a bit of a backlog, I'm afraid."

"We need a break with this one. It's getting ridiculous." Revie tapped the folder with his pen.

"It's narrowing down though, isn't it? This can't be a stranger. It's not random, is it?"

"No, it isn't. We have probably already spoken to the murderer, so we need to go back over the people we know and investigate them a bit more thoroughly."

"That's your job, not mine," said Dr Jordan and got up to leave the room.

DC Eve came in at the same time and said, "Sir. Laura Yates is downstairs and she wants to speak to you. She's in the interview room."

"Oh, is she? I'd better pop down and have a word," said Revie. "Thank you, Doctor, I'll have a think as usual and wait for my mind to sort it out for me. Jackson!" he shouted suddenly.

DS Jackson got up from his desk with a sigh and his colleagues grinned as he did so.

"We've got Laura Yates to have a word with," Revie said to him as they walked down the stairs.

"I gather that she wants to tell us something," said Jackson.

"We will soon find out what that is, wont we?"

Pushing open the door, they saw Laura sitting at the table and Jackson hardly recognised the voluptuous woman he had first met at the Yates. This Laura looked much thinner and drawn and nearer her age of 42.

"Have you had some tea, Laura?" asked Revie.

"No, I don't want any," she replied shortly.

"I'll get us all some tea, we haven't had ours yet."

"Good idea sergeant. Help us all to relax." Revie agreed.

"I can't relax," said Laura, "I don't think I will ever relax again." She began to sob while Revie watched and waited.

He was trying to decide whether the sobs were genuine, or for effect.

Jackson brought in a tray of tea and three Penguin biscuits. Laura smiled at him gratefully and Jackson smiled back.

Revie made a mental note to tell Jackson to back off her. Laura was looking for another man.

"Right, Laura. What is it we can do for you?" he asked.

"There is no way that Richard would kill himself. He wasn't the type. I've thought about it over and over and he wouldn't have killed himself any more than he would have killed the others. If you knew the kind of life he had, you would know that he wasn't violent. I've never known him hit or threaten anybody. Well, not without a good reason."

She sobbed again and Revie kept his experienced eyes on her. There was something wrong.

"But he left a note," said Revie. "A note confessing to the crimes we have been investigating."

"But, why? Why would he do it? He had a lifetime to kill his father. Why pick that day? It wasn't any different to any other day. He wasn't acting different."

"Had he found out about your affair with David Farrington at that point?"

Laura glared at him, "I didn't begin a relationship with David until well after Thomas's funeral. I wouldn't even call it a relationship, more of a fling."

"It seemed more than a fling when we called round the other day," said Jackson.

"Did it?" she answered. "Well it wasn't. If you knew me better sergeant, you would know that there are very few people I take seriously."

"What would you call it?" asked Revie.

"Look, I came in to tell you that Richard and I were thinking of getting back together."

320

"Really?" interrupted Jackson.

"Yes, we were."

"When did you decide this?" asked Revie.

"The past few days," said Laura. "We had been talking and saying that perhaps we should reconsider. We've known each other for so long that it seemed wrong to let it all go."

"Are you sure you aren't coming up with this story so that you can inherit his estate, without solicitors arguing that you were divorcing?" asked Revie.

Laura Yates, instead of protesting said, "I think it's probably more to do with wishful thinking, Chief Inspector. I would have gone back to Richard if he had asked me. David is just good at sex and sex gets boring after a while you know. That's why some people have affairs and others can't be bothered. I am facing the possibility that I'm finally becoming a woman who can't be arsed with sex anymore."

"That's very truthful," said Jackson.

"And, as to the other part of your question, I've checked with my lawyer and I will get Richard's estate. Although the legal stuff was going ahead, nothing has been changed or signed since before we separated. I get the money anyway."

The two policemen looked at her and smiled. Laura smiled back.

"But of course that also means that at the time of Richard's death, the separation was still going through and his death has put a stop to that. You get the money now he's dead," said Revie calmly.

Laura had the grace to look guilty, but said, "We were going to get back together."

"What would you say if we told you that Richard was murdered and didn't kill himself, Laura?"

"I would say that I have been telling you that all along. How was he killed?"

"We can't say now, but it wasn't suicide."

"I knew it. I knew he was murdered."

"So, who do you think murdered him Laura?" asked Jackson.

"The same person who murdered all the others."

Jackson changed tack. "Where was the suicide note when you went in to see Richard?"

"I told you already. I couldn't see a note."

"Where did you check?"

"I checked on the floor, in his pockets and on the hall table. But there wasn't a note. I looked in the kitchen and the other downstairs rooms, but couldn't see one. Then David came in and asked what I was doing and I told him, so he went upstairs to check."

"And he couldn't see one either?" said Revie

"No."

"Did he find anything unusual at all?" persisted Revie.

"I don't think so. You will have to ask him. By the time he came down, I was outside on the lawn being sick. I didn't speak to him about it after that. First you lot came and then I left him and we haven't spoken since."

"Not at all?"

"No, Sergeant Jackson. David has been texting and trying to ring, but I haven't replied. I don't want anything more to do with him."

"What about the stuff you got from the Lambs?"

Laura looked surprised to be reminded of the event.

"That's history. Alice can have it back. I don't want it any more. David sorted it out for me because I wanted the things. He persuaded the Lambs to sell. But like I told you, I get bored easily and now I don't want that rubbish."

"What are you going to do?" said Revie.

Laura thought for a moment and said, "I'm going to see Anthony, so we can decide what we are going to do about the estate and then I'll sell everything and move away. Start again somewhere else."

"Who do you think the murderer is?"

She answered without hesitation, "No idea. It's not me and it wasn't Richard. It wouldn't be Anthony because he's not violent, just a pisshead. Janet is too timid and David, well he might be an idiot, but I've been with him most of the time this has been going on and I can't really say that he had the opportunity. Plus, he couldn't organise a piss up in a brewery. So, I don't know. Maybe it's one of those stuck up relatives of theirs."

"What motive would they have?" asked Revie.

"Well for one thing, Thomas shagged all the kids when they were small. Maybe it got too much for one of them. I don't know!"

"Did he molest you, when you were small Laura?"

"Can't remember. Maybe I escaped that dubious pleasure for some reason."

"Why did no one report Thomas Yates to the police?" asked Jackson.

"You should know, being a copper. There would have been loads of investigations, kids taken into care and a court case where it was a child's word against an adult and nothing will be done. The only way out for most people who have been abused is to ignore it, grow up and spend some time in therapy."

"Thank you, Laura," said Revie, holding open the door so she could leave.

"Wasn't the note found in his jeans pocket?" asked Jackson.

"Yes, it was. Sticking out for all to see," answered Revie.

"So, someone planted it."

"But, who?"

CHAPTER THIRTY EIGHT

"Where shall I put all this stuff of Grans?" asked Tom.

"Put it in the library!" shouted Eleanor in answer.

They hadn't got home until after midnight. Everyone was tired and feeling stressed following the dramas of yesterday. Elizabeth was making breakfast for the family who were coming in and out at different times, instead of the 9 o'clock mealtime she had requested.

That was annoying for her, "It's not a café you know." she said to Tom as he wandered in at quarter past.

"I know Auntie Elizabeth, but I've got loads to do today so I can catch up from yesterday. Just don't bother with me, I'll sort myself out."

Edith, however, enjoyed the comings and goings. It reminded her of the past.

"I like all of this," she said simply and Elizabeth stopped worrying about her silly problems and hugged her Mum.

"It's lovely to have you back. It's like the old days," she said.

"Is it, dear? I don't remember that, but it is nice to be with a family. Everyone is so friendly. Do you know that every morning, someone has been bringing me a cup of tea to my room? And giving me a whisky at night?"

"I know Mum. That was me!"

"Well, thank you dear! You are good to me, aren't you?"

Edith drank her tea and buttered her toast and enjoyed short conversations with different people. She was finding it difficult to differentiate between them all.

She had been seen by Eleanor's doctor and had one meeting with a psychiatrist. They were both of the conclusion that Edith was suffering from the early stages of Alzheimer's and that it had probably been brought on by the stress of her son's death. The outlook promised further dimming of her faculties. The family had talked and said they would do whatever was required to make her comfortable and safe. This meant she would be looked after at Eleanor's house initially, with constant checks on her progress.

In the short time Edith had been back with her family, they realised that they were unlikely to learn why she left and what had happened during the years in between.

"Gran, have you got a key to that leather case? The red one?" asked Tom.

"I don't keep keys anywhere, because I lose them," she said helpfully.

"Do you mind if we have a look for the keys after breakfast? Or I could just force it open. What do you think' Gran?"

"You do whatever you want dear. I'm sure that you know best Andrew."

Eleanor and Elizabeth looked across at each other and raised their eyebrows.

"Do you remember Andrew?"

"Of course I do! Why would I forget Andrew? He's my son and he's not dead you know. He's helping me and I'm helping him, just like we promised." Edith stubbed her cigarette hard against her plate.

"I'm going to force the lock Mum. I won't have to do too much damage, I don't think." Elizabeth was trying not to upset her.

Eleanor looked at her Mum and said,

"Ok. Do it in the library and that way we won't have any dramas in here."

"Mum, would you like to come over to the yard with me? I want to see the horses that are coming in today."

Eleanor was beginning to find it very limiting to have her invalid mother staying. She was used to doing what she wanted, when she wanted and no one ever questioning how long she was gone. Now she was checking on Edith all the time. She was hoping the burden would be spread amongst the sisters and not all landing on her doorstep.

"Yes dear! That would be nice. I will go up and get changed and then we can go over there. Will we be there for lunch?"

"No Mum, we are just going to go out of the kitchen door and walk over there. It won't take long and you can sit on one of the benches when the girl arrives to show me. It will be interesting to watch."

"Will it?" she asked.

"So, are you going to go?" asked Elizabeth.

"Where to, dear?"

"I think you should just go and do your thing, Eleanor. It will take forever if you try and - you know."

"Mum!"

Tom gave an alarmed shout from the hall.

"Mum. Come into the library!"

Within fifteen seconds, Tom had been joined in the library by Eleanor, Elizabeth, George, Emma and Daniel. He was standing in front of the opened red leather case which sat on a desk.

Emma drew in her breath and Elizabeth put her hand to her mouth.

Daniel said, "Oh no!"

"What does this mean?" said Eleanor.

The case was full of cash, jewellery, a gun and a box of bullets.

"I'd better check to see if it's loaded," said Tom.

"No, don't!" said Daniel and he reached over to stop his nephew. "We ought to tell the police about this."

"Do you think it's something they would be interested in?" asked Elizabeth.

"They will if it ends up being the murder weapon," said Tom pointedly.

"You think Mum is the murderer?" asked Eleanor incredulously.

"No, not necessarily. But she has got a gun hidden away, she knows all the victims and has been living secretly in the area for years," he pointed out.

"But we've seen what's she like!" said Elizabeth. "How could she work out how to kill people?"

"Are you listening to what you are saying? Mum, a murderer?"

"Who's a murderer?" asked Edith as she looked into the case.

No one had seen her enter the room.

"Mum, what do you know about the money and the gun in this suitcase?" asked Eleanor.

Edith said, "I moved some of my cash about because it was vanishing and I couldn't work out how. People would say to me that the price of living is going up all the time and I must accept that. But I moved it around from one case to another all the same. I didn't know how long I would have to wait where I was."

"What about the gun, Mum?"

"Now that gun is your brother's, isn't it? From when your father ran the gun club? I know some of the guns had to go to Mrs Thatcher, I don't know why she wanted them, but this one was saved wasn't it?"

"The police have been looking for a gun like this Mum, for the murders in Leeds. Did you take it with you when you left home that day?" asked Elizabeth.

"I must have done, I suppose," she answered.

"Have you killed anyone Mum?" asked Eleanor and was rewarded with a kick from Emma. Eleanor kicked her back. They were children again.

"I don't think so. Unless you count the baby I lost between you and Andrew. But I didn't know I was pregnant so I don't think it was really my fault I went riding that day."

"I don't mean that Mum, I mean shooting anyone," continued Eleanor.

Edith gazed at her family and smiled. She looked about 14 years old.

"I don't know what you mean."

Daniel tried another tack.

"Why did you leave home that day Edith? Why did you take all that money?"

"For the ransom! For Andrew's ransom!" she said loudly and swept out of the room.

"What are we going to do now?" said Tom.

"Count how much money is there Tom," instructed Daniel. "Then I think you had better get Michael over here."

"We are going to have to decide whether to call the police about this," said Eleanor.

"Do you think Mum is a murderer?" asked Emma.

"No, but look how she's acting. She might be involved in an innocent way and not realise it."

"Or she's putting it on," commented Eleanor.

"I don't think she's capable of that," said Elizabeth.

"There seems to be about two hundred thousand pounds here," said Tom. "You count it too, George."

Eleanor said, "We'll get in touch with my solicitor and I think I'd better get the psychiatrist involved. Between them they will keep her safe while the police investigate. We can't keep it secret, or we shall all be in the shit if it gets found out."

The others agreed and went their separate ways.

Half an hour later they met in the kitchen, joined by Michael who looked extremely worried.

"Where is she now?" he asked.

"She's having a shower," said Elizabeth.

"Look, sorry everyone, but I've got someone coming to bring me a horse in ten minutes. The solicitor wants me to take Mum to see him this afternoon and the psychiatrist straight afterwards. They will advise us, but I've got to go now," said Eleanor.

"How did we get to the point that all our lives are revolving around Mum?" asked Elizabeth.

"We always did revolve around her," answered Emma.

"She said the money was for Andrew's ransom," Tom informed his Grandfather.

"Where did she get that idea from?" he asked.

"She wouldn't answer that. She acts half the time as though she doesn't know what's going on and the other half as though she does. But even when she does understand, it's not like a normal person," explained Emma.

"I can't see how she would hurt anyone though, she's not like that," George noted. He liked his mother in law.

"I suppose the point is that she's not the person she was and the new Edith might commit murder," pointed out Daniel.

Edith walked into the kitchen while they talked and said, "I can't find the hairdryer. Does anyone know where the hairdryer is please?"

She was stark naked.

CHAPTER THIRTY NINE

Police have released further details about the death of Richard Yates.

First considered to be suicide, it had been widely speculated that Mr Yates had killed himself in response to the murder of his father and his neighbour. Now police are considering the possibility that Richard Yates has also been the victim of a murder.

Police are asking again for anyone with any information to contact their local police station or Crime Stoppers.

It has also been reported that Alice Lamb, who was seriously injured during the murderous attack on her sister, may now be regaining consciousness. Police are refusing to confirm whether or not this is the case.

Anthony paced around the front room.

He had just returned from a visit to his solicitor's office and had learned good and bad news. Even though he wanted to leave Janet and start up on his own, he had been disappointed that she wasn't there when he returned to the house.

She was in hospital with her mother. Mrs Banks had taken an unexpected turn for the worse and was apparently breathing her last. It was a bloody nuisance that it was happening just now after years and years of illness. Anthony should be getting the attention, not old Mrs Banks.

Anthony wanted to complain about Laura Yates still being the heir to his brother's estate and as a result owning half of his parent's house. He didn't like that at all. He needed as much money as he could to begin his new life.

But, at least his solicitor confirmed that his own divorce had gone far enough to ensure that Tina wouldn't get more than 50% of their marital property.

He really wanted a drink now. It was very difficult to stay sober when he was depressed, or when he was happy. Today he felt both in equal measures. He twanged the elastic band on his wrist. Janet didn't leave any drink around the house, so he would have to go out for it. Perhaps David had some.

He decided he would go next door and ask. David's van wasn't there, but Anthony knew where he kept his house keys and he was sure that David wouldn't mind him taking a couple of cans from the fridge. He could return them later.

With a spring in his step, he walked across the driveways and looked for the key under the shoe jack by the back door.

It wasn't there.

That was a blow. Perhaps David was keeping Laura out of the house now that they had split. But it also meant that Anthony couldn't get in. He thought that he would try his parent's house, Richard might have left something in the fridge.

He walked across the front lawns and down his old driveway. Passing the back door, he walked to the garage and took the house keys from the hook next to the spade.

Before he walked back to the door, Anthony leant against Richard's car and looked at the back of his childhood home.

What happened to those years since they were children? Nearly everyone was dead or moved on. He knew that most people felt like this from time to time, but honestly it must be worse for those that stayed in the same place. People who move on can reinvent themselves and make friendships without a rolling history.

He looked up to his old bedroom window. The same bedroom he had shared with Richard until he left to get married to Laura. Anthony stayed for three more years until he too married and left. The brothers would return rarely for visits, for they were never made welcome. Their mother would complain and nag and their father leer at their wives and take money from his sons. Neither wife wanted to be around Ellie or Thomas. That meant that events such as Christmas were never held at this house. When Anthony and Richard were small, Christmas had been spent at Granny and Grandad's house where there was a tree and presents and love.

Anthony hadn't felt any love from his parents and to be honest he was glad they were dead. But not Richard, Richard's death was a mistake.

Sometimes lately, Anthony imagined killing everyone. Had he killed them?

Laura was standing at his old bedroom window and waved to him. She was beckoning him in. What was she doing in the house?

Anthony walked in though the back door and Laura came downstairs to meet him in the hall.

"What are you doing here, Laura?"

335

"I've come for some of Richard's stuff and I'm going to take his car Anthony. It's better than mine."

"I hope you're not taking anything of mine or my parent's."

"I wouldn't do that. You know that I inherit Richard's estate, including his share of this house?"

"So I gather, it seems wrong somehow, I'm not so sure that Richard would want that."

"It is what it is, Anthony. Do you want to sell or keep it?"

"Sell it. Too much went on here. Even before everyone got murdered, there was enough going on."

"Perhaps we should arrange to come and clear everything out together. Get a skip and really sort the house out, then it stands a chance of selling."

"Richard thought it was haunted," said Anthony.

"Did he? Your Mum and Dad? God, Richard might be haunting it now."

"It certainly feels cold enough."

Suddenly, Laura went sheet white and sat down smartly on the bottom step. She put her head between her legs and said, "I should have done this in the first place."

"What do you mean Laura? Come to the house?"

"No. Put my head between my legs, Anthony. I'm pregnant."

Anthony sat down next to her and said, "Oh Laura. Are you pleased? Are you alright? Does David know?"

"Lots of questions. I'm alright and David doesn't know. It's nothing to do with him. The baby is Richard's." She sobbed uncontrollably.

Anthony put his arm around her.

"But how can you be sure Laura? I mean you haven't been with Richard for so long. You don't look pregnant."

"Because of how far along I am and the fact I haven't had period since I've been with David. And we used condoms, I insisted. I just thought it was the stress of everything. I've lost weight, not put it on. But the doctors have confirmed that in less than three months, I shall be giving birth to a Yates boy. What do you think of that, Anthony?"

"I don't know! I'm stumped! Did Richard know?"

"No, he didn't," she answered simply.

Suddenly the front door opened and the sound of wind chimes filled the hall. Anthony looked up and saw that there was a set of Leeds United football wind chimes hanging from the banister where Richard had so recently swung.

"Did you put them there?" asked Anthony.

"I did, to help his spirit move on. But the front door was locked and bolted."

"That means he's heard about the baby."

"Yes," she said. "I will do a DNA test when he's born. The doctor said that if you did a test too, then they could prove the link with the family. Will you do that?"

"Yes, of course," he replied. "I'm going to be an uncle. That's some good news then."

"So now you don't need to be so cross about the will. The money will go to my son now, so it's still in the family."

"No, I suppose not. Are you going to tell David? He might kick up a fuss."

"What about? He wouldn't want a child whether it was his or not. David isn't very family orientated."

"I thought he arranged to steal the clothes and jewellery for you?"

Laura turned on him.

"It wasn't stealing! I told David what I wanted and he went to see the Lambs the day before we went to collect the stuff. They were quite happy with the deal, I think they were short of money or something and David promised to pay them at the end of the month. He was expecting to get paid a big cheque from one of his customers then. It was all above board!"

"Ok! I'm sure it was. But what did the ladies say when you went in to see them that night. And why did you go so late?"

"Apparently, they wanted us to go when everyone would be watching TV, because they said they didn't want the neighbours to know their business. They said they wouldn't like people to know that they were skint. In the end I didn't go in, because David wanted me to stay outside."

"Why would he want you to do that? Stay outside I mean? You can't know whether the ladies were dead or alive when you collected the stuff?"

Laura was silent for a minute and said, "David has assured me that they were fine when he went in. If they died that night, then it was after we left. Perhaps someone saw us go in and thought it would be a good idea to frame us. I don't really know. It just seemed a laugh at the time. We had been drinking before we went in and smoking weed."

"With the baby?"

"I didn't know I was pregnant then, did I? I don't do either now."

Anthony suddenly remembered why he had called round in the first place, but decided that now was not an appropriate time to look for alcohol.

"How can you be sure that David didn't kill them when he went in?"

"Why would he do that? And anyway, he just acted the same when he came out as when he went in. He would have been different, wouldn't he?"

"How long was he in there?" asked Anthony.

"Not long, about fifteen minutes probably."

"That's quite a long time for you to wait."

"David shouted from the living room window to me and said the ladies hadn't quite got everything together. We were laughing because he said they were dressed in their jamas and that seemed funny to him." She smiled again at the recollection.

"David can be such fun, can't he Anthony? Trouble is he never seems to take anything seriously and now I'm going to have to. I would have got Richard back you know."

"You always could Laura. He really loved you."

"When I was next door, sometimes I was sure that I could hear him breathing. I don't know if he was in bed in that room or whether he was standing right up against the window."

"He might have been trying to listen to you."

"Yes, I thought that. And that meant that he heard us two as well. It seemed funny at the time. A bit of a kick I suppose. Oh, poor Richard!" She began to cry again.

"All that being so, who killed him Laura?"

"I'm not so sure that he was killed. The police could have it wrong. I think it was suicide, I'm sure it was. I've thought about it over and over and wondered if he just did it without thinking because of me. I started off thinking he was murdered, but I've changed my mind."

"They seem pretty sure that it was murder made to look like suicide. If it was, it must be someone we know. Someone with a motive to kill all of them, a motive we haven't spotted yet."

"Have you been trying to spot motives?"

"I don't think that I've actually been thinking about it at all. Not in a proactive way. I've been reacting to everything that's been happening, usually in a negative way."

"Like you have no control over what's gone on?" You haven't, have you? Unless you are the murderer, you have no control."

"I should have control."

"Are you the murderer, Anthony?"

"What would you do if I was, Laura?"

"So long as you hadn't killed Richard, I wouldn't say anything. Did you kill Richard?"

"I haven't killed anyone. Ever."

CHAPTER FORTY

Patsy Prentice stood in front of her wardrobe, trying to decide what she should wear from the poor show she saw there.

Some clothes would never fit her, because she had gained at least two dress sizes since Andrew died and the rest seemed old fashioned or tatty. She shut the door again and tried the chest of drawers, where sadly the result was the same. There was no way that she was going to impress anyone this evening.

The phone call had come out of the blue. She hadn't seen Ken since three months after Andrew died. He had promised undying love and a future together if only she were free.

But once she became free, he said that they should take it slowly because Andrew's death looked suspicious. And then once her mother in law started her questioning, he said leave it to him, he will deal with it. When she disappeared, Patsy wondered how exactly he had dealt with it.

"Don't be ridiculous," Ken said, when she asked if he were anything to do with it.

"It's just that you said that you would sort her out," she said.

"Well as it turns out, I didn't have to, did I?"

"I suppose not," she answered.

It wasn't so much that Ken was wonderful in comparison to Andrew. It was just that he paid attention to her and romantic attention was a part of marriage which Andrew ignored. What Ken saw in her had confused her at the beginning of the relationship, but he constantly told her that she was beautiful and the woman of his dreams. Patsy began to feel that life was almost worth living and subsequently became daily unhappier with her lot.

So when Ken suggested that they should scare Andrew away with phone calls and noises outside the house, Patsy was all too willing to agree.

Patsy immature and naïve, told Andrew about the feelings of being watched and followed. Initially sceptical, he began to see trouble at every turn. Sadly, Andrew was inherently nervous and careful, a fact he hid behind his athletic exterior and was solely due to the childhood he spent in Leeds.

Patsy was surprised how quickly Andrew agreed with her. That fateful night when she told him that she could hear screaming outside, Andrew went immediately outside and she assumed in his sleepy adrenaline driven state, had slipped on those dreadful steps.

Patsy heard Andrew scream when he fell, but she never told the police that she saw someone in the garden looking up at the bedroom window. She was sure that it was Ken, although he denied it later when asked. He told her that if she mentioned seeing anyone at all, it could open her up to a revenge attack and she should keep quiet. So she did.

Ken gradually became more distant, even failing to respond to her stories of noises continuing outside.

"Perhaps it's your dead husband coming back to haunt you for letting him die that night," he said cruelly.

"I didn't let him die!"

"Well you knew he was going to leave you and if he did that, you wouldn't get much would you? This way, you got the whole house and his money, no questions asked."

"It wasn't me who killed him!"

"Wasn't it? You wanted out of the marriage and you were always polishing the steps. If I told the police that you overheard him talking to his mother about leaving you, I bet they would be interested in that."

"I just wanted to be with you, that's all!" she said.

"Well it's not a good time at the moment. And if I'm honest, I'm not so sure that I want to be going out with a murderer."

Ken talked in this way over the next few weeks and gradually stopped contacting her. His phone was disconnected and then Patsy realised with horror, that in her stupidity, she had absolutely no idea where Ken lived.

The noises outside the house continued on and off over the years, but gradually these events grew further and further apart. Patsy, not wanting to let anyone know about her affair with Ken, withdrew into herself and eventually talked to no one. The more she considered the events surrounding Andrew's death and Edith's disappearance, the more it seemed to her that she could possibly have murdered Andrew. The children never contacted her, choosing to remain in contact with their rich and influential aunt.

Patsy thought Eleanor a controlling bitch, who wanted to run her family's life like one of her novels, with her typing fingers deciding what would happen next.

Bitch.

343

It had been so tempting to tell those policemen when they came around to see her that time, but at the last minute all she told them about was werewolves. That made her sound stupid she knew, but the noises had sounded like that! Of course, Patsy knew that she drank a little bit more than she ought, but that was only because of her nerves.

And there had been no help from anyone. Andrew's family had dropped her like a hot brick. Not that they gave her much attention when Andrew was alive. But it would have been nice to get a telephone call or something from time to time.

Patsy finally decided on an old sweatshirt of Andrew's. It was going to cover her body at least and make her look thinner. If she wore the skirt with the elasticated waist, then no one would be any the wiser. It was a pity there hadn't been a little more warning of the visit because it might be an idea to run a colour through her hair. It was definitely looking much greyer these days. Yes, Patsy felt that she was looking much greyer in the face too.

Finding a lipstick, she applied some and surveyed the result. It hadn't done much for her, but she left it on anyway. She patted her cheeks and saw colour come to them, but that didn't look very good either.

"I'll just have a quick drink," she said out loud. "Give me a bit of courage."

Patsy had no idea who the woman was who had rung. She just said that she knew that Patsy was an old friend of Ken and wondered if she minded her popping round? Apparently, she had something to discuss with her and it couldn't be done over the phone. Patsy reluctantly agreed to see her Friday evening and now she had an hour to wait for the visit.

What could it be about?

Patsy turned on the news and watched them talk about the record breaking high temperatures and then a motor sport accident. It was nice not to hear about another murder or suicide.

It had been so odd this year. All those people connected to Andrew dying and the police no nearer to solving the problem. She hoped to God they didn't intend to revisit Andrew's death. Patsy didn't think that she would be able to stand up to any questioning. But someone might be able to tell her where Ken had got to.

Perhaps this woman knew?

Her mind travelled back to Andrew.

He hadn't been so bad to her. In fact, he had probably been alright. She often suspected that he had affairs, but he always came back to her and never brought any of his trouble home. She expected that Andrew would have been amazed to know that she had had her little secret too.

Was it her fault that Andrew died? She couldn't recall actually wishing him dead, but there had been many times in the throes of passion with Ken that she considered Andrew gone. Was that enough to tempt fate? Was fate that capricious? That wasn't the right word, was it?

Suddenly Patsy laughed. She remembered Andrew telling her a tale from his childhood when one of his parents' friends had used the word capricious many times during one weekend sailing holiday with the family.

He left behind his copy of Readers Digest and when Edith read it, she noted that it was one of their words in that edition. The magazine used to choose unusual words which they described in every edition. The family found that highly amusing.

That was the sort of humour that Andrew's family had, a bit cruel, a bit odd. Not everyone understood.

There it was again!

A kind of howling, grumbling noise, right outside the window.

Patsy turned off the television and stood stock still, listening. The noise stopped and she strained her ears, desperate for a repeat of the noise but also praying that the night remained silent.

The lights went off. Patsy had closed the blinds in anticipation of her visitor and now the room was dark. She moved forward cautiously, putting out her hands so that she didn't fall.

The noises outside resumed, but this time seemed to be nearer the window. "Patsy! Patsy! Please come and help me!"

It sounded like Andrew. She was immediately transported back to the night of his death. Creeping forward into the kitchen, she stood in front of the door. Perhaps she should phone the police.

And tell them what?

"Please help me. Please!"

The sound was in the garden, definitely. She opened the back door tentatively and was relieved to see that the moon had come from behind a cloud and lit the lawn. There was nothing there.

She walked out onto the steps and felt a loud thump against the back of her head. She brought her hand up to her head and felt blood dripping.

Patsy felt another crack and fell back onto the steps.

As her eyes closed, she saw a shadowy figure peer down into her face.

CHAPTER FORTY ONE

"Is she going to be alright?" asked Jackson.

"The operation was a success, but we won't be able to speak to her for a few days. All she said to the paramedics was, 'Where's Ken? She said she wanted to talk about Ken. Oh and also she said I think Ken killed Andrew, it wasn't me."

Revie and Jackson were looking again at all the information they had collected during the past year. The Christmas decorations were hanging around the office, but the team didn't feel much like celebrating. There had been so many deaths and disasters this year that no one felt particularly Christmassy.

"Is everyone here? We'll have another discussion," asked Revie.

"They are. They are waiting for you," said Jackson.

"I know we keep going through this, but the story is added to all the time. We are missing something, so let's really listen and then think. Sergeant Jackson, let's go over again what the Patsy and Andrew Prentice story is."

"OK, Andrew had spoken to his mother and a couple of other people about his intention to leave his wife. He was going to go home. He thought that someone was bothering them, hanging around the property or telephoning them from time to time. Andrew sometimes had affairs, but nothing very serious. As far as I can gather, he hadn't made any enemies through that or anything else. There were a few rumours about Patsy having an affair too. A man has been seen calling at the house when Andrew wasn't there and continued visiting after his death. A shaven headed man, about 6 feet tall, drove a maroon Mercedes van, but no one has the number plate and it doesn't appear on any CCTV that we know of. Andrew was found in jogging bottoms and a tee shirt and no shoes. He was found lying with his head on the steps and blood coming from the back of his head. It was a cold night, below freezing and everything pointed to him slipping on the ice and hitting his head. It killed him pretty well instantly. Last Friday night, Patsy appeared to have been expecting someone as she had dressed differently and put on a bit of make-up.

She was found by a neighbour after his dog kept barking, so he went to investigate. It's lucky he did, because he found Patsy lying in the same position as her husband, with similar injuries. She's only said what you already know. The only telephone calls she received in the previous couple of days had been from withheld numbers. She doesn't seem to have a mobile number registered to her. Oh and she has nothing to do with her husband's family and she doesn't have any contact with her children."

"Thanks for that," said Revie.

"Now, can you go over everything we know about the Yates please Pearl?"

"Yes. Thomas Yates was born in London to a feckless mother and father who paid little attention to him and his brother. He met Ellie when they both holidayed in Blackpool one year and they married within a few months. They had two sons and I believe she had a few miscarriages. He was a paedophile, quite a predator who assaulted several local children, including some of the Prentice children, Janet Banks, Judith Buckley and also Tina

349

and Laura Yates, although she denies it. Most of the abuse took place at his house, the photographs and evidence point to that. We are assuming that it was him who took the photos. Unusually for a paedophile, he also had affairs with women of his own age. But mainly kids. He was a disgusting man. He's been at it since he arrived in Leeds really, so we don't know what made someone snap to murder him, that's if it's anything to do with the abuse. So far, we haven't had any actual sightings of anyone unusual around the place when he died. His sons were around and his neighbours, but no one saw anything out of the ordinary. He was last seen alive on the Thursday. Then when his son, Richard couldn't get hold of him, he found him shot dead on Saturday morning. He was shot with a small calibre pistol, in the chest. The shooter was apparently by the sofa and Thomas Yates was standing in front of the fire when the gun was fired. His wife Ellie Yates, was electrocuted by a washing machine a couple of years earlier. Investigations at the time decided that it was an accidental death. But reading through some of the notes on the event, someone said that the injuries were as though the earth on the machine wasn't connected. But checks on the machine later, showed that it was. The decision was made that the mother board had malfunctioned, possibly to do with Ellie using a screwdriver on it. Judith Buckley told me in a recent meeting, that Ellie had complained about the machine causing her problems for a few weeks.

I checked out the sons and discovered that Anthony had been stopped for drink driving that same morning, so he was in police custody at the time his mother was discovered. He had been having an on off affair with Janet Banks and following his father's death, he moved in with her. He didn't seem that taken with her and was using her more as a stop gap. Richard Yates discovered his father's body with David Farrington. Not long after the funeral, Laura Yates left Richard for David and moved in next door. Both brothers were going through a difficult financial and emotional time. I think Andrew has got the next part?"

"I have. Laura and David continued a loud and public affair and also drank heavily. They indulged in some light drug taking. Laura wanted some of the Lamb's possessions and apparently David arranged for the ladies to sell him the stuff. They collected this one night, at a pre-arranged time and according to David the ladies were well when he collected it. Laura tells us that she stayed outside, but is sure his manner didn't change and that he couldn't have attacked the sisters. There was no blood on any of their clothing. Richard told people he was hearing ghosts around the house and thought it could be his parents haunting him. He and Anthony had a conversation not long before Richards's death and their plan was for Anthony to move in with him, while they sorted out their future.

Without mentioning his feelings to anyone, Richard supposedly killed himself by hanging from the banisters. Anthony discovered the body and was closely followed in by Laura and David. Anthony and Laura insist there was no suicide note, David said he didn't look, but the paramedics found one in Richard's pocket. The note said that he had killed himself because he had killed his father and Sylvia Lamb. The post mortem has still not decided fully whether the death was a suicide or a murder. Family and friends say that he wouldn't kill himself and he wasn't a murderer. Since then, Anthony Yates has left Janet Banks and moved in with Laura Yates at her house in Wakefield. The one she previously shared with Richard. Their divorce hadn't gone

351

far enough for her not to inherit all of Richard's estate. She shares the Thomas Yates estate with Anthony. Anthony's divorce was far enough along for him not to have to give his ex-wife Tina anything more than was previously agreed. Tina is in another relationship and seems happy enough. Laura Yates has given birth to a boy last month called William Richard, who she insists is Richard's and not David's. David insists it is his and so she has arranged DNA tests for the baby, Anthony and David. I don't know what the results are yet. Anthony and Laura say they are not an item, just trying to sort their estates out. I expect that Janet Banks is a bit pissed off as her mother died not long before he went, so she was finally free."

"Is her mother's death suspicious in any way?" asked Jackson.

"No Sarge, she went to hospital and died there. She's been ill for years."

"It's a lot of information, isn't it guys? Keep attention on the story, because the clue is in the things we have been listening to. Don't forget that. The answers are in these details," Revie reminded them.

"I've been studying the Lamb story," DC Eve said. "I love the journal and have read it countless times. Most of it is like a diary, but some is gossip. I've got a feeling that they used to blackmail some people, judging by code words I've identified. I can show anyone those codes if they are interested. And the night they were shot, Yates and Farrington insist the Lambs were alive when they left that night. If that's true, someone was either already at the property or followed them in and shot the ladies. Why? If it was Yates and Farrington, why shoot the ladies for the clothes and jewellery? Out of the blue? Sort of doesn't

352

make sense and there was no unusual DNA found on them. But, what if the ladies knew that this murderous Mr X was somehow involved in the murder of Thomas Yates and tried to blackmail him? There had been a search downstairs, maybe for the journal, but it wasn't found. If that was the reason the ladies were shot, because they disturbed the search, it would make a lot more sense. Alice was shot first, on the stairs, by the same gun that killed Thomas Yates. But, there were no bloody footprints going from that body to upstairs, intimating that the murderer did not pass her on those stairs, unless he could fly. We checked the other steps up there, but haven't come to any satisfactory conclusions. Sylvia was shot twice by the same gun, once in the chest, then as she fell, another bullet hit her under the chin and up through her face. Smeared blood was found on the carpet near the bathroom at the end of the landing. Alice has regained consciousness several weeks ago, but may never be fully mentally able again and so isn't much help. The journal says a lot as I said, but mostly the interesting information is, them seeing Edith Prentice in the road outside and seeing the family coming and going around the Yates house. Many sightings marry up with the information we already have. She did see both Richard and Anthony at the house in the days prior to his murder. She saw Anthony at the house the morning of Ellie's death, but that was the same time he was supposedly being breathalysed. There is loads of stuff about his abuse of local children, again matching up with what we know. I think we will be able to refer to it, as and when we find out any more information."

"Thanks," said Revie. "Now, who's done the Prentices?"

"Me sir," answered DC Plummer, a relatively new addition to the team. "Edith Prentice spoke to her son in the weeks before his death, about his intention to leave his wife. He also told her about the noises and phone calls from a supposed stalker. He died from a fall that night as discussed, but Edith wouldn't let it drop. She was convinced it was murder and annoyed everyone with her ideas. Her family didn't seem to believe her. Then, after a few weeks she took her car, her dog and several thousand pounds cash and vanished. She wasn't discovered despite a long publicity campaign until we noticed that she was mentioned in the Lamb journal. Another appeal followed and she was found within hours. Lately, she has rapidly moved through stages of Alzheimer's and we cannot speak to her. She is being cared for in a nursing home. When she was found, she mentioned that she lost her car and her dog. She had been keeping some of her cash in a case she had at the house she rented and a lot more in a case next door. Also in that case was the murder weapon. Her fingerprints are on it, but not on the trigger. She said that it belonged to her son, but it doesn't seem to. She said that she needed the cash for Andrew's ransom and was waiting for him to be brought back to her. This was the only explanation she came up with, in the short period of time she was lucid. The prognosis is not good for her, but we have to treat her as the main suspect. She had only recently found out about the abuse her children suffered, so that could have been enough to turn her. As for the rest of that family, I can't tie anyone up to being in or around Leeds at any time the murders or attacks occurred. None of them seem to have a motive either. I understand about abuse being a motive, but they haven't bothered with old man Yates up to that point. They seem to have plenty of money, so again I don't know why they would risk it in any way?"

354

"Thanks everyone for that. I'm thinking that although you have all worked extremely well in your research, perhaps you should consider widening the area."

"In what way, boss?" asked Pearl.

"By looking at work colleagues, or staff or neighbours. Like I said, the detail that will catch this murderer is here somewhere. But, thank you everyone."

The team began talking amongst themselves and commenting on each other's work.

"Just so you know guys, I have sent up a Christmas wish to Santa that we solve this by Christmas Eve so we can all enjoy the holidays with our families. Plus, we will have a massive party to celebrate." said Revie.

He was rewarded with a ripple of applause.

CHAPTER FORTY TWO

Baby William was a surprisingly good baby and Laura a surprisingly besotted mother.

Anthony looked across the kitchen table and watched her breastfeed the boy. He considered how cosy they were in the warm kitchen, and wondered where it was all heading. Work on his father's house had slowed up considerably in the last few weeks of Laura's pregnancy and hadn't speeded up since the birth. Anthony wanted the place sold and the money safely in his account, the desire for a move abroad not having left.

He had a sneaking suspicion that Laura would like him to stay and take up the reins from Richard, or David. He wasn't sure he wanted that.

The letterbox clattered and Laura looked up.

"Perhaps it's in today's post?" she said.

He got up from the table and went to the front door.

Once David found out that Laura was pregnant, he insisted that the baby was his. Laura explained her story and that she was sure the baby was Richard's. David demanded that he take a DNA test too and after a week of arguing and messages going back and to, Laura finally agreed.

"It's for the best, Anthony, I can finish it once and for all," she said.

Anthony wasn't convinced. David had followed Laura back to her house more than once and frightened her. Anthony reassured her when he could, but was having enough trouble with Janet.

"I don't know why you want to move in with that slag," Janet said on more than one occasion.

"She's not a slag and I'm only staying in the guest room. We don't sleep together. She's carrying my dead brother's baby, for fucks sake!"

Janet remained unconvinced and said that she would wait for him.

"Now Mum's dead, I'm selling my house too and she has left me loads of money. There's enough for a business and a nice house in France, just like you always wanted."

Anthony said no, but in truth he was sorely tempted. It was useful to stay with Laura, but a baby?

He didn't really want a baby, or a wife. He wanted a bachelor life.

But, somehow, he had been attending antenatal classes and the birth and now he was changing nappies and getting up in the night. How the hell had that happened?

He picked up the letters from the mat and quickly shuffled through them. There was a letter from the DNA lab.

Today they would find out who was William's Daddy.

Handing the letter to Laura, he saw the colour drain from her face. Perhaps she wasn't so confident after all. She opened the envelope with one hand and began reading the letter it contained.

She scowled and read it through again. Then she handed it to Anthony.

"What does it mean Anthony? I can't work out what it means."

Anthony took it from her and read, then reread.

"From what I can gather here, William does not have the same paternal DNA as me or David. But they say that David and I have the same father. Oh, my God!"

"You and David are brothers? That doesn't make sense. That means that he's Richard's brother too."

"Not necessarily, Richard might not have the same father I suppose."

"But you two are brothers, aren't you? You look the same."

Anthony sat down, "Who knows? Oh God, that means that on top of everything else he was at it with the neighbour's wife!"

"So, does that mean they can't prove who William's father is?"

"No. It means that David isn't the father, I'm obviously not the father, but they can't confirm that Richard is. David has the same DNA as me, but not the same as Richard. We need to get some DNA from Richard. I wonder if they've got any from the post mortem? Or maybe we could get some of his from here? I wonder if that's too difficult?"

"I don't know. I'll have to ring them up. Someone will have to tell David. That won't go down well will it?"

"No. Shit, I wonder if we should tell the police too?"

"Why? What's the point of that?"

"I'm not sure, I suppose I've been used to letting them know everything this year," he said.

"Won't it be nice to have everything nicely tied up for Christmas?"

"I would love to have everything tied up for Christmas with my life sorted out. But I don't think my life ever will be. My life is mental."

"Don't get depressed Anthony, I can't be doing with that." Laura never pandered to his moods and he found he liked her approach.

"Shall I tell David?"

"Might as well. He's your brother after all."

Anthony, even after reading the letter and saying the words out loud, hadn't actually taken that fact on board.

He and Anthony and Richard were brothers.

"I'll go around to see him later. You ring up the pathologists and the DNA lab. Let's get this finished."

When Anthony called at David's house that evening, he tried to ignore Janet looking at him through the window of her house. He also noticed that the builders weren't getting on very quickly with the work at his place. In normal circumstances, he would have given the work to David, but that wasn't going to happen now.

David only let him in when told that there was surprising news from the lab.

"You've found out that I'm the Daddy, haven't you?" he said facetiously.

"No. I've found out that you and I are brothers."

Anthony waited for the news to sink in.

"How? What do you mean? How the hell have you come to that conclusion?"

"It's not my conclusion," said Anthony. "It's what the lab says. You and I have the same father."

He handed over a copy of the letter and let David read it for himself.

"So, your father fucked my mother?"

"That's one way of putting it."

"Where do we go from here? Can't they tell who the baby's father is?"

"Only after we get some of Richard's DNA from somewhere. We are going to try and get some from the police or coroner. Laura doesn't think that there is anything that will be any good at the house. That's what we were thinking."

"This is all very stupid and irritating, Anthony. Why have our lives got to be so fucking complicated? I've made some stupid decisions and done some stupid things lately. Now I'm wondering whether I would have made some of those decisions, if I had known the truth."

David looked confused and angry.

"We could all say that, David. We've all suffered a good deal. Why don't we draw a line under it? There's a baby ready to carry on the name. Let's all be friends."

"Why, Anthony? The baby won't be carrying on the name if he's mine, will he? It'll be the Yates name. I want my name on the certificate."

"But he isn't yours David, Laura is still sure he's Richard's. "

"It's a good job my Mum and Dad are dead. My Dad would kill me and my Mum if he found this out."

"Did you have any idea at all about this?" asked Anthony.

"You mean that my Mum was a whore?"

"Steady on David, there's no need to talk like that. You don't know the whole story, so don't call your Mum names."

"Alright, I'll call your father a fucking twat, is that better?"

Anthony didn't answer. He couldn't think of anything to say.

"Shall I let you know as soon as the other results are back?"

"Yes, tell me as soon as you know. And now brother of mine, you can leave my house."

As Anthony walked out of the room, David shouted after him, "We have something else in common now, Anthony! We've both shagged our brother's wife!"

Anthony stopped, thought about turning back and thumping David, but decided instead to leave the house. As he did, he bumped into Janet.

"How are you Anthony? Are you coping alright with the new baby keeping you awake?"

"I'm fine Janet and Laura's baby doesn't keep me awake. How are you?"

"Excellent! I'm just popping in to see David. Him being on his own same as me, means that we can help each other out. He needs me to do him a favour, apparently."

"Oh, that's kind, Janet. Look, I've a lot to do today and I need to get off. Take care of yourself!"

Janet watched him jog back to his car and noted how much energy he seemed to have now.

Anthony jumped into his car and drove away. Janet knocked on David's door and he shouted for her to come in.

"Janet, I need you to do something for me and not ask any questions. Please, I've got a few problems I need to sort out."

CHAPTER FORTY THREE

"I'm going over to see Mum today. Do you want to come with me, Dad?"

"Do you mind if I don't, Eleanor? It's very wearing going into that place. I can feel them draining the life blood from me. You go too often you know, love. She won't know it's you."

Michael seemed to have aged at least ten years since Edith arrived back. After Edith went missing he had enjoyed life and appeared to blossom and his daughters thought that perhaps he was better off without her. Now his wife was back, he had begun to wilt.

"I don't always feel so well," he said to his daughters when they asked. "It's like she's taking my energy away. I don't know whose energy she was using to survive when she was lost. But she's taking mine again now."

"No one's," said Eleanor, "That's why she started going loopy I should think. But maybe now she's in the home, you will start to feel better. I'm sure you will."

"I hope so too. It's muddled my head up a bit," he admitted.

Eleanor put on her jacket and considered that if they didn't buck Michael up, he could go down the same road as Edith and none of them wanted that.

"Dad, have you thought of going down to the Fowey house? You could take Flora with you. I'm pretty sure no one is there now. Ask Tom."

Michael seemed to cheer up. "Would you mind if I took Flora? I mean with your mother back?"

Eleanor smiled. "No, Dad, Mum isn't really back, is she? She's just here, that's all. I don't want you to stop enjoying yourself because of that, none of us do and Flora makes you happy."

"Oh! I thought you would want me to be a husband to her."

"No Dad. I don't think she will ever leave the home she's in now, do you?"

"That's really sad, Eleanor. Your mother was so..." he searched for the correct word. "Determined!"

"Yes, she was. And being in there will stop the police bothering her too."

"Do you think she had anything to do with the murders?" asked Michael for the umpteenth time.

"I can't see how, but I'm going to find out how that gun got into her case. It isn't hers and it certainly wasn't Andrew's."

"Or mine," said Michael. "But, neither her doctor nor her solicitor will let the police talk to her. So maybe it will be up to us to clear her name."

"Yes Dad."

"So, will you or I ask Tom if the cottage is free?"

"I don't mind Dad. You ask him, you should be able to get him on his phone today."

Eleanor left her Dad looking much more cheerful as she walked out of the kitchen.

They had found a lovely nursing home near Caernarfon, a grand country house where Edith was convinced she was staying with relatives. Eleanor went up to her mother's room and found her brushing her hair in front of a mirror.

"Hello Mum! How are you today?"

"Hello! Now, would you help me with my hair? I have guests for supper tonight."

Today, Eleanor must play the ladies maid.

She took the brush from Edith's hand and gently brushed her hair. Edith leant back into the hairbrush and closed her eyes.

"Would you like your hair up or down?"

"I think up today, don't you? That way I can wear the tiara."

"That's an excellent idea. Your hair is in wonderful condition. What do you think about having it coloured? Have you seen the hairdresser yet?"

"Not yet, would you arrange it for me? What colour do you think I should have in my hair?"

"When you had chestnut it suited you so well, but what about a honey blonde now? It will make you look so much younger."

Edith put her hand up to her hair and smiled.

"I've always had beautiful hair," she agreed.

"Mum? I was wondering if you had remembered anything else about the gun we found in your case. You know, the red leather case you had at the old cottage."

"I don't know about any gun. I just found it in my other case under the bed one day. I thought Andrew must have left it with me, the day he came around to see me."

Eleanor slowly continued to brush, frightened the moment would be broken and Edith would stop talking.

"Oh yes, which day did he come around?"

"He came around every so often, only when he could get away. You see his kidnappers didn't always keep a good eye on him and sometimes he escaped. I gave him money, so he could pay them to keep him alive and I expect he needed a safe place for the gun. If they found out he had a gun, they would kill him."

"He could have told the police though."

"He said the police weren't any good and he had to sort it out for himself."

"How did he get to your cottage?" asked Eleanor.

"In his van, he had a nice red van and he would take me for rides sometimes. We would go shopping and a few times we visited where I was born and the school I used to go to. He taxied me to his old house and we watched Patsy through the window. She didn't see us, it was so funny!"

Eleanor continued brushing but inside she was feeling sick. Was her mother having a lucid moment or making up more rubbish?

"Can you remember anything else then, Mum?"

"I know that Andrew will be worried now that you've moved me away from the cottage. I should have stayed, so he knew where to find me."

"Did he always look like Andrew?" Eleanor asked carefully.

"When he visited you mean? When he first came back I didn't recognise him. But after he explained that he has had some surgery, I understood. We used to talk about the old days a lot."

"You mean when we were all children?"

"Only from when you were very small, when we lived in Leeds. We never really got around to when we all got older. We talked about the people we used to know. We had fun."

"You are sure it was Andrew?"

Edith opened her eyes and turned to face Eleanor.

"Are you calling me stupid? I could dismiss you for that! Now please leave and send someone else to me."

Eleanor carefully put the brush on to the dressing table, kissed her mother on the head and left the room.

As she walked down the stairs, she met the nurse in charge and they went into the office.

"How is Mum doing now?"

"Your Mum is doing fine, but I have to tell you that unless you want her to have 24-hour nursing at home, it is likely that she will need to stay here or somewhere similar."

"I'm finding that a lot of the time she talks about just frivolous stuff and it doesn't mean much. But sometimes she says things that make real sense."

"That's how this condition takes people I'm afraid. It can be difficult to work out what is true and what is fantasy. Mainly it's all mixed up in her head and she forms it into a story in order to make sense of it. Are you still worried that the police will want to interview her? We won't allow it in any situation. They will never be allowed to interview her."

"No, I realise that," said Eleanor. "I'm trying to understand some things she just told me. Thank you very much Sister, we really appreciate what you are doing for her."

"And you will come to the Christmas party? Its next Thursday, we have carols and Santa and all the trimmings!"

"I shall do my very best," said Eleanor.

As she walked towards the car, Eleanor dialled a number.

"Is that Chief Inspector Revie? Its Eleanor Prentice, I think I have something to tell you."

CHAPTER FORTY FOUR

Chief Inspector Revie looked round the door and beckoned to his sergeant.

"I've just spoken to Eleanor Prentice," he said. "She's told me something strange."

"What's that?"

"She said her mother told her that Andrew was still alive and visited her regularly at the cottage she rented. Apparently, she gave him money and he had plastic surgery and he gave her the gun to hide."

"I thought that Mrs Prentice isn't very reliable in the sense department?" he said.

"She's not. But Miss Prentice seems to think that in the story she told her there is perhaps some truth. Mrs Prentice said that this Andrew used to talk to her about the days when they lived in Leeds and took her shopping and on trips back to where she used to live. She was convinced that Andrew had been kidnapped and only managed to get away every so often. She said that he drove her back to his old house and they watched his wife. They weren't telling the police because they are useless."

"Sounds a bit crazy to me, perhaps they are trying to put us off treating her as a suspect?"

"If that were so, I don't know why she is bothering to involve herself in a further story. She knows that we can't interview the mother, probably ever."

"Even so."

"If we take what Mrs Prentice said as true, it means that a man posing as her son regularly took money from her, drove her around the murder sites and persuaded her to hide the murder weapon."

Jackson sat back in his chair.

"If that is true, we are getting nearer, aren't we?"

"And if the story becomes public knowledge, Edith Prentice may be in danger."

As they pondered this new information, DC Eve popped her head round the door.

"Laura and Anthony Yates are downstairs and want to see you sir," she informed them.

"Let's go down and see them. Today is a day when all the information starts coming together. I'm sure of that."

Within ten minutes Revie and Jackson were sitting opposite Laura and Anthony. A pushchair alongside held a baby.

"So, this is your son," said Revie and stroked the baby's hand. "He's a handsome little chap."

"Yes, he is," agreed Laura.

"Motherhood suits you," noted Jackson.

She smiled in response and said, "Thank you Sergeant Jackson, I like being a mother, so far!"

"What can we do for you, Mrs Yates?"

"We have been trying to sort out the paternity of young William. I know he's Richard's, but for the sake of legalities I decided to have DNA tests done."

"Yes, I heard about that. How did you get on?"

Anthony said, "Not very well actually. The test was done with my DNA and David Farrington insisted on a test too and when the results came back, it's caused a bit of a hoo-ha."

Laura continued, "It turns out that David and Anthony have the same father, but neither is the father of William. Well we knew that Anthony wasn't, but hoped that his DNA would prove Richard was the Dad because they were brothers. So now we need to know if there is some of Richard's DNA kept here somewhere and we can have that tested."

"I can check for you," said Revie.

"I want to prove that Richard is William's Dad. Have some good come out of all the horrible events this year."

"At least it all seems to have come to an end now. Have you any more clues, Chief Inspector Revie?"

"One or two Mr Yates, but we can't reveal them at the moment. Has anyone informed Mr Farrington of these developments?"

"I told him last Wednesday, the day we found out and he didn't take it very well. He called his mother a whore and Thomas Yates a... name."

"David can get very cross, Chief Inspector. But he doesn't often get violent. He always wants to get even."

"I was just thinking," chipped in Jackson. "All those tests prove, is that you and David have the same father, but not that your father is Thomas Yates. Whatever a further test says about William's paternity, it can't say that Thomas Yates is your father."

"So we need to do a test on Thomas Yates DNA. I bet there is some of that at the lab too. We will get it all tested," said Revie.

"I wonder if it's anything to do with the deaths? I don't know how, but maybe if someone found out about affairs and stuff?" asked Anthony.

"Who knows? It's worth checking into, I'm going to arrange that straight away."

"Is there anything else you have to tell us?" asked Jackson.

"No, only I didn't kill Sylvia Lamb and I'm sure that David told the truth when he said they were still alive."

"Have you had cause for doubt on that subject, Laura?"

"Not really, I suppose I've been dwelling on it. I mean I know it wasn't Anthony and I don't want it to be Richard and I want you to find out soon and stop all the killings. I'm worried for my baby."

"Why is that Laura?" asked Revie.

"No idea. Perhaps my instincts are on red alert from giving birth. I feel quite vulnerable, like I know something I don't know I know."

"I will look after you," said Anthony.

Laura looked at him, as if for the first time.

"I'm not so sure that I want you to, Anthony."

After they left, Revie and Jackson went back to the office.

"Arrange for those DNA tests sergeant. Let's see what happens about that."

"Will do," he said.

DC Pearl came over and said, "Boss, Patsy Prentice has regained consciousness and the doctor says that we can have five minutes with her. Do you want me to go?"

"Go with AA and see what you can get from her. See what you can find out about this Ken."

DC Pearl was pleased with the responsibility and winked at Eve as he walked past her desk.

"Eve! I want you to look through the Lamb journal and note the entries where the Lambs say they saw Edith Prentice. See if anyone else is mentioned being seen at those times with her."

"OK sir."

"You think that Farrington is our man?" asked Jackson.

"It's pointing to him, isn't it? But it could still be Anthony Yates. He's the one who has ended up with all the money, his brother's wife and maybe his son."

"Plus, Patsy Prentice said it was a woman who attacked her."

"No, she said a woman rang her and arranged to meet her."

"If Pearl hasn't left yet, tell him to get permission from her to look round her house. We may come up with something there."

"What about the house that Edith Prentice rented? Should we look through that one again, too?"

"Why not? Can't hurt, can it?"

"I'll get the key from the landlord," said Jackson.

"Sir?" said DC Eve. "I've looked through my notes from the journal and Mrs Prentice was seen on several occasions, but just walking up and down the street looking into gardens and houses. They didn't say that she was with anyone or talking to anyone. They noticed that she carried a large bag because they liked it and thought it was expensive."

"Is that all? You look as though there is something else?" asked Jackson.

"Well there is. It's something else that they have written in the journal. It's only an ordinary entry, you know about not a great deal. But it refers to the layout of the house. Can I go back to the Lamb house and take a look? Can you come with me, Sarge?"

"Yes, I can. Is it important enough to go this afternoon, Eve?"

"I think so, sarge. I hope it's relevant."

"I've got some DNA testing to sort out first and then I'll come along with you and see what the excitement is about."

CHAPTER FORTY FIVE

"So, what's the mystery, Carol? What have you got on your mind?"

They were walking towards the Lamb house. Alice was still in hospital and as time went on, it seemed increasingly unlikely that she would ever leave. The estate was being managed by a solicitor, as there had been no next of kin designated by the two ladies.

"The more I've read their journal Sarge, the more I feel I know them and I got to know the house and their lives without realising that I had. Like watching a soap, I suppose."

"So you want to go around the house to check what?"

"I want to check something out. I'm thinking if I say it out loud it might not work, but if it does, it's gold."

"Are you thinking that if your idea works out, you want the credit?" asked Jackson.

She turned to him and said, "Perhaps I do."

"I can understand that."

"Would you mind just following my lead? Let me ramble on?"

"Unless you start causing damage, then yes, I will."

Eve unlocked the door and walked through the back kitchen into the main kitchen. Then she went around the units and appliances. She poked, prodded and opened and shut doors and drawers.

"What are we looking for?"

"See if you can find anything that resembles a key, a lock or a lever," she said.

"That will open a secret door?" he asked.

She smiled in response. But after a few minutes of searching they came up with nothing.

"Let's go through," she said.

They walked through the hall and into the sitting room where the journal had been kept. Jackson walked over to the window and looked across the road.

"This street has changed a bit during the last year," he commented.

"I know. The ladies should have been sitting at this window watching the street get ready for Christmas and maybe thinking about their own decorations and plans. It's a bit sad really."

Eve answered. "They were going to a couple of parties. They always did. One big party was held across the road at the Farrington house, where all the neighbours would be. They were quite excited!"

"And now it will never be the same again."

"It feels haunted in here, doesn't it?" said Eve.

"Hmmm. I'm not so sure I believe in that. I've been in too many murder scenes to start thinking that way," said Jackson.

"When we came last, we saw that Alice was shot on the stairs from about here." She stood in the hallway looking up and holding an imaginary gun.

"And there is the question of how the shooter got up the stairs when there was no way to pass the body and there was blood everywhere."

"Exactly. We will go upstairs now, ignoring that part of the story and go to Sylvia's bedroom. "She opened the door and bang, bang, she was shot dead."

"Then we either assume that the clothing and jewellery was stolen at this point, or it had been taken away about half an hour before, by Yates and Farrington," said Jackson.

"But, whichever story is correct, the shooter had to get away from here without leaving a blood trail."

"There was blood along the landing," he said and walked towards the bathroom. "But it stopped here."

They stood in front of the marble dresser at the end of the landing.

"Recognise this?" she asked.

"This table thing here?" he asked.

"Yes. Seen it somewhere else?"

"In someone else's house, you mean?"

"Yes and also in this house."

Jackson thought. "There's one in the kitchen isn't there? Here?"

"And where else?"

"Don't know."

"The Yates house?"

"Bedroom. Yea, I remember."

"Well I think they are all connected," she said.

"To each other?" he laughed.

"No, but what if these two are connected in this house?"

Jackson stopped and said, "let's see if we can get it to move."

They looked underneath the table top and to either side of the table and then suddenly.

Click.

"Right at the back," said Jackson. "A wooden lock."

The dresser pulled away from the wall and it was apparent that it was hinged like a door.

"There's a cupboard behind," said Eve. "Shall I go in?"

"Ok. Do it."

She scrambled in and pushed the back wall of the cupboard.

"There's a ladder here, Sarge. What's the betting that it leads down to the kitchen?"

"This was a clever idea, Carol. You've done well."

He took his phone and called in.

"We need forensics back at the Lamb house sir. DC Eve has hit the jackpot."

Eve sat outside and said, "Will this help me with my promotion? I'm going to take my exams next year."

It won't do any harm," he agreed.

The wind blew around the corner and whirled towards them, picking up litter on the way.

"Carrier bags!" she said suddenly.

"Carrier bags?"

"When I came here with Tony, a carrier bag flew into our faces and I put that carrier bag in the boot of the car. There are carrier bags in the drawer upstairs."

"Your point being?"

"Maybe the carrier bag was used to put things in, or a change of clothes or something."

"Is the bag still in the car?"

"Don't know, we only took it as a joke about recycling. It will be in the car we took that day," she said.

"You said you saw a similar piece at the Yates house?"

"In the front bedroom," she said.

"On the dividing wall," he said, "I remember that."

"Christ! You don't think that's relevant, do you?"

"Being on the dividing wall? A way to get from one house to the other without anyone knowing?" said Jackson.

"How the hell could he do that without anyone knowing? Farrington, I mean?"

"Because he's a fucking builder, like his father," said Jackson.

They were looking at the houses opposite wondering if the case was really coming together after so long.

"We've got to talk to the boss. We've got to get David Farrington into the station. Start asking him some questions."

Two vans pulled up and the forensics team climbed out.

Jackson went to have a word with them, directing them to the search area. Eve stayed watching the houses opposite and saw David Farrington standing at his bedroom window, looking right back at her.

Neither averted their gaze.

Suddenly David moved his head sharply to the Yates house next door and stared at the window. Eve looked across following his stare and saw a man staring back at him.

DS Jackson tapped her on the shoulder and said, "The boss is on his way with some uniforms. They are going to arrest Farrington and search his house. Someone is ringing Anthony Yates and getting access to his house too."

"Looks like someone is already in there," she said.

Jackson looked and answered, "He says to wait for him before we do anything, so we will just keep watch from here."

CHAPTER FORTY SIX

By the time DCI Revie arrived with two police cars and an ARV, forensics had found blood splatters in the hidden cupboards. Most telling, they found a piece of jewellery.

David Farrington would be arrested shortly.

Revie led the team across the road and with the back and front of the house covered by officers, he knocked on the door.

There was no answer and he knocked again.

"If you don't let us come in David, we will break the door down. Please let us in."

There was no answer and Revie moved away as a member of the team forcibly opened the door.

"Go in slowly guys, he may have another gun."

The team held back, while the armed police did their job. They finally called that the house was clear and they could enter.

"They need to check next door sir," said Eve urgently. "We think he can get in there from this house."

"How so?"

"We had an idea that there is a similar hidden door like at the Lambs. We only just thought of it before you got here. Now, David Farrington has vanished while we've been watching, so I think they need to check it out."

Revie passed the information on and the operation was repeated at the Yates house. A crowd of neighbours was beginning to gather in the street outside. It seemed the year was going to end as it had begun.

This house was called clear too and the team entered. Jackson and Eve went straight up to the front bedroom and looked along the dividing wall. In the chimney breast was a pine and marble shelf surrounded by an ornate panel.

It was part of the wall and so during the renovations at the property had been left intact.

Jackson used the same wooden key method and heard a satisfying click as it swung away from the wall. They could see a small compartment in the chimney and a pine panel which led to the bedroom next door.

"You go through Eve," he said. "You're a bit smaller than me."

"Ha-ha," she acknowledged and squeezed herself into the hole. But before she could push through to the other side, she stopped and picked something up.

Handing it to Jackson, she said, "Look at this, Sarge."

He took it from her and said, "A photograph of a boy, a boy eating a bag of sweets and smiling."

He looked closer, "It looks like it was taken on that window sill there," he said pointing to the bay.

Jackson bagged it and encouraged Eve forward with a shake of his hand. She turned a handle and a small door opened, leaving her looking at DC Pearl. He almost jumped out of his skin.

"Fucking hell Carol! What are you doing?"

"Finding out how David Farrington skipped from one house to the other," she informed him.

Chief Inspector Revie shouted her from the Yates room, "Well done with your idea, Eve. That was a good call."

"Where's Farrington?" asked Jackson.

"He must have gone through here and out of the back door while we were knocking at his. Then he could have skipped over the fence and into the alleys," said Revie.

The old stone alleys ran criss-cross all over Applewyke, between houses and along streets. They were still used as shortcuts around the town. David Farrington would know them, like he knew the back of his hand.

"He could be anywhere now," said Jackson.

"Think where he is likely to go," said Revie.

They were disturbed by a uniformed officer walking into the bedroom and saying, "There's an Anthony Yates outside sir, says it's his house."

"Ask him to come up will you, constable, let's see if he has any ideas."

Anthony Yates stood in the bedroom and looked at the hole in the wall with genuine surprise.

"Do you know anything about this, Anthony?"

"No, I fucking don't! It goes through to next door, what the fuck!"

"We came to arrest David Farrington and he appears to have escaped through here and got away. Where do you think he will have gone?"

"Arrest David? What for? What's he done?"

"Does he have anywhere else that he could go?"

"No, like where? What's he done?"

"What do you know about this doorway?" asked Jackson.

"I don't know anything! I thought it was a dressing table. I can't understand how it's a door!"

"Do you recognise this boy?" said Revie as he held the photograph up to Anthony's face.

"No, wait, that's been taken in this room, hasn't it? I think its David. Where did you get it from?"

"We found it in there," said Jackson, pointing to the doorway.

Anthony sat down on a box in the middle of the room and began shaking.

"I don't think I can take much more," he said and promptly fainted.

Paramedics from the waiting ambulance said he was probably in shock and they would take him to the hospital for a check-up.

Anthony heard one of the neighbours say to another, "That's the last of them now. I expect he's the one who's done it all."

"If he is the murderer," said Revie as they walked down stairs. "It could be Laura Yates who rang Patsy Prentice."

"Or it could be Laura Yates in league with David Farrington. It's difficult to keep up with her."

"She seemed pretty genuine when she spoke to us. In any case sergeant, get in touch with her. She might know where Farrington has gone."

"She might know about this doorway too," said Jackson.

"I heard that David was seeing Janet Banks," said Revie.

"It's very incestuous round here isn't it?" noted Jackson.

As it turned out, no one had to get in touch with Laura as she arrived in her little car as they were speaking.

She got out and said, "bush telegraph I'm afraid, I got a telephone call. What's happening?"

"Quite a lot Laura, could you come with us please? Where's the baby?"

"My sister, she's staying with me at the moment. Where's Anthony? He said he was on his way to see the house."

"Just come with us."

Revie led her into the Farrington house and she suddenly became aware of all that was going on.

"There's police everywhere! Has there been another murder?"

"No, but we have reason to suspect that David Farrington has been involved in at least one," Jackson informed her.

"David? That doesn't make sense. Are you talking about the Lambs? I've explained about that, they were still alive when he left there."

"Come and look at this," said Jackson and he took her up to the bedroom.

"Have you seen this before?" he asked Laura, while pointing at the dresser.

"Of course, it's always been there. David's father built it I think."

"Have you seen it do this?" asked Revie as he turned the lock. The door swung open revealing the doorway to next door.

385

"Oh my God!" said Laura. "Has that been there all the time? I had no idea."

"David knew it was there. We think he has been using it to get into the Yates house and possibly commit murder," said Jackson.

"I don't believe it!" she said.

"He's vanished after escaping through here, have you any idea where he could have gone?"

"No, there isn't anywhere else. Have you tried his workshop on Town Street?"

"Yes, they are looking there now."

"May I go through there?" she asked.

Revie answered, "open house, why not?"

Laura bent down and with some difficulty squeezed herself through and into the main bedroom next door.

"Wow, this is hard to believe," she said.

"Wasn't very lithe through there, was she?" said Jackson.

"No," answered Revie. "I really don't think that she's been through there before."

The two men followed her through and Jackson said, "I'm afraid Anthony has been taken to hospital."

"Oh no! Why?"

"He fainted. I think it's all got a bit much for him. He's in the General if you want to go and see him," said Revie.

"Yes, I will," she answered. "You know Anthony wanted that unit taken down on this side, but I told him it was too nice. I never, for one second thought that it led to next

386

door. Anthony can't have known either, nor Richard. He certainly never mentioned it."

When Ellie and Thomas were alive, it was just covered in crap. I wonder if that's why David wanted to do the renovations here? Even after all the trouble, he still asked me to give him the work, he said he was skint."

"You've spoken to him recently?" asked Jackson.

"Only about the DNA testing really, did you manage to sort that out?"

"Not had long enough to do anything. But we will let you know as soon as we know something."

"William is Richard's son, however the DNA test pans out for the rest of them. I just hope we haven't opened another can of worms."

She walked out of the room, but reaching the top of the stairs she added. "You think David came through there and killed Ellie, Thomas and Richard, don't you?"

"The night you fetched the clothes from the Lamb's, the night they were murdered, what was David wearing?" asked Revie.

"Erm... Jeans, white tee shirt and trainers. Pretty well what he always wears," she answered.

"Does he have more than one set of those clothes?"

"About six," she said. "Although sometimes his tee shirt is grey or black, but mostly it's white."

" Thank you," answered Jackson. "Perhaps you will call us later and let us know how Anthony is?"

"Of course," she said and skipped down the stairs.

CHAPTER FORTY SEVEN

"Phone call for you, boss," said DC Pearl and handed him the phone.

"Detective Chief Inspector Revie," he answered.

"Hello! This is David Farrington."

"Mr Farrington, I can't say that I was expecting you to call."

Upon hearing this, the rest of the team fell silent and Revie put the call on speakerphone. Jackson put in a request on his own phone, asking for David Farrington's call to be traced.

"I wanted you to know that I'm sorry for all that's happened and I want to give myself up. But first, there are one or two jobs I need to finish."

"And what would they be?"

"I can't say, just yet. But I have posted a blog explaining what has happened so far. Once you've read it, I'm sure that someone as clever as you will be able to work it out. That DNA thing threw me, so now I have to speed up my plan. As long as I complete everything I set out to do, then I will be safe."

"Can you give me an idea where I might find this blog?"

"On the internet, where do you think it would be?"

"I realise that David, I was thinking more about the name it might be under."

"Use your big police team to find it," he said. "I'm afraid I've a journey to make."

The phone went dead.

"It seems we need to start looking for a blog. Let's also hope that he hasn't been writing it for the past year, explaining what he has been doing," said Revie. "And we have missed it."

Jackson finished his call and said, "they've traced the call to Holden."

"Where Edith Prentice had that house," said Eve.

"Yes, does he have any connection to the landlord there?" asked Jackson.

"I have no idea. The landlord is called, she flicked through her notes. "Mr K Davies."

"Ken," said Pearl.

"It doesn't say, but I didn't investigate that very much. It's on my to-do list," she said.

"So, we need to find him as well, don't we?" said Jackson.

"In case he's the Ken who knew Patsy," said Eve.

"Do we have contact details for him?" asked Jackson.

"Only via the Holden house, I'll find them though," said Eve.

"Go over there Pearl and see what's going on. A car is already on its way."

"I've found it!" said DC Eve, half an hour later.

"That was quick," said Jackson.

"He wrote it yesterday. Do you want me to read it out or print it off?" she asked.

"Read it out, let's have a five-minute break," said Revie.

The room went quiet and Jackson shut the door.

DC Eve flushed and began her monologue.

My name is David Farrington, a builder's son from Applewyke. I wasn't going to write anything about this at first, but I'm getting the idea that the police are on to me. I don't want to be caught yet as I still have things to do.

In order to make you understand, I have to tell you a bit about my childhood. My Mum and Dad were just ordinary people. Dad was a builder and Mum stayed at home cleaning and cooking.

When I was little they didn't like me going out much and made me stay in the house. I soon learned that if I stood in the bay window, I could hear everything that went on in the bedroom next door. Uncle Thomas was having fun with loads of other kids and never me. Those children were special. Sometimes he would close his curtains but leave the side curtain open so that I could look in. Everyone seemed to be having a lot of fun. They were sweets and photographs.

When I got older, about 4, Uncle Thomas let me come into the room and watch. He let me take some pictures and then I knew I was special too. More special than the others because they didn't know I was watching. He had a curtain that drew in front of the bay, so I could sit behind it, like I was on stage. It was great.

Nobody told any grownups because Uncle Thomas said that they would put a stop to the fun and he would have to kill anyone who told. Plus, he would have to kill their family too. You can understand why he would have to. He was so kind to everybody and gave them sweets. Nobody ever talked anyway because we all wanted to keep it secret.

But I was the most special. Uncle Thomas showed me what to do and how to enjoy myself and how to help him enjoy himself. When we got older he didn't bother with my friends anymore and so he didn't need me to help him and I missed that a lot. Then he stopped asking me round and I would stand at the bedroom window waiting to see him and sometimes he would be there, but not very often.

Even before I left school, my Dad taught me joinery and electrics and stuff. He used to do work for the Yates and one time he built them a pine and marble unit. He made one on this side too. I used the passage when I was a kid, Uncle Thomas made the passage. I think he had my Dad help him make it, because sometimes he liked to help Thomas play, or something. I used to wonder how it got to be there, but now I wonder if Thomas made it so he could shag my Mum. But it came in useful when I lived here, when I was on my own. I could use the one on my side and then skip through. I could watch them when they were sleeping and frighten them when they weren't. I built some at the Lamb's house too, because they wanted to hide that ladder. I suggested the passage, so that they could surprise people when they came around sometimes. Some sort of party trick with visitors wondering how they got downstairs without being seen. They liked the idea anyway.

Those stuck up Prentices left and got rich and famous and didn't bother about us anymore. We all married and got on with our lives. Then I found out my wife was having an affair, so I divorced her and came back here after both my parents died.

That was alright, until I discovered who she was having an affair with. Andrew Prentice, that's fucking who, one of the fucking specials. I found that out about the same time I noticed Thomas Yates was playing with kids from the new estate.

So, I thought I'm going to put a stop to this. I started to follow Andrew and that's how I met his wife. Dowdy old trout, no wonder he was looking for it elsewhere. She didn't take much seducing and I fucked around with her while I learned a lot about the Prentice family. I told her I was called Ken, my father's name not mine. The best lies must always contain some truth, they say.

I decided that he should be the first to go and all I had to do was make him think he had burglars. The night he had to die, I just upped my game, polished the steps and waited for him to come down. I whacked him with a sandbag, easy. Dead, no more affairs for you Mr Prentice. But then his nosy parker fucking mother wouldn't let it drop. Where is he? What happened to my son? It wasn't an accident! Stupid cow went on and on, so one day I followed her from Patsy's house and convinced her that he had been kidnapped and we needed a lot of money to save him. She must have been pretty stupid or senile or desperate because she brought £250,000 with her.

I let her rent my house and took money from her regularly to help me out. That house used to be my mother's and I haven't bothered changing the name on anything. It was useful leaving it in her maiden name. Sometimes old Ma Prentice seemed to think that things were a bit odd, but I soon got her back on track. That car of hers was too obvious, so we had to get rid of that pretty quick. She might have found her way home. That bloody dog of hers didn't like me so I gave it to Judith Buckley.

Now I could carry on my mission.

Next to go was that fat, ugly, nasty bitch Ellie Yates. Once she complained about her stupid washing machine, I knew what to do. I waited until she was on her own and went round to 'fix' it. I disconnected the earth and told her make sure that when she used it she must support it with one hand on the machine and one on the sink. I waited with her and made sure there was plenty of water about.

What a display! She shook a lot and the lights went out, there was smoke and sparks. Lovely! I connected the earth, made all as it should be and went upstairs and through the door. You know that Anthony had been in my house, pissed and asleep just before I killed his mother? Twat, I sent him on his way and he got done for drinking and driving. That was a bonus!

Now I had to bide my time. I knew I was going to kill Thomas Yates, but had to be careful not to do it too quickly. I didn't want to draw attention to myself.

The gun was my father's. I kept it in the shed of that rental house along with bullets. I only had twenty bullets, so they all had to count. Edith Prentice looked after it for me between missions and didn't even know.

One night I saw him being visited by Anthony and Richard and arguing with both of them. I waited for them to leave and let myself in through the door upstairs. Boy was he surprised to see me in the room. I asked why he had stopped looking after me and making me special and he said that I had never been special. Can you believe it! After all I did for him!

So, I shot him. He still looked surprised while he was bleeding on the floor. I don't think he died straight away. He couldn't move but his eyes were following me, so I put his glasses on. Then I left.

No one saw me. But then I worked out that the Lambs might have been watching. They were always looking at people and being nosy. I'd heard about a journal and thought I might have to get it.

Then that slag Laura came on to me, so I started shagging her and once Richard found out, she came to live with me. When she wanted the jewellery and clothes, I had a reason to be over at the Lambs and involve her in a murder. I spoke to the old women and they said that they wouldn't sell. That made me mad, so I took Laura and the bag and inside was a change of clothes and the gun. I went in through the kitchen and looked for the diary. I was still looking when Alice came down and asked what I was doing. So, I shot her. Then I thought, I can't walk past her and instead I went up through the kitchen cupboard and onto the landing. Sylvia sat up and said she would call the police, so I shot her too. Then I got the things Laura wanted, put them in the leather bag and went into the passage again.

I changed my clothes and put the bloody ones in a carrier bag and went outside. Laura was so excited about the jewellery that she never noticed anything wrong. I think she started to suspect something after a while, because she changed towards me.

Richard was trying to get her back. I put a stop to that when I strangled him and hung him on the banisters. He wasn't dead and was really surprised to see me watching him hang! He wriggled a helluva lot before he died. I was stupid there, because I forgot the suicide note and had to go back and get it. That was the mistake that began to make people suspicious.

Then, I began to miss going next door and watching people sleep. And there was no one at home, I felt so lonely.

That cunt is trying to tell me I'm not the father of that child and Thomas might be my father and I might have killed my brother.

Now my head hurts.

I still have to kill Anthony and that stuck up writer bitch. She really thinks that she is better than us all.

I will do that and then tell you how I did it.

CHAPTER FORTY EIGHT

"We've established that David Farrington is our man and also that he's mad," said Jackson.

"Yes," agreed Revie. "We have to protect Eleanor Prentice, possibly her mother and Anthony Yates."

"What about Alice Lamb?" asked Eve.

"We haven't got enough people to protect everyone. We will just have to warn them. Maybe get them to move out until we find him."

"With Edith Prentice, we can let the home know. They will have their own security."

"Sir!" said Eve, "Tony's on the phone."

"Yes," said Revie into the receiver.

"He's not at the house, but he's been here. There's a lot of mess as though he's been looking for something. I spoke to the neighbour and she said he was driving a maroon Mercedes. She didn't get the registration number. It's got red seats and it's a van. She said he drove away very quickly."

"Any CCTV anywhere?"

"At the local garage, the neighbour said he went there and so I'm waiting for the manager to sort it out as we speak."

"Ring me back as soon as you know."

He ended the call.

"Anthony Yates has left hospital and is back with Laura," said Eve.

"Tell him to go to a hotel or anywhere safe with Laura and her baby," instructed Revie.

DC Eve gave instructions to Anthony on the phone. When she finished, she said, "they are going to stay at her sister's, he said Farrington doesn't know where she lives."

"I hope not," said Revie.

Eleanor Prentice could not be reached on her mobile or the landline. Revie left messages on both for her to call him as a matter of urgency. Details of Farrington and the van had been distributed among the police forces.

"I've got an instinct he's going to Wales," said Revie.

Andrew handed an envelope to Revie.

"The DNA results, boss," he said.

Revie opened the envelope slowly.

"It's like the Oscars," quipped Andrew.

"And the winner is!" said Jackson.

Revie read through the letter and said, "Right everyone. Thomas Yates was the father of Anthony and David Farrington but not the father of Richard. Richard is the father of William, so Laura was right."

"And the baby doesn't have any bad blood, if there's such a thing," noted Eve.

"She will glad to hear that," said Jackson.

The investigation was going nowhere fast as the night progressed.

David Farrington did not show up on phone pings or CCTV until 7am the following morning.

"He's on the phone again," said AA.

"Hello," said Revie, "Where are you David?"

"Somewhere, did you find my blog yet?"

"We certainly did, but we haven't had time to read it. What's in it?" Revie asked.

"I should let you read it. I think it explains my missions and how I planned them, I'm quite proud of it."

"Are you going to let us come and speak to you David?"

"I don't think so. No."

"You haven't slept for hours now. You must be tired. I know we are all very tired."

"Well I'm not, I can rest later. Right now, I have to keep going."

David finished the call and Revie sat for a moment wondering what to do.

"Try Eleanor Prentice again and any of the numbers we have for the rest of that family. I've got a weird feeling about this."

"He's put more on the blog, sir," said Eve.

"Read it out for us, would you?"

I have been thinking about what I've been telling you and now I'm not so sure that the reasons I gave you are the correct ones. I know that I still have work to do in order to complete my mission. I've been told that over and over again. I'm being pulled towards the seaside and am looking forward to seeing old friends and family.

I do want the world to know that whatever happens, I have been a victim all my life. I have been pushed into doing things I never really wanted to do and in between

times have tried to enjoy myself and keep nasty memories at the back of mind. I've been told that I shouldn't do that because keeping things in your head makes you do things you really don't want to do, but you just HAVE to do them. I just try and swallow all my bad thoughts deep down and hide them in my stomach.

That's probably why I haven't always been able to make decisions without being pushed into them. I certainly feel as though I've been pushed into some decisions so maybe it's because of what I did as a boy.

I will write to you again as soon as I can, but while I'm travelling it's not so easy.

But I want you to know that IT CAN'T BE MY FAULT IF I AM BEING TOLD TO DO IT!!!!!!!

"Sounds as though he's hearing voices," said Jackson.

"Or getting ready to say that the voices made him do it," said Pearl.

"However, he is setting his defence out, we have to get hold of Eleanor Prentice somehow. Get in touch with her local police," instructed Revie. He was beginning to feel nervous and didn't want his team to notice.

"Have we traced his phone yet?" asked Jackson.

"They've narrowed down the area and he's definitely in Wales. North Wales," said Andrew.

"His phone is," Eve reminded them. "He might not be with his phone."

"He would have to have an accomplice for that to be true," said Jackson.

"Do we know where Janet Banks is?" asked Revie.

"I'm on it," said Eve.

"Tony says the van hasn't got any number plates. I'm checking with PNC any van that's registered to him or this Ken or any other person we know about," said Andrew, shouting from the phone call he was taking.

"Bring him back in," instructed Revie.

Jackson took a piece of paper from a female PC he hadn't noticed before. Eve saw him do a double take and then smile.

"This is Special Constable Josie Swan Sarge. She's helping us out today," she said.

"Well thank you, Josie. We need all the help we can get."

The others nudged and winked at each other.

"Right you lot. Edith Prentice was taken away from the Caernarfon home last night for a visit with her daughter Elizabeth. We've left a message on her phone. Eleanor Prentice hasn't got back in touch with us, but a girl called Tasha who works for her says that she just left this morning and they aren't sure when she will be back. They aren't bothered because she often goes out to see a horse or meet someone about her writing. She doesn't often tell anyone what she's up to, so they carry on regardless. Her father is down in Cornwall with a friend and her son is in Snowdonia somewhere with a group doing a charity walk."

"We have pinged Farrington's phone and he is in the Snowdonia area. We need to send in the local police. I think we should go there too."

Eve said, "Laura and the baby are still at her sister's and they are safe. Anthony has been taken back to hospital because he is beginning to show some signs of mental problems and they have decided to keep him in for some observation."

"Alice Lamb?"

"She's in the home and apparently safe," said Andrew.

"So apart from Eleanor Prentice, everyone is where they should be," said Revie. "I wonder why she didn't ring us back?"

Tony Pearl came in sat down at his chair and put his feet on his desk and began relating the story from the previous evening.

"The woman who lives next door to that house never shut up! She was convinced that there was something funny about Edith's family when she met them. She seemed to think that they had taken over their mother's life when she had been managing very nicely on her own. She drove me nuts. But at least the lead she gave me on the van was useful. She said that the van he drove was often kept in the garage."

"It wasn't when we checked, was it though? I wonder where he kept it then?" asked Jackson.

"Could be anywhere, but we have confirmed that the house belongs to Farrington. Ken is his father and his mother brought the house with her when they married and then Ken did it up to rent. They rented it out for years until Ken died and then David eventually let it to Edith Prentice. He didn't bother changing the name on anything and that's how he got away with it for so long," Eve informed them.

Jackson took another phone call, spoke for a while and then turned to the team.

"The Headloo have been to the Prentice house and say that Miss Prentice is definitely not there. They confirm what the girl said, that it would not be considered unusual for Miss Prentice just to go out. I've told them we need to find her and we need to find David Farrington. They are on their way to Snowdonia, but the signal up there is very iffy. All the details are being sent."

"Headloo?" asked Pearl.

"Heddlu," said Eve.

"Right."

CHAPTER FORTY NINE

When Eleanor received the phone call saying she was required urgently, she set off immediately, saying little to anyone else. The message was unmistakeable.

She had to get there straight away because her son was in danger. How the hell did he know where Tom was today? Perhaps he had rung up and pretended to be someone else or perhaps he followed Tom's tweets, it seemed thousands of others did. Yes, he probably found out that way.

She shouted to Tasha to look after the dogs until she got back a bit later. The horses would be sorted by the girls and they were used to her skipping off on some appointment or other. Eleanor paid them enough not to bother her, didn't she?

Now this was proper drama, David threatening Tom. It was pointless telling the police until she knew exactly what was going on. They had been very slow so far. She was good at thinking on the hoof and fully expected to solve this problem before it escalated into anything serious.

Eleanor drove the Range Rover fast. A good driver with no fear, she overtook and cornered with professional skill and was making good time.

Tom and the guides he was sub-contracting for the day would already be at Pen y Pass in order to escort the charity walkers to the summit. She knew they were taking the Pyg track up and coming back down to Llanberis. But how did David know that? By the time she arrived there, Tom's group would be already on their way. Where the fuck she was going to park, she had no idea. He said that

404

she must meet him in the café and he wanted to sort some things out with her.

It was Saturday. There had been heavy falls of snow the previous week and walkers and climbers would flock there. There would be the usual mixture of climbers wanting to practice their winter skills and walkers wanting to experience the white, majestic beauty of Snowdonia. The fact there were still two weeks to Christmas, made the adventure more exciting for them. There would be hundreds of people there, so he couldn't really do anything out of the ordinary without drawing attention to himself. She must keep one step ahead of him. She knew this mountain better than him.

There would be no way in hell that she would get a parking place at Pen y Pass at 8.30, when she estimated she would arrive. That rope would be across the car park and an attendant keeping everyone away.

If he was parked there, he would have to park before 8 o'clock. He couldn't have phoned her from there though, because there was no signal.

Eleanor decided she would have to park at Nant Peris and get the Sherpa back to Pen y Pass. At the car park, she put on her coat, boots and rucksack, took out a pound coin and walked to the bus stop.

She looked around the car park to see if she could see him. But he wasn't there.

The red bus pulled up and she boarded, gave the driver her pound and sat down. On board were a mixture of groups laughing and joking and solitaries lost in their own thoughts and plans. Ten minutes later they were all getting out at Pen y Pass car park.

Eleanor decided to go to the toilet and then into the café.

There he was.

Beside him were two cups of drinking chocolate and two pieces of cake.

"Here you are," he said and pushed a drink and cake towards her.

"I'm not hungry," she answered.

"We'll have it anyway, it's cold outside. We should set off soon."

"Where are we going?" she asked while taking a tentative sip of her drink. He wouldn't have poisoned it, would he?

"I was thinking that we should set off up the mountain as soon as we finish this," he said.

"OK. I hadn't realised you were so interested in climbing mountains David."

"I haven't done any for a while, but I had some kit back at the cottage from the olden days. I'm quite looking forward to this. It should be a good day out!"

"I'm glad you are so happy about it. Have you told anyone else?"

"That I'm meeting you? No. I've told someone that I had some more jobs to do and that was about it. I haven't said where I was going."

"I see."

"What's the plan do you think?" asked David.

"Follow our noses up the Pyg track? That's the way Tom has taken his group."

"I think I saw them go."

"Watching him, were you?"

"I was here very early. They arrived when it was still dark and I watched them from the car. They wouldn't have given me a second look."

"They got off alright?"

"Well they all set off about half an hour ago. There were about 60 of them I think, but they were all laughing and joking. We'll see how long that lasts."

Eleanor scowled and finished off her chocolate. She would have to watch him like a hawk.

She took out her phone.

"You won't be able to use that in here," he said.

"There's no signal anyway. You don't get a signal anywhere on the mountain."

"Really? I thought you could get a signal the further up you went."

"No that's a fallacy. That's why it's so difficult doing rescues up here. They have to rely on radios."

"Must have got it wrong then," he answered.

"I only wanted to see the time," she said and put the phone in her pocket. She needed to keep it accessible. Tom and his group were getting further ahead and she needed to catch up. There must be a way that she could deal with David and look after Tom at the same time.

"We had better go," he said.

He patted his jacket pocket and winked at her. "I have a gun in here," he said.

Eleanor glared at him.

There were still lots of people coming into the café and the two of them shrugged past the crowd and joined the line of climbers making their way through the snow.

Eleanor knew that she must keep her wits about her, watch everything he did. She must do something before he got to Tom.

"Are you warm enough in that jacket David? And those boots look a bit uncomfortable."

"Are you trying to worry me Eleanor?"

"No not at all, I'm just thinking of things to talk about. When was the last time you climbed Snowdon?"

"About 20 years ago on a lad's weekend. It was bloody hard work and I was much fitter then. Today is going to be hard work, but I quite fancy getting to the top."

"You think that's a possibility today? "

"Why not?" he answered cheerfully.

There was plenty of snow about, but as most people were staying on the path, it was relatively safe. The sky, clear and blue gave a wonderful view of the Glyders and Llanberis Pass.

On they trudged, side by side and every so often overtook slower climbers in front. Eleanor worked out that if they continued at this speed, they should be able to see Tom and the group where the Pyg Track met the Miners Track. She needed to divert David without him knowing she was doing it.

"Which track did you climb last time?" she asked him.

"Track? We just followed everyone else up and down!" he answered.

"So, you didn't really study the mountain before you climbed it?"

"Don't be daft Eleanor, I'm not that interested," he chuckled.

Eleanor increased her pace and was pleased to see that David was beginning to struggle. That would help her.

What may also help her was the mist which was beginning to drop. Although not forecast, it looked as though visibility would be restricted the higher they climbed.

She stepped relentlessly up, satisfied to hear his heavy breathing behind her. Eleanor had a strong competitive streak and wanted to win any little challenge she set herself. Even if the other person didn't realise it was a competition.

They arrived at Bwlch y Moch. The Pyg track continued to the left. To the right lay Crib Goch, the pyramid shaped mountain which appeared tall and menacing as the mist rhythmically moved in front of it.

Now you see it, now you don't.

"Is that the summit?" asked David.

"Yes," Eleanor said.

"We are doing well then. Is that the way Tom went?"

"Yes."

Eleanor knew perfectly well that the group had continued along the Pyg track.

She also knew that Crib Goch is not the summit of Snowdon.

But it was a very dangerous route to take, snow or no snow.

"This walk of theirs is taking them to the summit and back down again?"

"Yes, but they aren't coming down this way, they are going down the Llanberis Path."

"We'd better get a move on then," he said.

"Why have you chosen now to meet me David? You are taking quite a risk, aren't you?" said Eleanor.

"I want to know how the plan has gone so wrong. I only wanted a few people to die. Just the guilty ones and it seems to have got a bit out of hand. I thought the long-term plan would see me rich and safe. Now the police have decided that I'm their killer and I don't see how I will ever be able to go home again."

"Well you are their killer, aren't you? You didn't cover your tracks well enough if you wanted to get away with it. Perhaps you killed the wrong people. Why have you threatened my son? Why have you decided that you want to kill me after all this time?" asked Eleanor.

"Because it's your fault, you know it's your fault. He wouldn't have been able to do it if it hadn't been for you."

"What do you mean?" she asked.

"You were the first. He practised on you, he told me that later. You taught him how to do it on someone so young," David told her.

The mist was quite heavy now and Eleanor noted that no one had followed them. Anyone with a drop of sense wouldn't come this way today. But David had little sense, she knew that.

410

She pressed on.

She knew that now she could phone for help; the signal was better up here. While David was trudging with his head down, Eleanor quietly took her phone out and found Chief Inspector Revie's number. She typed a text giving the bare details of where she was and with whom and pressed 'send'.

"Will we catch up with them soon?" he asked.

"They had an hour start, but will have been travelling slower than us. We will be able to see them as soon as we get up to the next ridge," she said.

"Good, I'm starting to get tired," he said, as he trailed in her wake.

"You said on the phone that the police have been following you? What makes you think they won't follow you here?" asked Eleanor.

"Yes, they have. It's a bloody nuisance. I don't know if they are still following me now. But I'm expecting you to get me out of it. You are rich enough to help me set up abroad aren't you? Then with the money I'm getting from you, I will be able to start a new life. I will be free from everything then. How long now before we reach Tom?"

"I would say another half an hour. That's all."

"And he definitely has the money on him?"

"I didn't say that David. I said he has the key to the place where I keep my cash. A place the taxman can't get to."

"Then when I've got the key you can take me down again safely and show me where to go. After that you and Tom will be free of me."

411

"We ought to get on David, this mist is coming down pretty thick and we could lose our way very easily."

"And we can't have that Eleanor. Before we catch up with Tom, will you answer a question for me?"

"Maybe," answered Eleanor.

"What did you think of that blog of mine?"

CHAPTER FIFTY

Police are appealing for the public's help in locating David Farrington of Leeds. Mr Farrington is wanted in connection with the recent spate of murders and attacks which have occurred in the area. He may be travelling towards North Wales.

They have asked people to be on the lookout for a maroon Mercedes van, which they believe he may be driving. The following photograph was taken recently and the police do not believe he has changed his appearance since the picture was taken.

Police are warning the public not to approach David Farrington, but contact Yorkshire police, Crime Stoppers or their local police.

"I haven't had time to look at any blog," she answered.

"You promised you would read it!"

"And as I promised, I will. As soon as I am back safe with my son," she answered.

"When you look at everything I've written, you can see much more clearly how you have been involved, even when you didn't know that you were. The police won't be able to see it though."

"Yes. I'm sure," she answered doubtfully.

"It's quite exciting, isn't it? Once they find out that between us, we solved all those problems for them?"

"Yes, very exciting. Now, they must literally be over the next ridge, that little one there. Are you getting tired? Your boots are looking a bit wet and slippery."

"You know, I thought these boots would be good for today, but I think my feet must have grown or something."

"The boots could have shrunk over the years. They are very last century, aren't they?"

"I'm noticing that my feet are slipping the further up we climb. Are you sure we are on the right bit? No one else has come this way."

"There are people ahead and there will be people behind us. It's just because the visibility is getting worse that we can't see people so easily," reassured Eleanor.

"Are you sure you know where we are going?"

"Of course, I've done this hundreds of times." She knew that now she had the upper hand, because David was panicking.

"I must be getting nervous or cold. I'm shaking. I'm not so sure that this jacket is up to much," he grumbled.

"Is the jacket old too?" asked Eleanor.

"Yes, quite old. Should I take it off do you think?"

"Perhaps best, then it will have chance to dry out. This mist is probably seeping through."

She helped him take the jacket off, realising that the cold weather was making him lose some of his common sense.

"I'll hang it from the back of my rucksack," she told him. "You flap your arms about for a few minutes and then you can put on a spare jacket of mine."

"Thanks," he said and clapped his arms around his shoulders, back and to.

The mist was very thick now. They were virtually blind. Eleanor knew that she would have to be careful and quick. The mist could lift at any moment and the skies would clear. It all had to be finished by the time that happened.

"Did you tell anyone that you were coming here David?" she asked for the second time.

"Nobody," he answered. "I rang the police and told them that they should read the blog and that I had to finish the mission. That was right, wasn't it?"

"So no one apart from me knows that you are here?" she repeated.

"No. I want this to work as much as you do. How high up are we? I can't see a thing! Can I put that jacket on now please?"

He stood shivering in front of her. She thought how ill he looked and stupid.

"Of course David," she said.

"I'll get the spare jacket out now and you just go over there. That's where Tom always rests his group for five minutes."

"Where?" he asked.

"Straight ahead, there's a bench," she said. "That's right, follow your nose!"

As he walked, Eleanor began to shout, "No! Please no! Help me! Someone please help me!"

David turned to look at her, his face a picture of bewilderment.

415

But it was too late.

The ground gave way under his feet and he vanished from sight, screaming.

Eleanor walked towards the edge, now a metre shorter than it had been. She threw David's coat after him and stepped back. On cue, the mist lifted and the skies cleared.

The Pyg track below was visible and she could see people running back towards the spot where David had fallen. He was lying motionless halfway between her and the track. He was caught on a ledge on the slope below.

"I hope he's dead," she said quietly. "He must be dead."

She lay down where she was and did not shout or try and attract attention, deciding that a woman in shock would probably not necessarily react. After all she had just escaped the clutches of a murderer, hadn't she?

She saw some people in red jackets taking charge and took out her binoculars to have a look. They were making their way up the snow towards David. They were probably Mountain Rescue. Surely, they couldn't help David survive that fall? It took them fifteen minutes to reach him and she saw them checking him over and moving him slightly.

Eleanor almost jumped out of her skin when behind her she heard, "Rescue 122 to MRT. In bound to your location ETA 5 minutes. Listening on ground to air."

She rolled over on to her back, so that she was facing the noise which appeared to be coming from the two men wearing red jackets. They were from the same Mountain Rescue team as the people below and the message was coming from a radio.

"Are you alright?" asked one.

The other knelt beside her and she lay there stunned for a second. She would have to play the correct part now.

"Keep down," said his colleague and he also crouched on the ground.

There was a deafening sound and a downward rush of air as a huge yellow helicopter flew slowly over them. Snow was blown from the side of the mountain and everyone within sight of it crouched or sat on the ground.

A winch man came down with a stretcher which he unclipped and went to help with the casualty. The helicopter circled slowly around the lake and the mountain until summoned back. The cable was lowered again and the stretcher containing the body of David Farrington attached. They watched the stretcher and the winch man return inside and the helicopter move away north. As it flew over her again, Eleanor attempted to stand up but was restrained by her rescuers.

"The down wash from the helicopter is very dangerous. It can blow you off the edge," said a rescuer.

"Are you alright?" the man asked kindly. "Are you something to do with the man they have just picked up?"

"Am I safe?" she asked. "He tried to kill me and then suddenly he fell over the edge."

"You know who he is?" asked the man.

"Yes, he's David Farrington. He's a murderer and he wanted to murder me. Is he dead? Am I safe? They know he has a gun? It's in his jacket."

"No, I don't expect they do." He made a hand gesture to his colleague, who immediately sent a message over the airwaves. He received one back.

"Ok, do you think you can manage to walk back down? Or we can bring the stretcher to you? What's your name? "

"I'm Eleanor Prentice. That man was trying to kill me and my son. My son is on the mountain somewhere with a group."

"Your son isn't Tom Prentice, is he?" asked the rescuer.

"Yes, do you know him?" she asked feebly.

"I do and I know who you are too," he answered.

"Oh!" she said and as she did, two more Mountain Rescuers appeared.

"Need any help?" asked one.

"I'm alright to walk back down," said Eleanor. "I'm not hurt, just a bit shocked."

"Are you sure?" asked another.

"To be honest, I would rather walk down."

"Is that ok with you guys?" her rescuer asked his colleagues.

"Fine," said one. "We need a break down there. We've been out since dawn."

"The police are on their way," said another rescuer.

"Good," answered Eleanor.

"How on earth did you end up here?"

"He's been on the run from the police and he rang and told me that if I didn't meet him he was going to find my son on the mountain and kill him. I wasn't to tell anyone."

She stopped speaking for effect and said, "I suppose I should have told someone. But he's killed before, so…."

"Come on, let's get you down," said one.

Eleanor began to walk with them and was surprised to find that her legs were quite wobbly. She brushed herself down and took a chocolate bar from her pocket. She ate, then drank some water offered by a rescuer and began to descend.

"Be really careful down here," said the only woman in the group.

"I will. He thought Tom had come this way you know, he thought it was the Pyg track and I didn't correct him. I would rather I fell than he hurt my son."

"You knew this was Crib Goch?"

"Of course and that it's dangerous, especially on days like this. But it was the only way I could buy some time," she explained.

"Very clever," was the comment.

"It was, until he started to realise that I was taking him the wrong way and he went mental. He said he was going to kill me and went to get his gun. I slipped and sort of fell down and suddenly he was gone. He didn't struggle or anything, he just went."

"Snow cornice," said one. "They've been forming but aren't solid enough to carry a person's weight."

Everyone nodded their heads in agreement and descended.

When they reached the Pyg track, one or two walkers asked questions of the Mountain Rescuers and said they had been hearing that the bloke in the helicopter was the murderer the police had been after. They said they couldn't comment.

419

Eleanor noticed that one of her rescuers was talking discreetly on the phone and guessed it was something to do with her and the police.

Her phone began ringing and she took it out of her pocket.

"Bore da Tom!" she said brightly.

"Mum! Are you alright! I've just heard that you were something to do with the helicopter, is that right?"

"It is! But don't worry, I'm absolutely fine. I just had a bit of an adventure."

"Do you want me to come and meet you?" he asked.

"No. You carry on with your work and I will catch up with you in Llanberis. That's where you are finishing up isn't it?"

"Yes Mum, but..."

"I'm fine, not a scratch. I will tell you all when I see you later. Bye bye!"

"You are going to have a lot to tell him, aren't you?" said one of her helpers.

Back at the car park, they were met by two policemen.

"Would you mind sitting in the car with us, Miss Prentice?"

"Not at all," she answered and climbed in.

While she made herself comfortable in the back, she heard them stand down the Armed Response team.

"We need a statement about all this," said the sergeant. "Though I think you might have to give one to the Yorkshire team. They are on their way too."

"Popular at the moment, aren't I?"

"So it would seem. How are you feeling? Do you want to see a paramedic or anyone?"

"No. Thank you, I'm fine. As long as I know my son is safe and that murderer is dead, I am happy."

"We are not sure he's dead yet," said the constable.

"No, right. But I won't be sorry if he is," she said truthfully.

"I shouldn't think you would be. If he's done the things he's supposed to have done," said the sergeant.

He spoke into his radio for a few minutes, he turned to Eleanor and said, "DCI Revie will come to your house later this evening to interview you."

"Can you take me down to Llanberis to meet my son? To the mountain railway station please?"

CHAPTER FIFTY ONE

Police have not yet confirmed that the man who fell from Mount Snowdon today is David Farrington, who they have been looking for in connection with the murder of Andrew Prentice, Ellie Yates, Thomas Yates, Richard Yates, Sylvia Lamb and the attempted murder of Alice Lamb and Patsy Prentice.

Police will release a statement later today.

"I hate it when they say Mount Snowdon," said Tom as he turned off the radio.

They were sitting in his Range Rover in the car park at Llanberis. Having been dropped off by the local police, Eleanor and Tom had agreed to meet up with the Yorkshire murder team later that evening.

"I know," answered Eleanor.

"What a day Mum. Do you want me to take you home and then bring your car back tomorrow?"

"No, take me to Nant Peris and I'll follow you home. I'm fine to drive."

"Ok. So what actually happened? Why would you come over here without telling anyone and meet a murderer?"

"He told me he would shoot you if I didn't meet him. I don't know if he really wanted to kill you, but he knew that to threaten it was the best way to get me over here. He wanted money and I told him that you had a key to a cash box. He wanted half a million, but I don't think he had considered how much space that would take up in cash. I expect he just wanted a spectacular, or something. I've no idea why he killed everyone else, but it's something to do with our childhood and I'm part of that. I'm going to tell the police that I came just because he said, but I deliberately engineered it so that he went up Crib Goch instead of the Pyg track."

"Were you going to push him over?" asked Tom.

"I hadn't really thought that far ahead. But I soon saw that he wasn't a winter climber by any stretch of the imagination, I thought that I could probably trick him somehow. I thought it would work out for the best. Things usually do."

"And then he fell through a cornice?"

"That was lucky, wasn't it?"

"Yes, it was. And the police version is?"

"That I went with him unwillingly and when he went up Crib Goch I didn't correct him. As the weather got worse, I was willing to die up there rather than have you hurt."

"Thanks for that Mum! Why didn't he have his jacket on?"

"I persuaded him to take it off on the mountain and then threw it after him when he fell. He was getting hypothermia so wasn't paying attention."

"Don't tell the police that."

"I won't. I'll say he took it off himself, I'm not going to say a great deal to them actually."

"Best way."

"I've no idea why he decided to come over here, the police should tell us more. I just went defensive when cornered and I honestly didn't care whether he died or not. He killed my brother."

"I know Mum. Are you really alright?"

Before she could answer, there was a knock at the window and Tom wound it down.

"He's dead mate, the bloke who attacked your Mum. Oh, hello Mrs Prentice, I didn't realise you were there."

"Thanks for letting us know, John." Tom grinned at his friend and shut the window.

The gossip grapevine in the North Wales outdoor community moves fast.

"So that's that, he's dead," said Tom.

"That's that," agreed Eleanor. "Hopefully we can all get on with our lives now."

"Maybe, until the next drama. I'll take you back to your car, this mist is coming down pretty thick again."

"Did your day go well?" she asked.

"Yea fine, the group was capable so the weather didn't hurt. Plus, there was quite a lot of excitement with the helicopters and the body and my Mum being attacked. They'll spread the word and I'll get more business!"

It was seven o'clock by the time Revie and Jackson knocked at the door of Plas Cerrig. Eleanor and Tom had showered and were preparing to eat.

"Do come in!" Eleanor said to the officers. "Would you like to eat with us? There's plenty!"

The men looked hungrily at the food and said they would love to eat.

"I understand that David is dead, Chief Inspector," said Eleanor.

"Yes, he is. Perhaps if you keep the clothes you wore today to one side and then as soon as the post mortem is finished, we can decide if we need them or not."

"Do you think my mother killed him?" asked Tom.

"No, not at all, everything points to the fact he fell accidentally. What we need to clear up is how he actually came to his end," reassured Jackson.

"I can tell you as we eat if you like and then I will write it in a statement for you. Would that suit?"

"Yes, it would." answered Revie. "This food is very welcome. It's been a long day."

"It's been an unusual day, that's for sure," agreed Eleanor.

She proceeded to tell them her version of events and then asked some questions.

"How did you know he was coming over here?"

"He rang us and we managed to track his phone. We thought he was coming to you, but of course we sent officers to the house first."

"And I wasn't there, because he had threatened Tom."

"We left you a lot of messages. You should have called us," said Jackson.

"Hindsight is a wonderful thing sergeant. I'm very busy at the moment and I just wanted to get to David quickly and stop him hurting Tom. That's all."

"How could you do that halfway up a mountain?" asked Jackson.

"I have always visualised the end result of any situation, then all I have to do is go forward in my day and deal with what comes up. It hasn't failed me yet."

"Right," said Jackson. Arrogant Drama Queen, he thought.

"All the attacks will stop now, Chief Inspector," said Tom. "That should make it easier for you."

"I hope so. I wanted to get it cleared up before Christmas. But somehow it feels as though there are still some loose ends."

"You will work it out," said Eleanor.

"I generally do," he answered.

"So, where to after this?" asked Tom. "You could stay here but I expect that's against the rules or something."

"Yes, it probably is," agreed Revie.

"Did David Farrington make any contact with you prior to today?" asked Jackson.

"The only time I have seen him since we left Leeds when we were children, was the day we came for that interview with you Chief Inspector. My father and I went for a drive and ended up seeing him and going into his house. He was horrid, so Dad and I left as soon as we could. But I did tell you about it at the time."

"Yes, yes you did. We are still at a loss as to why he could keep on with these attacks all on his own," said Revie.

"What made you suspect him as your man though?" asked Tom.

"Just narrowing things down, that's all. He was your mother's landlord, for example."

"No! Was he really? What a good job we got her out of the way, he might have killed her too."

"Can you remember anything else he said to you today? Something you think may help us?" asked Jackson.

"No, I don't think so. He seemed to think that the police would know why he had done it all. He said he had been writing to you."

"In a manner of speaking, there is still a lot to go through on the evidence side. But, at least there won't have to be a trial. We have to get to Bangor and then see what conclusions we can come to. Thanks for the food. Goodbye."

CHAPTER FIFTY TWO

Two days before Christmas, Anthony Yates went shopping with Laura. They were preparing for 'a nice family Christmas', as Laura informed him.

Anthony wasn't really sure what was happening. He appeared to be in some sort of relationship with his sister in law, where plans were being made for months ahead. It seemed that she had always wanted to live abroad, so why didn't they all do it as a family?

He wanted to be on his own, live the life of a new singleton. But now Laura was rich, or going to be. She had the marital home, half the parental home and they had recently learned that David had left her his complete estate. The estate could well be substantial. Laura was trying to convince Anthony, with his share of his marital home and his share of his parent's home, they would be able to purchase a huge property in France.

It was a mesmerising choice.

Either of them could have had fun with lawyers, who would argue about who was actually entitled to each estate. Anthony was really David's next of kin and Thomas had left his estate to his sons. His sons were Anthony and David and not Richard, so would Laura really be entitled?

"We can fight about it and give thousands to lawyers. Or stay together and have a fabulous life in another country. It's the only thing that makes sense, isn't it?" she said.

Anthony Yates hadn't decided what he was doing yet. However, here he was, walking through the centre of Leeds pushing a baby and shopping for tinsel.

Not very rock and roll.

#

Janet Banks was devastated.

She had expected to be with Anthony. She had put up with his drunken spells and his depression and his rages. She had even been prepared to defend him when she believed he had something to do with the death of his parents. Now her mother was dead and Anthony was with Laura and she was on her own. Those favours she did for David, well perhaps she could use the information as leverage later on.

She had heard that they were going to move abroad, just like she had planned.

Janet decided to sell her house anyway and move abroad too. Maybe she would move somewhere near to Anthony. After all, she had planned for them to be together forever, hadn't she? And with everyone being dead or sick or going to move away, this street would not be the same. No more generations of families knowing each other and what they got up to, for good or for ill. She rather fancied being a neighbour to Anthony and Laura again.

She would put her house up for sale and keep a chatty friendship with the two of them and wait and see.

#

Judith Buckley was cleaning her house with more vigour than usual. She hoovered and polished and rearranged over and over again. Today she realised that the edges of the windows had a tiny amount of black mould on them.

That meant the toothbrush. She must bring out the toothbrush and place it in baking soda and scrub and scrub.

Judith began to develop a cleaning obsession soon after her first miscarriage. The anxiety that those shocks produced had been almost unbearable. She washed her hands and checked the door was locked over and over. After a while, the cleaning obsession became her new anxiety.

Judith was well aware that this need for cleanliness was closely related to the filthy pig hole of a house lived in by the Yates. Perhaps it had been a germ or dirt which had caused her to miscarry her eight babies.

Eight.

If she cleaned everywhere properly, she would be safe.

She had been horrified that day when David arrived with a little dog and told her that he was taking it to be destroyed.

"I'm taking it for a friend," he explained. "The dog has bitten a couple of people and yesterday bit a child. Her owner can't bring herself to do it and I volunteered."

"But that's terrible!" said Judith.

"Got to be done," said David.

"I'll have her," said Judith suddenly. An image of eight little dead souls, lost without their Mummy had come into her mind.

"Dogs are vermin," he said, "It'll shit and piss everywhere."

"Well then I will have something to clean up, wont I?"

And so Judith became the carer of the tiniest, sweetest little dog she had ever seen.

She called her Baby.

Only now of course, it turns out that the dog had belonged to Edith Prentice and she wanted her back. At least the family wanted her back. The little dog, her very own baby of three years was to be taken away.

They were coming for her this afternoon because they wanted Baby and Edith to be reunited for Christmas. It was very cruel and Baby would miss her very much. They shouldn't be separated from each other, it wasn't fair.

Judith was going to put up the Christmas decorations and a tree and Baby would help. The tree was only small, but pretty and looked so nice and twinkly. Judith and Baby always had the best Christmases together. But this morning's phone call from Eleanor Prentice informed her that someone would be collecting Baby this afternoon.

She wouldn't bother putting up the decorations this year. She didn't think that she would be bothered with anything else, ever.

She scrubbed the window as Baby sat on the sofa and watched.

#

Alice Lamb lived in a residential home near Leeds.

The wills which had been left with their solicitor many years prior, made each sister the other's heir. The estates had turned out to be considerable.

But Alice's care was also costing a fortune and the executors were in the process of selling the house in order to help fund it. Alice would never get better. She was in a persistent vegetative state and knew nothing about the care she was receiving.

431

A couple of the nurses had said that they were sure Alice would sometimes try and communicate with them. They had seen her eyelids flicker and once they saw her lift her fingers.

But Alice was elderly and the doctor said that there was no point in investigating the problem any further. They didn't feel the need to pursue a cure. She was receiving the most expensive care where she was and that was all that could be expected.

#

Patsy Prentice returned to her lonely house in a taxi. No one accompanied her and there was no one waiting for her when she arrived.

She soon realised how damp the place became without the heating on and had to spend the best part of an hour getting the boiler working. And the bed needed changing and the washing done.

There was nothing worth eating in the cupboards and Patsy had to throw out everything from the freezer and fridge as there had apparently been a power cut while she was in hospital.

Three months is a long time to be hospitalised and ill. In books and films there is always someone to sort out the house. Even when there is no family, the neighbours rally around and make everything wonderful. As it was, Patsy suspected that her bank account would be overdrawn, her bills unpaid and maybe some threatening letters from service suppliers.

There had been no visits or messages from her children.

She sat down on the armchair and cried uncontrollably. When finally the flow of tears stopped, Patsy went to the sideboard and saw with immense satisfaction that she still had plenty of whisky.

#

Edith Prentice remained in the residential home in Caernarfon. She still considered it to be an expensive hotel and gave instructions to the staff on a regular basis.

The trips out with her family were welcome and enjoyed immensely, but forgotten as soon as they were over. The nurse there had said that showing her the dog may help some memory return.

Her last consultation revealed very little.

"How old are you?"

"Six. I'm six years old."

"And, where are you?"

"I'm in my bedroom. Asleep."

"Are you on my own?"

"Yes, there's only me in the bed. We sleep top and tail at Grandma's house, not here."

"And what is different about this night?"

"Grandad is here."

"Does your Grandad usually visit you?"

"Not at this house. We moved to this house a few months ago and left Grandad and Grandma at their old house. I miss them."

"They are visiting you?"

"I suppose, but it's a bit odd."

"Why is that?"

"Because he's sitting in his chair."

"His chair? What kind of chair?"

"The chair that he always sits on. But it's in his rose garden. He loves his rose garden and he taught me how to kill slugs. Slugs eat the roses you see."

"I know. Slugs are difficult to get rid of. Can you see the garden from your bed?"

"Yes, it's so beautiful and smells so nice. I don't know why Grandad is sitting in his chair though. He's usually working in the garden, never sitting. He said I should always work and not sit about."

"Carry on."

"He's talking to me. He's saying that I must look after the others and be a big girl. He's very happy and says that I must remember that."

"Did you remember that?"

"I think so. I love my Grandad and my Grandma."

"What about your parents. Do you love your parents?"

"I suppose so."

"Let's move on to the next day. What's happening now?"

"I've just got back from school and Ellie is in the kitchen. She starts school soon and doesn't want to go. I'm supposed to walk her there, but I don't want to do that because she's miserable."

"And what is Ellie doing?"

"She's grinning and pulling faces at me. Oh!"

"What's the matter?"

"She just said that Grandad is dead! He died yesterday and Ellie is still pulling faces. I hate her."

"How do you feel about that news?"

"I said good. Because I know he's happy and not in pain. He said that I had to remember that. Oww! That really hurt!"

"What hurt?"

"My mother just hit me over the head because Ellie went and told her that I am glad Grandad is dead. She told Mum that I said 'Good' when I heard, so Mum is angry again. I have to go to bed straight away. It's not fair."

"Did you get to see your Grandad at the funeral?"

"No, I wasn't allowed to go. Grandma said that when Grandad died, he pointed to the window and said Jesus and then dropped dead. I saw a corpse candle once."

"A corpse candle?"

"Once when I was walking in the dark on a lonely road and saw it in front of me. It was really scary."

"I don't know what that is."

"It's a real candle flame, quite big and supposed to foretell unhappiness and death. My brother died not long after that."

"Do you think about death a lot?"

"Not much, apart from having a lot of dead relatives and seeing ghosts and wondering about what will happen when I die. You know the usual."

"The usual?"

435

"Yes, the usual. I wish that some people I know were dead. Well there's one person I wish was dead."

"Who do you wish was dead?"

There was a long silence.

"Who do you wish was dead?"

"I want to stop this now. I've said enough and there's nothing left to say. Just because I wish he was dead doesn't mean that I killed him you know."

"Nevertheless, for the sake of the session shall we carry on for a while?"

"I don't want to carry on anymore. I'm finished."

"It's not really a case of you wanting to finish, is it?"

"I don't want to do it anymore. I want to stop now."

"This would be good time to continue, we are making some progress finally. Who do you wish was dead?"

"If I say, then I will get the blame and it wasn't me."

"If it wasn't you then it has already happened and you seem to be referring to something which was going to happen."

"I suppose. But you seem to be making a big thing about it and that upsets me."

"Did you do it?"

"No. No I didn't. I'm glad he's dead and if I could get away with killing him then I would have done it. But no, I didn't kill him."

Edith left the consulting room and went into the hallway.

The decorations were up and when Edith supervised the tree hangings while the nurses let her help.

"It's lovely for you to help us, Mrs Prentice. So many of the other residents aren't interested."

"Well I'm good at interior design. You ask anyone! As soon as my house sale goes through, I'm going to arrange the décor myself. My father, the Chief Constable of Yorkshire is overseeing the sale. It shouldn't be too long now."

"No, it won't be long Mrs Prentice. We shall miss you when you go. But you will be here for Christmas, won't you?"

"I'm going to the seaside for a few days. I think someone is coming to pick me up."

"That will be nice," said one. "Here we have two fairies. Which one do you prefer?"

#

DCI Revie sat in front of his desk, staring at a folder which contained details of the Yates case.

The killer of all the dead people named and accounted for. Everything was sorted for Christmas, just like he wanted.

It was just that something didn't seem quite right.

"Come on boss! We are going to do the presents now." DC Eve poked her head round the door. She was grinning from ear to ear. The whole team had been ecstatic since Farrington's death.

"I'm coming. But will you sort out the Lamb journal for me? And your notes on it?"

"Why? That's all finished, isn't it? You want it right now?"

"We can do this present thing first and then I want the journal and the notes on my desk."

"Ok, but you have to come out now. Everyone's waiting for you."

Revie got up and walked into the main office. Christmas wasn't really his time of year. He liked working. He liked having everyone around him and at his command while they pursued a common goal. Christmas was only a great time if you had a lovely family around you. Revie's experience of life showed that very few people have a lovely family around them. Christmas accentuated that fact.

Revie had no one to visit. He would rather be working.

The office was loud and full of joviality. There was no alcohol allowed, but the energy level was high. Revie noticed Jackson paying a lot of attention to Josie Swan. He would have to keep an eye on that. Jackson often let his head be ruled by his...

"What did you get sir?" asked Pearl.

"A pink I phone cover," he answered, holding it in the air.

"That should come in handy," said Pearl.

"Hmmmm. What time is everyone meeting tonight?"

"8 o'clock boss, are you definitely coming?"

"I'll be there," he answered and went back into his office.

Eve had been as good as her word and left the journal and her notes on his desk. He was going to read through them, if it took all Christmas to do it.

CHAPTER FIFTY THREE

"Mum!" shouted Tom. "Where are you?"

"In the library!" she shouted back.

"What time are we setting off for this dinner?"

"In an hour, I just have to finish this."

Tom came into the library and said, "Are we going to go through with it?"

"I think so, don't you? If we buy them through our property company and then through an agent, no one will know it's us."

"It's going to be hell of an investment."

"But we are going to get them cheap, aren't we? People don't want to live in murder houses, they get creeped out."

"So, run it by me again, exactly why we are making this investment?"

"We buy dirt cheap, the Yates house, Farrington house, Banks house and the Lamb house. We renovate and convert into flats. We should get two flats from the three smaller houses and at least six from the Lambs. We make money, we save tax."

"It doesn't bother you that the houses are all houses of death?"

"Naaa, I don't care now that Uncle Thomas is dead. And I will like owning his house, it puts me back in control."

"You feel out of control?"

"No, I have done in the past, but not now. Now I will control everywhere that has ever caused me trouble."

"I think I understand that," said Tom.

"There you are little Betty!" Eleanor said. "How are you settling in?"

"She seems to be feeling a bit lost since she got back," said Tash. She was staying at the house tonight to look after all the dogs.

"Do you think she's missing Judith?" asked Eleanor.

"Perhaps, are you thinking that we should have left her there?"

"She will settle in soon; the other dogs will make her welcome. Come on puppy!" said Eleanor. "How did Judith take it?"

"She seemed very quiet, a bit depressed really. She said that she wished she could be allowed to keep her. But I didn't have time to hang about, so I just put the dog in my car and drove back. She called her Baby you know!"

"Silly woman," said Eleanor.

"Right one hour, be ready Mum, you know what you're like."

"I promise. Get the car ready, I'm dressed and Tash is taking care of the house. Let me finish these last few notes for the end of my book."

Eleanor turned back to the computer.

She had worried for a while whether the journal would reveal some clue to the police about her involvement. But so far it hadn't. The first evidence they missed from the leather tome was the fact her mother had been seen walking along the street from time to time. But how could they know what her mother looked like now? No, the woman they saw was her. She was the same age now as her mother the last time they had seen her. It was a natural mistake to make, but a very lucky one.

The little conversation between the killer and her when she called that day ensured that her father wasn't suspicious. She didn't blame her father, just her mother. That stupid woman had allowed it all to happen. The day she confessed to having had an affair with her brother in law and that he was probably the father of her only son almost broke her mind. Her mother had always been so much closer to her son than her daughters. Did that explain why her brother had never been one of the specials? Did he know that he was his son?

But she didn't kill her brother. When her stupid mother decided to go crazy after his death, no one could grieve properly. She was stealing all the grieving limelight. The rest of them did the organising and the coping, while she did the drama. At least that gave her the opportunity to bump into the widow's new boyfriend when she visited that day. Who would have thought it was him, after all those years? He had been so pliable and gullible, ridiculously so.

She had thought that she would have to blackmail him to do what she expected, but he just wanted to impress the girl of his childhood fantasies. They met secretly and she found out everything about the lives of the residents of the old street.

Everything he did was under her instruction. Except for the night she entered the house of her uncle through that silly doorway. He had been so surprised to see her standing in the doorway just like she had done as a child. Only this time, she carried a gun. She had huge fun reminding him of everything he had done to her. He couldn't believe that she remembered everything. Like she could fucking forget.

He had begged, just like she had begged him all those years earlier. She remembered smiling when she shot him and the warm feeling it gave her to see him drop, bleeding to the floor. It was a tiring drive, there and back overnight. No one noticed or questioned. Her father was suspicious, but he would never tell.

But things hadn't gone quite to plan. She heard about the women and their journal and she had to hatch another plan. Secreting herself in the cupboarded stairwell, she shot the women at the prearranged time. By the time he arrived, they had only to transfer the crap his girlfriend wanted into his bag. They laughed about the silly tart waiting outside. They wouldn't have laughed so much if they had realised one of the old crones was still alive.

Then he became so clingy and demanding. He thought they would be together as soon as the job was completed. He wanted to leave the country and set up in advance of her arrival, stupid fucking bastard. What she had to do now, was get rid of him.

Would she ever be found out?

"Have you finished Mum? We need to go."

"I have, but I've decided that I might go with a different ending. I think I give too much away with this one. Either that or I shall have to change all the names. It's good for the reader to be kept in suspense."

443

"Probably," he answered.

"Right, you can drive. I'm going to get pissed and probably stoned," said Eleanor as she picked up her very expensive large bag.